Against
All Odds

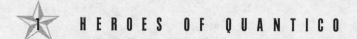

1 HEROES OF QUANTICO

AGAINST ALL ODDS

IRENE HANNON

Revell

a division of Baker Publishing Group
Grand Rapids, Michigan

© 2009 by Irene Hannon

Published by Revell
a division of Baker Publishing Group
P.O. Box 6287, Grand Rapids, MI 49516-6287
www.revellbooks.com

Second printing, March 2009

Printed in the United States of America

Library of Congress Cataloging-in-Publication Data
Hannon, Irene.
    Against all odds : a novel / Irene Hannon.
        p.   cm. — (Heroes of Quantico ; bk. 1)
    ISBN 978-0-8007-3310-0 (pbk.)
    1. United States. Federal Bureau of Investigation—Fiction. 2. Government investigators—Fiction. I. Title.
    PS3558.A4793A7 2009
    813'.54—dc22   2008041926

To my father, James Hannon,
who always wanted me to write a mystery.

I hope suspense counts, Dad . . .
because this series is for you!

PROLOGUE

"Sir? I think you need to hear this."

With a preoccupied frown, David Callahan looked up from the security briefing in his hand. His aide, Salam Farah, stood on the threshold of his small office deep inside the fortified U.S. Embassy compound in Kabul, Afghanistan. The man was holding a tape recorder and a single sheet of paper.

"A new message from the terrorists?" David lowered the briefing to his desk.

"Yes. And another personal threat."

"I'm not interested in threats directed at me." David waved the comment aside. "Let our security people worry about them."

"This one is different, sir."

After forty years in the diplomatic service, most of them spent dealing with volatile situations in the world's hot spots, David had learned to trust his instincts about people. And in the two months he'd been back in Afghanistan trying to help stabilize the local government, he'd come to respect Salam's judgment. His aide wouldn't raise a red flag unless there was good cause.

"All right." David adjusted his wire-rimmed glasses and held out his hand. "Let's see what they have to say."

In silence, Salam set the recorder on the desk, pressed the play button, and passed the sheet of paper to David.

As the spoken message was relayed in Pashto, the language favored by the Taliban, David scanned the translation. The warning was similar to those that had come before: convince the country's struggling fledgling government to release a dozen incarcerated terrorists and pay a twenty-million-dollar ransom, or the three U.S. hostages that had been kidnapped a week ago would die.

But as he read the last line, he understood Salam's concern. The nature of the personal threat had, indeed, changed.

If you do not convince the government to meet our demands, your daughter will be our next target.

His pulse slammed into high gear.

"When did this arrive?" A thread of tension wove through his clipped question.

"Half an hour ago. It's been in translation."

"Was it delivered in the usual manner?"

"Yes."

Meaning a randomly selected seven- or eight-year-old boy had been paid a few afghanis—the equivalent of a dime—to thrust the tape into the hands of the first U.S. soldier he saw at busy Massood Square, not far from the main gate of the embassy. The young, nimble couriers always managed to slip into the crowd or dart through the traffic before they could be restrained. It was a simple, expedient delivery method that left no clue about the origin of the messages.

Swiveling toward the small window in his office, David considered his options.

The official stance from Washington was clear—the United States didn't negotiate with terrorists. Nevertheless, secret deals were sometimes bartered that allowed the government to save hostages while maintaining its hard-line public stance. While he'd been assigned to broker a couple of those clandestine arrangements during his career, David had never recommended that course of action. Had never even considered recommending it.

Until now.

Because he wanted to protect Monica—even if she wanted nothing to do with him.

As he stared out the window at the jagged, unforgiving peaks of the distant Hindu Kush Mountains, snow-covered on this frigid February day, he was keenly aware of the moral dilemma he faced. If he'd been unwilling to advise covert bargaining to save the lives of the three American hostages, how could he in good conscience change his stance now just because his own daughter had become a target?

Whoever had masterminded this latest threat had thrown him a cunning, world-class curveball.

For thirty eternal seconds he wrestled with his dilemma. But when he swung back toward Salam, there was steel in his voice.

"Get Washington on the phone."

1

Evan Cooper had never liked predawn pages.

In his four years on the FBI's Hostage Rescue Team, he'd pulled his share of all-nighters. And those were fine. He'd much rather stay up until the sun rose than be awakened by that rude alert. Especially on a Saturday after a late night of partying.

Stifling a groan, he groped around the top of his nightstand until his fingers closed over his BlackBerry. Once he'd killed the piercing noise, he peered at his watch in the darkness, forcing his bleary eyes to focus. According to the LED dial, it was four in the morning. Two hours of sleep.

Not enough.

Resigned, Coop clicked on his in-box. Normally, his adrenaline would already be pumping as he speculated about what crisis had escalated to the point that the nation's most elite civilian tactical force would be called in. But in his present condition, the address line did little more than arouse mild curiosity in his sleep-fogged brain. Why had the page been directed to him alone rather than to his full team, as usual?

Squinting in the dark, Coop scanned the clipped directive from Les Coplin, head of the HRT.

Meet me at Quantico ASAP.

No explanation. No clue about why this meeting couldn't wait until a decent hour. Just a summons.

In other words, typical Les.

After four years of this drill, Coop simply shifted into autopilot. And thirty minutes later, he found himself striding down the too-bright corridor toward Les's office with no actual recollection of getting dressed, driving to Quantico, going through security, or parking his car.

It was almost scary.

"You look about as alert as I feel."

At the wry comment, Coop glanced over his shoulder. Mark Sanders closed the distance between them in a few long strides and fell into step beside him.

"One too many beers last night?" Mark queried.

"At least." Coop didn't figure it would do any good to deny the obvious. Mark had been by his side most of the evening. "I take it you got a page too?"

"Yep." He scanned the deserted hallway. "Looks like it's just you and me, kid. A two-man job. This might be interesting."

Maybe, Coop conceded. *After I wake up.*

"How come you're so perky?" Coop gave Mark a suspicious look. The two of them were often teamed up on missions that called for partners, and their on-the-job pairing had led to a solid friendship. "You had as much to drink as I did."

"I also stopped for a cup of coffee at the quick shop on the way in."

"Smart."

"I thought so." Mark's lips quirked into a smirk. "Hey, maybe Les will take pity on you and offer you some of his special brew."

The commander's thick-as-motor-oil sludge was legendary— and universally abhorred. But Coop was desperate. "I might take him up on it."

"Whoa!" Mark's eyebrows shot up. "You did have a rough night. Or else you're getting old."

"Thanks a lot, buddy." In truth, he felt every one of his thirty-eight years this morning.

Chuckling, Mark stopped outside Les's office and slapped Coop on the back. "Hey, what are friends for?" He lifted his hand to knock but froze as a gruff voice bellowed through the door.

"Don't just stand there. Come on in!"

Rolling his eyes, Mark pushed the door open and stepped aside, ushering Coop in first.

"Now you decide to be polite," Coop muttered under his breath as he passed.

Mark's soft chuckle was the only response.

"Sit." Les waved them into chairs and fished out some file folders from the sea of papers on his desk. He worked the stub of his ever-present, unlit cigar between his teeth as he scrutinized the men across from him.

"You two look like something the cat dragged in." He turned to Coop. "Especially you. Get some caffeine." He motioned to a coffeemaker on a small table against the wall.

After exchanging a look with Mark, Coop rose in silence and filled a disposable cup three-quarters full, stirring in two packets of creamer to cut the bitterness of the noxious swill that masqueraded as coffee. Nothing got past Les, Coop reflected. One quick, assessing glance was all it had taken for the man to figure out who had fared the worse from a night of barhopping.

His astute powers of observation were no surprise, though. A former green beret and HRT operator, Les had headed the Hostage Rescue Team for the past two years. And he'd earned the respect of every HRT member with his keen insights and cut-to-the-chase manner. He'd also earned the nickname Bulldog, thanks to his stocky build, close-cropped gray hair, and square jaw—not to mention his tenacious determination.

As Coop retook his seat, grimacing at his first sip of the vile brew, he ignored the twitch in Mark's lips and focused on Les.

"I've got a job for you two. Ever hear of David Callahan?"

Mark shot Coop a silent query. At the almost imperceptible shake of his partner's head, he answered for both of them. "No."

"Didn't think so. He keeps a low profile. Here's some background you can review later." He tossed a file across the desk, and Coop fumbled with his coffee as he grabbed for it, the murky liquid sloshing dangerously close to the rim of the cup.

Les scowled at him and chewed his cigar. "Keep drinking that coffee." Settling back in his chair, he ignored the flush that rose on Coop's neck. "David Callahan works for the State Department. Has for forty years. He's been in about every hot spot in the world where the United States has a vested interest. By reputation, he's a savvy diplomat and a tough but fair negotiator. When you see the secretary of state shaking hands with foreign leaders after a diplomatic coup, you can bet David Callahan had a hand in it. I assume you're both versed on the current hostage situation in Afghanistan."

It was a statement, not a question.

To Coop's relief, Mark took pity on him and accepted the volley. The coffee was starting to work, but he wasn't yet ready to dive into this game.

"Yes. The basics, anyway. An unidentified terrorist group kidnapped three Americans a week ago and is demanding the release of a number of extremists who are in custody, as well as a large ransom. The hostages are a wire service reporter, the director of a humanitarian organization, and a State Department employee. The last I heard, things were at a stalemate."

"That's right. It's a dicey situation. Callahan is holding firm to our nonnegotiation policy with terrorists, but he's facing immense pressure to convince the State Department and the Afghan government to reconsider that stance. And the terrorists just raised the stakes."

Leaning forward, Les passed a file to Mark. "Background on Monica Callahan, David's daughter."

14

"How is she involved?" Mark took the file.

"She isn't. Yet. And it's up to you to keep it that way."

"I'm not sure I understand." Twin creases appeared on Mark's brow.

"Three hours ago, the terrorists gave David Callahan a vested interest in the outcome by threatening his daughter." Les turned to Coop. "You with us?"

"Yes, sir. But I'm not sure I understand, either. Shouldn't this be handled by State Department personnel?"

"In general, yes. David Callahan's own security is being managed internally. But he wanted the best available protection for his daughter. And he went to the highest levels to get it."

"The secretary of state asked for HRT involvement?" Mark sent Les a surprised look.

"No one *asked* for anything. It was an order." Les chewed on his cigar for a few seconds. "And it came from the White House."

Stunned, Coop stared at him. "The White House?"

"The coffee must be kicking in. Good." Les worked his cigar to the other side of his mouth. "Now that I have your full attention, we can talk about your assignment."

"Is the daughter in Afghanistan?" Mark asked.

"No. Much closer to home. Richmond, Virginia. I want you and Coop on dignitary protection duty 24/7 until this hostage situation is resolved."

"That could be weeks," Coop said.

"And your point is . . ." Les pinned him with a piercing look.

Coop took a fortifying gulp of his coffee and remained silent.

"That's what I figured." Les removed his cigar long enough to take a swig from his own mug. "We'll work the intelligence angle from here and try to intercept any imminent threats. I need you two on the ground with Monica Callahan to provide physical protection." He passed another file over to Mark. "Classified intelligence on the hostage situation and terrorist cells in the U.S. that could be connected to it."

"Is a safe house being arranged?"

At Mark's question, Les leaned back in his chair and squinted. Not a good sign, Coop knew. Their boss only squinted in tense situations—or if things weren't going as planned.

"That would be the most effective way to deal with the situation. And we're securing a location now. But we have a challenge to deal with first."

As Coop leaned forward to wedge his coffee cup into a tiny bare spot on Les's desk, he exchanged a glance with Mark. His partner's concerned expression mirrored Coop's reaction. When Les said "challenge," he meant "problem." And with the White House watching over their shoulders, problems were not a good thing.

"I'm assuming you'll explain that." Coop's even, controlled tone reflected none of his sudden unease.

"The lady isn't aware of the danger because she hasn't responded to her father's calls. As you'll discover from her file, they've been estranged for many years." Les delivered his bombshell matter-of-factly. "So your first challenge, gentlemen, will be to convince her she needs protecting and get her on board with the program—despite her feelings about her father."

The last vestiges of fuzziness vanished from Coop's brain. They were supposed to protect an uncooperative subject from a terrorist threat with the White House looking over their shoulders.

Wonderful.

From the set of his jaw, Mark wasn't any more thrilled by the assignment than he was, Coop deduced.

Dignitary protection details were bad enough under the best conditions. No one on the HRT had joined the group to play

16

nursemaid to high-powered, pampered VIPs. And that's what these gigs amounted to in most cases, as he and Mark knew firsthand. You stashed the person in a safe house and babysat until you got the all clear.

In other words, you were bored out of your mind.

But he'd take that kind of assignment in a heartbeat compared to the one Les had handed them. One wrong step, and their careers would be toast.

"We'll feed you intelligence as we get it," Les continued. "And we'll proceed on the assumption that you'll convince Ms. Callahan it's in her best interest to cooperate. In the meantime, get up to speed on those files and head down to Richmond. I want you on the job by nine o'clock. The local field office is handling covert surveillance until you get there. Any questions?"

Coop and Mark exchanged a look but remained silent.

"Okay. Stay in touch. And good luck."

Rising, Coop gripped the file folder on David Callahan and picked up his coffee. As he followed Mark out the door, he glanced at the murky dregs sloshing in the bottom of the cup. They turned his stomach.

And the assignment Les had handed them was having the same effect.

As for luck . . . he had a feeling they were going to need a whole lot more than that to emerge from this job unscathed.

2

Two hours later, Coop angled his wrist on the steering wheel and checked his watch. Not bad. At this rate, they should be in Richmond well before the nine o'clock deadline Les had given them.

"You want any breakfast?"

At Mark's question, Coop flicked a quick look in his direction. When his partner inclined his head toward a pair of familiar yellow arches at the top of the highway off-ramp up ahead, Coop grimaced.

"I'll take that as a no," Mark said.

"I'm still tasting the grounds from Les's so-called coffee. But I'll pull off if you're hungry."

"I can wait awhile."

Coop didn't offer again. The mere thought of food was enough to make him queasy. "Finding anything interesting?" He nodded toward the briefing material in Mark's lap. His partner had been engrossed in it since they pulled onto the highway, and Coop had been content to drive in silence.

"David Callahan is impressive."

"He must be to have enough clout to pull off this kind of security. And to have Oval Office connections."

"Sounds like he's earned a few favors. The man has been in more hot spots than a Bedouin's camel."

"Remind me to appreciate your humor later, when I feel more human." Coop gave him a sardonic look. "Too bad we weren't

18

assigned to *his* security detail. Given the level of scrutiny on this job, I have a feeling that would have been safer than babysitting his daughter."

"Hey, look at it this way." Mark fished a photo out of the file and positioned it in his partner's field of vision. "If we have to babysit, at least she's a babe."

Babe was a good word to describe Monica Callahan, Coop conceded as he examined the head shot. Shiny, russet-colored hair framed her oval face and skimmed her shoulders, the tapered blunt cut providing fullness and bounce. Bangs swept to either side of her smooth forehead, and intelligent, deep green eyes stared into the camera with a disarming frankness. Her lips were curved in an ever-so-slight smile, as if she was thinking about some private joke.

For some reason, Coop got stuck on her lips. They were full and soft and oh-so-appealing. *Kissable* was the word that came to mind. And very . . .

"Watch the road," Mark suggested mildly, his expression amused as the car began to drift toward the shoulder.

Jerking his focus back to the highway, Coop made a course correction.

"I thought this would get your attention." Mark grinned and slid the photo back into the file. "Why don't you pull over and we'll switch places? Once you're up to speed on the files, we can talk about a game plan."

"Okay by me."

Thirty minutes later, Coop closed the file on Monica Callahan. "I'm impressed."

"There aren't any slouches in that family, that's for sure."

"How many people do you know who've written a bestselling book at age thirty-four?"

"Zero. Until now. What was the name of it again?"

"Talk the Walk."

19

"Clever."

"And that's just for starters. PhD in communications. College professor. Business trainer and communications consultant. Sought-after speaker. She's one busy lady."

"Who is not going to take kindly to having her life disrupted, I suspect."

Flipping open the file again, Coop gave it one more quick scan. "I didn't see anything in here about why she and her father are estranged, did you?"

"Nope."

"That's going to complicate things."

"Tell me about it."

In the distance, Coop spotted another pair of yellow arches. "I think I could face some food now. Besides, I don't want to go into this on an empty stomach."

"You don't have to twist my arm." Mark flipped on his turn signal.

As his partner edged into the right lane, Coop surveyed the bleak February landscape outside his window. A light dusting of snow covered the ground, and the temperature was hovering at the freezing mark. The scene was cold. Inhospitable. Ominous.

Like this assignment.

His gut clenched into a knot, and an unsettling feeling of apprehension swept over him. "I don't have good vibes about this mission."

At his quiet comment, Mark shot him a surprised look. "That doesn't sound like you."

Twin furrows dented Coop's brow. Mark was right. He couldn't remember ever being intimidated by an assignment, from busting up a lethal drug ring in Puerto Rico to high-risk international fugitive pickups to quelling a prison riot. He was used to danger.

Yet this job spooked him, for reasons he couldn't articulate. He just had a gut feeling they were walking onto a minefield. And in general, he trusted his instincts.

This case, however, was a little different. The intense scrutiny that White House involvement implied could, in itself, account for his trepidation, he supposed. Until they scoped out the job and met the woman they'd been assigned to protect, he needed to keep his concerns in check. There was no reason for both of them to worry unnecessarily.

"Sorry." He tried to massage away the dull headache pounding behind his temples. "Chalk it up to too many beers and not enough sleep."

"Maybe food will help."

"Maybe."

As Mark turned onto the exit ramp, Coop hoped his partner was right. Monica Callahan's refusal to take her father's calls wasn't a good sign, but perhaps she would listen to reason in person. Based on her file, she sounded like an intelligent, articulate, mature person. Someone who would be able to put her personal feelings aside and look at the situation in a logical manner. Who would listen to—and follow—the recommendations of experts. Who would do her best to make their job easy.

He hoped.

Chin propped in hand, Monica reread the conclusion of the thesis written by a graduate student she was advising. Not a bad first effort. But not up to this student's capabilities, either. The analysis of the research project wasn't thorough enough. Fortunately, it was only a first draft.

She wrote some comments in red at the end, hesitating once to wonder if she was being too critical. No, she decided. She was no harder on her students than she was on herself. She finished the sentence, then set the sheaf of papers aside.

Reaching for her mug, Monica took a sip of the cooling coffee and checked the clock on the wall in her home office. Eight-thirty. She'd been working for more than two hours already. Not an ideal way to spend a Saturday morning, but her speaking schedule had been heavy since the release of her book a month ago, and she had a lot of catching up to do. Good thing she wasn't trying to teach a class this semester too.

She glanced at the phone on her desk, glad she'd turned it off. Shutting out the world always helped her focus. But it had been a bit harder than usual to tune things out today after the disturbing call in the early hours of the morning from her father. Or rather, from her father's office. *How like him to have an underling place a personal call rather than dial it himself*, she thought in disgust. Family matters had always been relegated to a distant second place in his life, well behind his job.

But she was grateful it hadn't been him on the line. After the man had identified himself and asked her to hold for her father, she'd had a chance to recover from her shock and regroup. Though she was curious about his reasons for contacting her after a gap of more years than she cared to count, she'd long ago decided that David Callahan had no place in her life. So severing the connection—and leaving the phone off the hook—had not only bought her an uninterrupted morning of work, it had sent a strong message to her father.

At least she hoped it had.

Because she had no interest in what the man had to say.

Monica Callahan was as stunning in person as her photo had suggested.

That was Coop's quick assessment when she opened her door in answer to Mark's knock at 8:45. She was also tall—five-seven or eight, he estimated, using his own six-foot-two frame as reference—and her snug, worn jeans and body-hugging black turtleneck confirmed that her slender figure was rounded in all the appropriate places.

"May I help you?" Her green eyes were cordial, and she had a voice as smooth as warm honey.

"Ms. Callahan, I'm Mark Sanders and this is Evan Cooper with the FBI." Mark flashed his credentials. "May we come in?"

Surprise rippled across her face, followed by suspicion. "If this has anything to do with my father, I'm not interested."

The slender hope for an easy, uncomplicated mission that Coop had been nurturing began to shrivel.

"Ms. Callahan, we're here because a number of people in positions of authority have reason to believe you're in danger." Coop tried for a calm, reasonable tone.

Monica's eyes narrowed, and she aimed a hostile look at him. "Including my father?"

"Among others."

"My father hasn't played any role in my life in years. I don't intend to let him start now."

As she began to ease the door closed, Coop had a split second to consider their options. Unfortunately, there weren't many. Les had been clear about their mission—protect Monica Callahan. They could do it the easy way or the hard way. And Coop much preferred the easy way. It was too cold to lurk around outside doing surveillance on her small, well-kept bungalow, as the field agents from the Richmond office had been doing until they arrived. They had to convince her to listen to reason.

But they wouldn't have that opportunity if she shut the door in their faces. He and Mark had discussed their strategy if she balked, and he implemented it now.

"If you value your life, I suggest you give us a chance to explain the situation."

At Coop's blunt statement, Monica froze. Then she lifted her chin slightly. "That sounds like a threat." Her gaze didn't waver.

Neither did Coop's. "It is. But the threat isn't from us. It seems you're on the radar screen of a terrorist group that plays for keeps."

The slight dilation of her pupils and the twitch of a muscle near the corner of her mouth told Coop his scare tactic had worked. They had her attention. That was the first step.

"If you'll give us a few minutes, we'll explain," he offered, warming his tone a couple of degrees.

"Do I have a choice?"

"Yes, ma'am," Mark spoke up. "We can't force you to cooperate. But our assignment is to protect you, and we'll do that to the best of our ability with or without your assistance. We'll stay out of your way if you prefer, but our job will be much easier if we work together."

After looking from one man to the other, Monica's lips flattened into a grim line and she stepped back. "Fine. Come in. I'll listen to what you have to say."

As Mark followed her in, Coop did a quick visual sweep of the neighborhood. According to the two field agents who'd been on-site prior to their arrival, everything looked normal. Nor did there seem to be any suspicious activity now. The quiet, tree-shaded neighborhood of small homes appeared to be deserted on this cold February morning, as if everyone was sleeping in. The very thing he wished he was doing, Coop thought with a sigh.

Stepping inside the door, he twisted the lock. Not even a deadbolt, he noted with a frown. An intruder's dream. Break the glass side panels beside the front door, reach in, and flip the lock. Gaining entry would be a piece of cake.

"Something wrong?"

At the frosty question, Coop turned. Monica had stopped in her small foyer and was watching him, hands on hips, her posture tense. Over her shoulder, Mark gave a slight shake of his head, as if to say, "This isn't going to be easy."

Amen, thought Coop.

"Just looking at your locks." He tried for a conversational tone, hoping to diffuse the almost palpable tension. "Do you have a security system?"

"I've never needed one."

He ignored the challenge in her words. "If there's somewhere we could all sit down, we'll fill you in on the situation."

After a brief hesitation, she led the way into the living room to the left of the foyer. Decorated in a casual, contemporary style, it featured neutral-toned furniture accented with bright throw pillows that picked up the predominant hues in the colorful impressionist prints hanging on the ivory walls. A thick oval of glass supported by a granite base served as a coffee table. On top was a small vase of fresh flowers, a bowl of M&Ms, and an ornate, old-fashioned music box that seemed out of character with the clean, simple lines of the room. Built-in bookcases, filled to overflowing, flanked a bay window on the far wall.

Monica chose a chair upholstered in a subtle geometric pattern formed by shades of gray interspersed with magenta flecks. Gripping a throw pillow against her abdomen, she crossed her legs and glared at the intruders. Mark perched on the arm of the dove-gray couch, leaving a teak chair with an upholstered seat to Coop.

When Monica remained silent, Mark folded his arms across his chest and looked at Coop. He'd taken the lead when they'd knocked on the door, but now he seemed content to let his partner do the talking.

Thanks a lot, Coop signaled with his eyes.

The merest twitch of Mark's lips told Coop his message had been received.

Turning his attention to Monica, Coop plunged in. Considering that the atmosphere couldn't get any more strained, he figured they might as well lay their cards on the table. "Are you aware of the current hostage situation in Afghanistan?"

"Yes." Monica regarded him warily.

"Your father is involved. And he's been receiving threats from the kidnappers."

"I would think he's used to that sort of thing by now, given the nature of his work."

"The threat has been extended to include you."

Her expression grew skeptical. "You're suggesting that terrorists in Afghanistan are targeting me? Here in Richmond?"

"Terrorist groups have cells everywhere."

"Aren't you being a little dramatic?"

"Your father doesn't think so. Neither does the White House."

"The White House?" Her face went blank with shock.

"It seems your father has connections in high places."

Coop gave her time to process his bombshell, watching as shock gave way to resentment.

"You're saying these terrorists are hoping to get my father to give in to their demands by threatening me?" she clarified.

"More or less."

Tossing the throw pillow aside, she rose in agitation and strode to one of the front windows. As she stared out, she shook her head and gave a bitter laugh. "Well, the joke's on them. He couldn't care less. I—"

She broke off in mid-sentence as Coop took her arm and eased her back, stepping between her and the window as he pulled down the shade.

"What are you doing?" She gave him a confused look.

"Trying to prevent you from being a target."

She drew a sharp breath, almost as if she'd been slapped. "You're serious about this."

"Dead serious." Coop nodded to Mark, and the other man rose to draw the rest of the shades. The day was already overcast, and the room grew dim.

"If you're trying to make my day even gloomier, you're succeeding. And that's quite a feat, since I'm a pretty upbeat person in general." Monica reached out to flip on a lamp.

A tremor ran through her voice, undermining her attempt at sarcasm and bravado. And her hand wasn't quite steady, Coop noted. Good. Healthy fear was an asset in a situation like this, as was spunk.

"We're trying to give you a realistic idea of what you're up against if the threat is serious," Coop countered.

"Is it?" She gave him a direct, assessing look.

"We have no reason to believe it isn't." Coop directed his next comment to his partner. "Why don't you brief Ms. Callahan on the basics from the file we reviewed en route."

They retook their seats, and Coop let Mark have the floor. His rundown earned her rapt attention, giving Coop a chance to observe her reactions—and admire her classic profile. Monica Callahan was a beautiful woman. Not to mention smart, talented, and successful. Yet according to her file, she was unattached. Why? Of all the unanswered questions about this job, that one intrigued him the most.

". . . want me to do?"

Only the tail end of her question registered, and Coop forced himself to refocus.

"The easiest way for us to protect you is for you to disappear until the threat is neutralized," Mark responded.

"Disappear?" She gave him a puzzled look.

"To a safe house," Coop jumped in. "A place only a handful of people know about."

"And how long will it take for this threat to be . . . neutralized? These hostage situations have been known to drag on for weeks."

Mark and Coop exchanged a look. If they wanted Monica Callahan's trust and cooperation, Coop suspected nothing less than absolute honesty would suffice.

"We'd like to think this will be over in a matter of days. Or sooner. But you're right. There are no guarantees."

Already Coop was beginning to recognize—and dislike—the sudden firming of her jaw that indicated she was going to dig in her heels.

"I have obligations to fulfill."

"Ms. Callahan, let me give it to you straight." Coop leaned forward and clasped his hands between his knees, his gaze intent. "If you won't follow our suggestions, our ability to protect you will be compromised."

"That's my problem, isn't it?"

"Not when the Oval Office is involved."

Anger flared for a brief second in her eyes. Once it died down, she returned Coop's look without flinching. "I'm sorry to complicate your lives. But the fact is, we're talking about *my* life here. And frankly, I think everyone is overreacting. The notion that a terrorist group would single me out is ludicrous. And other than one sentence in a terrorist missive, you've given me no reason to believe the threat is serious. Look around you."

She waved her hand in an encompassing arc. "I lead a quiet, ordinary, orderly life in a quiet, ordinary neighborhood. This is not terrorist territory. So let me give it to you straight too. I'm not leaving my home. I'll reschedule whatever commitments I can if that will make your job easier, but I'm not going to put my life on hold because of my father. That's my best offer."

As Coop and Mark exchanged a quick glance, she rose. "Why

don't you gentlemen talk about this while I put on another pot of coffee. If you can come up with a reasonable plan, I'll listen."

Coop rose before she took two steps. "I'd appreciate it if you'd let me take a look first."

She halted and angled toward him, crossing her arms tight to her body. "You guys are determined to make me paranoid, aren't you?"

"No, ma'am. We just want to keep you safe," Mark spoke up.

Tight-lipped, she nodded toward the kitchen. "Help yourself."

As Coop passed, he could feel the tension emanating from her body. He wanted to reassure her they'd do their best to disrupt her life as little as possible, but in reality their presence would be intrusive. And she was stuck with them, in one way or another, until the hostage crisis in the Mideast was resolved.

He secured the kitchen as quickly as he could, and when he returned she disappeared down the hall without a word.

Silence settled into the room as she exited. Mark moved closer to Coop and perched on the edge of the couch. "The lady is not happy."

"Tell me about it." Coop raked his fingers through his hair and shook his head. "I don't think she's going to budge from this place, and the house has serious security issues."

"I noticed."

"We may need to call in some local field agents for perimeter security."

"Agreed."

"You and I are going to have to stick close. As in inside. And she is not going to appreciate having her space invaded 24/7."

"I'd say that's a fair assessment. But to be honest, I'm more concerned about her security away from here. We need to get a handle on her commitments for the next few days and put together an ops plan. We may have to request some backup."

The headache that had begun to fade started pounding again in Coop's temples with renewed vigor. "You want to put in the call to Les?"

"Nope." Mark folded his arms across his chest. "I ran interference for you this morning in his office. It's your turn to step into the line of fire."

"Any suggestions?" Coop took the handoff without argument. Mark had done him a favor earlier when his brain had felt pickled; it was only fair he return it.

"Pray?"

"Very funny."

"Hey, maybe it's not such bad advice." Mark's quick grin faded. "I can tell you one thing, though. Les is *not* going to be happy."

"I can tell you something else. We're going to need all the help we can get to pull this job off."

3

It wasn't fair.

Monica gave the button on the coffee grinder an angry jab. As she gripped the edge of the counter in a futile attempt to restore some sense of stability to her shaken world, the grating noise was an audible parallel to the silent churning in her stomach. Why, after all these years, after she'd finally moved past the hurt and guilt and betrayal, had her father reappeared to disrupt her life again?

Resentment bubbled up inside her, seeking release.

But she shouldn't be taking it out on the two men in the next room, she acknowledged, remorse pricking her conscience. It wasn't their fault her father had abandoned her and her mother. Nor did they bear any blame for her unresolved feelings about her unhappy family history. They were just trying to do their job.

By rote, she put the ground coffee into a filter, slid it into the coffeemaker, and poured in a carafe of water. Whatever anger she felt should be directed toward the source, she reminded herself. Her father. Once again, his job had impinged on her life, setting into motion a chain of events that had, according to the two men in her living room, sucked her into a web of danger. Assuming that was true, she'd be a fool not to cooperate with their efforts to protect her.

So she would. On her terms. Like it or not, the FBI would have to carry out its assignment without taking over her life.

And judging by the reaction of the two men when she'd delivered that ultimatum, they didn't like it.

Not one little bit.

"The message has been delivered."

Tariq al-Hashemi, seated cross-legged on the dirt floor, looked up from the map he was studying. The setting sun streaked in through the small, grimy window in the mud wall of the half-ruined building on the outskirts of Kandahar, spotlighting his aide's youthful, impatient face. He'd been that way once too. Long ago. But life had snuffed out both youth and haste. Now, though he was just shy of forty-five, he knew he looked twenty years older. The mirror didn't lie. Deep creases lined his cheeks and forehead beneath his black turban. Gray flecks peppered his dark beard, and his loose-fitting pants and black robe hung on his gaunt frame. But he used the sharp intensity of his dark eyes to temper his aged appearance.

"Good. Any problems?" he asked.

"No."

Positioning his body so the weak sunlight could better illuminate the map in his lap, Tariq resumed his perusal.

After a few moments, sensing the man in the doorway hadn't accepted his dismissal, Tariq pinned him with a steely look. "What is it, Anis?"

"Are there any further instructions?"

"No. Now we wait."

"But it has been a week already. And the Americans are not responding."

Tariq's nostrils flared with anger. There had been a time when no one—no one—questioned his decisions. His fall from grace had been humiliating enough, but the loss of power and

32

authority was even more difficult to bear. Allah willing, he would regain both. Soon. He was becoming a major player in the country's massive opium trade, and funds were beginning to flow in. If all went according to plan, the kidnapping would not only raise additional money, it would bring the Americans to their knees.

One American in particular.

Rising in one lithe movement to his full five-foot-ten height, he threw his shoulders back and let his silent, penetrating stare bore into the other man until Anis shifted and dropped his gaze. Only then did Tariq speak.

"You are young, Anis. And inexperienced. You must learn that patience is our ally. And you must learn that there can be only one leader. If you are not willing to accept my decisions without question, you are free to leave."

Humiliation mottled the man's ebony complexion. "Of course. I beg your forgiveness." With a slight bow, he backed from the room.

A full sixty seconds passed before Tariq moved. Turning toward the window, he allowed the rigid line of his shoulders to ease slightly as he walked the short distance to the grimy pane. Though he changed locations often, the view from his succession of windows was predictable. Dusty, arid streets and crumbling buildings, or the endless, unforgiving expanse of desert. Poverty. Hunger. Despair. All the things he had known for most of his forty-four years. All the things he despised.

It was his hatred for privation that had propelled him to seek power and affluence, using whatever means were necessary—first as a recruit to the Taliban, later as an ally to the new government. And over time, he'd created a good life, one that allowed him to live in a degree of comfort far removed from his impoverished roots. Until an investigation into corruption within the new government had sent his world into a downward spiral.

And the mastermind behind the investigation that had led to his downfall?

Troubleshooter—and troublemaker—David Callahan.

Tariq watched as the sun set behind the distant mountains, throwing the barren desert terrain into bleak shadows. He'd accomplished much since his ignominious fall from power, he reflected in satisfaction. Once he'd wrestled his hot anger into submission and replaced it with a cold, hard, ruthless determination, he'd begun to reassemble his band of followers, all the while keeping tabs on the tottering government. Despite David Callahan's behind-the-scenes efforts to clean house early on, corruption had mushroomed and spun out of control after the diplomat left. It was only a matter of time until the government collapsed and the U.S. was ousted.

And Tariq intended to help things along.

From the moment he'd learned of David Callahan's return, he'd been formulating the plan that had been set into motion with the three back-to-back abductions a week ago. The hostages were now secured in a domed mud hut outside Kandahar, in one of a hundred small, anonymous villages that blended into the desert.

If David Callahan convinced U.S. and Afghanistan authorities to meet Tariq's demands in return for the release of the hostages, all the better. Such a coup would fill his coffers and expose a weakness—in the government and in David Callahan—that would make both vulnerable to future attacks.

However, knowing Callahan's tough stance on terrorists and the man's dismissal of personal threats, Tariq hadn't been surprised that the diplomat had ignored his demands. That's when he'd raised the stakes. Letting three strangers die rather than violate your principles was one thing.

Letting your only child die was another matter entirely.

As the fiery sun disappeared behind a jagged peak, snuffing

the light from the landscape, a sense of calm filled Tariq. He'd long ago grown immune to killing. Life was cheap. No one had cared when his wife and six-year-old son perished in a vicious blizzard in the refugee camp. Why should he care if others suffered similar fates? Tariq wanted power. And revenge. If necessary, death would be a means to that end.

He hoped David Callahan understood that.

Because if he didn't, people would die.

Including his daughter.

"Les? Coop. We're at Monica Callahan's."

"And?"

"She's not thrilled by our presence."

"That was a given, considering she's on the outs with her father. Did you convince her to move to a safe house? I've got one lined up about a hundred miles outside of Washington."

From his vantage point on the small front porch of Monica's bungalow, Coop considered his response as he surveyed the neighborhood. The place was starting to come alive, and he stepped to one side, behind a piece of lattice woven with a tapestry of dead vines. An older man in the house across the street exited the front door, clutching a bathrobe around his well-padded middle as he hustled toward a rolled-up newspaper on the walk. Farther down the block, a car pulled out of a driveway and headed in the opposite direction. Two kids on skateboards, oblivious to the cold, were having some sort of competition a few houses down. It looked like a normal Saturday morning.

If only it was.

"No." Dancing around Les's question wasn't going to win him any brownie points, Coop decided. "At this point, the best we've been able to do is convince her to alter her schedule somewhat to better accommodate our surveillance."

"Not good enough."

"We'll keep trying." Coop could picture Les squinting as the commander chomped on his cigar.

"Do that. White House or no White House, I can't afford to send a bunch of operators down there just because this woman is being unreasonable."

"Understood. But if she won't budge, we'll need some backup. We thought the local field office might be able to handle perimeter surveillance."

"They're not going to like that."

"I know." All HRT operators started their FBI careers as field agents, and Coop was well aware that the assignment he was proposing would take precious time away from an agent's regular cases. "But I didn't think going to local law enforcement for help would be an option."

"It isn't. This case is classified. We have to handle it ourselves."

The line went quiet, and Coop waited in silence. Les's cigar was getting a workout this morning.

"Okay. Regroup with the lady. Try again to get her to see reason. In the meantime, I'll talk to the Richmond SAC and lay some groundwork."

Since the special agent in charge of the Richmond field office had already sent two men out this morning to Monica Callahan's house, Coop had a feeling he wouldn't be surprised by the follow-up call. Nor would he be pleased.

"I'll be back in touch once we have a firm ops plan in place." A dark brown delivery van stopped two houses down, and Coop shifted position to keep it in sight. Despite the familiar logo on the side and the driver's standard uniform, he watched as the man jogged up to a door, deposited a package, rang the bell, and jogged back.

"Everything okay there at the moment?"

"Yes." Coop kept the van in sight until it disappeared around the corner at the end of the street. "My initial impression is that security at the house is pathetic, but we'll do a more thorough check and remedy what we can."

"Get back to me as soon as you have a plan."

"Will do." Coop slid his BlackBerry back into the holder on his belt and did one more visual scan of the neighborhood before slipping back inside.

As he turned from bolting the door, Monica was coming down the hall from the kitchen, carrying a tray laden with mugs, a coffeepot, cream and sugar, and a plate of coffeecake.

"Let me take that." He moved toward her and reached for the tray.

"I can handle it." She didn't relinquish her grip.

"I'm sure you can." He smiled, holding tight. Logic hadn't worked with her. Maybe charm would. "But I try to be a gentleman."

She considered him for several seconds as he braced for the already-too-familiar independent lift of her chin and prepared to counter whatever argument she raised.

Instead, to his surprise, her lips softened and she returned his smile, releasing the tray.

"Thanks. You can put it on the coffee table."

Without waiting for a response, she preceded him into the living room. As she leaned over to move aside the bowl of M&Ms, he couldn't help admire the way her snug jeans showed off her slim waist and trim hips.

A discreet cough from Mark redirected Coop's attention. His partner grinned as his gaze flicked back and forth between Coop and Monica, his silent commentary more eloquent than words. Had they been alone, Coop would have responded with an acerbic comeback. As it was, he did his best to ignore the other man.

"Is that enough room?"

Once more, Coop switched focus. Monica was watching him, her expression unreadable as she waited for him to deposit the tray on the table.

"Yes." He took his time setting it down, willing the hot flush on his neck to subside.

"Help yourself." She gestured to the tray as she poured herself a cup of coffee and kicked off her shoes. Tucking her feet under her, she settled into the same chair she'd vacated earlier.

Mark didn't wait for a second invitation. He filled a mug and took a generous piece of the cake.

"Did you two have breakfast?" Monica queried as Mark dug into the cake.

"Yes. Though you wouldn't know it by the way my partner is wolfing that down." Coop sent a pointed glance toward Mark as he poured some coffee.

"It happens to be very good coffeecake," Mark defended himself. "Tastes homemade."

"It is." Monica took a sip of her coffee.

"I'm impressed." Mark savored another bite. "Compared to that fast-food breakfast we ingested on our way down from Quantico, this is a real treat."

"Quantico?" Monica's hand stilled, and she looked from one to the other. "Isn't there an FBI office in Richmond?"

"Yes. But we're not field agents." Coop put a piece of cake on a napkin and took his seat. "We're with the Hostage Rescue Team."

"Hostage Rescue Team." She repeated the name slowly. "I don't understand." She reached for a handful of M&Ms, and Coop noted the slight tremor in her fingers.

"The HRT is a civilian counterterrorism unit. We provide

tactical resolution in hostage and high-risk law enforcement situations," Mark told her, spewing the official description of the unit.

She popped a couple of the M&Ms into her mouth, crunching down on them before she spoke. "I'm still confused. I'm not a hostage."

"And we want to keep it that way." As Coop leaned over to put his mug on the coffee table, the jacket of his suit gapped open to reveal the Glock tucked into a holster on his belt. The firearm caught—and held—Monica's attention, he noted. She popped some more M&Ms as he discreetly adjusted his jacket.

"The HRT also provides dignitary protection in special situations," Mark added.

"I'm not a dignitary."

"Your father is. Meaning you are too, by association. And the White House has concurred with his high-risk assessment. That's why we're here." Coop leaned forward again and clasped his hands together. "Our mission is straightforward, Ms. Callahan. Protect you until the hostage situation is resolved. The terrorists either aren't aware of—or don't care about—your estrangement from your father."

Her eyes narrowed. "You know about that?"

"The bare facts were in your file. Nothing more. I assume your father mentioned your . . . rift . . . when he arranged for security."

"Rift doesn't begin to cover it." She gripped her mug with both hands and stared into the dark depths. "My father has played almost no part in my life for the past twenty-four years. And he played only a small role prior to that. I haven't even seen him since he attended my mother's funeral ten years ago."

Her words were cold and threaded with bitterness and resentment. But Coop had caught the flicker of pain in her eyes, the momentary vulnerability, before she looked down. And he could relate. He'd had his own father troubles, and he knew what a lasting impact that could have. Monica Callahan's file had painted a picture of a successful, confident, has-her-act-together woman. While that seemed to be accurate as far as it went, he suspected it was incomplete. Whatever had happened between her and her father might be in her distant past, but it continued to cloud her present.

"We'll do our best to disrupt your life as little as possible," Coop promised, gentling his voice. "And we're sorry for the inconvenience."

Several seconds ticked by. The elegant curve of her throat quivered as she swallowed, and when she looked up, her features had softened.

"Actually, I'm the one who should apologize. I'm sorry if I've been a bit hostile. I'm not happy my father's problems have cascaded down to me, but that's not your fault. You're simply trying to do your job. That said, I can't disappear without disrupting a lot of people's lives. All I can do is lay low as much as possible and try to minimize your hassles. Can you live with that?"

It wasn't ideal, but at this point Coop was willing to take whatever cooperation they could get. A quick glance at Mark confirmed that his partner felt the same way.

"It's a start. Why don't we talk about your schedule for the next few days? That way we can assess risk and make some recommendations."

"Let me get my calendar." She rose, grabbed another handful of M&Ms, and headed down the hall.

Once she disappeared, Mark leaned toward Coop and spoke in a low tone. "At least she didn't throw us out."

"True. But it's not going to be easy. We'll still need local backup."

"Is Les taking care of it?"

"Yes. He's not happy about it, though. And the field office isn't going to be, either."

"Tough. Unless she's willing to move out of this house, we can't handle security on our own."

"Agreed. In the meantime, we need to keep pushing for the safe house."

"Why do I think the lady isn't going to bend on that?"

Frowning, Coop tapped one finger against the arm of his chair. "It might help if we knew what the problem is between her and her father."

"Maybe." Mark cocked his head. "Why don't you try turning on that charm again? It seemed to be very persuasive with the tray in the hall."

"Very funny."

"I'm more than half serious. And my keen observation skills tell me it wouldn't require much acting on your part to feign some interest."

The hot flush surged again on Coop's neck. "You're the one who called her a babe in the car."

"True. But our reactions in person were different. I noticed her assets. You salivated."

"I don't think I'm going to respond to that."

"No response is necessary. The evidence speaks for itself." He flashed a brief grin, and then his demeanor grew more serious. "But work on the safe house, okay?"

An odd inflection in Mark's voice put Coop on alert. "You sound worried."

"I am. You know how you said in the car you had bad feelings about this assignment? Well, they must be catching. In my opinion, the faster we can make Monica Callahan disappear, the better off everyone will be."

An ominous chill settled over Coop. In the three years he'd been paired with Mark on missions, he couldn't remember a

41

single occasion when both of them had been unnerved by a job. And he heartily concurred with Mark's conclusion. They needed to get Ms. Callahan out of sight. Sooner rather than later.

Only the lady wasn't interested in disappearing.

Maybe he'd have to resort to charm after all, Coop speculated. That wasn't a strategy he often used in this job.

But Mark was right in his assessment on that front too. Turning on the charm for Monica Callahan wouldn't be any hardship.

None at all.

4

She was going stir-crazy.

Only nine hours into this . . . arrangement . . . and she was ready to climb the walls.

Heaving a frustrated sigh, Monica rose from the desk in her home office and prowled around the small room, feeling like a caged animal. Or worse. At least animals in cages had a view of the world outside. In her cage, every shade, blind, and drape had been drawn, shutting out the weak February sun and casting a pall of gloom over her house—and her mood.

She'd holed up most of the day in her office, telling the two men who'd taken over her home that she needed to work. And that was true. Unfortunately, she'd accomplished a big fat zero. Although she'd tried her best to brainstorm themes for her next book, the surreal events of the day had rendered concentration impossible. Instead, she'd cleaned out files, sharpened pencils, rearranged the closet . . . anything to keep from thinking about her present situation.

Stopping at the window, she cracked the mini blinds just enough to peer out. Everything looked normal. The low-wattage dusk-to-dawn lantern attached to the back of her house faintly illuminated her small brick patio, revealing the neatly arranged wrought aluminum table and chairs, now under prudent cover for the winter.

Beyond the edge of the patio, darkness had claimed her yard. Once she'd considered nighttime to be a quiet, serene interlude.

That had changed the instant the FBI appeared on her doorstep. Tonight the darkness took on ominous tones, shrouding her yard in an inky, menacing cloak.

Thanks to her father.

A shiver ran through her, and Monica dropped into the over-stuffed easy chair beside her desk. Old and decrepit, its blue damask faded and worn, the piece was long overdue for the junk heap. But she'd salvaged it from her mother's apartment after Elaine Callahan died far too young of cancer. It was one of the few pieces she hadn't donated to charity or discarded.

Monica closed her eyes and rested her head against the familiar, lumpy back. Here, in the spot that always reminded her of the comfort and security of her mother's arms, she found a small measure of peace. In the succession of exotic locations she'd called home as a child, this chair had been the one constant, the refuge to which she retreated at the end of the day, climbing onto her mother's lap to listen to bedtime stories and words of wisdom.

"Forgiveness is hard, honey. But it's what God calls us to. Besides, as some wise person once said, holding a grudge is like drinking poison and expecting the other person to die. It hurts you a lot more than it hurts them."

Jolted, Monica opened her eyes and stared at the pool of light on the ceiling, cast by the lamp beside her. Her mother's voice echoed across the years, as clearly as if she was sitting in the room, reminding her of a painful, long-ago incident.

She'd been nine years old. With her father's nomadic lifestyle, it had been hard for Monica to break into the cliques at the succession of American schools she'd attended. But then she'd met Kathleen, also an only child, also the new kid in town. They'd bonded instantly, and Monica had been certain their friendship would last forever.

When Kathleen had dumped her a month later after being

recruited by the hottest clique in the school, Monica had been devastated. Hurt had turned to hate, and she'd let anger consume her . . . until her mother had pulled her onto her lap in this chair one night for a heart-to-heart.

"But what she did was wrong," Monica had protested after her mother counseled forgiveness.

"Of course it was wrong. Otherwise you wouldn't have to forgive her."

"But why do I have to do that? She hasn't even said she's sorry."

"You don't have to wait for someone to apologize to forgive them. Maybe she's embarrassed. Or doesn't know how to bring it up. Some people have difficulty finding the words to say 'I'm sorry.' But you can still forgive her. And if you tell her that, it might help the two of you patch things up."

For a couple of days, Monica had pondered her mother's words. In the end, she'd taken her mother's advice, clinging to the hope Kathleen would, indeed, be moved by the generosity of her former friend.

But the magnanimous gesture had backfired. Kathleen had laughed at her. Laughed! And ridiculed her in front of her friends.

It was one of the few times Monica had been sorry she'd taken her mother's advice. And she'd struggled with forgiveness ever since.

Especially in relation to her father.

A discreet tap sounded on her door. Startled, she lifted her head from the back of the chair and checked her watch. Six o'clock. She'd been hiding in her office for eight hours, subsisting on the M&Ms she'd confiscated from the living room. No wonder the FBI was checking up on her.

Rising, Monica moved to the door and pulled it open. The guy named Coop was standing on the other side. A slight five o'clock shadow darkened his jaw, highlighting the cleft in his chin. He'd also ditched his jacket, loosened his tie, and rolled up the sleeves of his white shirt to reveal muscular forearms peppered with dark hair. She couldn't help noticing his ringless left hand.

"We were getting ready to order some pizza and wondered if you'd like to join us. We figured you must be getting hungry by now." He flashed her a grin, but she didn't miss his quick sweep of the room behind her. Nor fail to notice that his gaze came to rest on the half empty bowl of M&Ms. "Or maybe not."

Her face grew warm. "Comfort food. They're a great stress reliever. I'm usually able to limit myself to three or four, but"— she inspected the bowl—"I guess I got carried away today."

He gave her a quick, discreet scan. "That obviously doesn't happen too often." Without waiting for her to reply, he turned up the wattage on his grin. "How about switching to pizza for dinner?"

"Now that's a notch up on the nutritional scale." The ghost of a smile played at her lips as she found herself responding to his grin. The man was charming, no question about it. Charming enough to coax her to dinner, if not to a safe house, though he'd given that his best shot this morning as they were going over her schedule.

"Hey, considering some of the food I've eaten on missions, pizza gets an A-plus on nutrition. It has everything . . . protein, starch, calcium, vegetables."

"Okay. You sold me. I'll be out in a few minutes."

"Any preferences?"

"Just load it up. I like everything."

"A woman after my own heart." The grin was back, and as he propped one shoulder on the door frame and leaned a hair closer, an odd hum zipped along her nerve endings. "Can I share a secret with you? I was afraid you might be one of those plain cheese pizza types. And I'm way too hungry for that."

She had to clear her throat before she could speak. "I'm glad I could do something to make this assignment more pleasant for you. I'm sure you're not thrilled about giving up your weekend, either."

He shrugged. "Missions come first. And not always at the most convenient times. You learn to live with it."

Once more flashing that endearing grin—the one that tucked a deep dimple into his left cheek—he pushed away from the door and headed down the hall.

As she watched him go, her heart gave a little flutter. One she had no trouble identifying as attraction. Interesting, she mused. It seemed that unless she was careful, the man who had come to protect her from physical danger could represent danger of an entirely different sort. Evan Cooper, with his broad shoulders, dark brown hair, and intense, deep brown eyes, was the kind of man who could turn a woman's head—and steal her heart—without half trying. Even a mature, practical woman who wasn't usually susceptible to the ephemeral quality of male charm.

Like her.

But forewarned was forearmed, she reminded herself. There was nothing abnormal about finding a handsome man appealing. Her response to his charm was no more than a physical reaction. Dangerous only if she let her emotions get carried away, if she forgot that it took a whole lot more than physical attraction to sustain a relationship.

She wouldn't let that happen.

Besides, she had no interest in a man whose career came first. And Evan Cooper had already made it clear that his did.

"She'll be out in a few minutes. Let's get two large with everything."

As Coop took his seat, Mark tapped in a number on his BlackBerry and placed their order. After he finished, Coop picked up one of the pieces of paper littering the kitchen table.

"Okay, I want to be sure we've got everything covered. Church tomorrow was a nonnegotiable commitment. We'll stick close, field agents will provide backup."

"Check."

"By tomorrow night, Les will have two more operators down here to take over the night security detail. Then we'll go to twelve-on, twelve-off shifts."

"Check."

"On Monday morning, she's got a presentation at the Jefferson Hotel for a national convention of insurance executives. We'll have the field agents do a sweep before we arrive and instruct them to stick close during the presentation. We can run down there tomorrow and look the place over once the other security detail arrives."

"What are we going to do about that book signing on Wednesday in Norfolk?"

"I don't like it. It's too public."

"I'm not the one you need to convince."

"Since when did I become the negotiator on this gig?" Coop sent an irritated glance in Mark's direction.

"The lady likes you."

Coop snorted. "Yeah. Right. I'm one of the guys who turned her life upside down, remember?"

"She seems to have recognized she was misplacing blame and has moved past that. She even apologized for giving us a less-than-hospitable reception."

"That doesn't mean she likes us. Tolerate might be a better description."

"I didn't say she likes *us*. I said she likes you."

With an impatient shake of his head, Coop dismissed his partner's opinion. "You're nuts."

"Nope. Observant. You'd have noticed it too, if you were looking at the situation objectively."

"Are you questioning my judgment?"

"Only when it comes to the lady. I have every confidence in your professional abilities."

Coop narrowed his eyes. "I don't mix business and pleasure. You know that."

"There's a first time for everything."

"This isn't it."

"Okay. Fine. Whatever." Mark started to gather up the papers on the kitchen table. "But I stand by what I said about the lady's feelings. And I still think you're the best person to convince her to cancel the book signing."

Ignoring the comment, Coop pulled out his BlackBerry on the pretext of checking messages. "You want to notify the agents out front to intercept the pizza guy?"

"Sure."

The smirk on Mark's face told Coop his partner knew he was employing evasive maneuvers. That was the one disadvantage of being paired with someone for years. They got to know you too well. But he didn't really care that Mark had picked up on his interest in Monica.

He just hoped Monica hadn't.

When Mark pulled his BlackBerry off his belt a few minutes later and skimmed a message, Coop sent him a questioning look.

"Pizza's here. One of the agents is bringing it up. Looks like you'll finally get to meet Nick."

"Your buddy from the academy?"

"Yep. I was hoping he'd be spared this assignment. Trust me,

49

I'll never hear the end of this. As he's sure to remind me, we didn't go through new-agent training together so he could do my grunt work."

The doorbell rang, and they rose.

"I'll cover the door from the hall." Coop pulled out his Glock.

With a nod, Mark drew his own gun and moved toward the foyer. Peering through the peephole in the door, he opened it just enough to admit a tall, sandy-haired man with startling blue eyes and a lean, athletic build, who was juggling two pizza boxes and a six-pack of soda.

"Your order, sir." He grinned as Mark holstered his gun.

"Very funny."

"Hey, I always wanted to do undercover work. First I get to spend my Saturday night playing the invisible man, and now I get to try being a pizza delivery boy. My life is complete."

"You forgot stand-up comic." Coop stepped into the foyer, grinning.

"*Try* being the operative word on that one," Mark added wryly. "Hand over the pizzas."

"What, no tip?" Nick feigned insult.

"Sure. How about this? Don't push your luck."

"Cute." He dumped the pizzas and soda into Mark's arms.

"Since Mark doesn't seem inclined to introduce us, I'm Evan Cooper." Coop moved forward and extended his hand. "You must be Nick Bradley."

"That's right." Nick took his hand in a firm grip.

"I've heard a lot about you."

"I'll just bet. So you got stuck with this guy as a partner, huh?" He planted his fists on his hips and aimed a look in Mark's direction.

"Yeah. But he's not that bad, once you get used to his idiosyncrasies."

"Does he still like to—"

"So how's life in Richmond?" Mark cut him off.

"Touchy, aren't we?" Nick grinned but took the hint. "Life in Richmond has been good. Up until today, when this little assignment forced me to cancel out on one great chick. Sounds like you guys have a hot potato on your hands with this job."

"That's a good description for it." Coop took their dinner out of Mark's hands. "We appreciate your support."

"Goes with the territory. We'll be close if you need us."

"Any action out there?" Mark asked.

"Other than a couple of teenagers necking in a car down the street, all is quiet. Enjoy the pizza." With a grin and a wave, Nick slipped out.

"Nice guy." Coop handed the six-pack to Mark as they headed for the kitchen.

"Yeah. We had some good times at the academy."

"Has he been in Richmond long?"

"About three years. He's due for a transfer soon."

A movement in the doorway caught their attention.

"I thought I smelled pizza." Monica gave them a tentative smile.

She'd touched up her lipstick and run a brush through her shiny russet hair, Coop noted, and her color was a bit higher than it had been earlier.

"It just arrived. Would you like a soda?" Mark offered.

"I have soda here. You didn't have to order that."

"The Bureau's paying the bill. Enjoy it." Coop pulled out a chair for her at the small dinette table.

As she slipped past him to take it, he caught a faint whiff of some subtle, pleasing fragrance he couldn't quite identify. While he wasn't usually given to poetic musings, it brought to mind idyllic, carefree summer days and happy endings.

"Coop?"

51

Mark's voice pulled him back to the present, and he had a feeling this wasn't his partner's first attempt to get his attention.

"What?"

"Ms. Callahan asked if we want glasses for our sodas."

"No. Thanks."

As Coop took his seat, Monica reached for a piece of pizza. "Is there any rule against using first names in your line of work? This Ms. Callahan business is going to get old very fast."

"The customer calls the shots. First names are fine with us if that's what you prefer." Coop snared a piece of pizza too.

"Definitely." She took a bite and surveyed the stack of papers off to the side of the table. "Why do I think you gentlemen have been planning my life for me?"

"We've been arranging security coverage here, at church, and for your speech at the Jefferson," Mark confirmed.

"What about the book signing?"

Mark shot Coop a look but remained silent.

"We're taking this a couple of days at a time," Coop replied.

"Why is it okay for me to do the convention speech, but the book signing freaks you out?" Monica directed the question to Coop as she took a hearty bite of pizza.

"The Jefferson is easier to secure. The speech is part of a private event in a place where we can control the access points. The signing is in a bookstore at a public mall. It's far more risky."

She finished off her first slice of pizza and took another. "I'll think about it, okay?"

"We'd appreciate it."

"In the meantime, why don't we go over our plan while we eat." Mark wiped his hands on a paper napkin and pulled out one of the papers from the stack. "The HRT is sending another two-man security detail down here tomorrow. We'll work twelve-hour shifts. The Richmond field office will provide exterior surveillance at the house and will give us additional support for the outside commitments you can't change."

"What about church tomorrow?" Monica asked.

"Coop and I will go with you, and the Richmond office will provide backup."

"Do you honestly think I'll be in danger at church?" She gave them a skeptical look.

"No place is safe, except a safe house." Coop leveled a direct look at her. "The kind of people we're dealing with hold very little sacred, Monica. Including life—as 9/11 proved."

At his grim tone, some of the color drained from her face. She set her half-eaten slice of pizza on her plate and clenched her hands in her lap.

"I still can't believe I'm in the middle of some terrorist plot. I'm sure you guys are used to this kind of situation, but the whole thing is surreal to me. It seems more like a thriller movie than real life."

"People in pretty high positions think it's very real." Mark took a swig of his soda, his expression somber.

As she lifted her own glass, the sudden, intrusive ring of the phone on the counter shattered the insular quiet of the room. Her arm jerked, sloshing dark liquid on the table. Mark tossed some napkins on the puddle.

"Sorry." She gave him a shaky smile and started to rise.

"Just so you know, we've put a tap on your phone. We want a recording of any messages or conversations."

At Coop's quiet comment, she sank back into her chair, letting the call roll to her answering machine.

"Hi, Monica. Sorry I missed you. I was hoping you might be available for lunch on Monday. Give me a ring."

The male voice on the line left no name or number.

Interesting, Coop reflected. According to her file, she had no close relatives. Based on a conversation earlier in the day as they'd gone over her schedule, she'd indicated there was no one close enough to her to merit an alert about her unavailability for the next few days. He tilted his head and regarded her.

"Matt Haley." She took a deep breath, let it out slowly. "A colleague. I've been reviewing a paper he hopes to get published. I expect he wants to get together to discuss it. I can put him off for a few days. Or have him come here."

"If he comes here, our presence will raise questions. Put him off." Coop's decisive tone left little room for argument.

"Okay. No problem." Monica tipped her head toward the counter. "By the way, how do you know they—whoever 'they' are—haven't also tapped the phone?"

"We already checked."

Monica drew a shaky breath and reached up to massage her temples.

"Headache?" Coop gentled his voice.

She summoned up the semblance of a smile. "Yes. I'm afraid I'm not used to all this cloak-and-dagger stuff. If you gentlemen will excuse me, I think I'm going to take a couple of aspirin and call it a night." She rose, waving them down as they started to stand. "Finish your pizza."

They remained silent until the soft click of a door told them she was out of hearing range.

"I think she's beginning to realize the situation is as dangerous as it is inconvenient." Mark sopped up the remainder of the spilled soda and deposited the soggy napkins in the empty pizza box.

"Yeah."

"We have her to ourselves all day tomorrow until the other HRT security team arrives. My advice is work on the book signing." He yawned and stretched. "And now I'm going to get a little shut-eye on the couch. Unless you want me to take the first shift."

"No. Go ahead. I can hold out for a while."

As Mark disappeared into the living room, Coop gathered up the remnants of their dinner. Half of the second pizza was untouched, and he slid the box into the refrigerator. He and Mark had cleaned their plates, but Monica's contained the half-eaten piece she'd abandoned when the phone rang. He slid it into the garbage.

In the back of the house, he could hear the water running, perhaps indicating a glass being filled. He was sorry she had a headache, sorry she was frightened.

But if that was the worst thing that happened to her during this assignment, he could live with it.

"Yes?" Tariq nodded to Anis as he answered his cell phone, and the man rose from his cross-legged position on the floor and left the room.

"It is as you suspected. They are watching the house."

The connection was excellent. If he didn't know Nouri was halfway across the world, a couple of hundred yards away from Monica Callahan's house, Tariq would think he was in the next room. Technology had its uses.

"How many?"

"Two men inside. It appears there are two more outside."

"Who are they?"

"We're checking with our contacts. Not local police. They may be State Department security personnel or FBI."

"Is there any activity that indicates they're planning to leave?"

"No. The lights have been dimmed for the night. All appears quiet."

"Does the security in place present a problem for the next step?"

"It shouldn't, assuming they leave the house at some point. We only need a few minutes."

Tariq took Nouri at his word. His older brother's son headed up his most experienced U.S. cell and had personally checked out Monica Callahan's house weeks ago. His loyalty was solid, and he would carry out Tariq's bidding without question. With the funds Tariq was funneling his way, he could buy any information he needed.

"Good. Alert me of any changes in status."

"I will."

The line went dead. Unlike Anis, Nouri hadn't questioned Tariq's strategy or his timing. He would find a place for Nouri in his organization when he regained power, Tariq resolved.

For now, however, he would wait. The enhanced security around Monica Callahan indicated her father wasn't dismissing the threat to her as cavalierly as he dismissed those directed toward him. But in truth, Tariq had been prepared for a more dramatic response. He'd expected the woman to be whisked away to some secret location. Not that it mattered. Nouri was prepared for all contingencies.

The next forty-eight hours were critical. If David Callahan didn't reconsider his stance by then, he would take the next step. And the one after that. And the final one. After all, he didn't need the diplomat to achieve his goal. He could regain power without his help. In fact, some of his supporters advocated the man's elimination.

Yet Callahan's influence was powerful, and Tariq planned to use it if he could. If anyone could convince the American president to meet the terrorist demands, it was the respected diplomat. That was the easier route to success, and Tariq always took the easy way, if possible.

Besides, the benefits to Callahan's cooperation were substantial. The list of prisoners whose release Tariq had demanded included key supporters, interspersed among red herrings. And the ransom money would help him buy the arms and influence he needed to achieve his coup.

Humiliating David Callahan by forcing him to renege on his principles and negotiate with terrorists in order to save his daughter was a bonus.

But in the end, with or without Callahan's help, Tariq would reach his goal.

No matter what it took.

No matter who had to die.

5

By seven Sunday morning, the sun hadn't yet crested the distant, jagged peaks of the Hindu Kush Mountains visible outside the window of David Callahan's office. Wiping a weary hand down his face, he stared at the distant, shadowed landscape. In between, hidden from his sight but vivid in his mind, lay the cacophony that was Kabul, where destroyed and decaying buildings offered mute testimony to decades of division and violence.

Violence that now threatened his family.

He'd done everything he could to protect Monica. Gone to the highest levels to ensure the best security available. Called in favors. Pulled strings. Taken measures he would never have considered employing on his own behalf. She was as well guarded as was humanly possible.

But that didn't ease his worry.

Nor muffle the voice of his conscience.

She wouldn't be in danger if you'd done what Elaine asked years ago and taken a different job. One that would have allowed you to be a real husband and father.

Like a looped recording, that refrain had replayed over and over in his mind during the long, dark night. In general, David didn't believe in dwelling on regrets. Besides, he had few—on a professional level, anyway. His career had been everything he'd hoped it would be. There was very little about it he would change.

On the other hand, his decision to forfeit his family gave him pause. Had he known twenty-four years ago what he knew now, his choice might have been different. At the time, however, he'd accepted the sacrifice because he believed what he did was important, that it made a difference and contributed to the greater good.

But that wasn't the only reason.

The sun found a crevice in the remote, isolated peaks and aimed an illuminating shaft of light through it, exposing the cracks and fissures in the distant mountains—and the blemishes on his soul. Though he'd danced around it for years, in truth his other reasons for choosing career over family had been selfish. He'd liked the adrenaline rush of working with the movers and shakers of the world. Liked feeling important. Liked the power and prestige and perks that came with the job. And he'd grown arrogant too, believing no one could do his job as well as he could.

In the end, the position came to matter to him more than the work itself. Not that he didn't do a good job. That was well documented. As was his fearlessness in the face of personal threats, a trait praised and respected by foes and allies alike.

But the accolades were unearned, he acknowledged. His willingness to stand up to terrorists reflected indifference, not courage. He just didn't care about his own safety. He'd done everything he wanted to do professionally. He had no personal life. He was sixty-six years old. Bottom line, it didn't much matter to him if the Lord took him next week or in ten years.

Closing his eyes, he rested his head against the back of his chair and let fatigue numb his mind.

"Sir? Are you all right?"

The sound of his aide's voice roused David from his light doze. An hour had passed, he noted with a discreet glance at his watch. Neutralizing his expression, he swiveled his chair toward the door.

"Yes, Salam. Good morning." He wasn't surprised the man had come in on a Sunday. They'd all been working long hours since the abductions.

"Good morning, sir. Have you been here all night?"

The man's quick perusal of his attire reminded David he had on the same clothes he'd worn yesterday. About two in the morning he'd returned to his utilitarian room in the low-rise barracks that honeycombed the embassy compound, but he'd simply stretched out on the narrow bed fully clothed. When sleep had eluded him, he'd given up and returned to his office.

"I went back to my quarters for a couple of hours. I'll run over later to shower and change. Would you check on my daughter's status as soon as you can?"

"Yes, sir. Can I get you some coffee?"

"That would be good. Thanks."

Five minutes later, Salam returned, a steaming disposable cup in hand.

"I spoke with our contact at the FBI. Two men are with her now, and a second team will be dispatched later today. HRT security is being supplemented with field agents."

"She's still at home?" The news jolted him.

"Yes, sir. She refused to go to a safe house."

Not good. He needed to convince her to disappear until this was over. But how?

In his professional life, dealing with hostage situations and terrorists and high-level government officials, he was confident in his abilities. In his personal life, with his own family, he was far less secure. Communicating what was in his head had always been easy; when it came to expressing what was in his heart, he'd been a dismal failure.

He could call Monica again, but she'd hung up on him yesterday before he could pick up the phone. Considering he'd thrown her life into chaos in the interim, he suspected she'd be even less inclined to talk with him today.

"Would you like me to try and ring your daughter again?" It was as if Salam had read his mind.

"No. She's had a long day. It's possible she's already gone to bed."

"Perhaps later?"

"Perhaps."

With a slight bow, the man left the room.

For his own peace of mind, if nothing else, David knew he had to try again to reach Monica. And maybe she would be more receptive to his call now that she'd had a chance to think the situation through.

But somehow he doubted it.

The minutes were crawling by, and it took every ounce of Coop's willpower to keep from nodding off. His late night and early morning were finally catching up with him.

He checked his watch. Almost midnight. Soon he could pass the baton to Mark and get some much-needed rest. In the meantime, however, he had to find something to do to keep himself awake. Listening to late-night talk radio wasn't cutting it.

Flipping off the small radio tucked beside a sugar canister on the kitchen counter, Coop refilled his mug, almost wishing for a cup of Les's high-octane brew.

Almost.

As he swallowed a scalding sip of caffeine, he ran a finger lightly down the worn cover on the Bible beside the coffeemaker. He'd noticed it earlier. In light of its presence, and Monica's insistence that church tomorrow was a nonnegotiable commitment, it didn't take FBI training to deduce that her faith was important to her. The "what" was clear.

He was more intrigued by the "why."

Religion had never been more than a blip on Coop's radar screen. Aside from obligatory church attendance on Christmas and Easter, it had played very little role in his growing-up years. And as an adult, he'd given it no more than an occasional passing thought. Few of his colleagues put much stock in it, either. Their jobs demanded that they base decisions on facts and empirical evidence. Lives often depended on it—including their own. As a result, Coop had a healthy respect for logic and deductive reasoning.

That's why religion had never appealed to him. It seemed to be based more on feelings and blind faith than facts. Not the kind of thing he would expect to appeal to intelligent, well-educated people.

Yet Monica Callahan was both.

It didn't make sense.

And he was too tired to try and figure it out tonight.

Turning away from the Bible, Coop wandered into the dim living room. Mark was sprawled on the couch, his breathing shallow and regular. The ability to sleep anywhere, under any conditions, was one of the skills HRT operators cultivated. But Coop knew that at the slightest sound, Mark would wake instantly and reach for his Glock. It was an instinctive reaction for all operators—on duty and off.

The floor-to-ceiling bookcases drew Coop, and he moved across the room, his shoes silent on the plush carpet. A quick skim of the titles suggested Monica's reading taste was eclectic, ranging from biography to philosophy to literary fiction to cooking. There were even some romance novels in the mix.

On a shelf of communication-related books, one title stopped him.

Talk the Walk.

Her own book.

Tucked unobtrusively among the other volumes.

Interesting. And impressive. Most authors of bestselling books would display a copy in a prominent place in their homes. Monica had chosen to slip hers in among the rest of her collection. Modesty, it seemed, was among her virtues.

Easing the book off the shelf, he returned to the kitchen. As he sat at the table, he flipped the volume over to read the endorsement on the back from a well-known relationship expert, himself an author of a dozen books and host of a weekly radio program.

"Monica Callahan has taken a popular axiom and turned it on its ear. We've all heard about the importance of walking the talk—practicing what we preach. Ms. Callahan presents a compelling case that the opposite is also true. That buying your wife flowers, or giving an employee a raise, or attending your child's ballet recital isn't enough. While those things do communicate that you care, Ms. Callahan contends that people need to hear the words too—because words are the window to the heart. I concur, and I highly recommend this book. It will improve every relationship in your life."

Intrigued, Coop opened the book and began to read. Less than twenty pages into it he'd already recognized his own behavior in two of the examples she'd used to illustrate her points.

But then, why should that surprise him? Words had never come easy for him. After all, he'd had no example to follow. He didn't remember his mother, and his father's expressions of affection had been few and far between.

The book covered that too, in a chapter devoted to reasons why people struggle with words. There was a whole list on page 102, and it included lack of role models.

But a different reason jumped out at him.

Fear.

Coop frowned. He could see how fear might cause a verbal communication problem for some people, but he didn't think it applied in his case. He attributed his reticence to prudence, and considered it an asset, not a liability. A reflection of strength. Independence, self-reliance, and autonomy were good things.

But they can also be lonely.

That unbidden—and unwanted—thought took him by surprise. In general, he shied away from introspection. It reeked of self-indulgence and narcissism, and he considered it a waste of time.

Besides, it's scary.

Where in the world was that annoying little voice coming from?

Irritated, Coop closed the book. Enough of this. He had too much on his mind to waste energy indulging in psychoanalysis, let alone try to deal with the double whammy of the "whys" behind Monica's faith and his own reticence. He must be over-tired. That had to be the explanation for his uncharacteristic reflective mood.

"Hey . . . it's way past midnight. Why didn't you wake me?"

Startled, Coop glanced up. Mark was leaning against the door frame, stifling a huge yawn. His brown hair was sticking up at odd angles, and his shirt couldn't be more wrinkled if it had spent the past two weeks crumpled into a ball in the corner of a suitcase.

"You look like you could use some coffee." Coop rose and poured him a cup.

"You didn't answer my question."

"I wasn't that tired."

"Yeah?" Mark gave him a suspicious look as Coop handed him a mug of black coffee. "Why not? You were half comatose in Les's office yesterday morning, and you haven't had any sleep since then."

"Second wind, I guess."

Clearly unconvinced, Mark surveyed the table. His eyebrows rose when he spotted Monica's book. "I see you've been doing some reading. Any good?"

"Interesting."

"Must be, if it kept you going for"—Mark checked his watch—"forty-three hours, with only two hours of sleep."

"Why don't you read it?" Coop rinsed his cup and set it on the counter, deciding that offense was the best defense. "You might learn a few things."

"Hey, I talk the walk. I know how to use words."

"Too many, sometimes."

"Very funny. Go get some rest. Maybe sleep will improve your mood."

"There's nothing wrong with my mood."

"Uh-huh." Mark picked up the book and shoved it against Coop's chest with a smug look. "And take this with you. It might help spice up your social life. Remember: women like guys who talk. You're the one who could learn a few things."

Grasping the book, Coop turned his back and headed for the couch, dismissing the temptation to refute Mark's assessment.

Because once again, his partner was right.

Six hours later, when the ringing phone brought Coop instantly awake, he felt a little more human. The restorative power of a few hours of sleep never failed to astound him.

Swinging his legs to the floor, he joined Mark in the kitchen as the answering machine kicked in.

"This is Salam Farah from the U.S. embassy in Kabul. I am trying to put a call through to Monica Callahan from her father."

As the accented voice spoke, Coop strode forward and checked the caller ID, a feature that had been added to her phone yesterday. The number on the digital display matched the one he'd memorized in David Callahan's file. He picked up the handset.

"Mr. Farah? Evan Cooper with the FBI. If you'll hold a moment, I'll see if Ms. Callahan is awake."

Depressing the mute button, he turned to find Monica in the doorway, rubbing her eyes. She was dressed in a loose-fitting pair of sweatpants and a sweatshirt, her hair tangled, her face makeup free. It was apparent the ringing phone had roused her too.

"A call from your father." Coop kept his finger on the mute button.

"I don't want to speak with him." Her jaw firmed into a stubborn line.

"What would you like me to say?"

"I don't really care."

Giving her an appraising look, Coop released the mute button. "Mr. Farah, Ms. Callahan would prefer not to accept her father's call. However, I'd be happy to speak with him instead."

The room went silent.

"Mr. Cooper?"

"Yes, sir. Good morning."

The diplomat dispensed with the niceties. "How is my daughter?"

"Fine, sir."

"I understand she's refused to go to a safe house."

Coop eyed Monica. Her arms were crossed over her chest and her shoulders were rigid.

"That's correct."

"You need to change her mind."

"I understand, sir. We're continuing to work on that."

"Until you succeed, use every means at your disposal to protect her . . . and give her my love."

"I will, sir."

The line went dead.

Replacing the phone in its cradle, Coop turned to Monica. "He sends his love."

Bitterness tightened her features. "The man doesn't know the meaning of the word."

A few more seconds of strained silence ticked by as Coop studied her. He considered asking how she'd slept, but the dark circles under her eyes gave him his answer.

What he really wanted to know was why there was such antipathy between father and daughter. It was difficult to draw too many conclusions from his brief phone conversation with David Callahan, but the man sounded sincerely concerned—and in the diplomat's request to pass on his love to Monica, Coop was certain he'd heard a catch in his voice. Monica also seemed like a caring, empathetic person. It was puzzling. And Coop didn't like unsolved puzzles.

"I hate to impose, but would you mind if I borrowed your guest bath for a quick shower? We'll check into a hotel as soon as the other security team arrives, but in the meantime I'd hate to show up at your church looking disreputable." Mark's request, delivered with a grin, eased the taut atmosphere.

"Of course. Let me get you some towels."

As she disappeared down the hall, Mark edged closer to Coop. "Here's your chance to work on the safe house. And find out what gives between her and her father."

Draining his cup, Mark followed Monica down the hall. Coop heard the murmur of voices, the closing of a door, and then Monica reappeared and headed for the coffeemaker. Propping a hip against the counter, Coop took a sip from his own mug, watching as she rested a hand on the Bible before filling a cup.

"I noticed the Bible yesterday. Interesting place to keep it," he remarked.

"It's a good way to start the day. It centers me." She lifted the cup to her lips and looked at him over the rim. "I'm sorry if my insistence on attending church this morning is complicating things."

"We have it covered." He watched, momentarily distracted, as her lips tested the temperature of the liquid. "Mind if I ask you a question?"

Her expression grew wary. "Depends on the question."

"It's related to religion."

"Okay." She dropped her guard a fraction.

"My experience of Christianity is pretty much limited to an occasional visit to church for a wedding or funeral, but I seem to recall that one of the basic tenets is forgiveness. I'm having difficulty reconciling your obvious commitment to your faith with your bitterness toward your father."

Although his comment was met with silence—and a cold stare—he caught the flicker of conflict in Monica's eyes. Apparently he wasn't the only one having difficulty reconciling the two.

"I guess you minded the question." He cradled his mug in his hands and watched her.

"I didn't hear one."

"Touché." He kept his tone casual and let a smile tease the corners of his mouth, hoping his relaxed approach would suggest conversation rather than confrontation. He was on shaky ground, and he knew it. But if understanding the rift helped him keep her safe, he'd risk pushing for information. "Let me rephrase. How do you justify your feelings toward your father in light of what your faith teaches?"

She took a long, slow sip of her coffee as she considered his question. Coop half expected her to brush it off. But to his surprise, she responded. "I can't. But I can't help how I feel, either."

Coop let a few beats of silence tick by as he studied her. "You don't strike me as the type to hold a grudge without just cause. What did he do to you, Monica?"

The quiet question was laid on a foundation of steel, and the subtle arch of her eyebrows told him she'd picked up on that.

"It's a long story."

"Mark takes long showers. And we don't have to leave for church for a couple of hours."

"Why do you want to hear it?" She'd turned the tables on him. And he wasn't sure how to answer. While there were security motivations behind his probing, in truth there were personal reasons too. But he couldn't tell her that.

Gripping his mug, he chose his words with care. "I've always believed you can never have too much information about anything—or anyone—you're involved with."

She hesitated, as if debating her next move. "How about I give you the highlights?"

He let out the breath he hadn't realized he'd been holding in. "Fair enough."

She took a seat at the table, and he moved to the counter to refill his cup. As he lifted the coffeepot, his gaze fell on the Bible. If he was a praying man, he'd be tempted to send a plea heavenward at this point, asking for God's help and guidance. He could use both for the professional part of this assignment. Keeping Monica Callahan safe when she ventured out into the world was going to be a challenge.

But he was also worried about his own safety—in the emotional, not physical, sense. He'd worked with beautiful women on other assignments. Had dated more than his share of gorgeous females. And while many had tried, none had ever managed to tap into his deeper emotions.

Yet in one short day, the woman across the room—with zero effort—had breached the defenses around his heart.

He didn't know how she had accomplished that feat. All he knew was that he was on dangerous ground. And that if he wasn't careful, he'd be tempted to violate his long-standing vow to keep his distance in relationships.

Grasping the mug with one hand, he touched the Bible with the other. No question about it. Prayers would come in handy about now.

6

It didn't take a PhD in communications to figure out Monica was already having second thoughts about her offer, Coop concluded as he took a seat at the table. Uncertainty flickered in her eyes, and wariness lurked in their depths. But he wasn't about to let this opportunity slip away if he could help it.

"Why don't you tell me about your mother first?"

To his relief, his backdoor approach worked. The barest hint of a smile tugged at her lips, and her tense grip on her mug relaxed.

"Mom was great. We were best friends as well as mother and daughter, and there's no one I admire more. She didn't have a college degree, but she was smart and had an exceptional facility for languages. Wherever we lived, she became conversant in the local dialect within months. After she and dad divorced, she was able to turn that into a lucrative career as a translator."

"How old were you when they separated?"

"Ten."

"That must have been tough."

To his surprise, she shook her head. "Actually, it wasn't. Dad was never around much anyway. He traveled a lot, and he worked long hours when he was in town. After the divorce, Mom and I came back to the U.S., and for the first time in my life I had a permanent home. That meant a lot to me. Stability is very important to children."

"So are two parents."

"Not if they're unhappy. Kids pick up those vibes." She took a sip of coffee and gave him an assessing look. "I get the feeling you didn't grow up in an ideal environment, either."

His fingers tightened on his mug. "Why do you say that?"

"There was a touch of melancholy in your voice when you mentioned two parents."

Jolted, Coop struggled to maintain a neutral expression, buying himself a few seconds by sipping his own coffee. Either she was very good or he was slipping. When soliciting information, he was always careful to get more than he gave. Yet she'd picked up some subtle, revealing nuance. A "proceed with caution" warning began to flash in his mind.

"My mom died when I was three, so I have no memories of a mother." He recited the bare facts impassively.

"I'm sorry."

He shrugged. "You play the hand you're dealt. I survived. At least both of your parents were living."

"True." She traced a circle of moisture on the table with one finger. "But death might have been easier to accept than rejection."

The soft, pain-laced words told Coop they were getting close to the heart of the rift.

"You think your father rejected you?" His gentle response was more statement than query.

"What else should I think?" Bitterness darkened her green irises. "When forced to pick between career and family, my father picked career."

"What do you mean by 'forced'?"

Twin furrows appeared on her brow. "Sorry. Bad word choice. My mother's *request* was reasonable—and long overdue. After being dragged around to hot spots all over the world for years, she finally gave my father a choice. Take a domestic State Department job or end the marriage. At the time, we were in Tel Aviv. We'd been in Beirut before that, and there was talk Baghdad would be the next move. Mom wanted more stability—

and safety—for me. My father chose to stay overseas. End of story."

"And you've resented him ever since."

"Do you blame me?" Her eyes flashed, daring him to challenge the validity of her feelings.

"No. But that was a long time ago. His concern now seems genuine."

"Too little, too late."

"Are you saying he didn't keep in touch after the divorce?"

"He provided child support, if that's what you mean. And he always sent a check for my birthday and Christmas." Her tone was dismissive.

"You mean he had no personal contact all those years?"

She wadded a paper napkin into a small, tight ball. "On rare occasions he'd stop by to visit me," she conceded, "but the encounters were always awkward. My father may be a great diplomat, but he had no idea how to relate to his own child. Or his wife. He's a very emotionally enclosed guy. The kind of person who never lets anyone get close."

That description fit his own father to a T, Coop reflected. But there'd been a valid reason for his dad's withdrawal. Not that it was any consolation to a child suddenly bereft of a mother and in desperate need of love and nurturing. All Coop had understood was that joy and warmth had disappeared overnight from his life.

"What are you thinking?"

At the prompt from Monica, Coop wiped all expression from his face. He had a feeling she was again seeing more than he intended to reveal. "Why do you ask?"

"You were far away for a minute. In a place that wasn't very happy."

He shifted in his chair, beginning to regret he'd opened this whole can of worms. Her intuitive ability was unsettling. "I suppose we all have some memories from our childhood that wouldn't be suitable material for a Norman Rockwell painting. My dad wasn't the most demonstrative guy, either."

"But he didn't walk out on you."

"No."

The conversation lagged. Coop took another sip of his cooling coffee, listening as Mark shut off the shower. He'd gotten the information he wanted. And he better understood Monica's bitterness. Though years had passed, the hurt and betrayal she'd felt when her father chose career over family remained. And it was possible she nursed a sense of guilt, believing the marriage had been sacrificed to give her a more stable childhood. That was a boatload of emotion to haul around for twenty-plus years.

But if the exchange had given him insights into Monica, it had also opened his eyes to a few things about himself. Monica's description of David Callahan as emotionally enclosed and unwilling to let anyone get close not only fit his own father, it fit him too. And he wasn't sure he liked being put in the same category as those two men.

"You know, I was lucky in a way."

Monica's unexpected comment deflected the disturbing direction of Coop's thoughts, and he latched on to it. "How so?"

"My mom countered my dad's rejection as best she could. She gave me absolute love and did everything she could to bolster my self-esteem. Plus, she helped me establish a firm foundation of faith. No matter what happens, or how other people treat us, I came to believe we're always loved by God unconditionally. And that we're called to follow his example."

Unconditional love. An appealing—if unrealistic—concept, Coop reflected.

"What about forgiveness? Isn't that part of love? Doesn't your faith call you to that too?" It was time to bring the conversation full circle, he decided.

"Yes." She rested her chin in her hand and shook her head. "But I struggle with it. My father has never even tried to apologize."

"Is that a condition for forgiveness?"

"No." She stared into the dark depths of her half-empty mug. "But I got burned once by forgiving someone I cared about. It was a hard lesson—and not easy to forget."

"A man?"

The question hung for a moment between them.

"Sorry." Coop felt heat surge on his neck. It was one thing to ask about her relationship with her father. That was personal but relevant to the job he'd been sent to do. This wasn't. "None of my business."

She regarded him for a few moments, her expression unreadable. "As a matter of fact, no. It was a childhood friend."

He didn't try to figure out why he was relieved by her response.

"You know, I feel at a distinct disadvantage here." Monica sat back in her chair, watching him. "You read all about me in that dossier they gave you. And I've spent the past fifteen minutes spilling my guts about my past. It seems only fair that the man I'm entrusting my life to would share a little of his own background."

While the comment had been made lightly, Coop heard the serious undercurrent. But though her logic was sound, he wasn't comfortable talking about his past with anyone. Even Mark, who was almost like a brother, knew only the barest details about Coop's childhood.

"There isn't much to tell."

"How come I don't buy that?"

He tried a different tack. "A lot of my work is classified."

"I'm not talking about your work."

The bathroom door opened, offering Coop an out. *Thank you, God!*

Rising, he drained his cold coffee and headed toward the sink

75

to rinse the empty mug. "My turn. I'm in desperate need of a shower and shave and clean clothes."

When he risked a glance at her, she was still sitting at the table. Still watching him. She didn't say anything as he made a beeline for the hall. Nor did he. In fact, he hadn't said all that much in general during their little tête-à-tête.

Nevertheless, he had a disturbing sense she had discovered far more about him than he had planned to reveal.

And despite the title of her book, she'd figured it out without a whole lot of words.

As his cell phone began to vibrate, Tariq withdrew it from the folds in his robe and checked the number. Nouri.

"Shall we leave?" One of the two turbaned figures sitting across from him on the rough concrete floor started to rise.

"No need." Tariq waved him down as he answered the phone. "Yes?"

"They left the house. We followed them to her church."

"She is maintaining her schedule, then."

"It appears so. There has been no change in the convention agenda, either."

"Security?"

"Two men close by today. There are others in the crowd at the church. FBI agents. The funds you provided were useful in obtaining information."

"Let me know if you need more. You are prepared to implement the next step if it becomes necessary?"

"All is ready."

"I am pleased. Remain in touch."

Ending the call, Tariq slipped the phone back into his robe and glanced at the men seated before him. His most trusted lieutenants. Still, they knew only pieces of the plan. And neither could identify more than a few behind-the-scenes players. It was safer that way. Trust was good—and necessary—to achieve his goal. But in limited quantities. He needed Mahmud and Sayed; the former had arranged the kidnappings, the latter was maintaining security on the hostages. They would be instrumental in coordinating the next steps in Afghanistan. After that . . . he would see.

"All is well in America, I hope?"

Tariq studied Mahmud before answering. Despite the black beard and smooth skin of youth, he had the shrewdness of a much older man. And despite his deferential attitude, Tariq knew he had his own ambitions.

"Yes. Everything proceeds according to plan." He motioned for Sayed to continue. "You were telling us of the hostages."

"They are secure. One of the men is ill, but it matters not. They may die soon anyway." He lifted one shoulder in an indifferent shrug. "We are ready to execute at your command."

"Good." The slightly rotund Sayed was older than Tariq, and the leader valued his blind obedience and ruthless disregard for life. He was a good man to oversee hostages. "Mahmud, you will return to Kabul tonight and await further instructions."

"Shall I begin to arrange for David Callahan's . . . demise?"

Like Anis, Mahmud tended to push for information and question commands. His more subtle approach, however, made his impertinence no more palatable to Tariq.

"That has not yet been decided." Tariq gave Mahmud a cool look. "Our focus now is on the daughter."

"Does that not seem the more . . . difficult . . . road? Killing Callahan would send a strong message."

With an effort, Tariq kept his temper in check. He needed Mahmud. For now. "Are you questioning my judgment, Mahmud?"

"No, of course you know best. I am simply trying to under-stand."

"It is not important that you understand, just that you fol-low."

When a flush darkened the man's cheeks, confirming the effectiveness of the rebuke, Tariq threw him a crumb.

"A stronger message will be sent if we carry out a threat to his daughter on U.S. soil: if we can reach a high-ranking diplomat's daughter in her own land, think what we can do here. Such a coup will demonstrate our power and influence. Now do you understand, Mahmud?"

"Yes. Thank you."

"The shadows grow long. It is time to return to your duties."

Rising in unison, both men bowed and exited.

Left alone, Tariq sat motionless. A shiver ran through him, the feeble rays of the late afternoon sun unable to dispel the descending evening chill in the small room. Tucking his chin into his coat, he shifted on the stained cushion that insulated him from the cold concrete. One day soon, he would regain the power he'd lost. No longer would he spend his winters in unheated hovels, forced to rely on men whose ambition was stronger than their loyalty or endure the impertinent question-ing of subordinates.

Only one man stood in his path.

And one way or another, he'd bring David Callahan to his knees. He'd settle for humiliating the man, forcing him to vio-late every principle he'd ever espoused by giving concessions to the terrorists. If that didn't work, however, he'd give Mahmud permission to take him out. That tactic wasn't as politically expedient. Nor would it make as strong a statement.

But on a personal level, it would be eminently satisfying.

78

"We have a new development, sir."

David adjusted his glasses and looked up. Since his call to Monica had been rebuffed two hours ago, he'd been finding it difficult to concentrate. Welcoming the distraction, he motioned for Salam to enter. "What is it?"

"We've received a message from someone who claims to have information on the whereabouts of the hostages."

A surge of adrenaline shot through David, though he did his best to rein in his excitement. False leads were common in situations like these. In all likelihood, this would be a dead end. But he also knew that on occasion a legitimate tip surfaced. And he couldn't contain his hope that this was one of them.

"Go on." He leaned forward, resting his elbows on his desk and lacing his fingers together.

"It arrived in the usual way. A young boy in Massood Square passed it to a soldier."

Another surge of adrenaline, this one impossible to subdue. Few people outside the intelligence community knew about the kidnappers' preferred delivery method. Its use suggested the message did, indeed, come from an insider.

"An intelligence briefing is scheduled in fifteen minutes, sir. Washington will join in by conference call."

"Thank you, Salam." David picked up a notebook and rose. "I know it's late and you've been here all weekend, but can you stay until after the briefing in case we need to take some immediate action?"

"Of course, sir."

"I'll be back as soon as it's over."

As he exited his office and strode down the hall to the conference room, David tried to temper his optimism. This could amount to nothing. Even if the tip was genuine, there was no guarantee it would produce results.

But he prayed it did. He'd seen too many hostage situations

79

end in tragedy, and with each one he'd been less able to stomach the senseless loss of life. The hostages might have been strangers to him, but he'd met their desperate families, felt their terror, sensed their frustration and their helplessness.

This time, he was experiencing those emotions firsthand. And he now understood why families always grasped at the slightest hope.

Because he was doing the same thing.

An hour later, David left the meeting feeling more encouraged than he had since the three Americans had been abducted. The intelligence experts considered the tip to be authentic, most likely from someone within the group responsible for the kidnappings. Someone who was disenchanted with the leadership, had ambitions of his own, or was simply greedy, they'd theorized. While the three-million-dollar payment demanded wasn't insignificant, it was a small price to pay if the information led them to the hostages.

That had been David's assessment when his opinion had been solicited during the meeting. And he'd been able to offer it in good conscience. With or without the threat to Monica, he considered buying information a prudent course in this situation. It was their best hope of finding the hostages, and it might allow them to resolve the situation without giving in to the kidnappers' original demands.

The president had concurred.

It was the instructions for obtaining the information that gave everyone—except him—pause.

David was to be the courier for the payment. Tomorrow afternoon at two, he was to go into the city accompanied only by his driver. The money was to be in U.S. currency and stuffed into a Mickey Mouse backpack. After the driver dropped him at Chahr Chatta Bazaar, Kabul's most crowded marketplace, David was to walk slowly down the narrow, pedestrian street.

During his stroll, a young boy would approach him with a pigeon in a cage and say, "I would someday like to go to Disney World." That would be David's cue to hand over the money, return to his car, and leave. No tricks, no tracking devices, no tails. If the informant was satisfied all had been done according to his instructions, David would not be harmed and the promised information would be delivered in Massood Square by the usual method.

The fear among those attending the meeting was that the arrangements had all the markings of a trap. David would be completely vulnerable.

He couldn't argue with that. But the risk didn't faze him.

Still, convincing the White House and the intelligence community that the risk was worth taking had required every nuance of skill he'd developed in his forty years of diplomacy and negotiating.

But in the end, he'd succeeded. Tomorrow he would drive into Kabul and follow the informant's instructions to the letter.

And if all went well, if he wasn't walking into a trap, if the informant followed through on his promise to provide the information, if they could find the hostages before the terrorists grew impatient and killed them . . . the end of the crisis might be in sight.

That was a lot of ifs, he acknowledged. But it was the only hope they had of locating the hostages. And David was willing to put his life on the line to rescue them.

And to keep his daughter safe.

7

The organ swelled for the final song, and Monica reached for the hymnal in the rack on the pew in front of her. The service had been the one normal thing in her life since the FBI invasion yesterday morning, and she hated for it to end.

For the past sixty minutes, she'd done her best to pretend the two tall men who sat behind her in the last pew, on the aisle, were there to praise God, not protect her. And to forget that some of the unfamiliar faces in the congregation weren't pious visitors seeking Sunday worship but on-duty federal agents.

Carrying guns.

In church.

It was surreal.

A touch on her shoulder reminded her of Coop's instruction as they'd entered the church. *Leave ahead of the crowd.* Reluctantly she replaced the hymnal and angled toward him. He tipped his head toward the aisle as his partner exited the pew ahead of him. Picking up her coat, she edged out and fell into step behind Mark, aware that Coop was close on her heels. As Mark pushed open the door to the vestibule, Coop's lean fingers closed around her upper arm in a firm but gentle grip.

"Give him a chance to verify everything is secure."

His warm breath caressed her cheek as he leaned close to speak, and she came to an abrupt halt. He was a mere whisper away, his body shielding hers from behind as his partner conferred with a couple of dark-suited men and a woman in a black skirt and royal blue blazer. Taking her coat, he held it as she slipped her arms into the sleeves.

A few seconds later, Mark rejoined them.

"We're clear. The car's in the portico. Let's make it quick."

Flanked by the two men, Monica crossed the marble floor, her heels clicking in rhythm to the soaring notes of "Amazing Grace." The three people Mark had been talking with spread out in the vestibule as a few members of the congregation wandered out. One of the agents pretended to read the bulletin board. Another checked his watch. The woman riffled through her handbag, as if searching for her keys. Yet Monica knew all were keenly attuned to their surroundings, watching for any indication of trouble.

Protecting her.

As they approached the exterior door, Mark stepped ahead. Lifting his left arm, he spoke softly. Monica hadn't even noticed the unobtrusive earpieces the two men wore, nor the inconspicuous mikes at their wrists, until they arrived at the church. There, she'd learned that all of the security people were linked by these discreet communication devices.

Without slowing his pace, Mark pushed through the door. As he exchanged a few succinct comments with the agent standing on the other side, Coop kept a firm grip on Monica's arm. When the agent leaned over to open the door of the SUV parked a few feet away, she found herself being hustled forward and eased into the backseat. Coop slid in beside her and Mark claimed the front passenger seat while the agent took the wheel. Their exit was accomplished with such speed and smoothness that they were pulling out of the parking lot as the organ finished the first verse.

"Wow. That was pretty impressive." Monica drew a deep breath. "I take it you two have been through this drill a few times."

"A few." Coop glanced over his shoulder as he responded.

"Checking for a tail?" Her question was only half in jest. The level of security for this little outing had demonstrated how seriously the threat against her was being taken. And convinced her the danger was more real than she'd been willing to concede.

Switching his attention to the road ahead, Coop watched as a car pulled out from the curb and took up a position in front of them.

"Did he just cut in front of us?" Monica's own antennas were up now, and her pulse tripped into a staccato beat. She leaned forward, gripping the edge of her seat.

"Yes." Coop settled back, his posture relaxed. "But he's on our side."

The pieces began to fall into place, and Monica tipped her head toward the car behind them. "That one too?"

"Yes. Buckle up." He adjusted his seat belt.

"Did we have an . . . escort . . . on the way to church too?"

"Yes."

They were also taking a circuitous route back to her house, as they had on the way to church, she noticed. When she'd teased them about their navigational skill earlier, Coop had explained it was safer to operate "out of pattern," as he'd put it.

She hadn't missed the disturbing implication. They were concerned that someone had been watching her long enough to know her habits.

Trying to stifle a sudden wave of panic, Monica groped for her seat belt and pulled it out. But as she tried to buckle it, it slipped from her shaky grasp, retracting with a thump that startled Mark and had him reaching toward his belt.

"Sorry." Hot color flamed in her cheeks.

"Let me." Coop released his own belt and leaned across her. His broad shoulder pressed against her as he grasped the buckle and pulled it out, and his fingers brushed her hip when he engaged it.

For some reason, her respiration went haywire. In other circumstances, she might attribute her reaction to the tall, dark man beside her, who reeked of masculinity and whose very presence evoked strength and competence.

But as appealing as he was, she suspected her response was due more to the sudden realization that this situation was a whole lot more perilous than she'd wanted to admit. She knew little about law enforcement, but she doubted elaborate security measures like the ones being taken on her behalf were employed without very good reason.

"I had no idea a simple visit to church was going to take this much coordination. The security was quite involved, wasn't it?"

At the slight quiver in her voice, Coop turned to her. Though she was doing her best to control it, he saw a flicker of fear in her eyes. And concluded that the full reality of the situation was sinking in.

On a professional level, he considered that a good sign. Fear often induced caution—and cooperation.

But on a personal level, it tightened his gut. Monica had been put in danger through no fault of her own, and while they would do their best to protect her, there were no guarantees. Especially in a situation involving terrorists who held nothing sacred. Least of all life.

As an HRT operator, he wanted to scare her into following their advice and working with them.

As a man, he wanted to alleviate her fears despite his own growing concern.

In the end, he chose to temper his response, reassuring her without downplaying the danger.

"It took some coordination, but I'd rather err on the side of caution than be caught unprepared." He kept his tone conversational. "Besides, we've handled situations far more complicated."

85

She stared out the tinted window in silence for a few seconds, giving Coop a chance to admire her classic profile.

"What about my speech tomorrow? And the book signing later in the week?"

"What about them?"

"Are they going to be a huge hassle for you?"

"We'll worry about the book signing as it gets closer. After the other security team arrives later today, Mark and I will go over and check out the setup at the hotel. Our preference is that you cancel the speech, but I expect we'll be able to contain the venue without major problems if we bring in enough manpower."

"All this time and effort expended on my behalf . . ." Her words trailed off. "If I cancel the speech at this late date, though, it will be a major problem for the organization."

"Then we'll deal with it."

"I'm sorry for causing all this trouble."

She was hunched into the corner of her seat, looking so alone and vulnerable that Coop had an unsettling urge to entwine his fingers with hers in a gesture of comfort and support.

He restrained the unprofessional impulse by engaging his hands in another task. Pulling out his BlackBerry, he punched in some numbers.

"You're not the one causing the trouble." He directed his next comment to Mark. "I'll check with the agents on duty at Monica's."

"Good idea."

After a clipped conversation, Coop slipped the device back into the holder on his belt.

"Everything okay?" Mark shot him a glance in the rearview mirror.

"Yes. We're good." Coop checked on Monica. She was still pressed into the corner of her seat, her head angled toward the window.

"Hey." He said the word softly, and dismissing protocol considerations he rested his fingers on the back of her hand. It was like ice.

She twisted toward him, her gaze dropping to their connected hands. For an instant he thought she was going to pull away. When she didn't, he continued.

"None of this is your fault, Monica. We'll deal with the speech. After that, we'd like you to reconsider the safe house. That will allow us to give you the best possible protection until this is all over. Will you think about it?"

She regarded him for a few moments. He saw a chill ripple through her before she gave a slow nod. "Okay."

"Good." Resisting the urge to give her hand an encouraging squeeze, he smiled and retracted his fingers. "Crank up the heat a little, would you, Mark?"

"Sure."

His partner complied, and the chill in the car dissipated. But Monica still felt cold.

All except for the back of her hand where Coop's fingers had rested.

"Will it bother you guys if I do some cooking?"

At the question, Coop and Mark stopped discussing the hotel floor plan spread out on the kitchen table and turned to Monica, who stood in the doorway. She'd exchanged the burgundy wool suit she'd worn to church for snug jeans and a soft green sweater that matched her eyes, Coop noted in a swift, appreciative scan.

"Not at all. Are we in your way?" He gestured toward the large sheets of paper.

"No." She spared the material no more than a quick look.

Turning, she busied herself at the counter. "I thought I'd make chicken divan for dinner, unless you prefer pizza again."

"You don't have to feed us, Monica."

She stopped what she was doing but didn't respond at once to Coop's comment. He raised a brow at Mark, who shrugged.

"When I'm on edge, it helps to cook. Unless you'd rather order out." She said it without turning around, her tone subdued.

People coped with stress in a lot of ways, especially when confined. And Coop thought he'd seen them all. Video games, TV, solitaire, crossword puzzles—and less innocent means of escape like drinking and smoking. His own coping mechanism was reading. Mark preferred listening to music.

Cooking was a new one for him. But he was open to whatever worked. Monica was wound as tight as a spring. If she didn't find some way to release her tension, she'd snap. He'd witnessed it on a number of occasions. And he didn't want to see it happen to her.

"If we're taking a vote, chicken divan gets mine," Mark spoke up. "I've eaten enough pizza for two lifetimes."

"I'll second that," Coop added.

He watched her shoulders ease a fraction. And kept watching her until Mark kicked him under the table and spoke in a low, amused voice.

"Focus, buddy. We were talking about securing access points, remember?"

For the rest of the afternoon, Coop did his best to give their operations plan his full attention. He even positioned himself with his back to Monica. But his awareness of her was an almost tangible thing, disconcerting in its intensity. And totally beyond his experience.

No woman had ever affected him this way—and he had no clue why Monica did. Yes, she was beautiful. And smart. And sensitive. She seemed like a kind, caring, ethical person. Yet he'd met other women who shared many of those qualities, and he'd given them no more than a passing glance.

But for whatever reason, Monica Callahan appealed to him in a way no other woman ever had.

And that scared him.

He could deal with things he understood. But he didn't have a clue why he was drawn to her. There was no logical explanation for the aura of . . . specialness . . . about her. And he didn't like things he couldn't explain. Puzzles without solutions. Riddles without answers. Missions with too many unknowns. Situations requiring faith rather than facts for resolution.

"If you guys are at a breaking point and can clear the table, I'll put dinner out."

At Monica's comment, Mark turned to her with a grin. "Breaking point or not, I can't resist those aromas any longer. I'm operating on the fumes of that sausage and egg muffin Nick delivered this morning, along with a lecture on our bad eating habits. And I think hunger is undermining my partner's concentration, anyway."

Checking to confirm that Coop got his double entendre, Mark gave his partner a smirk and began to gather up the papers littering the table.

"Can I help you with anything?" Coop rose as Mark finished clearing the table and headed for the living room to deposit their afternoon's work.

"You could set the table, if you like." Monica wiped her hands on a towel and shed her oversized apron as she spoke. "The plates are in the cabinet on the far right and the utensils are in the drawer by the coffeemaker."

While he set three places, Coop assessed Monica. The strain around her mouth had eased, and the almost palpable tension he'd felt emanating from her earlier had dissipated. Most of her makeup, light to begin with, had been wiped clean by the steam from the stove, leaving only an endearing streak of flour on her cheek.

As she moved back and forth between the counter and the table with appetizing platters of food, Coop realized she'd plunged into her cooking with a vengeance. She deposited a large casserole of chicken divan, the meat and broccoli laced with a creamy sauce, in the center. A heaping bowl of mashed potatoes and an oversized bowl of salad shared the remaining space with a basket of what appeared to be homemade biscuits. And a tray of fresh-baked chocolate chip cookies was cooling on the counter.

Stunned, he gave the food another quick survey. "You did all this in the past"—he checked his watch—"three hours?"

"It's nothing special. They're all simple, basic recipes."

"Trust me, Monica." Mark grinned at her as he reentered the kitchen and perused the table. "For two bachelors who subsist on fast food and Chinese takeout, this is a gourmet feast."

"I'm not sure I'd go that far. But it's hearty, anyway. Let's eat while it's hot."

"You don't have to twist my arm. Milady." Mark pulled out a chair for her with a flourish, eliciting a giggle.

A giggle.

Coop could hardly get Monica to smile, let alone giggle. He shot Mark a dark look as the other man sat down.

"Hey, buddy, are you going to join us or what?" Mark's expression was all innocence.

In silence, Coop took the remaining place.

"Give me a sec, okay?" Without waiting for a response, Monica bowed her head and closed her eyes. Her prayer was brief, but it was long enough for Coop to pin Mark with another narrow-eyed warning—which the other man ignored.

"Okay, this is family style, so help yourself," Monica invited, raising her head.

After they'd all filled their plates and taken the edge off their hunger, she brought the conversation around to her speech.

"Now that you've had a chance to review the hotel layout and talk about security, are you comfortable with the setup?"

"We'll know more after we go over there tonight and check it out in person," Coop responded.

"But what's your initial assessment?"

"It should be doable with minimal risk," Mark said. "We'll have agents from the local office planted in the audience and among the hotel staff, and Coop and I will stick close."

"There's a food service entrance near the stage that has outside egress, and we'll use that coming and going," Coop added. "It will allow us to enter and exit without going through the crowd."

"I usually use a cordless mike and move around."

"We'd prefer you to stay behind the podium this time." Mark took a second helping of mashed potatoes.

She toyed with her salad. "I guess you don't want me wandering through the audience during the Q&A, either."

"No," the two men replied in unison.

"See? Great minds think alike." Mark grinned and lifted a forkful of potatoes. "Did you put garlic in these?"

"Yes."

"I thought so. They're great."

"Thanks." Monica smiled and picked up the basket. "Have another biscuit too."

"Don't mind if I do." Mark helped himself. "These are fabulous."

"Coop?" She turned toward him.

"Thanks. I second my partner's compliment. These remind me of the biscuits my stepmother makes."

"I didn't know you had a stepmother." She set the basket down and gave him her full attention.

A man could drown in those green pools she called eyes,

he reflected, forcing himself to concentrate on buttering his biscuit. "My father remarried when I was sixteen. I was only home for another year before I left for college, but I remember her great meals. And I always enjoyed the care packages of homemade cookies and brownies she used to send me in college."

"You never told me that."

Coop responded to Mark's comment with a shrug. He'd never told anyone about his stepmother's kindness. He didn't talk about personal history. Or he hadn't until the past twenty-four hours. "It wasn't a big deal."

"Hey, brownies and cookies are always a big deal." Mark winked at Monica, eliciting a soft chuckle.

Although Coop wasn't thrilled with Mark's flirty attitude toward the woman sitting between them, he supposed it could be a diversionary tactic. Mark was as attuned to nuances as Coop was, and Monica's stress was obvious. Often in tense situations they used lighthearted banter to put someone at ease. That was probably what Mark was doing.

He hoped.

Coop's BlackBerry began to vibrate, and he pulled it from its holder. Monica's smile faded as she watched him, and the tense atmosphere their casual dinner had managed to lighten grew heavy again.

"Are the reinforcements here?" Mark laid his napkin on the table as Coop ended the brief call.

"They will be in two minutes." Coop downed the other half of his biscuit in one large bite and wiped his mouth with his napkin. "We'll help you clean up before we head out," he told Monica. Rising, he reached for one of the bowls and her plate, noting that despite all she'd cooked, she'd eaten very little herself.

"No, that's okay. It will give me something to do." She stood and gestured toward the cookies. "Do you have time for dessert?"

"We always have time for dessert." Mark grinned and answered for both of them. "And my guess is our replacements wouldn't mind having some, either, while we brief them."

The doorbell rang, and Coop moved toward the hall, Mark behind him. "Stay here," he told Monica.

Mark dropped back once they entered the foyer while Coop checked the peephole. A pair of tall, formidable-looking men in suits stood on the other side, one with black hair and a rugged, intense face, the other with dark auburn hair and penetrating eyes. Two of the HRT's top operators. Les wasn't taking any chances with this gig, Coop reflected as he swung the door open.

The men stepped inside quickly, and as Mark holstered his Glock they exchanged greetings.

"Have you guys been fully briefed?" Coop tossed the question over his shoulder, leading the way to the kitchen.

"We reviewed the intel on the drive down," the auburn-haired man replied.

"Good. We'll bring you up to speed in a minute." Coop ushered them into the kitchen. "Monica, let me introduce you to the night shift."

As Coop spoke, she turned and braced herself against the counter, gripping the edge.

"Rick Hooper"—Coop tipped his head toward the dark-haired man—"and Shaun MacDonald . . . or Mac, as we call him."

Though her smile seemed forced, she moved forward and held out her hand.

"I already told them they're just in time for KP duty." Mark grinned and gave her a wink as she greeted the newcomers.

"He's kidding, of course," Monica assured them. "But you are in time for chocolate chip cookies and coffee, if that interests you."

"Sounds good. Thanks." Mac flashed her a smile.

The men helped themselves, disappearing into the living room one by one until only Coop was left.

"We need a few minutes to sort through things," he told her.

She swallowed and gave a jerky nod. "I'll stay out of your way." Angling toward the sink, she busied herself with cleanup duties.

Coop traced the rigid line of her shoulders, her tense posture mute testimony to her stress. As was the way she fumbled a bowl. It dropped into the sink, splashing her with soapy water.

Snagging a dish towel, he moved forward and handed it to her in silence. As she dabbed at her face, he couldn't tell whether the moisture around her eyes was water—or tears.

"Monica." He spoke softly, waiting until she looked up before continuing. "It will be okay."

She searched his eyes, as if seeking the truth. His demeanor must have soothed her, because after several seconds her features eased.

"I'm just a little jumpy. But I trust you guys."

He managed to paste on a confident smile, but as he headed toward the living room he could only hope they deserved the faith she'd placed in them.

Forty-five minutes later, when Coop reappeared in the kitchen, Monica folded her arms and faced him across the room.

"Mark and I are heading over to check out the hotel." He snagged his jacket off the back of a chair and shrugged into it. "We'll be back to relieve Rick and Mac at six tomorrow morning."

"Okay."

She watched as he settled his jacket on his shoulders, expecting him to leave at once. Instead, he hesitated, as if uncertain about something. Such behavior from a man who usually projected authority and confidence rattled her.

"Is something wrong?" She braced herself.

"I have some news."

"Good or bad?"

"It may be good."

"That doesn't sound very definitive." She gave him a wary look.

"I just talked to my boss in Quantico. It appears someone in the terrorist group responsible for the kidnappings is willing to sell information about the location of the hostages."

"Isn't that good?"

"If it's authentic. The security people who analyzed the communication think there's a high probability it's legit. In all likelihood it came from an insider with his own agenda. But it could also be a trap."

"What do you mean?"

"Your father has been designated as the courier for the money."

It took her only a couple of seconds to process that piece of information and reach the obvious conclusion. "The terrorists may be trying to lure him out of the embassy so they can . . ." She didn't finish the sentence.

"It's possible. He's been told to come alone."

"Where?"

"A crowded marketplace."

"Is he going to do it?"

"Yes."

"Why?"

"That's a question you'd have to ask him." He propped a shoulder against the door frame and slipped one hand into the pocket of his slacks. "I can place a call to the embassy if you want to talk to him."

A brief flicker of indecision delayed her response for a fraction of a second. "No."

"If you change your mind, let Rick or Mac know. They can put the call through."

"Thanks."

Once again he hesitated. "Are you okay?"

He seemed as surprised by the soft question as she was.

"Yes." A tremor ran through her word, exposing the lie.

His gaze dropped to her lips, then rose again to her eyes, holding them captive. "Monica?"

One word. That was all he said. But she heard much more. *Tell me the truth. I care. I want to know how you really feel.*

Several silent seconds ticked by as she considered how to respond.

"I'm not sure." Her voice was little more than a whisper as she responded to his unspoken entreaty. "This has been very hard. And scary."

"I know. But we'll do our best to get you through it."

Under his probing scrutiny, Monica felt her composure begin to disintegrate. Since Coop and Mark had turned her world upside down yesterday morning, she'd been struggling to appear poised and confident and strong.

Except she didn't feel strong now. She felt off balance and unsure, especially in light of this latest bombshell, with its unsettling implications. And in desperate need of something solid and safe and dependable to cling to. Something or someone.

Someone like Coop.

Even as the thought echoed in her mind, she dismissed it as absurd. The man was a stranger to her.

But she couldn't dismiss as easily the powerful urge to walk across the room and lean into him, to let his muscular arms enfold her. Protect her. Shelter her. The urge was so compelling she took an involuntary step back to counter it.

"Thanks." A single word was all she could get past her tight throat.

His eyes narrowed a bit at her retreat. "Try to get some sleep tonight. You're in good hands."

"I will."

With a final assessing look, Coop disappeared down the hall. A couple of minutes later, she heard the front door open, then click shut.

He was gone.

Taking with him whatever residual peace of mind she'd been clinging to. His departure left her feeling abandoned. And uneasy.

This is ridiculous, she berated herself, grabbing a dishcloth to give the spotless counter another vigorous scrubbing. Rick and Mac were in her living room. They were HRT operators too. Just as competent and qualified as Coop and Mark. Hadn't Coop himself said she was in good hands?

She believed that. She did.

The problem was, they weren't Coop's hands.

And for whatever reason, that made a huge difference.

8

"May God go with you, sir."

Hoisting the bulging Mickey Mouse backpack onto one shoulder, David gave Salam the ghost of a smile. "Thank you. I hope he's listening."

It was time. Buttoning his fleece-lined coat against the frosty air, David strode down the hall and exited the office building. His State Department security team was clustered around his car, and every member looked nervous. He understood that. Their job was to protect him, not let him walk into a potential trap. Once the decision had been taken out of their hands, they'd lobbied for at least a few security precautions.

But David's only concession to their concerns had been a bulletproof vest. Too much was at stake to play games with the informant. He wasn't about to jeopardize this opportunity by going in armed or wired, as security had suggested.

Besides, no safety measure would shield him from a bomb. He knew that as well as they did.

With a nod to the security team, he slid into the backseat. The door shut behind him. The car moved forward. After a brief pause at the main gate, they pulled onto Airport Road, leaving behind the protection of the walled, heavily fortified embassy.

And as the car headed toward Pushtunistan Square and the bridge that would take them over the Kabul River, David Callahan wondered if this was the day he would die.

"Nouri?" Tariq pressed the cell phone to his ear and peered through the smudged glass, hating the dirt and indigence and destitution that surrounded him. He could afford better, thanks to the opium trade. But he needed to lay low, hide in an obscure hole until this operation was finished. After that, his sacrifices would pay dividends.

"Yes."

"Is the speech still to be given?" He turned his back on the view. David Callahan had not responded to the threat to his daughter. It was time to take the next step.

"My source says there has been no change."

"Good. That is your window. Use it."

"I understand. It will be done."

The line went dead.

Three thirty-seven.

Squinting at the LED dial on her bedside clock, Monica leaned closer to verify that only twenty sleepless minutes had crawled by since she'd last allowed herself to check the time.

Slowly she sank back onto her pillow and did the math, factoring in the time difference between Richmond and Kabul.

In less than an hour, her father would risk his life in the hope of saving three hostages.

And her.

The refrain that had been echoing in her mind since Coop told her the news replayed again.

He's willing to die to keep you safe.

But it's his job.

99

People don't choose to die for a job. People die for principles—or love.

He never told me he loved me.

Maybe he's telling you now, in his own way.

But I wanted to hear the words.

It takes more courage to die than to speak. Yet you didn't even have the courage to call him.

The guilt pressed down on her, relentless as the oppressive, humid heat of a Richmond summer day, and she swallowed past the sudden pressure of tears in her throat.

Struggling into a sitting position, she flipped on her bedside lamp and reached for the Bible she'd brought in with her from the kitchen. She held it unopened in her unsteady hands, her thumbs brushing the worn cover. She didn't need to turn to Exodus to know what the Lord thought about stiff-necked people. And she didn't need to flip to Ephesians to be reminded of his opinion on bitterness, indignation, and reviling. Or his instruction to be merciful and forgiving.

As Coop—a confessed lukewarm Christian, at best—had pointed out, forgiveness was at the heart of her faith. Everyone knew that.

She also knew it was one of her biggest failings. At least in terms of her father.

On that front, her mother had been a far better Christian, Monica acknowledged. Elaine Callahan had forgiven her husband long ago. Yes, she'd been disappointed in her marriage. And yes, she'd placed the bulk of the responsibility for its demise on him. Yet somewhere along the way, she'd not only found the grace and charity to forgive him, she'd come to feel sorry for him. And she'd encouraged Monica to do the same.

But after taking her mother's advice on forgiveness once—with disastrous results—Monica had resolved never to repeat that mistake.

100

Now, in the quiet of her room, far removed from whatever peril David Callahan was facing at this very moment, she knew she had to start down that difficult path. Clenching her fingers around the Bible, she closed her eyes.

Lord, I know I should have done this years ago. But bitterness is powerful, and fear can be paralyzing. I ask you to help me overcome both and to follow the example you set. Please forgive me for my stubbornness. And please keep my father safe.

For a full minute, Monica let the prayer resonate in her mind as she recalled the old Chinese proverb: a journey of a thousand miles begins with a single step. She'd taken that step tonight. Tomorrow, she would take the next one. In the interim, she had to trust that the Lord would keep her father safe. It was beyond her power to do anything else.

Determined to put aside her worries, Monica flipped off the light. If she didn't get some sleep, she'd be a zombie when she delivered her speech tomorrow—correction: today.

Staring at the dark ceiling, she thought of her mother's antidote for a sleepless night: warm milk with a dash of vanilla and a sprinkle of cinnamon. She hadn't had one of those tonics in years. Hadn't *needed* one. But if ever a situation called for comfort food—or drink—this was it. Too bad her house had been taken over by the FBI. She wasn't about to traipse out there again in the ratty sweat suit she liked to sleep in. And she didn't have the energy to get up and change.

She punched her pillow into a different shape and turned on her side.

Thirty minutes later, she was still wide awake, still trying to imagine what was happening in Kabul.

She had to think about something else.

The reconnaissance trip to the Jefferson Hotel popped into her mind. She'd half expected Coop to call afterward and tell her how it had gone, but then, why should he? As he'd said when he left, she was in good hands.

Hands.

An image of Coop's fingers resting on hers in the car flashed through her mind. He had nice hands, well proportioned, with lean, powerful fingers that looked competent for any task. The kind of hands that could exhibit strength—or gentleness. What would it be like to be touched with gentleness by Coop? Monica wondered. To let those strong, skilled fingers work magic against her skin?

A flutter in her stomach warned her to rein in her imagination. Romantic fantasies were fine in appropriate situations. But this wasn't one of them. She'd just met the man. He was here on a job that was under intense scrutiny from the highest levels. He *had* to be nice to her. When this was over, in a day, or a week, or a couple of weeks, he'd walk out of her life as abruptly as he'd entered it.

Besides, he wasn't her type. He was too reticent. Too unwilling to open up, to share. And she'd vowed long ago to walk a wide circle around men like that. Relationships should be based on communication and trust, and Coop didn't strike her as the type who did either very well. His fast exit this morning when she'd tried to elicit a little personal information had been telling. If she was smart, she'd consider that a warning and keep her distance.

Nevertheless, she was intrigued by him. And it wasn't easy to forget the feel of his fingertips against her hand. What would it take to get the taciturn HRT operator to loosen up? What emotions were hidden under that calm, controlled veneer he presented to the world?

Dwelling on those questions, however, was not going to help her get to sleep, Monica concluded. Thoughts of Evan Cooper were *not* relaxing.

102

Determined to redirect her focus, she switched sides and forced her mind to replay an old movie she'd watched a couple of nights ago. An hour later, she managed to escape into an uneasy slumber.

There was just one little problem.

Coop had the starring role in all her dreams.

Except for the recurring one with her father, in which a bomb kept going off.

At David's direction, the embassy car dodged a bicycle and a horse-drawn cart to nose into the curb near the entrance to Chahr Chatta Bazaar.

"Wait for me here," he instructed the driver.

"Yes, sir. Good luck."

"Thank you."

Pushing open the door, David hefted the heavy backpack over one shoulder and stepped onto the pavement. He'd substituted wool slacks and a casual jacket for his customary suit, and he turned up the sheepskin collar to cut the cold, biting wind that whipped down the street, sending loose papers scuttling across the road.

Lord, please walk with me on this journey.

The spontaneous supplication surprised him. Although he was a believer, prayer played little role in his life. Nor did he attend church or read the Bible. But his mother had planted a seed of faith in him as a youngster, and it sometimes poked a tentative leaf or two above the ground in crisis situations. Today certainly qualified.

Without giving himself a chance to second-guess his courier role, David strode down the street and turned into the market.

He'd been here once before, on a much earlier State Department trip to Kabul, to sightsee. In those days, he'd been enamored by his exotic ports of call. While their allure had faded in the intervening years as the term *exotic* came to be interchangeable with *impoverished*, the memory of his first visit here remained vivid. And little had changed.

The roofs of the four arcades had disappeared, but the narrow cobblestone street retained the seventeenth-century feel he remembered. Despite the cold, turbaned merchants in flowing robes were doing a brisk business in tiny shops or from the backs of donkeys. A silk dealer was haggling loudly with a customer. A silversmith was seated cross-legged inside a doorway, fashioning an ornate piece of jewelry. Elaborate beaded hats and fine embroidery were displayed on the fronts of some shops. In others, all manner of textiles covered every available space, forming a colorful collage.

The merchandise was the only bright spot in the otherwise bleak, dingy setting.

As instructed, David traversed the street in an unhurried manner. And with a calmness that surprised him. He'd been afraid that when the moment arrived, fear would paralyze him. Instead, the opposite had happened. After all, there were far less meaningful ways to leave this world. He took some consolation in the fact that his death, if that was his fate this cold February day, would be for a noble cause.

Pausing, he closed his eyes and opened his heart.

Father, into your hands I commend my spirit. Please forgive me for all of my many mistakes and shortcomings. And bless Monica always with your grace. Let her never be lonely. Help her understand why—

". . . Disney World."

David missed the beginning of the sentence, but the last two words suddenly registered. His eyes flew open.

A young boy—no more than seven or eight, David estimated—

regarded him with solemn, dark eyes. His face was dirty, his nondescript clothing a mismatch of drab, ill-fitting items . . . and he held a bamboo birdcage containing a pigeon.

"Repeat." David said the word in Pashto.

The boy shifted from one foot to the other, darting a quick, nervous glance up and down the street, but he didn't comply with David's request. Instead, he pointed to the man's backpack.

"Repeat." David tried again, switching to Dari. He had to be sure this wasn't some freak coincidence, simply a young boy who'd been attracted by his Disney World backpack and was looking for a handout.

This time, the boy understood the instruction. In slow, deliberate English he repeated the words.

"I would someday like to go to Disney World."

This was it. David's heart began to pound. He eased the backpack off his shoulder and handed it to the youngster.

Dropping the pigeon cage at David's feet, the boy grabbed the backpack with both hands and wove his way down the street. In seconds he had disappeared.

Slowly David backed away from the cage. He didn't think it contained a bomb; there was nowhere to conceal one in the delicate mesh of bamboo. But there were plenty of shadowy doorways and tiny lanes where a sniper could be hiding. Now that his package had been delivered, David was expendable— if the informer had used the lure of information as no more than a ruse to generate some easy cash . . . and eliminate the courier.

Nevertheless, David followed the instructions and headed toward his waiting car, looking neither right nor left.

It was the longest walk of his life.

When he emerged from the market, the embassy car remained parked where he had left it. The driver started to get out as he approached, but he waved the man back into the vehicle and slipped into the backseat.

"Let's get out of here," he said.

"Yes, sir."

The ride back to the embassy was tense and quiet.

Not until they pulled into the compound and the gates swung shut behind them did David allow himself to believe his life had been spared. The informant had kept his bargain.

So far.

Now David prayed the man would honor the rest of it and supply the information they desperately needed.

"Ladies and gentlemen, communication isn't brain surgery, although the tools of the trade can be dangerous. Words, like scalpels, can cut. But so can silence." Monica waited, giving the audience in the Jefferson Hotel's ornate ballroom a few seconds to digest that thought.

"You know, I must admit I'm not much of a country music fan." Her gaze swept the audience and she smiled. "But there was a song a few years back that captured my key message today. It was called 'I Thought You Knew.' It's a song about the danger of assumptions, and wishing for a chance to say all the things you thought the other person knew.

"'I Thought You Knew' happens to be a love song. But the principle is true in all parts of our life. If you remember only one thing from my talk this morning, let it be this: don't make the mistake of assuming someone knows how you feel—in your professional life or your personal life. Talk the walk. Thank you."

Thunderous applause filled the room, and three hundred people rose to their feet as one. From his position to the right of the velvet-draped stage, facing the audience, Coop had a good view of the enthusiastic reception Monica's speech was being given. And the ovation was well deserved. For the past forty-five minutes, she'd made everyone in the room think, charmed them into laughter, and touched their hearts.

Including his.

No question about it. The lady knew her stuff.

He exchanged a glance with Mark, who stood at the front of the room on the other side of the stage. His partner grinned and gave a subtle thumbs-up signal.

As Monica launched into the Q&A session, fielding questions with consummate skill and a warmth that endeared her to the audience, Coop altered his position slightly to better observe the people approaching the mike positioned in the center aisle, beneath the huge crystal chandelier. They all looked like typical business types. No one exhibited any behavior that tripped a red alert. Everything seemed under control. A visual and audio check with the agents positioned at the exits and in the red-draped alcoves along the sides of the room confirmed that nothing was amiss. Still, he was glad they were in the home stretch.

Twenty minutes later, as the president of the organization joined Monica at the podium to end the Q&A, Coop and Mark slipped backstage to relieve the agents on duty there.

"Wasn't she great?" The man's enthusiastic question was met with another round of applause as his voice boomed through the mike. "*Talk the Walk* will be available for sale in the expo area, so be sure to pick up a copy. Ms. Callahan, thank you again. I know we all learned a lot this morning. Ladies and gentlemen, lunch is now served in the Empire Room."

As the man shook her hand and she exited into the wings, Coop and Mark were waiting to escort her. Once in the food service area, two more agents joined them. The four men formed a tight circle around Monica while they wove among stainless steel counters and racks of dirty dishes.

Coop spoke into the mike at his wrist as they approached the outside fire door where they'd entered, its alarm disengaged for her appearance.

"Okay, we're clear," he said to the two agents in the lead.

They pushed through the door, hustling Monica into the waiting SUV, which was book-ended by two nondescript vehicles. Coop climbed in beside her, and Mark took the front passenger seat. An agent she didn't recognize was behind the wheel. No one spoke until they were on the road and headed back to her house.

"That was quite a performance."

A flush crept over Monica's cheeks at Coop's compliment. "Thanks."

"I second that." Mark angled toward her. "You had them eating out of your hand."

Her color deepened. "You two are good for my ego. You can come to my speaking engagements anytime. Except I hope you can sit in the audience and enjoy the next one."

"I enjoyed this one. Didn't you, Coop?"

"Yes."

"Learn anything?"

Coop sent his partner a "knock it off" look.

"In case you haven't noticed, Monica, Coop's not the most talkative guy around." Mark ignored the other man's silent warning. "But I found him reading your book at two in the morning on Sunday, so maybe there's hope for him yet."

"You were reading my book?" Monica's speculative gaze came to rest on her seatmate.

"I was having a hard time staying awake that first night, and I like to read. I found it on your bookshelf. It sounded interesting." Coop felt a flush rise on his own neck.

She waited, as if she expected him to say more. When the silence lengthened, Mark shook his head.

"It might be nice to comment on the book," Mark prodded. The flush on Coop's neck rose higher.

"That's okay." Monica responded to Mark but smiled at Coop. "It's not everybody's cup of tea. What sort of books do you like to read?"

"Biography. But I was intrigued by your book. It kept me awake."

Rolling his eyes, Mark turned his back on his partner. "I give up."

Recognizing his faux pas, Coop tried to think of a way to mitigate it. But to his surprise, Monica reached over and laid her slender fingers on his hand—as he had done with her yesterday.

"Hey, it's okay. I'll take intrigued. And trust me, considering that a lot of my students use my book to cure insomnia, the fact it kept you awake until the wee hours is a compliment."

He added graciousness to her growing list of attributes.

"Don't you get nervous in front of a big audience like that?"

At Mark's query, Monica removed her hand. Coop missed the connection at once. "Not usually. You gain a comfort level with practice. I thought I might have a problem today, given all that's going on, but I attribute my calmness to you guys. I trust you to keep me safe."

"No pressure there." Mark grinned at her over his shoulder, but Coop heard the serious undercurrent in his partner's voice. And felt the same way.

Trust was good. It induced cooperation. But there was a downside too. When someone trusted you, it added to your burden. Increased your sense of responsibility. Failure became less of an option.

It hadn't taken Monica's profession of trust to solidify Coop's resolve to keep her safe, of course. He'd been determined to do that from the moment Les gave him and Mark this assignment. It was his job.

But in the past three days it had become more than that. He would do everything he could to live up to Monica's trust not only because it was his job but because he was coming to care about her far more than the duties of this assignment dictated.

There was one problem with keeping her safe, however. And it had nothing to do with his professional abilities. He was well trained and experienced. He was good at what he did. Skill wasn't an issue.

Luck, however, was.

Along the way, he'd learned a hard lesson. In his business, total commitment and tactical excellence didn't always equate to success. Sometimes, on rare occasion, an HRT mission failed.

Coop wasn't about to admit that to Monica.

But that unsettling reality compelled him to say a silent prayer that this assignment wouldn't be one of those exceptions.

9

"Sit tight while Mark sweeps the house." Coop directed his comment to Monica, then resumed scanning the neighborhood outside the SUV's windows.

"I've got the routine down. Don't worry."

Lowering his left wrist from near his mouth, Mark spoke from the front seat. "Nick says everything's been quiet since we left."

"Shouldn't take long, then."

The agent behind the wheel pulled into the driveway. As soon as the car came to a stop near the front walk, Mark slid from the front passenger seat and headed for the house while the escort vehicles continued down the street. Within a couple of hours of their arrival on Saturday, someone had made copies of her key for the agents on duty. She'd lost track of who all had one at this point, but she knew Mark and Coop did.

The driver stepped out of the vehicle as well. As Coop started to follow suit, Monica restrained him with a hand on his sleeve.

"Coop? I'd like to place that call to my father once we get inside."

She saw a flicker of surprise in his eyes—and a hint of warmth she classified as approval.

"No problem. I'll arrange it."

He took up a position on the other side of the car, and Monica settled back in her seat, grateful to have a couple of minutes to catch her breath.

She hadn't been surprised she'd slept late this morning, considering she hadn't nodded off until almost five. It had taken Coop's firm, repeated knock and concerned query through her door to rouse her at eight-thirty. Then it had been a mad dash to get ready for her speaking engagement and drive a winding route to the Jefferson. They'd arrived for her appearance with mere minutes to spare.

Given the hectic pace of her morning, there'd been no chance to call Kabul. But during the drive into Richmond, she'd had the opportunity to pepper Coop with questions about the outcome of her father's trip to the bazaar, and to reassure herself he was back in the embassy, safe and sound. There'd been no word yet from the informer, but hopes were high that the promised information would be passed on soon. If all went well, the hostage situation could be resolved in a matter of hours.

And Monica would have her life back.

As far as she was concerned, that couldn't happen soon enough. In the past few days, she'd learned she wasn't cut out for cloak-and-dagger stuff. But she was grateful it didn't seem to faze the FBI personnel assigned to protect her.

Her door opened, and Coop leaned down. "We're clear."

She took the hand he extended and swung one leg to the ground. The hem of her black A-line skirt inched toward her thigh, and she tugged it back into place—but not before Coop gave her exposed leg a discreet, appreciative scan.

He might not be the most communicative guy around, but Monica got the message loud and clear.

He found her attractive.

And for reasons she refused to consider, that pleased her.

"Let's wait on the call to my father until I change." Monica needed a few more minutes to let the adrenaline rush from her speech subside before jumping into another emotional fray.

"Okay." Coop fell into step beside her, his gaze sweeping their surroundings as they walked toward the porch.

The front door opened as they approached, and Mark ushered them in, closing it behind them. Monica watched as he locked the new deadbolt that had been installed Saturday afternoon while she was holed up in her office trying to pretend everything was normal.

"How about I order Chinese for a late lunch/early dinner?" Mark pocketed the key and grinned at Monica. "I know it can't compete with that great meal you fixed yesterday, but it would be easier than cooking again, after your busy morning."

"Chinese gets my vote," she confirmed with a smile. "Coop, if you'll give me fifteen minutes, I'll be ready for that call."

"No hurry."

As she headed down the hall, Monica knew her comment wasn't quite truthful. She doubted she'd ever be ready for a call to her father. But in light of his selfless gesture in the marketplace, she needed to take this first step toward forgiveness.

And trust that the Lord would guide her on the difficult journey ahead.

"I need a soda. Want one?" Mark moved toward the kitchen as Monica's door clicked shut.

"Sure."

Coop followed Mark, rotating the kinks from his shoulders. "I'm glad the speech is over."

"Me too. No matter how hard you try to secure a public venue, the margin for error is too high for my taste."

"I agree." Coop took the soda Mark handed him and pulled the tab. The hiss of carbonation as the pressure released was a good metaphor for his own dissipating tension now that the speech was safely behind them.

"You need to work on the book signing." Mark opened his own soda. "That one makes me nervous."

"How about we work on it together?"

"There's a better chance she'll listen to you."

"Are you going to start that again?" Coop took a long swallow from the can and gave his partner an irritated look.

"My eyes don't lie."

"What's that supposed to mean?"

"I see how the lady looks at you. It's not the same way she looks at me. Trust me, you have more . . . influence. Despite that remark about her book."

Heat warmed Coop's neck again. "Okay. I admit it. The compliment didn't come out quite the way I intended."

"Compliment? 'Your book kept me awake' was a compliment? Man, you're in worse shape than I thought. Now, smooth talker that I am, I'd be happy to give you a few—"

A scream pierced the air, cutting Mark off mid-sentence.

Choking on his soda, Coop drew his Glock and sprinted down the hall, Mark at his heels.

They heard a thud. Like the sound of someone falling. The screams ratcheted down to ragged, sobbing whimpers.

Coop stopped beside Monica's door, his pulse pounding. Mark took up a position on the opposite side.

With a nod to his partner, Coop pushed the door open, bracing himself for whatever lay on the other side.

It wasn't what he expected.

Monica lay sprawled on her back at the foot of the bed, braced on her elbows. Her chest was heaving, her eyes wide with shock and horror. There was no obvious sign of injury. A quick inspection of the attached bath and the open closet confirmed there was no one else in the room.

Dropping to one knee beside her, Coop laid a hand on her

shoulder, struggling to keep his panic from registering in his voice. "Monica, what happened? Are you hurt?"

He gave her a quick visual scan, spotting the blood on the fingers of her right hand at the same instant Mark spoke.

"Coop."

His partner was standing by an open drawer in Monica's dresser, his expression grim.

Rising, Coop covered the distance between them in three strides, keeping one eye on Monica.

At the dresser, he found the source of both the stains on her fingers and her terror.

The lingerie in the drawer was soaked with blood.

Fresh blood.

Cold terror gripped Coop. "Call Nick. We need backup ASAP. And get forensics. Including a K-9 bomb sniffer. I thought you swept this place?" Accusation—and anger—sharpened his voice.

"I didn't go through the drawers."

The response was delivered in a neutral rather than a confrontational or defensive tone—much to Mark's credit, Coop acknowledged, a muscle clenching in his jaw. His implication and implied indictment—were uncalled for. No one was more careful than Mark. After nearly three years of trusting each other with their lives, Coop knew that better than anyone. His anger was misdirected. "Sorry."

"No problem. Check her out." Mark jerked his head toward Monica and pulled out his BlackBerry.

Gun in hand, Coop moved back to Monica. She was sitting up now, hugging her knees to her chest as she stared at the blood on her fingers. And she was shaking. Badly.

As he dropped back down beside her, she drew a shaky breath. "I found the blood and backed up too fast. I t-tripped over the footboard."

115

Though she was making an obvious effort to control her panic, the catch in her voice was telling. He wanted to pull her into his arms and comfort her but settled for a gentle touch of her cheek. "Are you hurt?"

"No." Her focus remained on her fingers.

Pulling out his handkerchief, he cleaned them as best he could. Her hands were like ice. Balling the stained square of cotton, he set it on the floor and rose, holding out a hand.

"Let me help you up." He pulled her to her feet in one smooth, sure movement, maintaining his grip until he was certain her legs were steady enough to support her. "We need to leave here, Monica."

Somehow she managed to dredge up the trace of a smile. "That safe house you recommended is suddenly sounding very appealing."

"It's all arranged."

"Can I pack a few things?"

"No. We'll get you whatever you need later. The ERT won't want us to touch anything." He didn't mention the bomb-sniffing dog.

"ERT?"

"Evidence Response Team."

"The agents on duty will cover us to the SUV, and our escort vehicles are on their way back." Mark joined them, his gun still drawn. "You ready to move out?"

"Yes." Coop was as anxious to leave as Mark was. Whoever had drenched Monica's lingerie drawer with blood could have planted a bomb somewhere else in the house, though he doubted it.

A shiver ran through Monica, and she rubbed her upper arms. "Can I put that on?" She gestured toward the bed where a black turtleneck sweater lay.

Her attire suddenly registered, and Coop realized her ecru-colored camisole top with spaghetti straps wasn't meant to be a blouse. And that it was the same lacy garment that had peeked above the V of the business suit she'd worn for her speech, subtly softening the tailored garment—and kicking his hormones into overdrive.

Stifling his inappropriate thoughts, Coop reached past her, snagged the turtleneck, and handed it to her. Once she'd pulled it over her head and smoothed it over her jeans, he took her arm. "Let's move."

He let Mark lead the way. Nick was entering when they arrived at the front door, his expression somber as Coop helped Monica into her coat.

"The escort vehicles have been recalled and will join you at the end of the street." The agent shook his head. "I have no idea how anyone managed to get into this house. We've had it under surveillance the whole time, front and back."

"Figure it out." Coop didn't care if he sounded curt. A slip like this could have cost Monica her life. Would have, if the intruder had wanted it to. Meaning the intent hadn't been to kill but to send a very strong message that despite their best efforts, she was vulnerable. And that they could get to her whenever they chose.

It was not a comforting thought.

And Coop didn't even want to *think* about Washington's reaction to this incident.

Mark and two other agents surrounded them as Coop hustled Monica to the SUV, where the agent who'd driven them to the speech was again behind the wheel. Coop slid in beside her, and Mark rode shotgun.

"Until we sort this out, the safest place would probably be the field office." Mark turned to address Coop as the vehicle backed out of Monica's driveway under the watchful eye of the two on-duty agents.

"Agreed."

"You want to call Les?"

"Your turn."

Capitulating, Mark slid his BlackBerry out of its holster and began punching in numbers. "I hope the ERT can make some sense of this."

"Whoever pulled it off managed to elude experienced agents. My guess is they didn't leave any calling cards."

A heavy silence hung in the vehicle as Mark waited for his call to go through.

"Les? Mark. We've had an incident."

Coop listened to Mark's brief, monosyllabic conversation. Judging by his partner's tight-lipped expression, it was not going well.

Beside him, Monica shoved her hands into the pockets of her coat and snuggled deeper into its warmth. He could sense her almost tangible tension, and he felt as if someone had punched him in the gut. Earlier, she'd attributed her calmness during the speech to him and Mark. Her confident words echoed in his mind.

I trust you to keep me safe.

Judging by the fear and uncertainty now in her eyes, that trust and confidence had evaporated. She'd come to the conclusion that since they'd failed her once, she couldn't count on them to keep her safe in the future, either. He wished there was something he could say or do to restore her faith in them. But he had the disheartening feeling it was a lost cause.

Mark ended the call, and Coop redirected his attention to his partner. "What's the word?"

"He wants a full briefing on a secure line when we get to the office. In the meantime, he's going to notify the State Department."

"Okay." A muscle twitched in Coop's cheek.

"They weren't trying to kill me, were they?"

At Monica's soft question, he shot her a glance. And could tell she already knew the answer. All she wanted was confirmation. And he figured she had a right to know the truth.

"No."

"But they could have."

That comment gave Coop a bit more pause. "Yes."

"It's not your fault."

She was cutting him more slack than he was willing to cut himself. His jaw settled into a hard line. "We were in charge. The responsibility rests with us."

"The guy got through deadbolts and past federal agents, Coop. What more could you have done?"

He wished he knew. But that still didn't exonerate them. They were the experts. They should have been able to prevent this.

"Besides, it's really my fault."

He frowned. "What do you mean?"

"You and Mark told me I should go to a safe house on Saturday. I should have listened to you. But I thought everyone was overreacting. Including my father."

"Don't blame yourself, Monica."

"I'm sorry if this is going to cause you problems with your boss."

He was more worried about the reaction of the White House. But he didn't need to add that to her burden of guilt.

"We can handle it. Les has been in the field. He knows what we're up against in a situation like this." That didn't mean he was going to show them any mercy, but Monica didn't need to know that, either.

"I can talk to him if you want."

A smile tugged at one corner of his mouth as he imagined her going head-to-head with the Bulldog. "I appreciate the offer, but it won't be necessary."

"Maybe my willingness to go to the safe house now will smooth things out."

"That will help."

"Where is this place?"

"I don't know. Les will brief us at the field office."

"Will the safe house be . . . safe?"

Her gaze pinned him, demanding an honest answer. He wanted to tell her there was no way anyone could get to her there, but there were no guarantees in this business . . . despite all the precautions they might take. Today proved that.

"As safe as we can make it." It was the best he could offer.

A flicker of fear sparked in her eyes before she snuffed it out. "Okay. I know you'll do your best."

Coop appreciated the vote of confidence. It was more than they deserved after the episode at her house.

He just hoped they could live up to it.

"Who's in the room?" Les Coplin's voice boomed over the speaker phone on the secure line in the Richmond FBI field office.

"Mark and Dennis Powers." Coop leaned back in his seat, bracing for the interrogation to come. Mark and the Richmond SAC looked as on edge as he felt.

"Okay. I promised Washington answers. Do you have any?"

"Not yet. When we got back from the speech, Mark did a sweep of the house and everything seemed to be fine. The dead-bolts that were installed on Saturday were locked and there was no sign of forced entry."

"The two agents on duty this morning are on their way back to debrief," Dennis added. "We had one man in front and one in back while Ms. Callahan was gone. No one came anywhere near the house."

"That they noticed."

A flush surged on Dennis's neck. "They're two of my best agents. They wouldn't miss anything suspicious."

"Then how did someone get past them? Apparently with a key?"

"The ERT is en route to the house, along with a K-9 bomb sniffer. Until they have a chance to check it out, I can't answer that question."

"I want any information you get the second you get it."

"Understood."

"Where's Ms. Callahan?"

"In a vacant office down the hall," Mark chimed in.

"Is she doing all right?"

"She's pretty shaken up," Coop replied. "And she's agreed to go to a safe house."

"Good. Because at this point, that's not even negotiable. If I had a choice, I'd hand her over to the Marines at Quantico. This is a hot potato."

Les's comment about the Marines didn't exactly bolster Coop's confidence, and Mark's frown confirmed he felt the same way. But Coop couldn't deny that a Marine base might be more secure than a safe house. And Monica's safety had to come first.

"Do you think we should suggest that to her father?"

"No. He asked for the HRT, and he's going to get the HRT. I expect you boys to make it work."

The sound of shuffling papers came over the line, and Coop pictured Les squinting as he gummed his cigar from one side of his mouth to the other.

"We've got a gated house lined up ninety minutes outside of Washington, near Charlottesville. Belongs to a retired government official who's in Florida for the winter. The owner is an old navy buddy of David Callahan's. We've already had our people check it out and set up a command center on-site. Dennis, we're going to need your people as backup on this too. We can't pull in local law enforcement. This has to stay off the radar screen."

"No problem. We'll use agents from the Charlottesville, Lynchburg, and Fredericksburg offices."

"When we hang up, I'll fax you a layout of the house and directions. Coop and Mark, let me know once you have an ops plan in place. Dennis, get evidence from Ms. Callahan's house to Quantico ASAP. It's got top priority for analysis. Anything else we need to go over?"

"No," Coop responded after a raised-brow query to the other two men.

"All right. I've deferred Washington for the moment. But they want answers about how this breach happened. And so do I."

The line went dead.

"Not a happy camper." Dennis rubbed a hand over his short-cropped, gray-flecked brown hair. "And I can't say I blame him. Invisible enemies who go through locked doors make great sci-fi movie villains, but they don't exist in real life."

"Meaning we're dealing with flesh-and-blood opponents who must have left us some clues about how they pulled this off." Mark doodled on the pad of paper in front of him—a series of boxes with one side missing.

"If they did, the ERT will find it," Dennis said. "In the meantime, Ms. Callahan should be secure at the safe house."

Coop hoped Dennis was right.

But whoever these people were, they were good. Very good.

And the bad feeling he'd had Saturday about this assignment returned with a vengeance.

10

The ringing phone pulled David Callahan back from the fog of an exhausted sleep, and he groped for it on the Spartan nightstand in his embassy quarters, trying to jump-start his brain.

"Callahan." He swung his legs to the floor and reached for his glasses, sparing a quick glance at the clock. Twelve-thirty. After delivering the backpack of cash, he'd stayed in his office until almost eleven, hoping the informer would follow through on his end of the bargain. But eventually he'd succumbed to fatigue—and common sense. Losing sleep wasn't going to expedite the process. And the intelligence people would let him know if there were any developments.

Perhaps that's what this call was about.

Anticipation gave way to shock as he listened, however. The news about the security breach at Monica's house was not what he'd expected, and he struggled to rein in his burgeoning panic as the implications became clear.

When the call ended, he depressed the button on the phone, waited until he heard a dial tone, and punched in the number for the FBI.

"Can I interest you in some Chinese now?"

As the door to the vacant office opened, Monica looked up. Coop lifted an aromatic white bag in invitation while Mark grinned over his shoulder, waving a second bag. It was five in the afternoon, and lunchtime was long past, but she had no appetite. As the FBI had scurried to make plans for her safety, she'd had nothing to do but sit, brood, and try—with limited success—to erase the image of the blood in her lingerie drawer. Not an appetizing picture. Her only diversion had been when an agent fingerprinted her for a set of elimination prints to supply to the ERT scrutinizing her house. That hadn't been very appetizing either.

"I appreciate the offer, but I'm not very hungry."

The two men came in anyway and set the food on the empty desk in front of her. Mark snagged two side chairs that were against the wall and pulled them up. It appeared they weren't going to take no for an answer.

"You need to eat." Coop's comment confirmed her conclusion. Instead of taking one of the chairs, he settled a hip on the desk as Mark opened the food containers, blocking her view of his partner.

She could sense his scrutiny, but she stared at the center of his broad chest, focusing on one of the buttons on his white dress shirt. "I can't forget the blood."

He leaned close to hear her soft response. Close enough for her to see the gold flecks sparking in his deep brown irises when she looked up. And close enough for the kindness—and caring—in his eyes to tug at her heart.

"Images like that are hard to forget." His tone was gentle, understanding. "But all you've had today is a piece of toast and a handful of M&Ms. Will you at least eat a few bites while we go over our plans?"

He'd noticed what she'd eaten. Did any detail escape this man? And was he this attentive on every job? Or was there a personal element to his caring? She swallowed past the sudden, surprising longing that tightened her throat. "I'll try."

Her response was met with a warm, approving smile. Standing, he reached for a disposable plate and utensils and slid them toward her. "What do we have, Mark?"

"Cashew shrimp and"—his partner peered into the second container—"mongolian beef, maybe?"

"What would you like, Monica?" Coop picked up the rice container and put a dollop on her plate.

"The shrimp, thanks."

He spooned the garlicky mixture over her rice. Both men loaded up their plates with a generous helping of each of the dishes and dove in. She supposed they'd seen far worse than a drawer of blood-soaked lingerie, had learned long ago to steel themselves against such horror. But shock waves continued to reverberate through her.

When Coop caught her eye, then glanced at her plate, she got the hint. Picking up her fork, she scooped up some rice and shrimp. Under his watchful gaze, she forced herself to put the fork in her mouth. Chewed. Swallowed. For an instant her stomach churned, as if unsure whether to accept or reject the offering. She waited a few seconds, prepared to bolt for the ladies' room if necessary, but to her surprise, her stomach settled down and her appetite kicked in. She took another forkful, and Coop smiled at her.

After she'd eaten half of the food on her plate, he wiped his mouth on a paper napkin and picked up some layouts. "Ready to hear about your temporary home?"

"Sure."

"Keep eating while we run over this." He set a layout and an aerial photo beside her plate. The house was long and low, contemporary in design. It seemed to be situated on several very secluded acres, and the entire compound was surrounded by a tall, decorative wrought-iron fence. There was a swimming pool in the back, and a curving, circular drive in front. What appeared to be a small guest cottage stood apart from the main house near a wooded section of the backyard.

"Nice," Monica remarked.

"How the other half lives." Mark grinned as he continued to wolf down his combination lunch/dinner.

"The house has a state-of-the-art security system, including off-site video monitoring from two cameras. We'll be able to tap into that feed at our TOC—tactical operations center—in the guest house." He pointed to the smaller building. "A two-person HRT security team will be with you in the main house 24/7. Mark and I will be on days, Rick and Mac on nights. We'll also have field agents spaced around the fence to secure the perimeter of the property. There are a few ground rules too." Coop turned to Mark. "If you're done stuffing your face, why don't you run over them while I finish eating?"

"Hey, I'm a growing boy." Mark winked at Monica, and she managed to give him a whisper of a smile as he laid down his fork. "The rules are simple. Stay inside unless you're with one of us. Sections of the security system in the house will be left on, and opening an outside door will trip the alarm. We'll deactivate it only to let people in and out. You have free run of the house, and someone will always be a shout away. Don't hesitate to call for us if anything—and I mean anything—spooks you."

"Do you think they'll be able to figure out where I am?"

"Not if we can help it." Coop polished off the last bite of his food, pushed his plate away, and folded his hands on the desk. His jacket had been discarded long ago, and he'd loosened his tie and rolled his shirtsleeves to his elbows. The fine sprinkling of dark hair on his muscular forearms held Monica's attention for a brief moment before she raised her head and waited for him to continue.

"We don't think we were followed here, but considering these people have fooled us once, we're not assuming anything. We'll leave here between five and six, when the bulk of the employees go home, disguised, and we'll coordinate departures to ensure more than a dozen cars leave when we do. If anyone is watching, we're not going to make it easy for them to spot you—or to follow. I'll be in the car behind you, Mark will leave separately. Later this evening, we'll rendezvous at the safe house."

"But what if they do manage to follow us?"

"All agents are trained to watch for—and lose—tails." He paused, and she sensed an internal debate was taking place. "But we're not perfect, as today proved. When we talked to our boss earlier, he mentioned the possibility of moving you to the Quantico Marine base. It's not the protection your father asked for, but if you're more comfortable going that route, I can put in a call to Les."

Noting Mark's surprised expression, Monica frowned. "Is that what you recommend?"

"Security there is very tight." He sidestepped her question.

"Would you . . . and Mark . . . be there?"

"No. That's a military operation. But they have good people."

She considered the offer. "Do you think the risk is higher if I choose the safe house?"

"We'll minimize it as much as we can. Using agents from other towns for perimeter security will help. No one should be looking to those offices to provide any clues about your whereabouts."

As a diplomat's daughter, Monica had been on enough military bases in her life to know they were like small towns—lots of people, lots of hustle and bustle. Security was tight, especially at access points, but it could be breached. And she doubted she'd have the kind of dedicated, one-on-one protection there that the HRT and field agents would provide at the safe house.

Either way, there was risk, she realized. But she'd rather trust Coop and the FBI to protect her than a bunch of Marines she didn't know at Quantico.

"I'll go with the safe house."

"You're sure?" Coop's assessing stare drilled her.

Her gaze didn't waver. "Yes. I'd rather be with you guys."

A flash of warmth shot through his eyes before he angled away to sort through the papers on the table. Retrieving a blank piece, he pulled a pen from his pocket and placed both items in front of her. "Put together a list of anything you need—clothes, toiletries, whatever—and we'll see it's taken care of. Sizes too. If this goes on beyond—"

He paused and pulled his BlackBerry from its holster. As he checked the number of the incoming call, a muscle in his jaw tightened. "It's the embassy in Kabul." He pressed the talk button. "Cooper here . . . We're trying to find out, sir. The Evidence Response Team is on the scene, and we're preparing to transport Ms. Callahan to a safe house . . . Yes, sir. I understand. We're doing our best."

"Coop." Monica touched his elbow. "Let me talk to him."

Slanting a look over his shoulder, Coop spoke into the phone. "Sir, your daughter is here now, and she'd like to speak with you."

Silence fell in the room.

"Sir?" Coop listened, then handed the phone to Monica. "We'll be in the hall."

She took the phone and waited to speak until the door clicked shut behind the two men.

"It's Monica."

"Monica." Her father breathed the word more than said it. "Are you all right?"

"Yes. And the FBI is doing everything it can to protect me. What happened at my house was . . . bizarre."

"It could have been fatal."

She flinched at his blunt, but truthful, assessment. "Everyone understands that. But I don't know how it could have been avoided. The precautions that have been taken to protect me are very elaborate." She took a deep breath, praying for the strength to let go of bitterness and the courage to reach out. "I was going to call you earlier, before all this happened. I wanted to thank you for going to that bazaar. You took a huge risk."

"It was worth it."

The quiet, heartfelt words touched a place deep inside Monica, and she was jolted by a sudden insight. He hadn't said I love you. But she heard his unspoken message. *You* were worth it. Had he sent her such veiled messages in the past too? she wondered, shaken. Messages she'd been deaf to?

All at once, the elusive theme she'd been trying for weeks to nail down for her next book sharpened into focus: listening with the heart as well as the ears. It seemed that was a lesson she needed to learn too.

"I've been thinking a lot over the past few days about our relationship, and I . . . I'm sorry we've lost touch."

"I'm sorry too. And the fault is mine, Monica."

"Not all of it."

"I disagree. But maybe . . . after this is all over . . . we could debate the point in person. I'll be back in Washington for a debriefing as soon as the situation is resolved. If you have a free evening, perhaps we could meet for dinner. Or coffee, if you prefer."

She heard his trepidation, understood from the options he'd offered that he would meet her on her terms. That he didn't want to push her beyond her comfort level. But all at once she felt the need to push herself. "Dinner would be nice."

"I'll look forward to it." The warmth—and gratitude—in his tone was unmistakable.

"In the meantime, be careful."

"I always am. I'm more worried about you. Please follow the advice of your security people."

"Trust me, I've learned my lesson on that score. We're headed for a safe house in a few minutes, and I don't plan to set one foot outside until the all clear sounds."

"Good. I'll sleep better knowing that."

Another veiled message about love. This one she heard, communicated via his sincerity and the slight tremor in his words.

"Thanks again for the dinner invitation."

"It will be my pleasure. Good night, Monica."

"Good night."

As Monica tapped the end button, she realized her hand was shaking. But her heart felt a new and cleansing calm.

When the line went dead, David slowly set the phone back on his nightstand. Resting his elbows on his knees, he dropped his head into his hands. He'd started the call angry, determined to berate someone for not protecting his daughter. And he'd wanted reassurance.

He'd ended the call appeased—and reassured—in a far different manner and on a much broader scale than he'd expected. By Monica herself.

Rising from his narrow bunk, David walked over to the window in the tiny, impersonal room that was his temporary home. Tipping one of the slats in the blinds, he stared into the night. The compound was illuminated for security purposes, the artificial light giving an unnatural glow to the rows of white buildings that had staked a tentative claim on this dangerous land, creating a tiny oasis of calm in the midst of turmoil.

A sudden, unexpected yearning for the green, forested hills of Virginia he'd once called home filled David. He was tired of leading a nomadic life, he realized. Tired of dealing with unreasonable people. Tired of watching man's inhumanity to man. And tired of waking up to a world where no one cared about David, the man—only about David, the diplomat.

You were right, Elaine, when you told me years ago that one day I'd wind up a lonely man and second-guess my choice. That day has finally come.

An aching sense of regret tightened his throat. Not for the work itself. He'd accomplished a great deal of good in his life. Yet he'd given up so much to achieve it. Too much, he acknowledged, in the clarity of hindsight. But no more. He was sixty-six years old. It was time to go home.

Especially now that Monica had given him a reason to return.

"Ready?"

"Yes." Monica picked up a sheet of paper from the desk and handed it to Coop. "Here's the list of things I'll need. I tried to keep it to a minimum."

"Let me pass this on to someone. Stay put."

He had his earpiece in again, Monica noted, indicating he'd moved into heightened security mode. From a snippet of conversation she'd overheard between Mark and Coop as she'd stepped into the hall after her conversation with her father, she knew Coop had taken a big chance by giving her the option of requesting that her security be transferred to Quantico. It seemed the HRT commander didn't want to consider that alternative.

Coop's willingness to confront his boss to ensure her safety—and increase her comfort level—endeared him to her even more . . . and cemented her decision to go to the safe house.

"Okay, we're set." Coop handed over a keychain as he rejoined her. "Here are the keys to the car. It's parked two cars down on the right outside the exit. A dark blue Camry. You said you're familiar with that model?"

"Yes. My previous car was a Camry."

"Good." Coop's lips tipped up as he surveyed her, and she was again captivated by the dimple in his left cheek. "You know, I think I like you as a blonde."

With a self-conscious tug, Monica settled the long, curly wig on her head and smoothed down the unfamiliar suit. She appreciated his effort to tease away some of her tension. "I can't say I'm thrilled with your new glasses, though. And you've sprouted an awful lot of gray in the past hour. But you do look very different."

"That's the idea. Okay, you're clear on the directions?"

"Yes. Take Parham Road to 33, go north to Montpelier. Take 617 south to the I-64 entrance. Pull into the truck stop on the right. You'll pick me up there, outside the ladies' room, after I meet the agent inside and change."

"Very good. I'll be behind you the whole way, and another agent will be ahead of you. Others will be nearby. If anything seems suspicious, we'll close in immediately. The car you're in is armored and has bulletproof glass, so you don't need to worry about your safety."

"What about your car?"

One corner of his mouth hitched up. "I have a gun."

As if that would protect him from a drive-by shooting, she reflected. But he didn't give her a chance to express that thought.

"Let's go." Taking her arm, he guided her toward the front of the building.

"Where's Mark?"

"He left with the first group of employees about fifteen minutes ago, out the back door. We're leaving from the opposite side of the building. There's a small stand of trees on the edge of the parking lot that will help shield us from any curious eyes."

They headed toward a cluster of people near the front entrance, and Dennis Powers stepped forward.

"Are you ready?"

"Yes. Thanks again for your support."

The man acknowledged Coop's comment with a brief tip of his head, then addressed the small group. "Okay, people. Just like we talked about. The normal end of a workday. Chat, wave, but don't linger. Ms. Callahan, you can walk out with Agent Reynolds." He gestured toward a slender black-haired woman who looked to be in her early forties as he handed Monica a briefcase. "A final prop."

As Monica started to move forward, Coop restrained her with a hand on her arm. Surprised, she looked back at him.

"There's a mike in the briefcase. If you need help or notice anything suspicious, say the word. All of us will hear you."

"Okay."

She expected him to release her, but he maintained his grip for an instant longer than necessary. She didn't mind, but she was aware that his hesitation drew a few discreet but interested glances from the agents.

At last, with a slight encouraging squeeze, he dropped his arm and she joined the agent near the door.

When it was their turn to walk out of the building, Agent Reynolds gave her an easy smile and chatted about a recent movie, as if they were continuing a conversation they'd started inside. Monica did her best to pick up her cues and force her stiff lips upward, but she was out of her league here. Agent Reynolds paused for a moment at Monica's car, laughed about some line in the movie, then lifted her hand and waved, moving away.

Willing herself to stay calm, Monica slid into the seat and settled the briefcase beside her, watching for Coop. Thirty seconds later he exited, checked his watch, and hurried to a silver

Acura as if he was late. That was her cue to start her motor and pull out.

After backing out of the parking spot, Monica fell into line at the exit with the other cars. Once on Parham Road, a check in the rearview mirror confirmed that Coop was behind her.

She followed the instructions to the letter, and forty-five minutes later she pulled into the truck stop at the entrance to I-64. She parked and went into the ladies' room, turning on the faucet as instructed. A stall door opened, and a Richmond agent attired and wigged exactly the same as Monica stepped out. It was like looking in a mirror.

"Seeing double?" The agent grinned, lightening the atmosphere.

"Yes. It's kind of weird, isn't it?"

"Trust me. I've done far weirder things." She dropped her gaze a fraction and touched her ear, listening. "Mr. Cooper just pulled in," she informed Monica as she handed over the tote bag that was slung over her shoulder, along with a black jacket. "The clothes and wig I was wearing when I arrived are inside. After you change into them, stuff your clothes and wig in the bag and take it with you. Wait ten minutes. Your ride will be at the curb outside the door, in a blacked-out Suburban. He'll open the door as you approach."

"Thank you."

"Glad to help. Now I'll need your briefcase and keys." Monica handed them over, and the woman smoothed down a stray hair. "Where are you parked?"

"Three spots down on your left."

"Got it. Good luck."

She stepped out the door, and it clicked shut behind her.

Slipping into a stall, Monica yanked off the blonde wig and stripped off her suit. She found a pair of black jeans and a dark green turtleneck in the tote bag and quickly made the change. Then she tugged on the short black wig.

134

Ten minutes later, as she exited the ladies' room, the SUV was waiting three steps away. The door opened and she slid inside, pulling it shut behind her. The locks clicked into place.

"We're halfway there." Coop smiled at her. His hair was back to its normal color, still damp from a fast wash in the men's room, and he wore a cowboy hat pulled low over his eyes. A denim jacket and jeans completed the Western guise. The man looked as sexy in cowboy attire as he did in a suit, Monica decided. When he leaned closer and laid a hand on her arm, her breath jammed in her throat. "How are you holding up?"

"I'm hanging in." A tremor ran through her words, caused as much by his closeness as nerves. "But it's been a bizarre day. The speech feels like a week ago instead of seven hours."

"No argument there." He put the car in gear and headed for the entrance to the highway.

"I guess you guys are used to stuff like this."

"We've had our share of . . . interesting . . . assignments."

"Why do I think that's a huge understatement?"

He shot her an enigmatic smile but remained silent.

"Why do you do it?"

At her quiet question, he shot her a quick look in the darkness. "Do what?"

"This kind of work."

The lady didn't mince words, that was for sure, Coop reflected. And she asked questions he'd never asked himself. Difficult questions. Why *did* he do it?

Excitement, he supposed, checking for tails in the rearview mirror as he pondered her query. He liked experiences that gave him an adrenaline rush. And being one of the good guys had always appealed to him too. He believed in justice, and the FBI offered him the opportunity to put that belief into practice.

But if he were honest, if he dug way down, there was another reason he'd joined the HRT. The high risk, long absences, and 24/7 nature of the work gave him an excuse to avoid serious relationships. The women he dated might be attracted by the glamour of the job, might be happy to share a pleasant interlude with him, but when it came to settling down, they wanted more stability. And that suited him just fine.

"I didn't realize it was such a difficult question."

The speculative undercurrents in Monica's observation put him on alert, and he was grateful the night hid his features from her scrutiny as he responded.

"It's not." He relaxed his tense grip on the wheel and strove for a conversational tone. "I like law enforcement, and the HRT seemed like it would be an interesting challenge."

"A rather lonely life, though, I would guess."

His fingers tightened again, and he flexed them. "I'm too busy to be lonely."

"Hmm."

He didn't know what that meant, but to his relief she let the matter drop. He tried to do the same.

But for some reason he couldn't dismiss her comment. Until she'd entered his life, he'd never thought about being lonely. He'd been happy to go to work, train hard, and party away the weekends. It had seemed like a good life. Yes, there were occasions when it felt a little empty. But lonely? How could he be lonely when all he had to do was pick up the phone and call one of the dozen women currently in his little black book?

Because right now you can't even remember any of their names.

The annoying little voice that had appeared out of nowhere during the past weekend was becoming way too impertinent, Coop decided. So what if he couldn't remember any of their names? They were a great antidote to loneliness.

But the pleasure they offer is temporary. And it leaves you emptier than before.

Enough, Coop decided. He had too much on his mind to indulge in self-examination. He needed to think about the woman he was assigned to protect.

Except she was the cause of his sudden penchant for pensiveness, he realized, casting a quick glance at her. She'd tipped her head back and closed her eyes, her even breathing suggesting she might have drifted off to sleep. No surprise there. He suspected stress had played havoc with her sleep last night, and today had been traumatic. She needed rest. And she needed someone to lean on, someone she could count on to give her emotional support.

But he wasn't that person, he reminded himself. He had to keep his distance for both professional and personal reasons. Getting close to people gave them power over you. You came to depend on them. To need them.

Like he'd needed his father.

Yet no matter how hard he had tried, he'd never been able to elicit the words of praise and approval and love he had longed to hear from Jack Cooper. It had been a harsh lesson, but he'd learned it well, vowing never to let himself need anyone that much again. The risk was too high.

And he wasn't about to make an exception to that rule.

Even for the special woman beside him.

11

"Shall I arrange a courier to transmit the information to the embassy?" Impatience nipped at Anis's voice through the static on the cell phone.

"Not yet. My preparations are incomplete." The man glanced out the window into the predawn darkness. Now that he had the three million dollars in hand, his arrangements were falling into place.

"They will begin to think you do not intend to provide what you promised. Almost a day has passed since the package was delivered."

The man gave a careless shrug. "I honor my bargains, as they will discover. But in my own time. Are there any new developments?"

"Yes. Tariq has given me a message to send to the embassy. It is to be delivered later this morning in the usual way. He intends to begin killing the hostages one by one in forty-eight hours."

"Anything else?"

"No. He tells me little. I am no more than a servant to him."

Anis's undisguised bitterness brought a faint smile to the man's lips. Bitter people were useful. They could be bought— and felt justified in selling out. "You will not have to deal with Tariq much longer."

"It cannot be too soon."

"Return to your duties or you will be missed. I will call when it is time."

The line went dead.

Forty-eight hours. That was the window he had in which to complete his arrangements and disappear. Not a lot of time, but enough.

And before he vanished, he would give the U.S. more than it expected. Generous man that he was, he would throw in a bonus.

A smirk twisted his lips.

It was too bad he wouldn't be around to see Tariq's reaction.

"When did this arrive?" David pushed aside his lunch and sat back in his desk chair to stare at the message Salam had just handed him.

"Half an hour ago. Intelligence had it transcribed and sent a copy over." Salam lifted the tape player in his hand. "Do you want to hear it?"

"No. This tells me all I need to know." He read the words again.

We have given you sufficient time and warnings. You have forty-eight hours to meet our demands, or we will begin killing the hostages one by one. The first will die at noon on Thursday.

And the next time we target your daughter, the blood will be hers.

"Get Les Coplin on the line."

"Yes, sir." With a slight bow, Salam exited David's office.

Fighting down his panic, David tapped a finger on his desk. Forty-eight hours. The ultimatum they'd been waiting for since the day of the kidnappings had finally come. And he didn't doubt the terrorists would follow through on their threats.

He'd pinned his hopes for a resolution on their informant, praying he or she would follow through once the money was delivered. But thirty-two hours had elapsed, and no information had been supplied. It seemed the U.S. had been duped to the tune of three million dollars.

Yet if he had it to do again, he'd recommend the same response. It wasn't a great surprise that the informer had deceived them, but there had always been a chance he or she would honor the deal—and that chance, however slight, had justified the risk. Now that it hadn't panned out, however, they were left with only two options: meet the terrorists' demands in the hope of saving lives, or refuse to be blackmailed and watch innocent people die.

Including his daughter.

Unless the HRT did a superlative job.

Monica seemed to trust the men who had been assigned to guard her. But David wasn't that generous. They might be good at what they did, but so were the terrorists. And the kidnappers had one significant tactical advantage over the HRT operators.

They were ruthless.

No sooner had Coop drifted to sleep in the safe house than his BlackBerry began to vibrate.

It figured.

As his adrenaline surged, he grabbed the device off the nightstand and checked the caller ID. Les. They'd talked earlier, while Monica was settling into her room, and his boss had signed off for the night. A new development must have prompted this 2:00 a.m. call.

"Coop here."

"Callahan heard from the terrorists. Forty-eight hours and they start killing hostages."

Closing his eyes, Coop sucked in a sharp breath. "I take it there's no word from the informer."

"No. And there was more to the message. According to the terrorists, the next time they target his daughter, the blood will be hers."

A knot formed in Coop's stomach.

"Run me through the security protocol there."

At Les's gruff, clipped command, Coop swung his legs to the floor and forced himself to focus on tactical issues.

"I checked out the command center in the guest cottage after we talked earlier. The video feed from the two security cameras is good, and the agents on perimeter duty are wearing night-vision goggles. We have one man continuously patrolling each side. They're checking in with the command center every twenty minutes."

"How about the house itself?"

"The security system is adequate. We have it activated for all doors, and only the four HRT operators have the access code. If an outside door is opened anywhere in the house, the alarm sounds and the command center is alerted. That's been tested. Mac and Rick are on duty tonight."

Silence. Coop figured Les's cigar-of-the-day had to be a soggy mess by now.

"Okay. It sounds like everything is covered. We have an 8:30 conference call tomorrow with the lab here and the ERT from Richmond. They promised to have some answers about what happened at Ms. Callahan's house. I want you and Mark both on the line. Where is she now?"

"In bed."

"Stick close."

"That's the plan."

As Les severed the connection, Coop set his BlackBerry back on the nightstand and stretched out again. Like all HRT operators, he'd learned to grab sleep on a job whenever the opportunity presented itself. To turn the "alert" mechanism in his brain down to idle, ready to kick in again at a moment's notice but low enough to give his body the rest it needed to function at optimal efficiency.

Tonight, however, sleep eluded him. He should be tired enough to drift off, he reflected. It had been a long, stressful day. And there was plenty of security in place. Monica was safe.

But he couldn't get the terrorists' warning out of his mind. *Next time, the blood will be hers.*

"The message has been delivered to David Callahan. The clock is ticking." Tariq took a sip of hot tea, trying to dispel the evening chill, and adjusted the cell phone on his ear. "If we do not get a response within eighteen hours, you will take the next step. Have you located Ms. Callahan?"

"Yes. It was not difficult."

Nouri's dismissive response didn't fool Tariq. Finding a woman the FBI didn't want found would be an impossible challenge for most people. It had been easy for Nouri only because he was good. Very good, Tariq amended, pleased he'd chosen his nephew to manage the U.S. component of his plan. Karim would be proud of his son. Nouri's hate for the Americans, whose bombs had killed his father, exceeded even Tariq's. And hate was a powerful motivator.

"How did you manage it?" In general, Tariq asked few questions about Nouri's methodology. He knew the man had planned for any contingency, was even prepared to pilot a rented plane in case Monica Callahan was spirited away to some remote location. And he respected his nephew's technical expertise, was impressed by the network of sources he'd cultivated. But beating the FBI was tough. While Tariq had never doubted Nouri's ability to find the diplomat's daughter, he was curious how the man had accomplished it.

"We concealed motion-activated GPS tracking devices in the luggage of the HRT operators when they were away from their hotel. They arrived at their 'safe' house twelve hours ago."

Tariq's lips twisted into an appreciative smile at Nouri's mocking humor. And at the irony that the very men charged with protecting the woman had led his nephew straight to her. "What about the defenses there?"

"I've already hacked into the security system. I'm looking at a feed from the security cameras as we speak. The perimeter is patrolled. There are two agents in the house at all times."

"You have a plan?"

"Yes."

"You have the appropriate resources?"

"Yes. Zahir and I will handle this alone, and we are well equipped."

"Good luck. I will be in touch."

As Tariq slid his cell phone into the pocket of his robe, he shivered and eyed the sleeping mat on the floor with distaste. Once he was prone, the chill in the room would seep into his pores. But he needed to rest. There was much to do in the next two days.

And after that, he would leave this hovel and move to more comfortable quarters. Because before he was through, the ransom would be paid.

With or without David Callahan's help.

Tariq knew that once he began killing hostages, the U.S. would find some clandestine way to meet his demands. The American people had no stomach for watching innocent civilians die.

It was a weakness he intended to use to his advantage.

"I found your care package outside my door."

Turning from the coffeemaker, Coop smiled at Monica. She was dressed in a new pair of jeans and a long-sleeved pink shirt, and she was holding a large bag of M&Ms.

"Everything fit okay?"

"Perfect."

He gave her trim figure a quick, appreciative sweep. Perfect was a good word for it. "Let me know if you need anything else."

"Thanks, I will. However, I don't remember putting these on my 'necessities' list." She hefted the bag.

"After everything that happened yesterday, I decided comfort food qualified for that designation."

Her smile softened. "Thanks. I've already dipped in."

"Before breakfast?" He arched a brow in mock horror.

"Chocolate gets top billing any time of day in my book."

Chuckling, he gestured toward a large white bakery box on the counter beside a half-empty coffeepot. "I don't think that stuff is any healthier, but help yourself. You'll also find eggs, milk, butter, juice, and English muffins in the fridge."

"Where's Mark?" She wandered over to inspect the bakery box, still clutching her M&Ms.

"On his laptop in the office."

"I see you guys already ate." She surveyed the few remaining pastries and selected a caramel pecan Danish. Plopping it on a disposable plate, she headed for the refrigerator.

"An hour ago."

"Want some scrambled eggs?"

"Are you offering to cook?"

"Why not? I don't have anything else to do."

And cooking helped her deal with stress, Coop reminded himself, noting her death grip on the M&Ms. "Sure."

"How about Mark?"

"How about Mark what?" The other agent appeared in the kitchen holding an empty coffee mug.

"Would you like some scrambled eggs?"

"I could be persuaded."

"The man has a tapeworm, if you ask me." Coop flicked a wry grin his way.

"Not true. But I've sampled Monica's cooking, and I never pass up a well-prepared meal."

"I can't promise much this morning," she warned. "There's not a whole lot here to work with." She released her hold on the bag of M&Ms, setting them on the counter as she inspected the scant contents of the fridge.

"Trust me. Whatever you make will be far better than anything I've eaten so far today. I've already ingested my allotment of donuts for the week," Mark reassured her with a grin, refilling his mug.

On his way out of the kitchen he flipped on another light, and Monica sent him a grateful look as she dropped some English muffins in the toaster. "Thanks. It was feeling pretty dingy in here." Once again all of the shades, drapes, and blinds had been drawn, and though she could see sun peeking around the edges of the windows it wasn't enough to dispel the gloom lurking inside. After all of this was over, she was going to head somewhere warm and sunny for a week or two, she resolved, breaking eggs into a bowl.

"A penny for them."

Turning, she found Coop watching her, one hip propped against the counter as he sipped his coffee. Today he wore jeans and a blue oxford shirt that revealed a faint sprinkling of dark hair in the hollow at the base of his throat. While she couldn't fault his attractiveness in a suit, she decided the more casual attire enhanced his rugged masculinity and appeal. How many hearts had he broken? she wondered.

"Monica?"

Her cheeks grew warm and she angled away to pour the whisked eggs into a pan of sizzling butter. She wouldn't reveal that last thought for a million dollars, let alone a penny! "I was thinking about white sand and palm trees and sunshine. That's where I'm going for some R&R after this nightmare ends. I plan to live in my swimsuit for at least a week on a tropical island. Do you like the beach?"

When he didn't respond, Monica risked a peek at him. At his speculative expression—and the sudden banked fire in his eyes—her breath caught in her throat.

As their gazes locked, his demeanor went from intimate to impersonal in a heartbeat. "Sure." Pushing off from the counter, he set his cup on the table. "How can I help with breakfast?"

"Just let Mark know it's ready, okay?"

He disappeared down the hall, and Monica ladled the eggs over the toasted muffins, trying to regroup. She wasn't sure what had just happened here. But she did know one thing.

She'd have gladly paid far more than a penny for *his* thoughts.

"Great breakfast, Monica." Mark wiped his lips on a napkin. "Best scrambled eggs I ever had."

"I second that," Coop added.

As Monica murmured a thank-you, she noted the men had cleaned their plates—reinforcing their image as stereotypical bachelors who appreciated a rare home-cooked meal.

"We need to get ready for that conference call." Coop addressed Mark over the rim of his mug.

"Right." Mark stood and carried his empty plate to the sink.

"Is there news?" Monica directed her question to Coop.

"I hope so. The lab in Quantico and the ERT from Richmond will be patched into the call. We need some answers about how security was breached at your house."

"Nothing from the informer?"

"Not yet." He hadn't told her about the latest missive from the terrorists. The threat to her was nonspecific, and there was no reason to increase her already high stress level.

As he carried his plate to the sink, Monica put away the carton of juice. "I noticed a large library. Do you think it would be okay if I borrowed a book? Reading would help me pass the time."

"Of course. The owner said we should make ourselves at home." Coop paused in the doorway. "If you need us for anything, don't hesitate to interrupt."

"Okay."

Left alone, Monica cleaned up the breakfast dishes. The routine task left her mind free to dwell on the threat that hung over her, her father's safety, the fate of the three kidnapped hostages—and Coop's intimate expression earlier.

None of those thoughts brought her any peace of mind—or helped her sort through her jumbled emotions.

Reading would help her cope, she decided, giving the counter one last swipe. Especially if the library held one particular book.

"Is everyone on the line?"

"We're in, Les." Coop pushed the speaker button and set his BlackBerry on the polished desk in the safe house's mahogany-paneled study. He settled back in a dark green leather club chair, a twin to the one Mark had claimed.

"Dennis Powers here. I have Gary Krouse with me, the ERT lead technician at Ms. Callahan's house. Nick Bradley, who headed the security team, is also here."

"Good." Les's gravelly voice ground through the speaker. "Melanie Parks from our lab in Quantico is on the line too. Gary, why don't you start?"

"Okay." The sound of papers being shuffled broke the momentary silence. "We didn't find much in terms of physical evidence. No fingerprints, no footprints, no broken glass or wood slivers to indicate doors or windows had been jimmied. But we did find a few fibers on the laundry room floor, under the small trapdoor that leads to the house's crawl space. We pegged it as insulation."

"I can confirm that," Melanie said. "It was the standard fiberglass variety."

"Someone got into the house through the attic?" Coop leaned forward and clasped his hands between his knees, his shoulders taut.

"That's our conclusion," Nick said.

"But how did someone get into the attic? Mark and I checked it out the day we arrived. It's no more than a crawl space, with one very small vent at each end."

"Did you go up?"

"No. It's pretty tight quarters. We flashed a light around from the trapdoor. Ms. Callahan told us she hadn't been up there since she bought her house five years ago. It's empty."

"That's true," Nick agreed. "But on closer examination, we discovered an interesting feature. There's a small, hinged trapdoor on one side that leads to the garage. It's almost invisible unless you're on top of it."

"We checked the garage," Mark chimed in, exchanging a frown with Coop. "We didn't see a trapdoor."

"I'm not surprised. We had to tear the place apart to find it.

It's hidden behind a bulky painting tarp that's stored on a tall shelving unit."

"We tested the samples we received from the trapdoor, and the wood is of fairly recent vintage," Melanie added.

"Coop, while we continue this discussion, one of you check with Ms. Callahan and see if she installed a trapdoor in her garage in the past few months," Les said.

"Mark's already on his way." Coop raked his fingers through his hair and tried to sort out the new information. "Okay, assuming she isn't aware the door is there, are we concluding our intruder installed it sometime in the past few weeks in case he needed it?"

"That's my hypothesis," Nick said.

The door to the office opened, and Mark shook his head at Coop as he took his place again. "I spoke with Ms. Callahan. She had no idea the trapdoor was there. She hasn't painted in two years, and it was a plain wall when she put the tarp up there."

"She's sure?" Les asked.

"Yes. She was very definite about it."

"Okay. So we have a new trapdoor. That doesn't explain how the intruder got in—and got out—yesterday without detection." Les's tone was terse.

"A couple more pieces of information might help," Nick responded. "The garage has one window. We found it unlocked."

"It wasn't unlocked when we arrived Saturday. We checked," Mark said.

"The pane of glass in one of the grids had also been removed," Nick continued. "It was sitting on the floor of the garage beside the window. The glass was new. It appeared to have been held in place with minimal caulk. We believe the intruder broke the glass on his first trip in order to flip the lock, then replaced it so it could be easily removed on his next visit."

"And no one saw any of this?" Coop demanded.

"Most of Ms. Callahan's neighbors work, and there's a bush beside the garage that hides the window from the street," Nick responded.

"That still doesn't explain how he got in once the house was under surveillance," Coop pressed.

There was an uneasy silence at the implied criticism.

"Go ahead and give them your theory, Nick," Dennis said.

"Since Saturday, we've had people in the front and back of the house while it was empty, but when the HRT operators were on-site we stayed on the street and did random foot checks in the back. We think whoever did this was watching us long enough to determine that.

"Here's my take. Sometime on Sunday night, the intruder waited until we'd completed a foot check, then entered the garage through the window and gained access to the crawl space via the trapdoor. Monday morning, after Ms. Callahan left with Coop and Mark for her speaking engagement, he entered the house through the trapdoor in the laundry room, poured the blood in the drawer, and exited the way he came in."

"But how did he get away?" Mark asked.

"When Ms. Callahan returned after her speech, we pulled surveillance back to the front of the house, and he used that opportunity to leave through the garage window. We interviewed all of the neighbors, and one woman did notice a meter reader about the time all of you arrived back at the house. She wasn't able to give us a definitive description, however, and no one else saw anything out of the ordinary. I assume that was our man, and he simply strolled away through the adjacent backyards in his disguise. He was probably given an all-clear signal by an accomplice watching the house."

If Nick was right—and Coop couldn't fault the man's deductive reasoning—that meant the intruder had been in the attic all night.

While they slept.

A cold chill raced up his spine. Mark's shocked expression mirrored his own.

"By the way, in case anyone is interested, the blood in the drawer was canine, not human," Melanie added.

But it could have been theirs. The guy could have taken *all* of them out if he'd wanted to, Coop acknowledged, trying to swallow past the sudden sick feeling in the pit of his stomach.

Yet he hadn't. Under orders from the mastermind who'd planned the kidnappings in Afghanistan and launched a methodical campaign of terror against David Callahan and his daughter, the intruder had gone to elaborate lengths to send a very strong message. The delivery of it had been planned in frightening detail and executed with precision.

And according to the last message David Callahan had received, it was only going to get worse if the diplomat didn't convince the U.S. and Afghan governments to cave in to the terrorists' demands.

"These people are thorough." Les echoed Coop's thoughts, pulling him back to the moment. "I know the safe house and grounds were swept prior to your arrival, but do it again."

The concern in his boss's voice did nothing to relieve Coop's uneasiness. In his four years on the HRT, he'd never sensed even a hint of nervousness in the man.

"We'll take care of it right away," Coop promised.

"Do that. Anyone else have anything to add?" When silence ensued, Les ended the call. "Keep me informed."

The buzz of a dial tone signaled the broken connection, and Coop slowly leaned forward to turn off the phone.

"Nick painted a pretty disturbing scenario." Mark crossed an ankle over a knee and folded his hands on his stomach.

His partner's studied, relaxed posture was the antithesis of Mark's real reaction to the situation, Coop knew. When things

151

got dicey or dangerous, Mark adopted an outward calm designed to hide the churning in his gut. In general, Coop had a similar coping style. But it wasn't kicking in today. He kept picturing the intruder crouched in the crawl space during the long, cold night, clutching a container of blood. What kind of man would do that? What would *drive* a man to do that? And what might he do next?

It was the final question that troubled Coop the most.

"Coop?"

At Mark's prod, he focused on his partner. "I was just thinking about what you said. Disturbing is an understatement."

"Why don't you go keep Monica company while I rouse Rick and Mac and get the sweep started?" Mark stood. "I don't see any reason to add to her stress. The quieter we can do this, the better."

"I agree."

As Mark headed out the door, Coop drew in a slow, deep breath. The HRT operators and FBI agents assigned to Monica would do their best to protect her. He was confident of that.

But as the hours ticked by, he was less and less confident it would be enough.

12

As if sensing his presence, Monica looked up when Coop paused at the door to the library.

"Meeting over?" She closed her book.

"Yes." He stepped inside the room, pulling the door shut behind him.

"You look like you could use some M&Ms." Lifting the half-empty bag from the table beside her, she shook it as an enticement.

"No thanks." A grin tugged at his lips. "Chocolate isn't one of my vices."

"Good. That leaves more for me." She popped a few into her mouth. "I polished off most of these after Mark's visit. From his questions, I assume there's a new trapdoor in my garage."

Coop heard the strain behind the forced lightness of her remark. And saw it in her body posture. Although she'd kicked off her shoes and was seated in a comfortable armchair with one long leg tucked under her, her shoulders were stiff and her fingers were clenched around the book in her lap. A Bible, he noted.

"Yes. Mind if I join you?" He gestured toward the second overstuffed chair that faced the marble-mantled fireplace.

"No. I'd appreciate an update."

He crossed the room, his stride unhurried. Mimicking Mark's relaxed posture in the study, he crossed an ankle over a knee and proceeded to recite the lab findings and conclusion in a calm, straightforward tone.

There was little he could do, however, to sugarcoat the most disturbing part of the story. When Monica realized the intruder had been in the attic for the entire night, the color drained from her face and her lips parted slightly in shock.

"I don't understand, Coop." It was clear to him she was struggling to process the news, much as he had done. "If they wanted to use me to convince my father to cooperate, why didn't this man hurt me?"

"He would have had to go through us to get to you, and I suspect they aren't willing to take that risk." *Yet.* But he left that qualifier unspoken.

"I didn't think terrorists cared about personal risk."

"They don't. But the leader may not want to risk the mission. He needs you as a bargaining chip. He orchestrated this to send a strong message without confrontation or injury. My guess is he hopes your father will be intimidated enough by this incident to convince the powers-that-be to meet their demands."

"He won't be swayed."

Even to save his own daughter?

Coop tried to mask his censure, but Monica was too quick for him. She leaned forward, her expression earnest. "He's right, Coop. I've read enough about terrorists to know that giving in to their demands breeds more terrorism. And leads to even greater loss of life. The only way to stop the cycle of kidnapping, their apparent weapon of choice, is to render it unprofitable. If you meet their demands, it's an admission that terrorism works, and that leads to chaos, which leads to more terrorism. I don't remember much about my father growing up, but I do remember his position on that. And I agree with it. A threat to me shouldn't dissuade him from doing what's right."

Everything Monica had said with such passion was true, Coop conceded. He couldn't argue with her in principle. But how did you reconcile principle with the need to care for those you loved, when the two were in direct opposition? He imagined David Callahan was struggling with that very conflict now. And the diplomat was trusting the HRT to lessen that burden by keeping his daughter safe.

There was no way Coop wanted to disappoint him. For professional—and personal—reasons.

"I can see you have strong feelings on the subject." Coop maintained an even tone.

"Stronger than I realized." She took a deep breath and sank back into the chair, as if her speech had drained her energy. "I've been thinking a lot about the situation for the past few days. Whoever is behind this is smart. They've put my father in an untenable position by giving him a vested interest in the outcome. I don't want him to compromise his principles and bolster the terrorists' cause because of me. He has to do what's best in the larger context and take personal considerations out of it."

"That's easier said than done." When his voice came out more husky than he intended, Coop changed the subject. "Does that help?" He gestured toward the Bible she was clutching.

She blinked once, twice, as she shifted gears. "Yes. Very much."

"My brother puts a lot of stock in it too."

"I didn't know you had a brother."

He hadn't intended to share that with her, but she'd been studying him in that perceptive, disquieting way of hers, and he'd said the first thing that popped into his mind to distract her. Maybe she'd get the hint if he shifted the conversation away from personal subjects.

"Yeah. One brother. Where did you find that?" He gestured toward the Bible.

"On the table by the window. Where does your brother live?"

So much for his brief hope she'd pick up his cue to switch topics. "California."

155

"Is that where you're from?"

"No."

"So where did you grow up?"

"Pennsylvania."

"I've been there a couple of times. What part?"

"Pittsburgh."

"Nice town."

No response.

Crossing her legs, Monica pursed her lips and regarded him. "To use an old cliché, it's like pulling teeth to get information out of you. Is that the result of your FBI training, or are you just an uncommunicative sort of guy?"

As usual, she didn't mince any words. But then, words were her business. And it was clear she followed her own advice. When it came to letting people know how she felt, she talked the walk.

"Did anyone ever tell you that you ask a lot of questions?" he countered.

"It's called conversation, Coop. Besides, aren't you the man who told me a few days ago that you've always believed you could never have too much information about anything—or anyone—you're involved with? If putting my life in your hands doesn't constitute involvement, I don't know what does."

She'd thrown his own words back at him. Score one for the lady.

Rising, he shoved his hands in his pockets and moved a few steps away to stare down at the flickering flames in the gas fireplace. "I don't talk much about my past, Monica."

"Why not?"

"There doesn't seem to be much point. It's history. What's done is done."

"True. But we're all a product of our past, and a person's history often helps others understand who they are now. Without that background, it's hard to establish any kind of close relationship."

Which was exactly why he'd avoided sharing his past.

When the silence lengthened, Monica reached for her bag of M&Ms and rose. "Sorry. I didn't mean to pry. I think I'll check out the DVDs I saw in the hearth room off the kitchen and see if there are any old movies. I could use a classic musical comedy about now."

The security sweep would be in full progress, and Coop had promised Mark to keep Monica occupied—and unaware. He needed to extend this conversation. "You like old movies?"

"Doesn't everyone?" She headed for the door.

Desperate, he dangled some bait, hoping to snag her attention. "My brother was a John Wayne fan."

It worked. She hesitated and looked over her shoulder, as if waiting to see whether he would offer more.

"He's a good guy. A lawyer, with a lovely wife and three great kids." He doled out a few more pieces of information.

"I always wanted a brother or sister." She half turned toward him, as if testing the water. "Do you see him often?"

Digging deep, he dredged up an answer. "No. We have very different lifestyles. For one thing, he's into religion like you are."

"That's interesting."

"How so?" He gave her a wary look, unsure where her comment was leading—but pretty certain he wasn't going to like the direction.

"You grew up in the same environment. He has a strong faith, you don't. There must be a reason for that."

Suspicion confirmed. They were moving into restricted territory. But he didn't have a good exit strategy. If he avoided her implied question, she'd probably write him off and head out to find that old movie. Not good. He had to distract her. If that required stepping out of his comfort zone, he'd have to make the sacrifice.

"We didn't share quite the same environment."

That caught her attention. She took a couple of steps back into the room. "What do you mean?"

"It's a long story." Coop motioned to the chair she'd vacated. "You might want to sit."

To his relief, she retook her seat without another word, then sent an expectant look his way.

The ball was in his court.

"Adam is six years older than me." He moved closer to the fire and shoved his palms into his back pockets as he watched the flickering flames. "He was nine when our mother died of cancer, and he spent most of his waking hours after that with his best friend's family. His friend's mother became a surrogate mom for him."

Monica did the math. Coop had been three when his mother died. At nine, Adam would already have had a good grounding in maternal love. Plus, he'd been informally "adopted" by his best friend's family. His environment had been as normal as possible under the circumstances.

Coop, on the other hand, had been little more than a toddler. His memories of his mother would be vague or nonexistent, and his father had been distant. The result had been a childhood without warmth or love. No wonder the man was enclosed. He'd had no role model to follow during his formative years.

"Who took care of you after your mother died?" Monica watched his profile as she broached the question.

"We had a succession of housekeepers. Some better than others."

His dispassionate response was intended to communicate it hadn't mattered to him. But Monica sensed otherwise. The stiffness in his shoulders told her that hurt remained from those

158

long-ago days. And she understood the pain of having a cold, uncaring father. The difference was, she'd had a loving mother to compensate for her father's deficiencies. Coop hadn't.

"I see what you mean about you and your brother having different environments. Your dad sounds a lot like my dad."

"At least mine had his reasons." Coop continued to focus on the fire. "I learned later that after my mom died he almost had a nervous breakdown. They were very much in love, and he couldn't handle the loss. In the end, the only way he could cope was to shut down emotionally and throw himself into his work. I can't fault him for that, if it helped him survive. But it wasn't easy for a kid to live in that environment. Dad mellowed a lot after he married Estelle, but I was sixteen by then."

In other words, it had been too late to salvage the damage done in his childhood. Monica had no trouble reading between the lines of Coop's commentary. And it explained a lot.

"People react to adversity in a lot of different ways. I have a feeling your dad didn't mean to cut you off."

"I'm sure he didn't. He wasn't a bad man. And he tried to make amends when I was older. But I'd lost interest at that point. I had my own life, and I really didn't need him anymore."

For years, Monica had felt the same way about her own father. Yet deep inside she'd always yearned for that missing link. As she guessed Coop had.

"Did you two stay in touch?"

"On and off." The flickering flames cast shadows on his profile, highlighting crevices of fatigue and worry she hadn't noticed before. "He died last year. Heart attack." The muscles in his throat worked, and he fell silent.

Much as he might deny it, Coop's father had meant more to him than he was willing to admit, Monica concluded.

"I'm sorry." She voiced the sentiment softly.

"Yeah. Me too." He cleared his throat. "It could have been

so different. I didn't need much as a kid. I just wanted him to notice me."

I just wanted him to notice me.

The pressure of tears built behind Monica's eyes. A world of hurt was contained in that simple statement. And from what she knew of Coop, she was certain he'd tried his best to make that happen. When he'd failed, it had colored the rest of his life. The boy who'd craved recognition from his father had concluded it was too risky to pin his happiness on someone else's approval and acceptance. As a result, he'd become a strong, tough, high-achiever who kept others at arm's length.

She had no idea how to respond to his revelation.

As the silence in the room lengthened, Coop tried to figure out what had just happened. How had Monica managed to elicit such personal information? He'd never told any of that stuff to anyone. It exposed a vulnerability, and that was dangerous. It was time for some damage control.

Preparing to lighten the atmosphere, Coop turned back toward her to offer a teasing remark—only to have the words evaporate. There was a sheen of moisture in her eyes, shimmering in the golden light of the fire, and her features had softened with caring and empathy.

It was not the reaction he'd expected.

Once again, he was struck by her ability to delve deep and understand the meaning behind words, posture, behavior. She knew his father's disinterest had hurt him. That it still did, much as he'd tried to deny it to himself. And he had a feeling she also understood how that disinterest had shaped his life—and his relationships.

To his surprise, he didn't feel threatened or angry by her intrusion into private territory. In fact, just the opposite. It felt good to share his long-suppressed pain with someone. No, he corrected himself, not *someone*. Monica.

An unexpected rush of tenderness tugged at his heart, and he had the sudden urge to close the distance between them, to pull her to her feet and take her hands in his. To touch the silky skin of her cheek, bend his head and taste her soft lips.

And for once, his impulse to kiss a woman wasn't driven by hormones. He was drawn to Monica at a deeper level than that. Deep enough to imply there could be more to this relationship than mere physical attraction.

And that scared him. Enough to keep his feet firmly rooted to the spot. He wasn't ready for anything that hinted at commitment.

Summoning up the lazy smile he used in the bar scene, he jammed his fists into his pockets. "Sorry. That got a little heavy. I don't usually bore pretty ladies with my sordid past."

She gave him an assessing look, and he got the distinct impression that she'd recognized his flattery for what it was—a defense mechanism. An attempt to relegate her to the just-another-pretty-face category. And she wasn't buying.

But to his relief, she didn't call him on it.

"I wasn't bored. Thanks for sharing some of your background." She stood. "I think I'll go check out the DVDs now. I saw a shelf with quite a collection, and—"

"Wait a sec." He reached for his vibrating phone, checking the ID before putting it to his ear. Mark. "What's up?"

"We need to check out the library."

"Okay."

"We're done in the dining room, living room, and kitchen area. Can you think of an excuse to move to any of those?"

"Yes. Great timing. Thanks."

As Coop slipped the phone back on to his belt, he smiled at Monica. "Want some company for that movie?"

Surprise flickered across her face, then gave way to a pleased smile. "Sure. But I warn you, I go for the old ones."

161

"How old?"

"Filmed before you were born. *Way* before you were born, unless you're a lot older than you look. And I like comedies and musicals."

"I could go for a comedy."

"Not big on musicals, huh?"

"I can tolerate them in small doses."

"Okay." She grinned and turned back toward the door. "A comedy it is, then."

The house was quiet as he followed her out. Coop assumed the rest of the HRT team was laying low until he and Monica settled into the hearth room. By the time the movie was over, the sweep would be finished. The house would be as secure as they could get it.

He could only hope it would be secure enough.

13

A sudden vibration on the table in the coffee shop distracted Nouri from his laptop, and he picked up his cell phone. "Yes."

"The local police are continuing to patrol the road behind the house every thirty minutes. Agents on perimeter guard duty are checking in with their command center at twenty-minute intervals. There has been no variation in that pattern."

"Excellent." After Nouri had dropped him off half a mile from the safe house last night, it had taken Zahir close to two hours to move into a concealed position close enough to afford a good view of the compound and to allow his mini shotgun mike to pick up verbal communication from the patrolling agents. Then he'd spent twelve long, cold hours in a tree observing and listening.

Nouri took a sip of his cinnamon spice latte and set the disposable cup on the wooden table. He liked his colleague's style—quiet, competent, professional. Zahir did what he was asked to do without question or hesitation. A man like that was invaluable . . . even if he did have a few quirks.

"You do not have a large window." Zahir's comment was matter-of-fact.

"It is enough." From his table in the corner of the coffee shop, Nouri scanned the room. At two in the afternoon, he had the place almost to himself. "There has been no activity in the master bedroom?"

"None that I can see. It remained dark all night."

"That will be my access point. I will pick you up in thirty minutes."

Ending the call, Nouri went back to perusing his computer screen, angling it more toward the back wall of the shop and away from any curious glances. It had been easy to circumvent the firewall at the safe house's security monitoring firm, and the feed he'd tapped into from the cameras was excellent.

After watching it for much of the past twelve hours, he had a good sense of the level and pattern of protection being offered to David Callahan's daughter. The perimeter was patrolled by four agents, the activity at the small guest house indicated it was being used as the command post, and two agents remained on duty in the main house at all times.

It was a tight net, but not impenetrable.

He also had a good feel for the entire compound, thanks to the satellite photo on Mapquest that had provided an excellent aerial image.

The layout of the main house hadn't taken long to nail down, either. A web search had yielded the name of the owner, and that, in turn, had led him to a feature on the house in an architectural magazine two years ago. The photos were excellent . . . and the floor plan, while bare bones, did show room locations.

Thanks to the GPS devices still in the HRT operators' luggage, Nouri also knew they had deposited their bags in the guest cottage. Meaning that's where they were sleeping. He'd have found a way to work around it if they were staying in the main house, but their sleeping arrangement dovetailed nicely with his plans.

Last night, he'd saved two hours of the video feed from the security camera mounted on the corner of the tennis court—the one that panned the back of the house at regular intervals. It would be an easy matter to override the live feed when the time came. Unless the agent monitoring the cameras displayed remarkable diligence, Nouri doubted whether he would notice the quick blip on the screen or the date change in the bottom corner.

Closing down his laptop, he took a final sip of his latte. There were risks with this job. Big risks. One mistake, one miscalculation, could mean disaster.

But he didn't intend to fail. Tariq believed in him. And Nouri believed in the cause. Since his father's death and his uncle's downfall at the hands of the Americans, his hate for the United States had grown exponentially. He'd chosen to work for the demise of the country from within its borders, and his success rate had been phenomenal. He didn't lack for assignments from a variety of insurgent groups. And he took them all.

This job, however, was personal.

This job was vindication for his father and uncle.

Failure was not an option.

He would not make a mistake.

"Good morning, sir." Salam entered David's office and set a cup of coffee on the diplomat's desk.

"You're here early."

"It is difficult to sleep these days."

"Yes, it is." David rubbed a weary hand down his face. "At noon tomorrow they start killing hostages. That gives us only twenty-nine hours."

"Your government has discovered no leads?"

"No." Locating the hostages had been given the highest priority by every pertinent U.S. security agency, but there was simply nothing to go on.

"Perhaps the informer will decide to follow through on his bargain."

"I'm not counting on that at this point. It's been almost two days since I delivered the money. But I suppose we can always hope for a miracle."

His phone began to ring, and Salam exited with a slight bow. "I'll get that for you, sir."

Reaching for his coffee, David took a sip of the scalding brew. Not that he needed it to stay awake. Despite his sleepless night, the drumming tension in his pulse was producing more than enough adrenaline to keep him alert.

The intercom buzzed, and David picked up the receiver. "Yes?"

"Lindsay Barnes from the secretary of state's office is on line one, sir."

"Thank you." Setting his coffee down, David tapped the number to take the call from the secretary's aide. "Good morning, Lindsay."

"Good morning, sir. The secretary will be leaving Iraq tomorrow morning at five and would like to detour for a meeting with you at Bagram to discuss the hostage situation in person before heading back to Washington. His ETA is about eight hundred hours."

The secretary's impromptu visit didn't surprise David. The hostage situation was being given front-page coverage in every U.S. newspaper, and the government's response was being scrutinized by the American public. Each day that passed without a resolution saw the president's ratings slip in the polls. The fallout from the deaths of three American hostages could cause irreparable political damage to a man who had his eye on a second term.

The meeting at the U.S. air base thirty miles north of Kabul would be a last-ditch effort to discuss possible solutions and damage control. David would have liked to think it was being prompted by humanitarian concerns, but he'd been in the business too long to believe that was the only motivation for the summons to meet with the secretary. The president was a good, decent man—but the political pressure in this situation would be immense.

"I'll be waiting for him, Lindsay."

"I'll let him know. And I'll alert you if there are any changes to his itinerary."

As David replaced the receiver, he reached for his coffee again. To his surprise, he noted a tremor in his hand. Odd. He'd weathered these kinds of situations in the past without any visible sign of nerves.

But he'd never had a personal stake in one, either.

The president might be worried about political fallout. David was more worried about the impending loss of life. And about his daughter.

Monica might be ensconced in a safe house, but "safe" was a relative term. And until this crisis was over, he wasn't going to rest easy.

"Mind if I join you? I'll bring popcorn."

Turning away from the TV screen, Monica found Coop grinning at her from the doorway to the hearth room, waving a bag of microwaveable kernels.

"Didn't you get enough of old movies this afternoon?" She sent him a teasing smile, surprised and warmed by his unexpected presence. When he and Mark had disappeared after dinner, leaving her security in the hands of Rick and Mac, she'd assumed she wouldn't see him again until his 6:00 a.m. shift started on Wednesday.

"I have to admit I found it relaxing. They don't make comedies like that anymore. It did, however, convince me I never want to build a house."

167

Her smile broadened. "I might have to agree. *Mr. Blandings Builds His Dream House* can't be a favorite movie of architects or home construction companies."

"That would be a safe bet. I liked the scene where Cary Grant got locked in the closet." He chuckled, the sound a pleasing rumble in his chest. "I hoped I'd be in time to catch some of the late show."

"It's only nine o'clock. I don't think this qualifies as the late show."

"Depends on how tired you are." He scrutinized her face. "You need to get some sleep."

"Easier said than done." No sense pretending her nights had been anything but restless. The shadows under her eyes proved otherwise.

"You'll get through this, Monica. Things have to break sooner or later."

The huskiness in his voice tightened her throat, and she had to swallow before she could respond. "I know. I'd just prefer it to be sooner."

"Me too."

"I don't suppose there are any updates? Or that my father has heard from the informer?"

"No. I'd have let you know if there were any developments."

"I figured you would." She brushed her hair back with a hand that wasn't quite steady.

He observed her for a few seconds, then inclined his head toward the TV. "What's playing now in your movie marathon?"

"I'm afraid it's a musical. But it's winding down." She mustered the semblance of a smile.

As she spoke, Gene Kelly launched into the title song from *Singin' in the Rain* and began to dance his way through the thunderstorm.

"At least you picked a classic. How about that popcorn?"

"You mean the musical didn't scare you off?"

"Nope."

"Brave man. Sure. I'll have some. I ran out of these an hour ago." She lifted her empty, crumpled M&M bag.

"I'll have to put those on the resupply list." He winked. "Back in a minute."

The enticing aroma of fresh-popped corn filtered into the hearth room a couple of minutes later, and Coop reappeared soon after carrying one large bowl. He took a seat on the couch beside Monica and set the bowl between them.

"Dig in." He helped himself to a handful and turned his attention to the TV screen.

Although Monica followed his lead, she had difficulty concentrating as the movie wound down. Coop had changed into worn jeans and a black sweater that enhanced his dark good looks, and despite the bowl separating them she could feel his presence in an almost tangible way. It was reassuring and comforting . . . but also disturbing. His proximity caused her nerve endings to tingle in a strange, though not unpleasant, way, creating a physical awareness in her that defied reason.

It was odd, she reflected. She'd met dozens of eligible men over the past twenty years, at school, in the course of her work, at social events. None had attracted her as Coop did. And he wasn't even her type. He was too enclosed, too uncommunicative. Still, he'd done a pretty good job of loosening up this afternoon when he'd talked about his past, she admitted. But she suspected that had been an aberration. That he'd been acting against type, for reasons that eluded her.

His appeal must be related to his role as protector, she theorized, trying to apply logic to the situation. She was depending on him to keep her safe. And despite the popularity of women's lib, despite her own convictions about equal rights and standing on her own two feet, there was a certain romantic allure about the stereotypical archetype of a knight in shining armor. Thrust into a situation of high danger, where her life depended on the ability of Coop—and the other agents—to protect her, it was only logical that she'd be grateful for their help.

But gratitude didn't explain the zing that shot through her when she dug into the bowl for popcorn and found her hand resting against Coop's.

She snatched it back as if she'd been burned. "Sorry." The apology came out in a breathless whoosh.

"I didn't mind."

He gave her a slow smile that turned her insides to jelly and did nothing to stabilize her respiration.

"Do you want the last of the popcorn?" He motioned to the few kernels remaining in the bottom of the bowl.

"No thanks."

Gathering them up, he popped them in his mouth as the closing credits of the movie began to roll. "Do you have a third feature planned?"

"No. I think I've had my movie fix for a month, let alone a day."

"Heading to bed?"

She stared at him, fixated on the word *bed*.

He tilted his head and gave her a curious look. "What's wrong?"

"Nothing." *Everything!* Her heart was thudding in her chest as if she'd run a fifty-yard dash. What in the world was wrong with her? She wasn't some teenager suffering through her first crush. She was a thirty-four-year-old professional, mature woman. *Get a grip*, she admonished herself.

"Are you sure?" Skepticism narrowed his eyes.

"Yes. Absolutely." She had to leave. Now. Running away wasn't the most adult response to her unruly emotions, but she didn't trust herself to stay in Coop's presence. Not when she kept wondering what it would feel like to be wrapped in those strong arms.

As Monica picked up the Bible, obviously preparing to exit, Coop tried to interpret her expression. He'd seen that type of look before, and in a typical social situation, he'd classify it as longing. And invitation.

But this situation was neither typical nor social. Monica's emotions were running high for a lot of reasons, including fear. No surprise, considering her life was in danger and her world had been turned upside down. Perhaps the glimpse of yearning he'd seen was more a silent plea for reassurance than anything else. A reluctance to break the connection between them and retreat alone to her room with only worry for company.

Nor did he want her to retreat. To his surprise, their discussion earlier in the afternoon had been a cathartic experience. He still couldn't believe he'd opened up about his childhood. But he didn't regret it. Sharing the trauma with Monica had diminished the loneliness he hadn't even been aware of until the past few days. Eased it to the point that he'd reneged on his promise to himself to steer clear of her once he was off duty for the day.

Now he sat inches away from her, fighting a powerful urge to lean over and taste those soft lips that were dusted with salt and glistening with popcorn oil.

"I-I guess I'll call it a night."

Her shaky words, the slight dilation of her pupils, almost compelled him to step over the line between personal and professional conduct. But calling on every reserve of discipline he could muster, he managed to rein in his impulses.

"Good idea. Maybe that will give you some comfort." He tapped the Bible clutched in her hands.

Hugging the volume tight against her chest like a shield, she gave a slow, deliberate blink. As if she was shifting gears. "Whenever I feel in over my head or things seem to be spiraling out of control, this centers me."

"I envy you that consolation."

"It's yours for the asking."

He gave a quick, dismissive shake of his head. "You make faith sound easy."

"I don't mean to. It's not easy at all. There are days I struggle, especially if I don't understand why certain things are happening. Doubt is part of being human. But my core belief—that no matter what happens, God is with me—never wavers. And it's a great comfort to know that once you turn your life over to him, you never have to face anything alone again."

He draped an arm over the back of the sofa and angled toward her. "I don't think I could turn my life over to anyone. Letting go of control, relying on someone else . . . that requires a lot of trust."

"You trust Mark, don't you?"

"Yes. But that's different. We've worked together for three years. He's earned my trust."

"So has Jesus."

Her quiet response took him off guard. "How so?"

"He was an innocent man, wrongly accused, who died to pay the price for our sins. He redeemed us when we didn't deserve redemption. And he did it out of love. Pure, unselfish love. If that isn't enough to earn our trust—and our love—I don't know what is."

Coop knew the salvation story from the sporadic Bible classes he'd attended as a youth, but Monica's succinct summary of its significance suddenly struck a chord.

Dying to save innocent people was a concept Coop understood. Much of his work revolved around that very principle. But would he lay his life on the line for someone who didn't deserve to be saved? No.

Yet that's what Jesus had done. Motivated, according to Monica, by selfless love. And she believed his sacrifice had earned him allegiance.

On the rare occasions when Coop thought about God, he always pictured him as an oppressive, omnipotent dictator. A stern, faceless, impersonal judge.

By contrast, Monica seemed focused on the personal relationship she had with the Almighty. The God-man who had loved humans enough to die for them despite their imperfections and flaws and mistakes.

That concept put a whole different slant on religion, Coop reflected. A God like that would be worthy of the leap of faith he'd always shunned as irrational. There was a logic to it that appealed to him. And to his concept of loyalty.

"That kind of love is pretty amazing, isn't it?"

At Monica's gentle question, Coop drew a deep breath. "Yeah. It's a little hard to grasp."

"You said you enjoy reading . . . would you like to borrow this?" She held up the Bible. "It might give you a few insights. And some answers."

"I wouldn't want to take away your source of comfort."

"I've read it lots of times. My favorite verses are filed away up here." She smiled and tapped her head.

If someone had told him a few days ago he'd be interested in reading the Bible, Coop would have laughed. But considering the way his feelings for Monica had thrown him off balance—and given rise to some pretty uncharacteristic behavior—he figured anything that offered the possibility of answers was worth checking out.

"Okay. Thanks." He took the book from her and tucked it under his arm. "Let me ask you one more question. This concept of turning your life over to God—don't you find that diminishes your freedom? That it chips away at who you are as a unique individual?"

"No. I've had the opposite experience. Giving my life to God has been liberating because I know he loves me. And when you know you're loved, you trust the other person. That frees you to be exactly who you are. To reach inside and bring out the very best you have to offer without fear or pretense."

Interesting, Coop thought. Monica viewed love as liberating. He'd always viewed it as confining. Dangerous. Predicated on passing certain "tests."

But according to Monica, God gave love freely. No strings attached. Even when humans didn't deserve it, his love was constant.

Constant, unconditional love.

It was an awesome concept.

And not that difficult to grasp, Coop conceded, given that God was divine. It was logical that his love would be perfect.

Human love, however, was a whole different story. It often came with stipulations and contingencies, corrupted by selfishness and agendas. It could be used to manipulate and control. It could diminish.

That's why he'd vowed never to marry.

Monica Callahan was the first woman who'd managed to shake his resolve.

As she looked at him across the popcorn bowl, her expression placid, he realized that in the few short days he'd known her she'd already had a significant impact on his life. Her empathy and insights had forced him to reexamine some of his long-held beliefs. And to identify some issues he hadn't even recognized. Like loneliness.

In other words, she'd given him a lot to think about.

Forcing his lips into the semblance of a grin, he rose. "I'd say

174

it's about time to call it a night. You're sure you don't mind if I borrow this?" He lifted the Bible.

"No. I'm heading for bed anyway." She remained seated.

"Try to sleep. You're well guarded."

"I know. I trust you guys."

There was that word again.

Trust.

He understood earned trust on a professional level. His life sometimes depended on it. But in Monica's mind, trust was also inexorably linked with love. A far riskier proposition, as far as Coop was concerned. He could deal with putting his life in jeopardy. He was far less comfortable exposing his heart to peril.

Lifting a hand, he headed toward the door. In a day or two or three this assignment would be over. Monica's life would return to normal.

But thanks to her, Coop wasn't sure his ever would.

14

"Aren't you going to turn in? Six o'clock will be here way too soon."

"Later." Coop responded to Mark's question without shifting focus from the two computer screens in the guest cottage.

Instead of accepting his partner's answer, Mark ambled over to join him behind Fendler, the field agent who was seated at the cottage's kitchen table monitoring the feed from the security cameras. "Looks pretty quiet."

"Let's hope it stays that way."

"Everything okay at the house?"

"Yes."

"You were gone awhile."

"I took a stroll around the perimeter before I came back."

"You were still gone awhile."

"I didn't realize you'd miss me." Coop sent Mark a wry glance as he took a sip from the disposable cup in his hand. The coffee tasted stale, but it was better than Les's sludge.

"How's Monica doing?"

"She's tense."

"That's understandable. How are you doing?"

Shooting Mark a warning look, Coop took another sip of coffee. He wasn't about to discuss Monica in front of the field agent, and he knew where Mark was heading. "Good."

"Yeah?"

With one quick gulp, Coop drained the cardboard cup, crumpled it, and tossed it in the waste can. "I think I'll grab some sleep after all."

"Good idea. I'll join you."

The single bedroom in the guest cottage held two twin beds that could be joined to form a king. For the duration of this assignment, they'd been pushed as far apart as possible. With Mark close on his heels, Coop tossed his jacket on one of them and wished the cottage had two bedrooms instead of one.

"Close quarters." He pulled off his BlackBerry and set it on the nightstand between the beds.

"We've slept in tighter—and far less comfortable—places." Stepping around the four pieces of luggage that lined one side of the room they shared with the HRT operators on night shift, Mark stretched out on the other bed and linked his fingers behind his head. "Everything look okay outside?"

"Yes. But I don't like all the pines along the fence. They provide too much cover." Coop raked his fingers through his hair and prowled around the confined space.

"The perimeter is well patrolled. And if anyone did manage to get into the complex, the cameras would pick them up. Besides, the doors at the house are armed, and Rick or Mac would hear a window breaking. The place is as secure as we can make it short of adding another dozen agents and handcuffing Monica to one of us for the duration. And I doubt the lady would go along with that. Unless it was you, of course."

"Knock it off, Mark."

"Touchy, aren't we?"

"I told you before, I don't mix business and pleasure."

"This job will be over soon. What happens then?"

Returning to the bed, Coop retrieved the small Bible from the inside pocket of his jacket and sat on the edge of the mattress. "I don't know."

"What are you reading?" Mark propped himself up on one elbow.

"Nothing yet." He set the book on the nightstand, sorry he'd pulled it out in front of his partner.

"You're evading the question." Mark reached over and tilted the cover to read the title. "The Bible? Whoa!" He swung his legs to the floor and stared at Coop. "If Monica has you reading the Bible, this must be really serious."

"I haven't read it yet."

"But you're going to."

"Maybe."

"Why?"

"Call it intellectual curiosity."

"Nope. Don't buy it. You always dismissed religion as too emotional."

"I'm having some second thoughts."

"Because of Monica."

"No. Because some things she said made sense."

"Uh-huh." Mark stretched out again on the bed. "Like I said, this is serious."

"It's too soon to be serious."

"Not according to those old love songs. One look across a crowded room and all that."

"I don't believe in love at first sight."

"You didn't believe in religion, either. And look at you now. A Bible-toter, no less."

With a disgruntled snort, Coop heaved one of the decorative pillows on his bed at Mark. "Go to sleep, okay? I'm going to read for a while."

"Sure." Mark rolled onto his side and spoke over his shoulder. "I'd wish you sweet dreams, but I expect that's a given."

Coop could hear the grin in Mark's voice. But his partner was wrong about the sweet dreams. Or dreams, period. Worry wasn't likely to allow him the luxury of much sleep. For a moment, he considered telling that to Mark to counter his roommate's conclusion. But as a comeback, it felt flat.

Because as Mark would no doubt point out, the cause of either sweet dreams or insomnia would be the same.

Monica.

Nouri lifted the curtain on the window of the nondescript motel room and checked the parking lot. There were a few cars positioned in front of the row of doors spaced along the long, low building, but they were clustered more toward the entrance. The back end of the lot, near the last unit that they occupied, was deserted. And at thirty minutes past midnight, it was unlikely more overnight guests would show up.

"All is quiet?"

At Zahir's question, Nouri let the fabric drop back into place and returned to packing his equipment for tonight's mission. "Yes. I must have given a convincing performance when I told the desk clerk we were two weary salesmen who'd been on the road for days and wanted a nice, quiet spot to crash, as far away from any activity as possible. The closest car is eight or nine doors down."

"And you are not concerned about the security camera at the entrance?"

"No. I pulled the brim of my hat low and kept my chin down during check-in. Besides, we have done nothing to raise suspicion. You are rested enough for tonight's job?"

"I slept four hours." Zahir shrugged and pulled on a black, long-sleeved knit shirt. "I have done far more taxing work on much less sleep."

"You will have plenty of opportunity to catch up after we

return. We will have nothing to do except wait." He slid his extra laptop into its case, pulled a blue sweater over his black turtleneck, and secured the latches on his backpack. "Ready?"

"Yes."

Lifting the curtains once more, Nouri scanned the parking lot. "We're clear."

He flipped off the light, and in silence the two men stepped through the door and quickly covered the few steps to their car.

The drive to Charlottesville, using the meandering route they'd mapped out through the countryside, took fifty-five minutes. They pulled into the Holiday Inn right on schedule.

"I will be back in a few minutes." Nouri retrieved the laptop from the backseat and headed to the room he'd booked earlier in the day, of use to him only for its wireless Internet service and close proximity to the safe house. The night clerk gave him little more than a brief, disinterested glance as he passed, then refocused on his computer screen. Probably playing some kind of game, Nouri speculated. Just as he was about to do.

Once in the room, he wasted no time bringing up the feed from the security camera by the tennis court. Retrieving the video he'd saved from last night during this same period, he overlaid it on the live feed. When the image from the camera panning the grounds meshed with his saved file it took little more than a keystroke to switch the source of the image. No more than the barest blip marked the transition.

Five minutes later, he rejoined Zahir and put the key in the ignition. "We have one hour and fifty-five minutes."

Tariq took a sip of tea and did a cursory sweep of the scene outside his window, alert for any suspicious activity. In a few minutes, Anis would bring his noon meal.

But he had little interest in food. The pieces of his plan were falling into place, and soon David Callahan would know the power Tariq wielded. Even now, Nouri would be implementing his abduction scheme. As soon as the girl was secured, he would send a message to Callahan, letting him know she would die along with the first hostage twenty-four hours from now unless his demands were met.

If that pressure didn't work, he would follow through on his threats.

It would be a diplomatic disaster for the United States, and a political disaster for the shaky Afghan leadership. Public sentiment in America had already shifted against U.S. involvement in this part of the world, and Tariq's scheme would accelerate that change of heart. The American people had no stomach for messy, faraway wars that had no impact on their lives nor interfered with their daily visit to Starbucks. Eventually, the president would be forced to withdraw troops. It wouldn't take long after that for the faltering Afghan government to topple, leaving chaos in its wake.

And in chaos, there was opportunity.

"I have brought your dinner." Anis stood in the doorway, balancing a tray.

"Set it on the table."

With a slight bow, Anis complied while Tariq examined the meal with distaste. The woman who prepared his food seemed to know how to cook little besides rice, lentil soup, eggplant with yogurt sauce, and fried pastries filled with ground beef and chickpeas, all served with flat bread. It was a far cry from the gourmet fare he had enjoyed in his better days. And that he would enjoy again soon.

Straightening, Anis angled toward Tariq and held out his cell phone. "Mahmud is on the line. He said he tried to reach you on your phone, but the call would not go through. Perhaps your battery is dead?"

Tariq slipped his hand inside his robe and withdrew his phone. Much to his disgust, the battery was, indeed, dead. He exchanged it for Anis's phone. "See that it is charged."

After another slight bow, Anis retreated as Tariq put the phone to his ear. "Yes, Mahmud. What is it?"

"I have learned from one of my sources that David Callahan is planning to go to the U.S. air base tomorrow morning."

Tariq frowned. "Why?"

"I do not know. He may be leaving the country."

Was it possible? Tariq wondered. Would he leave mere hours before the first hostage was to be executed? Or was he going to the air base to confer with a high-level U.S. government official? Bagram often hosted such meetings. Tariq suspected the latter.

"Find out more."

"My source knows nothing else." Frustration and impatience nipped at Mahmud's words. "If he is leaving the country, we will lose our chance to use his death as a tactical measure."

"And if we take him out now, our efforts to use threats against his daughter to force him to convince his government to comply with our demands will have been wasted."

"I am not convinced that will work, anyway."

Anger coursed through Tariq. In person, Mahmud would never have had the audacity to voice such an opinion. The man knew Tariq demanded absolute compliance and obedience, that he didn't tolerate anything that even whispered of insubordination. It seemed the three-hundred-mile buffer between Kabul and Kandahar had given Mahmud the courage to speak his true thoughts.

While Tariq wasn't pleased with the man's insolence, it validated his growing impression that Mahmud was not a man who could be easily controlled. Or trusted.

When the silence lengthened, Mahmud spoke again, his tone conciliatory. As if he'd realized his mistake, Tariq deduced. "I am not as experienced as you, of course. If you believe letting David Callahan go to the air base is the best course, I am certain that it is."

"Call me if you learn more."

Pressing the end button, Tariq severed the connection.

He hoped his abrupt dismissal communicated his displeasure. And kept the man in line for the next couple of days. He might need to call on him if things didn't go as planned.

But once this was over, there would be consequences for Mahmud.

In the meantime, he had other sources he could call who might be able to find out more about David Callahan's little excursion.

Head bent against the wind, Sayed stepped into the small, obscure hut in the tiny desert village and looked from one guard to the other. "All is well?"

"Yes. They are docile, like lambs."

The two men laughed, and Sayed strolled over to the three hostages who were seated on a rug on the dirt floor against the far wall. A wracking cough convulsed the older man as he approached. The government employee, Sayed recalled. His gaze moved on to the reporter. The younger man's eyes held an interesting combination of defiance and fear. The woman next to him, one of those idealistic do-gooders, was trembling. They were probably wondering if they were going to die soon, Sayed reflected, his expression dispassionate. And perhaps they were.

But it wouldn't be at his hands. In twenty-four hours, when

the first hostage was scheduled to be executed, Sayed would be very far away.

As he exited, he nodded to the two additional armed guards who stood outside the entrance to the hut. Heading toward his quarters in the adjacent structure where lunch awaited him, he was struck by the irony of the situation.

If anyone was going to die tomorrow, the men bearing arms—not the hostages—would be the more likely casualties.

Officer Ed Martin reached for the cup of coffee in the holder beside the front seat of his patrol car and stifled a yawn. He never had gotten used to the night shift, even after twenty years of rotating through it. Sleeping during the day still felt unnatural to him. Especially for the first day or two after the shift rotation. Sometimes he just had to catch a couple of fifteen-minute catnaps in the driveway of one of the big unoccupied estates on the outskirts of Charlottesville.

But that wasn't an option tonight. He'd been told to cruise down a little-traveled secondary road every thirty minutes and to report in each time. The department had started the routine yesterday, but none of the officers had a clue why. Considering all the government bigwigs who had weekend places out this way, he figured some high-profile person must be staying at one of the compounds.

Now he was on his sixth pass of the night. Like the prior runs, it was uneventful. He saw no cars on the narrow, two-lane road. The houses on his right were shielded from view by privacy plantings and fences, and the undeveloped woods on his left were pitch dark. Maybe after this drive-by he could take a few minutes and . . .

"What the . . ." His headlights illuminated a figure in ragged attire weaving down the side of the road. He'd run into his share of street people in some parts of his beat, but never in this area.

Martin settled his coffee cup in the holder and depressed the transmit button on his radio. "Three-seven-oh-one. I have an unidentified person walking down Hanover Road. Looks like a homeless guy. I'm checking it out."

Angling the spotlight on the side of his car toward the figure, he spoke over the loudspeaker. "Sir, please turn toward me and keep your hands where I can see them."

The man stumbled to a stop and complied, shading his eyes from the bright light. He wore a knit cap pulled low on his forehead, and he tucked his chin into the turned-up collar of his worn coat.

Keeping his gaze fixed on the man, Martin opened his door and stepped out of the car, his hand on his Smith and Wesson. He took a couple of steps toward the figure.

"Sir, what are you doing out here in the middle of the night?"

No response.

"Do you have a place to stay?"

No response.

"What's your name?"

At the sudden press of cold steel against the base of his neck, Martin's fingers clenched around his gun.

"One move and you're dead."

The low, intense voice, close to his ear, convinced the officer the man meant business. He remained motionless.

"Good. I like people who follow directions."

The "indigent" man pulled a neck warmer up over the lower half of his face and strode toward the car, snapping on a pair of latex gloves. He leaned inside to kill the spotlight and the headlights.

"What do you want?" Martin strove for a calm tone as he tried to stem the fear coursing through his veins.

185

"I want you to call your dispatcher and tell them everything is okay. Tell them the man you saw on the road was a teenager coming home late from a party and hoping to sneak in the back way. Say you've alerted his parents, and they're on their way to pick him up. Keep one hand on the wheel and don't touch the emergency button. Do it now."

Martin slid into the driver's seat, debating his options. Two against one wasn't good odds. Especially when one of them had a gun pressed against his neck. But the timing of this incident wasn't coincidental. It had to be related to the increased patrols in the area. For all he knew, it might have national security implications. It was his duty to attempt to thwart these two from whatever mission had brought them here on this cold February night.

Yet he had a duty to his family too. At twelve and fifteen, his kids needed a father. And his wife didn't need a dead hero for a husband.

"Do it." The gun pressed harder against his neck.

Depressing the transmit button, Martin relayed the message his assailant had dictated.

"Very good. Now get out of the car and open the trunk."

His pulse pounding, Martin stood. His legs felt stiff. The man he'd spotted on the road stood by the trunk. He held a gun too. He still hadn't caught a glimpse of the other man, but he could sense his presence behind him.

When he reached the trunk, the man from the road moved behind him too. The imminent sense of danger intensified, and he fumbled with the keys. These two did not intend to let him walk away from this encounter, he realized, a cold knot forming in the pit of his stomach.

"Open it."

It was dark and difficult to see the lock. He felt for it, and when his fingers closed over the raised circle he fitted the key in and twisted it until the trunk released with a distinctive click.

"Lift it up."

He needed to get his hand on his gun. And this was his chance, Martin recognized. Perhaps his only one.

His heart thudding, he bent down. As he started to raise the lid, he waited until his hand was level with his gun. Then, in one swift movement, he transferred his hand to his gun and pivoted sideways, calling on every ounce of karate training he could recall to deliver a solid kick with his heel.

His boot connected. With what, he didn't know, but he heard a grunt as he started to draw his gun.

Martin had never expected to emerge unscathed from the encounter. At best, he had hoped to survive.

But he hadn't expected the silent, deadly thrust of a knife beneath his ribcage.

His hand convulsed on his holster as he gasped in pain and staggered back.

A second searing thrust followed.

His legs buckled, and he felt himself falling . . . falling . . . falling into a black abyss.

As his world went dark, he had one last thought.

He wasn't the only one who was going to die this night.

15

Zahir eased the police car down a dirt byway that led into the woods less than a quarter of a mile from the safe house.

"How did you find this spot?" Nouri adjusted the earpiece for his voice-activated microphone.

"I stumbled across it as I was working my way to the safe house the first night. Allah smiles on our mission."

That was a moot point, as far as Nouri was concerned. His work against the United States was motivated by hate, not religious fervor. In his opinion, suicide bombers were misguided fanatics who threw their lives away. He had no respect—or patience—for such foolish gestures. It was more noble to live for many missions than to die for one.

Zahir parked the police cruiser in front of their car. While he retrieved the mini boom mike from the trunk of the dark sedan, Nouri strapped on his equipment belt, flipping off the safety on the 40-caliber Sig Sauer he hoped he didn't have to use. Even with a silencer, a shot would be loud enough to sound the death knell on their operation. Pulling the trigger would be a last resort.

"How long do you need to get into position?" Nouri joined Zahir at the trunk and lifted out his backpack. He slung a small stepladder over his shoulder and checked his watch.

"Ten minutes. I plan to perch in the same tree on the neighbor's property that provided me good cover last night."

"Let me know the second the agent on the back perimeter checks in. My twenty-minute window begins then."

"I understand." Zahir tucked his night-vision binoculars inside his jacket and set off along the edge of the road, disappearing into the dark shadows of the pine trees.

Nouri followed more slowly. As he slipped on night-vision goggles, pulled a ski mask over his head, and tugged on latex surgical gloves, he forced himself to take deep, even breaths. Unlike his visit to Monica Callahan's house, tonight's venture involved great risk. The diplomat's daughter was well protected, and he needed both luck and skill to pull this off undetected. But he'd done his homework and his plan was solid. Lack of preparation wouldn't jeopardize his mission. He was as ready as he could be.

Eight minutes later, Zahir's voice sounded in his ear. "I am in position."

"I am ready whenever you give the word."

"The agent on the east perimeter is approaching the front of the property. The agent in the back is heading for the west corner. Stand by."

Nouri's heart began to pound as the minutes ticked by. One. Two. Three.

"The agent in back is at the corner. This is your best opportunity to get into position."

Crouching low, Nouri covered the short distance to the center of the back fence, an ornate wrought-iron affair. He unfolded the stepladder, climbed it, and pulled himself up and over the fence, dropping soundlessly to the other side on a carpet of needles behind the row of pine trees that lined the inside perimeter. Reaching through the iron uprights, he folded up the ladder and eased it through. As he crouched behind the trees, he slid the backpack off his shoulders and removed a knife from the sheath on his belt.

"I am ready."

"The agent at the back perimeter has just checked in with the command center. He is walking your direction. The agent on the east perimeter is in the front corner of the property."

"I will be back in touch as soon as the agent is disposed of."

Disturbing the foliage as little as possible, Nouri moved in among the branches of the pine trees until he had a view to the other side. With each second that ticked by, adrenaline pulsed through his veins. When the agent came into view, his grip on the knife tightened.

The man walked slowly, scanning the property. He approached Nouri's position. Glanced his way. Kept moving.

Silent as a cougar, Nouri sprang. He was on the man in one leap, his knees gripping the agent's back.

With his left hand, he reached around and yanked the man's jaw up. With his other hand, he sliced through the right carotid artery.

The man gasped.

Blood spurted.

Before the agent could call out, Nouri dropped to the ground and delivered a precise kick to the back of his legs, bringing him to his knees. Nouri gripped his windpipe and squeezed, cutting off the man's air supply. The man's eyes bulged, and his struggle grew weaker. Nouri increased the pressure.

Thirty seconds later, the agent slumped into unconsciousness.

Grabbing him under the arms, Nouri dragged him behind the pine trees. He removed the man's gun and tossed it a few feet away. Pushing up the agent's sleeve, he cut the wires leading to the mike at his wrist. Not that the man would be calling for help. He was already unconscious. And within five minutes he'd be dead.

Nouri pulled a cloth from his pocket, wiped the blood off his hands, and checked his watch. The entire attack had taken less than three minutes. Good. He was right on schedule.

"I am ready to move to the house."

"The agent on the east perimeter is beginning to walk toward the back of the property. I see no other activity. You should be clear to approach," Zahir reported.

Keeping low, Nouri passed the tennis court and approached the darkened master bedroom suite at the end of the sprawling structure. This was the part of the operation where he would be most exposed. That's why he'd practiced the sequence of actions over and over to achieve maximum efficiency of motion.

Dropping beside a bush that formed part of the foundation planting, he opened his backpack and withdrew a gas mask, ice pick, a loop of piano wire, and neoprene gloves. The last item out was a small Teflon-lined, Monel steel cylinder containing compressed fluorine gas he'd pilfered during a clandestine visit to a geology lab a couple of weeks before.

After adjusting the mask on his face, he pulled on the gloves, set the stepladder beside the window, and climbed two steps to put him at the same level as the top of the lower sash.

Pressing the cylinder against the glass opposite the handle on the safety lock, he released a jet of gas by opening a special fitting that was surrounded by a snug ring of charcoal. Almost instantly the glass vaporized, leaving a sizeable hole. He repeated the procedure on the inside glass of the double-pane window.

Once both holes were formed, he inserted the ice pick, the tip rubberized to minimize slippage. Exerting steady pressure, he pushed on the safety latch of the window until it opened halfway.

After repeating the procedure with the canister on the other side of the lock to create two more holes, he discarded the ice pick and retrieved his jerry-rigged piano wire instrument. It was designed like a needle threader, and had performed as expected when he'd tested it.

Squeezing the wire loop together, he eased it through the holes in the glass, then allowed it to bow open. Once he'd snagged the half-opened lock, it was a simple matter to pull until it released its hold on the lower sash.

After retracting the piano wire, Nouri removed his gas mask and dropped both items to the ground. Any toxic, pungent fumes not captured by the charcoal collar had had plenty of time to dissipate. He stripped off his gloves and discarded them too.

The sash slid up with very little pressure, and he climbed through. Easing it shut behind him, he checked the time. He had seven minutes left.

He moved across the room to the half-open door and paused to listen. All was silent.

Sliding along the hall wall, he approached the first door on the left. A bedroom, according to the floor plan he'd found. The only one that showed any evidence of night use, based on Zahir's surveillance.

The knob turned easily, noiseless, and he slipped inside, closing the door behind him.

He took a moment to scan the room. The muted glow of a dim nightlight revealed Monica Callahan sleeping in the queen-sized bed against the far wall, the pillow bunched under her head, one arm across her chest. The covers were in disarray, as if she'd had a restless night.

And it was only going to get worse.

He allowed himself one brief flicker of a smile as he pulled a small bottle and a cloth out of a pocket in his vest. Opening the container, he held the cloth against the top and tipped the bottle, letting the sweet-smelling liquid soak into the fabric. Returning the bottle to his pocket, he approached the bed.

Although he was silent, the woman stirred and her lashes

swept up as he drew close. He froze, but she glanced at the clock on her bedside table, not at him. By the time she looked his direction, he was beside her.

Before she could react, he flung his body over hers to restrain her movements, grasped her free arm, and pressed the cloth to her nose and mouth. She squirmed beneath him, her eyes wide with fright, and tried to scream. But the cloth muffled her cries.

In less than half a minute, she grew limp.

Nouri kept the cloth over her nose and mouth for another fifteen seconds, then moved off the bed and opened her window, speaking in a low voice to Zahir.

"I'm ready to leave the house. Where is the east perimeter guard?"

"At the back of the property. He just checked in with the control center. You only have four minutes until the agent at the back is scheduled to check in."

"I'm on my way. Get the car."

Nouri returned to the bed and lifted Monica. He eased her through the window, held her under the arms, and let her drop to the ground with a soft thud. A moment later he followed. After retrieving the stepladder, he slipped it over one shoulder and slung Monica over the other.

Keeping low, hugging the lush landscaping, he jogged toward the back fence.

As he brushed through the pines at the back of the property, he noted that the agent was lying where he'd left him.

Resetting the stepladder by the back fence, Nouri climbed up. All his hours of weight training paid off as he hefted the woman up and over. He let her legs dangle before releasing her to crumple in a heap. In one lithe movement, he scaled the fence and dropped beside her.

As he bent to lift her, he noted blood on her left temple—and

193

the rock beside it. Frowning, he pressed his fingers against her neck. Felt a pulse. Good. It would be a shame to get this far and have a misplaced rock put a damper on their plans.

Tossing her over his shoulder once more, he headed up the small incline toward the road. The dark sedan they'd rented was moving his direction, and as it drew to a stop Nouri heard the trunk release.

He moved to the back, lifted the lid, and dumped Monica inside. Closing the lid with a quiet click, he slid in beside Zahir.

The car was already rolling as he shut the door.

"The perimeter guard was due to check in three minutes ago. The timing on this was very close."

At Zahir's comment, Nouri turned to him. Despite the dim interior, he detected a thin film of moisture on the man's upper lip. Unusual. He'd never seen Zahir sweat. "I knew it would be." He began to strip off his gear and stash it in the duffel bag at his feet, pulling on the blue sweater he'd worn earlier at the Holiday Inn. "Do you want me to drive?"

"No. I know the route."

Nouri settled back in the seat. Zahir had never faltered in any of the high-pressure situations they'd encountered, and Nouri didn't expect him to now, despite his uncharacteristic tension. Yet this job had been the most daring they'd ever pulled off. His own nerves had flared a time or two.

It would soon be over, however. Once they arrived back at the motel, it was a waiting game. The next move was David Callahan's. As the Americans liked to say, the ball was in their court. If he didn't meet Tariq's demands, in less than twenty-four hours one hostage would die in Afghanistan.

And another would die here.

Something didn't feel right.

A tingle of alarm raced along Coop's spine as he stared at the dark ceiling in the guest cottage. He had no idea what had jolted him awake, but he wasn't inclined to ignore the prompting of his gut. It had saved his hide on more than one occasion.

Angling his head on the pillow, he checked the clock. Three in the morning. That meant he'd managed no more than a couple of fitful hours of sleep.

And he knew he wouldn't get any more until he confirmed that everything was okay.

His fingers groped for his earpiece in the dark, and he fitted it in place, listening. The silence was reassuring. Yet the niggle of disquiet didn't dissipate.

Grateful he'd elected to sleep in his clothes, he felt for his shoes on the dark floor. Found them. Slipped them on and tied them, taking care to make as little noise as possible. No need to disturb Mark's rest without a legitimate reason. Standing, he slid the wire for his mike down the sleeve of his shirt and clipped it to the cuff.

He was holstering his Glock when Fendler's voice sounded in his ear.

"Minard, you're three minutes past check-in. Respond."

Silence.

Coop tensed.

"Minard. Come in."

Silence.

Coop opened the bedroom door and strode toward the kitchen. "What's up?"

Fendler frowned. "I'm not getting a response from Minard. He's on the back perimeter."

"I'll check it out. Put the other guys on alert. Have Mac and Rick look in on Ms. Callahan."

Grabbing his jacket and a flashlight, Coop headed out the

door. Gun drawn, light off, he worked his way toward the rear of the property, alert to any movement around him. But the estate grounds were peaceful. Nothing seemed amiss.

Yet Minard's silence was chilling.

Suddenly his earpiece crackled to life. It was Mac's voice. Taut. Clipped.

"Ms. Callahan is gone. There are signs of a struggle in her bedroom and the window is open."

A wave of panic crashed over Coop, powerful enough to freeze his lungs. His step faltered. Monica gone? How was that possible?

Sucking in a deep breath, he swallowed past his choking fear and lifted his wrist to his mouth, barking out orders. "Fendler, get Mark up. Mac, Rick we need you out here to help search the grounds. I'm at the back fence." As he spoke, he flicked on the flashlight and strode along the perimeter, just inside the line of pine trees that shielded the property from the scrutiny of curious passers-by on the road. "Has anyone seen or heard anything suspicious in the past twenty minutes?"

The response from the agents on the security detail was negative.

"Okay. I'm halfway along the fence and I haven't . . ."

His flashlight passed over a section of ground, arced back. The grass was trampled. And stained. Red.

A muscle clenched in his jaw. He swept the flashlight around the area of struggle. Found a path of crushed grass and spots of fresh blood, as if someone had been dragged. Tracked it to the pine trees at the back of the property.

"Coop?"

Mark's query echoed in his ear. He ignored it as he followed the trail, the thud of his heart almost painful in his chest as he forced himself to push aside the branches.

Terry Minard was on the ground, his head and neck resting in a pool of blood, his throat slit, his eyes open and vacant.

Coop didn't need to feel for a pulse to know there was no life left in the man.

"Minard is dead." He delivered the news in a grim tone as he swept his light along the fence. Saw the stepladder. Spotted some blood on a rock on the other side of the fence.

And knew that Monica was gone.

"We need answers. Fast. Let's do a cursory search of the grounds, but my gut tells me Ms. Callahan isn't here. We need to secure the area and the road behind the property. Get it done, Fendler. I'm on my way to the house now."

As he sprinted toward the front door, Mark fell in beside him, his expression somber. "What happened?"

"Monica's gone. That's all we know."

"Do you want me to call Les?"

Someone had to, Coop realized. In his fear for Monica, protocol had slipped his mind. "I'll do it."

Pulling out his cell phone, he jabbed in Les's direct line as they entered the house. He remained in the foyer as Mark headed toward Monica's bedroom.

"Coplin." Even at three in the morning, the commander answered on the first ring. Sounding wide awake.

"Coop here. I . . . have bad news. Monica Callahan is missing."

"What!" At Les's bellow, Coop cringed and jerked the phone away from his ear. "What happened?"

"We're trying to determine that. Based on the evidence we have so far, the snatch appears to have happened sometime in the past twenty minutes."

"What evidence?"

"The agent patrolling the back perimeter checked in twenty

minutes ago. He didn't call in twenty minutes later, as scheduled. We found him by the fence. Dead."

The string of expletives Les uttered matched the way Coop felt.

"Okay. I'm calling in local law enforcement. We need coverage there, and we need it fast. I want every patrol officer in a fifty-mile radius alerted that an abduction has taken place. I'll call Dennis Powers and get the Richmond ERT out there ASAP. I want material in the lab as soon as they can get it here. Where are you now?"

"I just stepped into the house."

"Call me when you get a handle on what happened."

The line went dead.

As Coop slipped the phone back into its holder, he realized his hand was trembling. That had never happened to him on a case.

But he'd never been assigned to protect anyone like Monica, either.

Nor had an assignment ever gone so wrong.

And the outlook wasn't good. Even if every law enforcement agency in the area deployed all the manpower they could muster, it would be impossible to stop every car.

"You need to see this, Coop." Mark spoke from the doorway of the foyer.

"Yeah." Raking his hand through his hair, Coop strode toward the hall.

"Hey." Mark put a hand on his shoulder as Coop started to pass, detaining him for a brief moment. "We'll find her."

"We don't have a lot of time. And these guys are good."

"We're better."

"You couldn't prove that by what happened here tonight." Self-recrimination put a bitter edge on his words. Shrugging off

Mark's hand, Coop continued down the hall toward Monica's room, pausing on the threshold.

In a quick but thorough scan, Coop processed the scene. They wouldn't touch anything until the ERT arrived, but he could come to some pretty obvious conclusions from a visual sweep. The bed covers were in disarray, indicating a struggle. The window was open, pointing to the escape route. He tried not to fixate on the smears of blood that stained the sheets. At least there wasn't much of it. And it could be Minard's. The abductor couldn't have committed such a bloody murder without being splattered. His one consolation was that if the terrorists had gone to all this effort to get Monica out alive, they must intend to keep her that way.

For now.

He couldn't let himself think beyond that.

Focusing on the scene, he realized Rick was kneeling on the floor beside a piece of white cloth. As Coop watched, the other operator leaned down and sniffed the fabric.

"What is that?" Coop joined him, dropping down to balance on the balls of his feet.

"Chloroform."

"There's more to see in the master bedroom." Mark spoke quietly behind him.

They found Mac studying the window in the adjacent room. When Coop drew close, the man pointed out the two sets of holes by the lock. "I've never seen anything like that."

Twin furrows creased Coop's brow. "How do you make holes in glass?"

"I was never very good at chemistry, but I'm thinking they must have created some kind of chemical reaction that dissolved the glass."

"I'm going to take a look outside."

Mark fell into step beside him as he exited the room.

Two minutes later, they were staring down at the discarded gas mask, ice pick, some kind of wire loop, and heavy gloves. The kind used in labs.

"Mac was right. They must have used some kind of chemical to burn through the glass." Coop shook his head. "This is surreal. And how could they get her out through our tight security net? Backing up further, how did they know she was here to begin with?"

"I have no idea. But we'll figure it out. Les will put every resource at his disposal on this case."

Coop didn't doubt that. And with the clues left behind, they'd eventually be able to piece together how the terrorists had pulled off the kidnapping.

But he had a sick feeling the abductors had left very few clues that would help them solve the more critical mystery.

Where had they taken Monica?

16

She felt sick to her stomach.

Fighting down her roiling nausea, Monica pried her eyelids open.

Blackness.

Frowning, she squeezed her eyes shut. Opened them again. Nothing.

Why was it pitch dark? The dim nightlight in her room didn't provide much illumination, but it did delineate the shadowy outlines of the furnishings.

Shadowy.

A shadowy figure looming over her. Pressing a cloth to her . . .

A sudden physical jolt snapped her back to the present. Her cheek rose from the bed, hung suspended, slammed back against the mattress. The pulsating throb in her temple intensified.

Her pulse skyrocketed, and fear clawed at her throat.

This wasn't her bed.

Fighting to subdue her mushrooming panic, she explored with her fingers. She was lying on a hard surface covered with some sort of coarse, scratchy cloth. And what was that humming sound? Why was it so cold?

An abrupt swerving motion threw her against an unyielding surface, and she moaned again as pain shot through her head. Another wave of nausea swept over her.

This time she couldn't fight it off. Turning her head, she

spewed out last night's dinner, retching until her stomach ached and she lay limp and spent, shivering from cold and fear.

Her cheek pressed to the rough fabric, her fingers clenched into tight fists, she tried to remember what had happened. She'd tossed a lot during the night, she recalled. After finally falling asleep well past midnight, she'd awakened often, checking the clock on her bedside table each time. It had been 2:45 the last time she'd looked at the digital dial.

That's when she'd seen the shadowy figure beside her bed.

For an instant she'd thought it was one of the HRT operatives come to check on her. But she'd dismissed that at once. They never entered her room without knocking. Terrified, she'd opened her mouth to scream. But before she could utter a sound, a powerful body had pinned her to the bed while a strong hand clamped a rag over her nose and mouth, muzzling her. Suffocating her.

Then everything had gone black.

The reality crashed over her.

Despite the elaborate security measures, despite her hidden location, despite the presence of numerous, well-trained agents, it seemed the HRT hadn't been able to keep her safe after all.

But how had her abductors managed to get past nearly a dozen dedicated, skilled, armed agents committed to protecting her? Had men died trying to keep her safe?

Had Coop?

Please, Lord, no, she prayed, wracked now by a new fear.

All at once the rocking motion stopped and the humming noise ceased, refocusing her on the present danger. The sound had been the drone of an engine, she concluded, tensing. She was in a trunk. And the sudden quiet must mean they'd reached their destination.

A door slammed, confirming her conclusion. The vehicle vibrated as another door was pushed shut, suggesting there were at least two people in the car.

202

She heard low-pitched voices, the words indistinguishable. A key was inserted in the trunk lock. Struggling to control the tremors that shook her body, she lowered her eyelids to a mere slit and rested her wrist on her chest. It might be to her advantage if they thought she was still unconscious, but she needed to get some sense of what was happening.

The lid lifted. Dim light spilled into the trunk, and she was able to read the dial on her watch. Three forty-seven. An hour had passed since she'd spotted the shadowy figure in her room.

"She threw up." A man's voice. Laced with disgust.

"We'll deal with it later. Get her inside."

Arms slid under her knees, her shoulders. She was lifted. Pulled against a solid chest.

As the man turned, she looked up. Saw dark, hard eyes. Caught a glimpse of an illuminated Motel 6 sign at the far end of a parking lot. Heard the sound of a door opening. And realized that if they got her inside, she'd never escape.

In desperation, she pushed against the man's chest and jerked out of his arms. Her feet hit the pavement. She opened her mouth to scream. Prepared to run.

But before she could utter a sound, a fist smashed into her face.

Stunned, she reeled back. Pain shot through her head, and a gush of blood spurted from her nose as she staggered and fell. Her chin connected with the edge of the trunk, and she felt her skin tear.

In one swift, ruthless move, the man yanked her back into his arms and crushed her against him, pressing her throbbing face tight to his chest in a suffocating hold that had her clawing at his shirt as she fought for air.

Once inside, the door shut behind them, and the man threw her on a bed, clamping his hand over her mouth as he braced himself on one knee beside her. She thrashed, straining to focus her blurry vision, as a second man withdrew a knife and leaned close to press the point of the blade against her throat, his icy eyes inches from hers. She froze.

"If you utter one sound or make one wrong move, I will use this knife." His words were low and menacing. "Do you understand?"

When she didn't respond, he pressed the knife harder, breaking the skin. She gasped.

"Do you understand?"

Fighting down another wave of nausea and panic, Monica gave a slight nod.

"Good. Let us test that theory." He signaled to the other man, who slid his hand off her mouth. She felt the prick of the knife as she swallowed. Tasted blood. Remained silent and still.

"There is no one else staying nearby. Your cries will not be heard anyway. But we take no chances. One sound, and this"— he lifted the bloody knife and held it in front of her, inches from her throat—"will kill again tonight."

Again.

The implication slammed into her with the same sharp, breath-snatching force as the fist had moments ago.

Bile rose in her throat.

"I-I'm going to be sick." The words came out whispered, raw.

Motioning to the man who'd carried her inside, the knife-wielding figure she'd already deemed the leader moved aside.

"Take her to the bathroom."

Sinewy fingers closed over her arm, and she was yanked to her feet. When her legs buckled, she was half dragged, half carried past the sink and mirror at the far end of the room and shoved through a door, into the tiny, windowless chamber that housed the commode.

She barely made it. Kneeling on the floor, she retched into

the toilet, emptying what little remained in her stomach. The man towered over her, one shoulder propped against the doorway, arms folded against his chest. She saw no compassion, no mercy in his eyes. And knew these men would kill her without compunction if she didn't do exactly what they said. Would relish it, in fact.

But for now, it seemed, they wanted her alive.

That gave her only one tool to work with. Time. And perhaps not much of that. As soon as the throbbing in her head subsided enough to allow rational thought, she needed to figure out how to use that tool to her advantage.

The other man joined his compatriot and stared down at her.

"We should gag her." The man who'd punched her spoke.

"No. If she throws up again, she'll choke. We need her alive. For now." He touched the knife at his belt. "Clean her up."

Once more she was jerked upright. The sudden move caused the world to tilt, and she grabbed the edge of the sink as the man propped her against the wall beside it. While he twisted the faucet and dampened a washcloth, Monica ventured a look in the mirror.

And was sorry she had.

The battered woman who stared back at her bore little resemblance to the Monica Callahan she knew. One cheek was puffy and bruised, and blood continued to seep out of her nose. An abrasion on her temple capped a massive lump, and her hair was tangled and matted with blood. Her right eye was swollen and blackening, her lip was split, and the gash on her jaw was bleeding.

Iron fingers grasped her chin close to the injured spot, and she gasped as the man jerked her head around. He scrubbed at the blood, his pressure increasing when he encountered an abrasion, as if inflicting discomfort gave him pleasure.

Monica did her best to fight back the whimpers of pain clamoring for release. But she could do nothing to stop the tears that coursed down her cheeks, the salt stinging each raw patch of skin they encountered.

"That's good enough. Put her over there." The leader gestured to a blank wall on one side of the room.

Once more, Monica was propelled across the room. The other man positioned her with her back against the wall. Like a firing squad, she thought in panic, wondering for one brief, terrified instant if they were going to shoot her.

But instead of a gun, the man lifted a small digital camera. A bright flash blinded her.

That's when Monica understood.

She had become the fourth hostage.

More than an hour had passed, and they were no closer to knowing where Monica was than they'd been five minutes after they'd discovered her abduction. And with every second that ticked by, Coop knew the odds of finding her alive diminished exponentially.

Wiping a weary hand down his face, he reached for his BlackBerry as it began to vibrate. Checking the caller ID, he winced.

"Who is it?" Mark looked over from the new command center in the kitchen of the main house. Agents from the Charlottesville FBI office were arriving, and the Richmond ERT was en route.

"The embassy in Kabul. David Callahan, I suspect." Angling away from his partner, Coop braced for the call. "Cooper here."

"David Callahan. What happened?" Cold fury tightened the man's voice.

"I'm sorry, sir. We had excellent security here. We're still trying to determine how the abductors managed to breach it. An Evidence Response Team is on the way as we speak."

"I know that. I already talked to Les Coplin. I want to hear your version. How did they know where she was?"

"I don't know, sir."

"Where did they take her?"

"We're trying to determine that."

Silence. Coop could feel the man's seething anger—and his terror—as strongly as if the diplomat was standing inside the room instead of seven thousand miles away.

"Mr. Cooper, I trusted you and your team with my daughter's life." Tension chiseled his words into sharp arrow points. "*She* trusted you. The HRT is supposed to be the best civilian fighting force in the world. Yet you failed me. And her." He stopped. Drew a harsh breath. "Let me tell you what I expect now. Find her. Save her. Is that understood?"

"Yes, sir. We're doing our best."

"So far, that hasn't been good enough. Do better. I'll be in touch."

The line went dead.

For half a minute after the diplomat ended the call, Coop stood unmoving, mired in gnawing guilt, struggling to hold on to his composure. Finally, he pulled the phone from his ear and slid it back into the holder on his belt.

"What did he say?"

At Mark's quiet question, Coop closed his eyes. "Nothing I haven't already said to myself."

"This isn't your fault, Coop."

He turned toward his friend. "Then whose is it?"

"Everyone shares responsibility. We were all in this together.

But I don't know what else we could have done." Frowning, Mark raked his fingers through his hair and propped his clenched fists on his hips.

"We could have sent her to the Marine base."

"That may not have been any safer. Besides, she chose this route."

"Because she trusted us."

"We'll find her, Coop."

"We have some news." Rick set his BlackBerry on the table. "The police car patrolling out back was just found on a forest road a quarter of a mile up. The officer was in the trunk."

"Is he alive?" Mark asked.

"Barely. Two stab wounds. He's lost a lot of blood. It doesn't sound good."

"Any chance we could talk to him?"

"Not according to the officers on the scene. He's critical. Paramedics are on the way. I'm diverting some of the ERT technicians to that location. They might pick up some tire tracks or footprints."

"Lab work isn't going to give us answers fast enough." Coop joined the conversation, his lips settling into a thin, unyielding line as he paced. "Monica may be alive now, but she doesn't have a lot of time. These guys are playing for keeps."

"We're doing our best," Mark reminded him.

"I know. But as David Callahan pointed out, our best hasn't been good enough."

The twin creases on Mark's brow deepened. "That's a pretty harsh assessment."

"Maybe. But I can't disagree with him. Can you?"

His partner's silence was more eloquent than words.

"I want to review the security video." Coop headed for the door. "Let's go back to the guest cottage."

They walked through the early morning darkness in silence.

The feed from the security cameras was still playing on the monitors as they entered, but Fendler was preparing to shut things down.

"I'll meet you over there in a minute." Coop tipped his head toward the screens. "Pull up the video for the thirty-minute segment when the abduction occurred."

As Mark strode toward the kitchen, Coop detoured to their room to retrieve his watch from the nightstand. As he picked it up, his gaze fell on the Bible. The book Monica turned to for comfort and guidance and strength.

He rested the tips of his fingers on it, wishing it would infuse him with those very things. While the concept of faith and religion wasn't yet a comfortable fit for him, much of what Monica had said over the past few days made sense. And he'd liked what he read last night too. As he'd paged through Mark, one verse in particular had stuck with him. "For with God all things are possible."

He clung now to that hope, wanting to believe, as Monica did, that God would stand by them through this storm and bring them safely to shore.

I'm not much of a believer yet, Lord. But I'm trying. Monica believes in you, and I believe in her. I think, with her help, I could learn to believe as she does. Please . . . give me that chance. Let us find her before it's too late.

As a prayer, his plea was pathetic, Coop knew. But he hadn't had a lot of practice. Nor was he good with words. With talking the walk.

He had to trust that God would give more weight to intent than to execution.

"*Unless our demands are met, she dies with the first hostage.*" In shock, David reread the message that had been sent to the embassy's general email address and forwarded to him by security. The text chilled him. And the accompanying photo of Monica turned his blood to ice.

"Sir, are you still on the line?"

The voice of Bob Stevens, the embassy security chief, echoed in his ear. He was glad the man had called first to warn him about the graphic nature of the photo before sending the email.

"Yes. What's being done to trace this?"

"We've got our top cybercrime investigators already on it. Based on a preliminary look, however, it won't be easy to nail down the source. The header's been stripped. That doesn't leave us a lot to work with."

"Can we respond?"

"No. It's formatted as an announcement."

"I want the FBI on this too."

"Of course." The man's businesslike tone softened. "I'm sorry about your daughter, sir."

"Thank you." He cleared his throat, struggling to hold onto his composure. "I'm hoping there's a clue embedded somewhere in the message that will help us. Keep me informed."

Ending the call, David dropped the phone back in its cradle. He'd spent a lifetime in the most violent parts of the world, seen sights that could turn the most ironclad stomach. He wasn't a hard man, but he'd learned to steel himself against horror, to build up an immunity to cruelty and carnage. The only way he could do his job was to ignore concerns about individuals and focus on the needs of humanity as a whole. Nothing he had seen in forty-plus years of diplomatic service had shaken his commitment to that mode of operation.

Until now.

As he stared at the image of his daughter's battered face, his resolve wavered. The terrorists believed he had sufficient influence to convince the secretary of state and the Afghan government to release political prisoners and pay a twenty-million-dollar ransom. And, in truth, he did. He was a skilled negotiator. Good enough to convince those in power that, Monica's involvement aside, there were reasons to cooperate in this case. Behind the scenes, if not in the public eye. He'd accrued enough credibility and political capital in his four decades of diplomatic service to pull off that argument.

Doing so, however, went against every principle he believed in.

Yet how could he let Monica die?

It was the toughest moral choice he'd ever faced. And David didn't know how to resolve his dilemma.

But he did know one thing.

He had less than twenty-two hours to figure it out.

"What the . . . ?"

Coop's frown deepened as he stared at the screen displaying the feed from the camera mounted on the tennis court.

"What's wrong?" Mark joined him and scanned the monitor.

"Look at the date."

Mark leaned closer and squinted at the small digital date displayed in the bottom corner of the screen. Now it was his turn to frown. "That's yesterday's feed."

"Fendler." Coop summoned the agent, who was pouring a cup of coffee. "Is this video from tonight?"

"Yes." The man joined them. "Find something?"

"Check out the date."

As the agent bent toward the screen, he lifted his hand to take a sip—and froze. "That can't be right."

"Back it up for us. A couple of hours." Coop traded places

with him, leaning over the man's shoulder as Fendler took his seat, set the coffee aside, and began typing.

"Okay. This takes us back to midnight."

"Run it fast forward. Let's watch the date."

The man punched a few more keys, and they concentrated on the numbers at the bottom of the screen.

"There. Stop it there. Now back up a couple of minutes and run it forward at normal speed."

In silence, Fendler followed Coop's instructions.

"The date's correct on this section," Mark noted.

The video played in silence for four minutes, the attention of all three men riveted on the date.

At 1:36, there was an almost imperceptible blip on the screen as the nineteen changed to an eighteen.

The color faded from Fendler's face as he swore softly. "They must have hacked into the security system and switched out the video with stuff they recorded last night."

Coop wanted to vent his anger on the man seated inches away. It would feel good to punch him out, to place the blame for Monica's abduction on him. But the video merge had been so subtle, and the date so small, he knew he could have missed it too.

Jerking away from the table, he walked over to the kitchen doorway and slammed the heel of his hand against the unforgiving molding. He welcomed the pain that radiated up his arm.

"I'll call Les." Mark spoke quietly behind him but kept his distance.

"Fine."

He heard Mark pull out his BlackBerry. Heard him tap in Les's number. Tuned out the conversation. He didn't want to hear Les's response to this latest piece of information. If the bad news kept piling up, he wouldn't be surprised if the Bulldog yanked them back to Quantico and assigned them to desk duty for the rest of their careers. Unless the White House fired them first.

Why couldn't there be some good news for once?

"Coop."

At Mark's solemn tone, Coop slanted a look over his shoulder, steeling himself. The taut line of his partner's features confirmed that the streak of bad news wasn't yet over. "There's been a new development. Les wants us on speaker phone."

"Does he have information about Monica?" It was the hardest question Coop had ever asked, but avoiding it wasn't going to change the answer.

"Yes. She's alive." Mark inclined his head toward the bedroom. "Let's take the call in there."

Without waiting for a response, Mark strode toward the room, phone to his ear, talking in a voice too low for Coop to hear. Sitting on one of the beds, he motioned for Coop to join him as he depressed the mute button. "David Callahan heard from the kidnappers. Les is going to forward their email to us."

As Mark spoke, Coop's BlackBerry vibrated, indicating a high-priority message.

"It's here." He started to withdraw the device from his belt, but to his surprise Mark laid a hand on his arm, restraining him.

"Les warned me that it's not pretty."

With a curt nod, Coop pulled out the BlackBerry as Mark spoke into the phone. "Les, I'm putting you on speaker. The email just came in, and Coop is opening it. Hang on a second." He pushed the speaker button.

Steeling himself, Coop clicked on the email and angled the screen so both he and Mark could read the brief, chilling message from the terrorists.

Unless their luck changed, in twenty-two hours Monica would die.

"Did you open the attachment?" Les's disembodied voice cut through the silence.

"I'm doing that now." His fingers fumbling, dread knotting his stomach, Coop called up the photo.

He thought he'd prepared himself.

He was wrong.

As the image of Monica's battered face flashed on the screen, he sucked in a harsh breath, as if someone had delivered a sharp jab to his midsection. She looked as if she'd been in a street fight. Her porcelain skin was discolored with purple bruises and bloody abrasions. One eye was swollen almost shut, the other wide with fear. The pink sweat suit she'd been sleeping in was stained with blood.

He wanted to pick her up, cradle her in his arms, soothe away her pain.

And with his bare hands he wanted to kill the men who had hurt her.

"At least we know she's alive," Mark noted softly.

"I think we can assume they're going to keep her that way until 2:00 a.m. tomorrow," Les said. "They wouldn't have gone to all the trouble of taking her out of the house alive if they intended to kill her before their deadline."

"Is the email being traced?" Coop pushed the question past his stiff lips.

"We're working on it, but there's not much to go on. Whoever sent this knows computers. In all probability it's been forwarded several times. Trying to trace it will take more time than we have and could lead to a dead end, anyway."

"Maybe we can initiate further communication," Mark suggested. "Every contact provides another opportunity for us to get a handle on her location."

"The email was sent as an announcement," Les informed them. "David Callahan can't reply."

"He can respond through the media." Coop's initial shock at Monica's appearance was giving way to cold fury and a ruthless determination to win at this deadly game. Losing was not an option.

"What are you suggesting?" Les asked.

"I think Callahan should go public with this. Communicate with the terrorists via the media. Insist he be allowed to talk to his daughter before he'll consider their demands."

"There's no assurance they'll comply with that request," Les pointed out.

"We don't have anything to lose by trying. And if he can talk to Monica, she may say something that will give us a clue about her location. I guarantee she'll try if she gets half a chance. Words are her business. She'll use them to her advantage."

In the silence that followed, Coop suspected Les was breaking in his cigar of the day.

"Okay. Let me broach that idea to the State Department. I'll be back in touch."

As the connection was severed, Mark slid his BlackBerry back into its holder. "If the story breaks in Afghanistan, it won't be long until the U.S. press is all over it."

"That's not necessarily a bad thing." Coop stared at the photo of Monica on his screen. "Some of my best leads during my field agent days came from people who read news stories and called in tips."

"It will be harder to pull off a clandestine rescue if the press is breathing down our necks."

"I know." He closed the email and looked at Mark. A muscle jumped in his jaw. "But unless we use every resource available, we may not have a rescue to pull off."

17

Someone was standing over her. She could sense it.

Doing her best to tamp down her burgeoning fear, Monica opened her eyes. The man who had carried her in from the car was staring down at her.

She remained motionless, determined not to let him see how much his silent, unemotional perusal unnerved—and chilled—her. But when he reached down and stroked his fingers along her neck, her instincts kicked in and she recoiled.

At her reaction, a strange light glittered in his eyes. Monica saw malice. Evil.

From her prone position on one of the two double beds, she angled a frightened glance toward the utilitarian desk on the other side of the room. The leader had tossed his gear on the second double bed beside the wall containing the window and door, and he was intent on his computer screen. Oblivious to—or ignoring—his partner's activities.

When the man began to play with the bottom edge of her sweatshirt, Monica's gaze swung back to him. He tugged it up a bit, exposing her skin. Dread choked her, and horror. She shuddered.

Please, Lord, not this too! Please!

"I could use a little stress relief after the past couple of days." A sick smile curved his lips as he ran a finger across her bare midriff.

"Not now, Zahir."

At the leader's quiet command, her tormentor's hand stilled. Monica turned her head toward the man, sending him a silent plea with her eyes.

A mirthless, threatening smile twisted his lips. "Perhaps I'll let you have a go at her later. If she causes us any trouble."

With that, he returned to his work.

For several long moments, the other man stood unmoving, one finger resting against her skin. At last, after a painful jab, he withdrew it and moved away. Transferring the equipment on the second bed to the table, he stretched out and turned his head to watch her.

She looked the other way, unable to control the tremors coursing through her body. She'd been about to ask for a drink of water; her mouth was parched, and she wanted to rinse away the sour taste of vomit from her tongue. But she had no intention now of asking for any favors.

Shifting on the bed, she bit back a moan. Every inch of her body hurt, and the pounding in her head remained at jackhammer level. A lethargic weakness had robbed her limbs of all strength. Focus remained a problem too, with the edges of the objects in her sight blurring at regular intervals.

On the other hand, her thinking was a bit clearer. It was obvious that with her two abductors between her and the door, there was no way she'd be able to get past them even if she was operating at full strength. They would subdue any physical attempt to gain freedom as harshly as they'd checked her first effort. Yet there had to be some action she could take to help those who were searching for her.

She risked a peek at her watch. Six in the morning. More than three hours had passed since she'd been snatched from her room. By now, an all-out effort would be underway to find her. And she had no doubt Coop would be leading the charge.

217

Assuming he hadn't been injured . . . or worse . . . in the assault that led to her abduction.

But she wouldn't think about that now. Couldn't. It would paralyze her.

Instead, she tried to recall kidnapping scenarios she'd seen in movies and on TV. In general, the abductors contacted the person who was expected to pay the ransom, sending some kind of proof they had the victim. The picture the leader had snapped of her earlier suggested her captors had followed that pattern.

What usually happened next? She frowned, trying to think. Didn't people often demand to talk with the victim in order to verify they were alive? Might her father do that?

She didn't know. But it seemed like a reasonable possibility. And if they let her talk with her father, perhaps she could send him a clue about her whereabouts.

Closing her eyes, she blocked out everything—her pain, her terror, her fears about Coop, her awareness of the man watching her from the next bed—and concentrated on coming up with innocent-sounding phrases that might provide listeners with a hint about her location.

Because she had a feeling that might be her only hope of survival.

Tariq cast a scornful look around the dingy quarters in Kandahar he'd occupied for the past couple of days, a few miles from his previous lodging. He was tired of moving from one dive to another, but he wasn't going to get lax about security at this stage. If anyone happened to suspect his involvement in the kidnappings, a shifting target would be harder to hit. And once this was over, he'd lay low for a while in nicer surroundings and focus on working his contacts in the disintegrating government.

"You are prepared to begin the executions at noon tomorrow?" He directed the query to Sayed over his shoulder as he lit a dim light to dispel the early evening shadows.

"Of course." The man gave a slight, deferential bow. "We await your instruction."

"Excellent. All is proceeding as—"

"Many pardons." Anis paused in the doorway. He, too, gave a small bow.

"What is it?" Tariq glared at him, his curt tone expressing his displeasure at the interruption.

"Al Jazeera just reported that David Callahan has issued a statement. He will not consider your demands unless he is allowed to speak with his daughter."

Tariq's eyes narrowed in speculation. The counter ultimatum didn't surprise him. The diplomat was known as a tough negotiator, and Tariq had expected him to want proof his daughter still lived.

What did surprise him was Callahan's insinuation that he might consider the demands if his condition was met. And he wouldn't have communicated that unless he'd already discussed the possibility with the U.S. State Department.

It seemed he might be bending under pressure after all.

When Anis continued to hover in the doorway, Tariq sent him an impassive glance. "Is there more?"

"No. I thought . . . would you like me to do anything?"

"If I choose to respond, I will handle it myself."

At the dismissal, Anis once more bowed. After darting a quick look at Sayed, he exited.

"An interesting development." Sayed clasped his hands behind his back and rocked forward on his toes.

"I believe it is a good sign. I will arrange a call."

"If there is nothing else, I shall return to my duties."

"That is all for now. I will call you in the morning."

As Sayed exited, Tariq pulled out his cell phone. There were a number of people he could contact for advice about how best to set up a call with Callahan. But none with a better technical background than Nouri.

Besides, it was time he checked on his American hostage.

"I found out how they pinpointed our location."

At Mac's terse comment, Coop looked up from the table in the main house's command center, where he, Mark, and Rick had been reviewing the ERT's preliminary findings. While they now had a decent handle on how the abductors had pulled off their scheme, they were no closer to pinning down Monica's location than they'd been when they'd discovered she was missing five hours ago.

In silence, Mac held out his hand to display a small electronic gadget. "A GPS device. Motion activated. It tracked us straight here." Disgust laced his voice.

"Where was it?" Mark moved closer to examine it.

"Sewn into the lining of my luggage. A loose thread snagged on my shaving kit as I was packing, and when I tugged, the stitching gave. My guess is they left a similar present in all of our suitcases. Probably at the hotel in Richmond."

"You mean we led them to Monica ourselves?" Coop gaped at the device in shocked disbelief.

"Looks that way," Mac confirmed. "Not that it matters at this point, but you may want to check your luggage to test my theory."

Ten minutes later, after the three other operators searched their suitcases, Mac's theory was confirmed. Each of them found an identical device sewn into an unobtrusive corner of his luggage. An ERT technician took possession, but Coop had no hope the team would find any prints. The perpetrators were too careful, too thorough, to leave any evidence that would allow authorities to trace the crime to them.

And if they were that careful in the small things, Coop knew the odds of them leaving any clues about their current location were next to nothing.

He couldn't decide what to do.

Distress knotting his stomach, David regarded the sandwich Salam had ordered for him as he'd left for the day. Though it was long past dinnertime and he'd eaten nothing since breakfast, he had no interest in food. Swiveling around, he searched the darkness outside the window in his office. Night hid the mountains from his view, but he knew they were there, looming and oppressive.

Like the decision he faced.

In twelve hours, he would meet with the secretary of state. He could hold fast to his traditional "no negotiation" posture, or he could deviate from his principles and go with a recommendation that might save the lives of the hostages—and his daughter—while attempting to preserve the United States's public position.

It was a gut-wrenching position to be in.

The sudden, jarring ring of the phone startled him, and he snatched the receiver from the cradle.

"Callahan."

"Bob Stevens. A package addressed to you was tossed at the embassy gate from a passing motorcycle about forty-five minutes ago. The guards thought it might be a bomb, but it turned out to be a cell phone."

"Was there a note?" David's grip on the phone tightened.

"No. But we assume this means the terrorists intend to honor your request. It doesn't have speakerphone capability, but we're retrofitting it to allow us all to listen in on the call, and we're attaching a recording device."

"Did you contact the FBI?"

"I spoke to Les Coplin five minutes ago. He's briefing his HRT operators. We'd like to set up a conference call in ten minutes in my office."

"I'll be right over."

Pushing his untouched sandwich aside, David picked up a notepad. As he reached for a pen, a spasm of pain shot up his arm, tightening the already tense muscles in his neck. The stress was taking a toll, he acknowledged. When this was over, he intended to take a long-overdue vacation. Spend some time with his daughter. And seriously consider turning this job over to a younger man.

"Coop, Mark, are you in?" Les's voice boomed over Coop's speakerphone as he and Mark sat at the table in the guest house kitchen, now devoid of the monitors that had done nothing to stop the kidnapping.

"We're here," Coop replied.

"In Kabul, we have Bob Stevens, head of embassy security, and David Callahan on the line," Les informed them.

"I also have a couple of my technical people sitting in," Bob added. "To bring everyone up to speed, David is wearing an earpiece and I'll be able to communicate with him during his conversation with his daughter. If you want me to pass on any instructions, speak into the phone. David will be in an adjacent room, and the conversation will be piped into this room so we'll be able to speak freely."

"Mr. Callahan, you need to ask Monica some question only she would be able to answer," Coop said. "We need to verify it's her on the line."

Several beats of silence passed before David responded, panic and frustration lacing his words. "I can't think of anything."

Based on the confidences Monica had shared about her rocky relationship with her father, Coop wasn't surprised by the man's inability to come up with a personal question. "Ask her what her favorite comfort food is."

"I assume you know the correct answer?" David's query came out stiff.

"Yes."

The tension between the two men was almost palpable.

"Okay. Good." Les redirected the conversation. "Bob, you said no hint was given about the timing on the call?" He sounded as frustrated as Coop felt.

"No."

"Then I guess we all hang tight and wait," Les said.

"It could be hours." Mark frowned and tapped a finger against the table.

"Do you have anything better to do?"

At Les's sharp retort, color flooded Mark's face. He remained silent.

"I didn't think so. Bob, we'll be standing by."

"When the call comes in, we'll let it ring six or seven times. That should give us all a chance to get connected. In the interim, we're going to do what we can to find out when this phone was activated and try to set up a trace on the incoming call. But my guess is they'll piggyback off of a couple of throwaway cell phones. We aren't going to have enough time to track the call back to the originating phone. And I expect the conversation will be brief. Most of it may even be scripted."

Bob Stevens's conclusions were sound, Coop acknowledged. The call might do no more than reassure them Monica was alive. But he hoped—prayed—the severity of her injuries hadn't interfered with her mental capabilities. Because he knew that if she could, she would do everything in her power to give them the clue to her whereabouts that they desperately needed.

Monica watched as the leader stood, stretched, moved toward the sink. Her bladder was growing uncomfortable, but she'd held off broaching the subject as long as possible, unwilling to direct a request to the man lying on the bed across from her. Her skin was crawling from his relentless scrutiny, and the notion of him coming close again sickened her.

"Excuse me . . ."

The leader paused at the foot of the bed and gave her a dispassionate perusal.

"I need to use the bathroom."

Zahir started to stand, but Nouri waved him back and spoke in the language they'd been using for their sparse conversation during the past few hours. Monica assumed it was some Middle Eastern dialect. He motioned for her to rise.

Relieved, Monica swung her legs over the far side of the bed, appalled by their wobbliness. She was afraid they wouldn't support her, but she'd crawl before she would give the man in the next bed an excuse to wrap his sinewy arms around her again.

Scooting to the edge of the bed, she steadied herself on the wall and stood. Her legs held. Barely. They shook as she lurched her way to the bathroom using the wall for support.

The leader let her pass, and to her relief didn't stop her from closing the door. It was odd, the small favors you could be grateful for in the midst of a horrendous situation, she reflected.

Two minutes later, as she sank back onto the side of her bed, the leader pulled out his cell phone. After a couple of exchanges, he switched to English and moved beside her, pulling the knife out of the sheath on his belt.

Whatever strength she'd had in her legs fled. Her pulse tripled. The breath hitched in her throat. Was this the end already? Had her efforts to hone and practice phrases she could use in a phone conversation with her father been for nothing?

Lord, please, give me more time! I don't want to die yet!

"A call is being made to your father. You will ask him to meet our demands. If you say one word that provides any information about where you are, you will not live past the phone call." He leaned close and pressed the point of the knife to her throat, as he had earlier. "Do you understand?"

She gave a slight nod.

Satisfied, he depressed the speaker button and set the phone on the bed. "We are ready."

"Place the call." The instruction given on the other end of the line came through sharp and clear.

The leader knelt on the bed behind her and gripped her hair, pulling it to force her head back slightly. She felt the sharp point of the knife against her neck. When she swallowed, the tip pricked her skin. She was almost afraid to breathe.

Sixty seconds later, Monica heard her father's voice. It sounded grainy and distant, but his anxiety and tension came through loud and clear.

"Hello?"

"Dad?" The word was little more than a croak.

"Monica? Is that you?"

"Yes."

"Are you okay?"

This was it. She had to make every second count. Her captors could cut off the call at any moment.

"I'm a l-little banged up from the drive." She struggled to supply her lungs with oxygen. "I'm ready to come home, Dad. Be like Tom Bodett and leave the l-light on for me, okay?"

The tip of the knife pushed deeper into her skin, and she gasped. She'd known the reference was risky. Had the terrorists recognized it? Her body rigid, she gripped the bedspread, bunching the fabric in her fingers.

"Monica? Monica, are you all right? Are they hurting you?"

The leader leaned close to her ear. "Tell him to meet our demands."

They'd missed her reference. *Thank you, God!*

"I'm okay. I just w-want to come home."

"We're working on that, honey." Her father's static-laced words came over the line. "I need you to tell us what your favorite comfort food is."

Puzzled, Monica frowned. Why would her father ask that? Besides, he didn't even know the answer.

Then the significance dawned. Coop must have suggested the question to verify it was her on the other end of the phone. Meaning he was okay. Relief coursed through her.

"M&Ms. Listen, I don't want to end up like that journalist I saw on the Sunday night news program a couple of weeks ago, who was killed by terrorists. Do what they ask, okay?"

The leader snatched the phone from her ear, depressed the end button, and removed the knife from her throat. "Now we will see how much your father loves you."

Leaving her on the side of the bed, he returned to his computer.

The hammering in her head had subsided earlier, while she'd lain unmoving. Now it resumed with a vengeance. Easing onto

226

her back, Monica focused on the ceiling and tried to ride out the waves of pain.

At least she'd done her best in the phone call, she consoled herself. She'd come up with several clues, all couched in innocent-sounding phrases, and she'd managed to work all of them into the conversation. There was nothing else she could do.

Except pray that Coop and the HRT would decipher her message.

18

As the terrorists severed the connection, Coop rested his elbows on the table in the guest cottage and dropped his head into his hands, tuning out the follow-up dialogue taking place on the conference call. It had been Monica on the other end of the line, no question about it. And her shaky, faltering voice had twisted his gut into knots.

Yet some positives had come out of the call, he acknowledged, forcing the left side of his brain to engage. For one thing, they had confirmation she was alive. For another, she'd packed a lot of information into the brief exchange with her father. A few of her comments had struck him as odd, and he suspected she'd been trying to send a message.

"Did anyone get anything out of the call that could help us find my daughter?" David's taut question pulled him back to the conversation.

"We need to hear it again. Bob, we'd like a transcript and a recording ASAP," Les responded.

"Our technicians are already working on that. We should have it to you in minutes. Any initial thoughts?"

"The sound was pretty garbled. I suspect the call was piggybacked through a couple of cell phones, as we expected." Mark doodled on a pad of paper in front of him, his expression pensive.

"I agree," Les concurred.

"Did she give the correct answer to the comfort-food question?" David asked.

"Yes." The analytical side of Coop's brain was now firing on all cylinders. "She also made some interesting comments. I think there are clues embedded in them."

"The remark about the drive was helpful," Mark concurred. "If she was transported by car, our search radius is more restricted."

"Possibly to within sixty minutes. I think her reference to the Sunday night news program was deliberate," Coop said.

"That may be a stretch." Les didn't attempt to hide his skepticism. "Considering the ordeal she's been through, there's a good chance she's not fully lucid. We all know what a trauma spike can do to victims."

Coop had witnessed the phenomenon often. Casualties of violence often shut down or became incoherent and confused until the effects of the trauma subsided, rendering them useless in the initial investigation. And Monica was a prime candidate for a spike. She'd been drugged, injured, and kidnapped. Her life was in imminent danger. She would be fighting debilitating terror with every breath she took.

But she was strong. And Coop was convinced that despite all she'd been through, she'd worked hard to help herself in the only way she could. With words.

"I don't buy it in this case," Coop countered. "I think she was giving us leads."

"I'd like to believe that." David joined in the discussion. "And I think you're right about the *60 Minutes* reference. What about that Tom Bodett allusion? Who is he?"

"He's been the spokesman for Motel 6 for years. That bit about leaving the light on was a direct lift from his tagline," Mark supplied.

"You think they're keeping her at a motel?" Incredulity raised the pitch of Les's voice.

"I think it's the only clue we have at the moment. And it's

not a bad plan from their point of view. Without Monica's hint, motels wouldn't even be on our radar screen."

Once again, David Callahan sided with Coop. "I'm not an intelligence expert, but this makes sense. Monica is smart. And she knows words. My instincts tell me she chose the ones she used with very strategic intent."

"Okay. We'll check it out. Mark, Coop, stay on the line. Bob, Mr. Callahan, we'll keep you apprised of our progress."

After the Kabul connection went silent, Les spoke again. "I've been doing a computer search as we spoke. There's one Motel 6 within a fifty-mile radius of Charlottesville. It's in Harrisonburg. Thirty-four miles away. At sixty miles, they have locations in Fredericksburg and Ashland. None of their other motels would be reachable by car in less than an hour. Dennis can have agents in his different jurisdictions make the initial contact with the facilities."

"This has to be handled with kid gloves," Coop cautioned. "If the abductors get any inkling we're on to them, this will get ugly very fast."

"I'm sure he knows that. But I'll remind him. I'm also going to put your team here on alert. If this pans out, I want them standing by for a rescue mission."

"Mark and I could accompany the agent to the motel in Harrisonburg. It's the closest one to Charlottesville and fits best with the sixty-minute time frame, assuming they took an indirect route as a precaution."

"I'll discuss it with Dennis and get back with you. Stand by." Les ended the call.

"Monica did good." Mark tossed out the comment as Coop slid his BlackBerry back onto his belt.

"Yeah."

"She's pretty amazing, considering all she's been through."

"Yeah."

"My gut tells me this is going to turn out okay."

"Not if this motel lead ends up being a wild goose chase." Coop raked his fingers through his hair. "But it's all we have. Other than a partial tire impression that suggests the abductors drove a midsize car, the ERT has come up with zip."

"They're still working the scene."

"I'm not overly optimistic." Coop stood. "Let's pack up. There's nothing else we can do here. I want to be ready to head to Harrisonburg once Les clears it with Dennis."

Without waiting for a reply, he strode toward the bedroom. A couple of minutes later, Mark joined him.

As they gathered up their gear, Coop was grateful for Mark's silence. He needed a chance to regroup after seeing the shocking picture of Monica, hearing her tremulous voice, feeling her fear. To find a way to deal with—and control—his roiling emotions.

But he had few coping mechanisms in his arsenal. Emotional involvement had never been an issue on a mission. Knowing it would compromise his ability to do his job, he'd steered a wide berth around that complication. To be an effective HRT operator, you needed absolute and complete focus. Personal feelings had to be put aside. Period.

This job, however, was different. This time he cared about the outcome not just as a dedicated professional, but as a man.

When this was over, when they found Monica—and they *would* find her—he needed to figure out how this woman had managed to infiltrate his soul in a handful of days.

But for now, he had to look at this as a job. He couldn't afford to let emotion cloud his judgment. To save Monica, he needed to operate at top efficiency. To use the clues she'd given them to track her down.

And this time he didn't intend to fail her.

A chilling wind whipped up the silty ground, and Sayed dipped his head as he passed the two guards at the entrance to the mud hut. He ducked through the doorway, casting an indifferent glance at the three hostages sleeping on mats on the drafty dirt floor. The older man's cough was worse, he noted.

"All is well?" He directed the query to one of the two rifle-toting guards inside.

"Yes. They sleep. Perhaps for the last time." The man smirked. "Tomorrow is a big day. And we are ready to follow your instructions." He lifted the gun.

"Good. I have been called for a late meeting with Tariq. I am confident he will have some directives. Stay vigilant." Sayed exited, sparing the hostages no further attention.

Once back in his quarters in the adjacent hut, he opened his cell phone and tapped in a series of numbers. As he waited for the call to go through, his lips curved into a slight smile. To-morrow at this late hour he would be far away from the sand and cold and primitive conditions he'd endured for most of his fifty-nine years. No longer would he have to risk his life in the company of men he didn't trust. His departure had been long in the planning, but the outcome would be worth the wait.

With the money David Callahan had delivered in the market, along with the funds he'd skimmed off the top of the opium-trading operation he oversaw for Tariq, Sayed could spend the rest of his life in comfort. The ten percent he'd paid his "accountant" to deposit the funds in an untraceable Swiss bank account had been money well spent. Likewise the small sum he'd paid the disenchanted Anis for information.

Unlike Tariq, Sayed didn't crave power or great wealth. The modest property he'd purchased in Brazil was more than adequate for his needs. Add in some good wine, fine cigars, decent food . . . a woman now and then . . . what more could a man want?

"Yes?" The clipped question interrupted his musings.

"All is ready?" Sayed kept his voice low.

"Your papers are prepared and your tickets are in my hands. They will be passed to you at the airport according to our arrangements."

"Excellent. I am leaving now."

Closing his phone, he exited the hut and strode toward his car without a backward look. Pointing it toward Kandahar, he disappeared into the darkness in a cloud of dust. Once out of sight of the village, he altered his direction and headed toward Kabul.

Everything had gone according to plan, he reflected with satisfaction. The guards were used to his late meetings with Tariq. They wouldn't begin to suspect trouble until tomorrow morning, after he was on the plane. And with the falsified papers that awaited him in Kabul, there would be no way to trace him.

He had just one more task to complete. One last debt to pay. And that would be taken care of in five or six hours, as he approached the outskirts of the city. The simple phone call would take no more than thirty seconds. But it would give David Callahan the information his government had bought for the price of Sayed's dream.

Plus a bonus that would eliminate any possibility of retribution.

The man was stonewalling.

Through narrowed eyes, Coop watched as Kurt Renner, the FBI agent he and Mark had accompanied from the Charlottesville office, questioned the general manager of the Harrisonburg Motel 6. The fifty-something supervisor was a typical petty bureaucrat who was making the most of his rare moment of importance. Coop had run into his type in past investigations. They typically crumbled under pressure—which he was itching to apply.

"Mr. Nieman, as I explained, we're in the midst of a confidential investigation." Renner's tone was courteous, but Coop heard the stirrings of frustration. "I understand your concern about protecting the privacy of guests at your facility. However, this is a life-threatening situation where every minute counts."

"But don't you fellas need a search warrant to look at records? On TV, no one ever turns over information without one."

The man's habit of running his hand over the long strands of hair he'd draped over his bald spot was getting on Coop's nerves. If Renner didn't make some headway soon, Coop intended to jump in. They couldn't afford to waste precious minutes being polite to this pompous jerk.

"It's on the way, Mr. Nieman. But we may not need it if you'll answer a few simple questions. Unless you have something to hide, that is."

Good move, Coop thought. The man's pasty complexion went a shade paler and his cocky attitude wilted a bit.

"No, of c-course not."

The stammer was a good sign too.

"We could also go to your area manager if you feel you can't cooperate."

"No, no. That's not necessary. I'll answer what I can."

"We appreciate that. We need to know if anyone of Middle Eastern descent checked in during the past week. And if they're still here."

The man shifted in his seat and did that annoying hair-rub motion again. "That sounds like profiling. Isn't that illegal?"

He'd had it. Slanting a look at Mark, Coop stood, using the intimidating height advantage that had worked well for him in interrogations during his field agent days. Shoving the edges of his suit jacket back, he propped his fists on his hips and stared down at the man.

"Mr. Nieman, we will get the information we need." His words were slow, deliberate. "The legal authorization to check your records and view your front desk security video is being processed as we speak. But let me give it to you straight." He settled his hands on the desk, palms flat, and leaned into the man's face, invading his personal space. The manager's eyelid twitched. "A woman's life hangs in the balance. Minutes matter. If she dies because you didn't cooperate, there will be repercussions."

Pinning the man with an intent look, Coop waited him out, hoping the subtle, nonspecific threat would make him crack. It had worked in the past. He prayed it worked now.

The man blinked. Shifted in his seat. Tugged at his tie. His Adam's apple bobbed. "Okay. What do you need?"

Instead of backing off at once, Coop held his position for another ten seconds—until he was confident the man realized they were through playing games. Then he straightened up and folded his arms across his chest. "We need to talk to your desk clerks, check your guest records for the past week, and review video if we discover anything suspicious. We may also need to talk to your housekeeping staff."

"I'll arrange it."

Reaching over, Coop shoved the man's phone in front of him. "Do it now."

At one in the morning, David Callahan gave up any hope of sleeping.

Swinging his legs to the floor, he sat on the edge of the narrow bunk in his quarters. He'd had no updates from the FBI or embassy security in the past two hours, meaning there was

235

no news. He knew the investigation was focusing on the motel chain Monica had referenced, and he could only hope the terrorists would buy the FBI some time by honoring their promise to keep her alive until the noon deadline.

Long before that, however, he had a decision to make.

Restless, he rose and moved to the small desk in his room, grappling with his impossible situation. What recommendation should he give when he met with the secretary of state in seven hours? Though he'd been hoping . . . praying . . . for wisdom and guidance, the solution to his dilemma continued to elude him.

He picked up a pen and pulled a sheet of paper toward him, flipping on the desk light. Perhaps if he put his thoughts on paper it would help. That technique had served him well in negotiation situations. Few people knew that his renowned extemporaneous eloquence was a sham. Prior to diplomatic sessions, he always developed and practiced key points verbatim.

He scribbled some notes, but he couldn't focus on his meeting with the secretary of state. Instead, he found himself thinking about what he would say to Monica if she sat across from him now. Pulling a clean sheet of paper toward him, he jotted a few thoughts. A few more. Began to write in earnest.

Thirty minutes later, when the shrill ring of his phone pierced the silence, his hand jerked, sending a squiggle across the page. He dropped the pen and snatched up the receiver, his heart pounding.

"Callahan."

"Bob Stevens. I'm sorry to disturb you, sir, but I just heard from Les Coplin. They think they've identified your daughter's location."

Gratitude, relief, hope, anxiety . . . David couldn't even identify the flood of emotions that cascaded over him.

"Tell me everything you know."

"Stop it there."

At Coop's command, the FBI technician froze the frame on the front desk video from the Harrisonburg Motel 6, capturing a man with his head low, his features shaded by the brim of a hat.

"That has to be him." Coop leaned forward, resting his hands on the table that had been set up in the empty warehouse they'd commandeered as a tactical operations center half a mile from the motel.

"I can't tell for sure if he's Middle Eastern." Mark scrutinized the image, checked the registration. "The name doesn't fit the ethnic background, either. Joe West."

"If he's our man, the name's a fake. And notice the gloves. He wasn't taking any chances about leaving prints."

"He did a good job keeping his face angled away from the camera too," Mark observed as he watched the video.

"Suspicious in itself. But the desk clerk we interviewed said he looked Middle Eastern. And consider the rest of the facts. He checked in two days ago and is still there—with a co-worker no one's seen. He asked for a quiet room at the far end of the building. He paid in cash. And housekeeping told us the Do Not Disturb sign has been on the door since he arrived."

"I agree it looks suspicious. But it's not conclusive."

Expelling a frustrated breath, Coop shot Mark an impatient look. "It's all we have. None of the guests at the other two locations raised any alarms. Most were one-night stays. The clerks said none of them looked Middle Eastern."

"You're assuming our suspects have darker complexions."

"They're terrorists. Affiliated with a kidnapping in Afghanistan. Do you think we should be looking for guys who are blond and blue-eyed?" Coop glared at his partner.

"Hey." Mark lifted his hands, palms out. "I'm just trying to play the devil's advocate. If we make too many assumptions, we could overlook critical pieces of information."

A beat of silence passed while the two men regarded each other.

"Sorry." Coop rubbed his neck. "But we don't have the luxury of time. I think we have to draw some reasonable conclusions and proceed on that basis. However, I'm open to better ideas."

"I think you're on the right track. But I don't want to move so fast we make mistakes. We're not going to get a second chance at this."

That sobering truth helped center Coop. They'd have one opportunity to get Monica out alive. They couldn't blow it. And thorough, logical preparation was the key to success for this operation, as it was for all their missions.

"I agree we need to confirm Monica is in there before we take any action. But in the meantime, I want our team ready to move."

Pulling out his BlackBerry, Coop punched in Les's number, watching Mark during his brief conversation with Quantico.

"They're on their way." He slipped the phone back into its holder. "Les says the story just broke on national TV. He doesn't want to alert the media to our location so they're coming in by Suburbans rather than chopper. He's bringing the rest of our assault team, plus three guys from one of the sniper teams. ETA is two hours. He wants an ops plan ready when he gets here."

"Les is coming?" Mark gave him an incredulous look. The HRT commander never went on missions.

"Yes. White House pressure, I suspect." But the chief's presence was fine with Coop. Les had been a stellar HRT operator, and he was a decisive leader. Coop couldn't think of anyone he'd rather have as mission commander than the Bulldog.

Especially when the stakes were this high.

One hundred and twenty-two minutes later, at 5:34 p.m., the warehouse doors swung open to admit two blacked-out Suburbans. Before the first vehicle came to a full stop, Les Coplin emerged. Cigar clamped between his teeth, he stepped back into his field commander role with reassuring ease.

Spotting Mark and Coop, he wove through the FBI personnel already at the warehouse, leaving the HRT operators to retrieve their gear. "Okay, give me an update." He planted his knuckles on his hips and squinted at them.

"We think they have Monica in the last unit at the end." Coop gestured toward a video monitor that had been set up in the command center. The camera was focused on the unit he'd referenced. "There are two people registered in the room. A field agent has taken over front-desk duty and is telling potential guests there's no vacancy."

"How many people are registered now?"

"Ten of the rooms are occupied. All toward the front of the motel," Mark responded.

"We need to clear them out."

"Agents disguised as housekeepers are doing that now. We're transporting guests off-site but leaving their cars in place. We've had local law enforcement close off the road and secure the outer perimeter, and we have agents on covert surveillance. One of them set up the exterior video feed we're watching."

Les peered at the screen. "Is that their car?"

"That's our assumption," Coop said. "We tried to get a read on the license, but it's caked with mud and illegible. However, the size of the car fits the profile of the tire tracks the ERT found."

"Do you have a blueprint of the facility?"

"Yes." Coop led the way to a table where the detailed drawing

239

had been spread out, pointing to the schematic as he spoke. "There's an air duct on one side of the last room. We plan to snake a fiber-optic camera through the ductwork to get a look at what's happening in there."

"How are you going to cover any noise?" Les chewed the cigar to the other side of his mouth.

"We're placing two agents in the adjacent room, posing as a couple with a baby. We'll send them in with some audio of a baby crying and they'll turn up the volume on the TV. That should mask any noise from the duct while they get the camera in position. We're setting up a feed over there." He gestured to a second video monitor off to the side, where two technicians were focused on their task. "As soon as the agents are in the room, we'll also have audio. They're going in with a stethoscope mike."

"Sounds like a plan. I've already got one of our language specialists on standby. She can interpret if the conversation isn't in English." Les scanned the cavernous room, zeroing in on the special agent in charge of the Richmond office. "I need to talk with Dennis. Brief your team on the setup. We'll regroup in a minute and get the snipers in position. Once the video feed comes in and we verify that Monica Callahan is in there, we'll talk about an assault plan. What's the timing on a data feed from the room?"

"The agents are on their way. We should have audio and video in fifteen or twenty minutes."

"Sounds like everything is covered. Get your guys up to speed."

Les headed across the room, and Coop waved over the other five members of their assault team. No matter the amount of planning, in the end success or failure would come down to the actions these men took in the space of a few critical seconds. There was a razor-thin margin for error.

As the team assembled around him, Coop knew he was surrounded by the best in the business. They'd worked as a cohesive, well-oiled unit for years, amassing an impressive success rate with high-risk operations.

And he didn't intend for this one to tarnish that record.

19

The muffled sound of a slamming car door echoed in the silent motel room with the same impact as a gunshot. Without moving from his computer, Nouri drew his pistol and glanced at Zahir, motioning toward the window as a second car door slammed.

Noiseless as a stalking panther, his partner rose and eased the drape open enough to see out without being seen. "It's a couple. With a baby. They're taking luggage out of the trunk."

The door to the adjoining unit opened. The muted sound of voices came through the wall.

"He's bringing in more luggage. And some sort of collapsible baby pen."

The door shut again. Zahir let the drape fall into place and exchanged a look with Nouri. "I don't like this. Why have they put someone in that unit now, after two days?"

The baby started to cry. Within seconds the muffled sobs swelled to a piercing wail.

"Perhaps that's the reason." Nouri reholstered his gun. "The desk clerk may not have wanted the baby to disturb the other guests."

"And perhaps it is not as innocent as it seems."

Suspicion was a good thing, and Nouri respected it. Better to be cautious than careless. Taken to extremes, however, it could lead to overreaction and unwarranted risk-taking. In general, Zahir was levelheaded. But Nouri had worked with him often enough to learn the man didn't like to be idle. Give him a surveillance job, and he could sit for hours immobile in a tree. Confine him to a motel room with nothing to do, and he grew increasingly restless—and paranoid. A dangerous combination.

The TV was turned on in the adjoining room, the volume raised to compete with the howls of the baby. When Zahir began to pace, Nouri decided a distraction was in order. "Why don't you do a weapons check?"

In silence, Zahir strode across the room, opened the closet, removed two large cases. He set one on the floor beside the bed near the door, the other on top. Flipping the locks, he yanked up the lid. "I am tired of hiding in this hole."

"In eight hours this hole will be history. Let us not jeopardize our great success with impatience. You have done well, Zahir. Tariq will be proud."

The compliment seemed to mollify his partner. For the moment, anyway.

Focusing once more on his computer screen, Nouri maintained a calm demeanor. But he, too, was concerned about their neighbors. The arrival of the couple could be meaningless, as he'd suggested to Zahir. Or it could be significant. There was no way to know.

With singular focus, he reviewed the abduction step-by-step, dissecting each component of the plan, analyzing the execution, until he was satisfied there had been no errors in strategy or implementation. It had been a precise, flawless operation. No one could know where they were.

Now, just one task remained.

He cast a dispassionate glance at the diplomat's daughter. She lay unmoving, curled on one side under the bedspread, her face bruised and swollen, her features etched with pain.

At least she didn't have much longer to suffer.

Because in eight hours, no matter what David Callahan decided, she would die.

New fear coursing through her, Monica risked a peek at the arsenal being laid out on the adjacent bed. Though she hadn't understood the exchange between her captors, she sensed the guests in the adjoining room had raised a red flag. While the leader's demeanor was calm, his posture was alert and watchful. The other man radiated tension, slapping the weapons on the bed with leashed aggression.

She gave her watch a discreet check. Almost six o'clock. Night had fallen again. Hours had passed since the phone call with her father. She'd done her best to pass on information to the FBI. But she must have failed. If they'd understood her clues, surely she would have been rescued by now.

Could she use the presence of guests in the next room to her benefit? If she screamed, they might alert the motel management. But it would also put them—and their baby—at risk. She'd seen the blood-stained knife on the leader's belt and didn't doubt he'd use it again on anyone who got in his way, as he had at least once already. And she didn't want to be responsible for any more loss of life—even if it came at the cost of her own.

Monica wanted to believe there was still a chance for everything to end well. Prayed there was. But her hope was ebbing, along with her residual strength.

And as each minute ticked by, she fought a growing fear that unless the HRT rescued her soon, she wouldn't live to see another morning.

"There she is! Hold for a minute!" As Coop barked the order into the mike at his wrist, the breath he'd been holding hissed through his teeth. The last few seconds, since the picture from the fiber-optic camera had flashed on the screen in the tactical operations center, had been the longest of his life. The HRT team clustered closer to the monitor as he issued another command. "Zoom in."

The agent in the motel room adjacent to the abductors complied.

As the image of Monica lying on the bed grew larger, Coop's stomach clenched. She was huddled on her side, her body hidden under the bedspread, but he had a clear view of her bloody, bruised features. He watched as she attempted to turn on her back, as her face contorted with pain, as she gave up the effort.

She was in worse shape than he'd thought.

But she was alive.

And he intended to keep her that way.

"We need to see the rest of the room." Les chewed the end of his cigar. "Pan the whole area."

The camera roamed over the room, halting at Les's instruction on the bed with the weapons. A man in dark attire stood with his back to the camera.

"Assault rifle, submachine gun, handguns . . . it looks like they're preparing for a siege." Mark inspected the cache, arms folded across his chest.

"Let's find the other guy. Keep panning," Les said. The camera moved on. "Hold it. Aim down as much as you can. I think there's someone seated against the wall between the rooms."

The camera shifted. "That's the best I can do," the agent said.

"Good enough. I see a leg and an arm . . . wait, he's getting up."

The operators watched in silence as the second man rose, stretched, walked over to inspect the weapons.

"They're both wearing pistols, but they're not wired." Coop scrutinized the image. "These guys don't plan to blow themselves up if we get too close."

"A definite plus," Mark remarked.

"Is anyone seeing explosives of any kind?" Les's question to the team drew a negative response. "Me, neither. Another plus. But we already know these guys have no qualms about killing. Pulling this thing off without casualties on our side will be tricky. Surprise will be our best tactical advantage."

"I assume we're not even going to consider bringing in a negotiator." Coop positioned the comment as a statement, not a question, though they all knew the rules about deadly force. Tactical resolutions were a last resort, used only after every other solution had been tried. And in hostage situations, it was standard procedure to call in negotiators from the FBI's Critical Incident Response Group.

But in this case, Coop knew CIRG mediators would do more harm than good. Terrorists didn't negotiate, and they couldn't be trusted. Yet Les would face intense scrutiny if he violated protocol. Be subjected to an internal investigation that would include, at minimum, an administrative inquiry.

Narrowing his eyes, the commander studied the video monitor in silence. Chewed his cigar. Shifted it to the other side of his mouth.

"If we alert them to our presence, Monica Callahan is a dead woman." At Mark's quiet comment supporting his position, Coop sent him a brief look of gratitude.

More silence.

The operators waited for Les's instructions as he squinted at the screen.

"We could try luring them out in the open," he said at last. "But I don't believe we can do that without arousing suspicion. So we breach. We identify ourselves." He paused and surveyed the assembled group, his next words slow and deliberate. "And *when* they reach for their guns, we take them out. Am I clear?"

The subtle difference between "when" and "if" wasn't lost on any of the operators. Nor was Les's decision to reject negotiation as an option. He was giving them the authority to put a quick, clean end to a perilous situation.

"Yes." Coop spoke for all of them.

"We also need to have some EMTs on hand."

"I can take care of that." Dennis had been watching from the background, and he stepped forward now.

"Good. Have a medevac chopper on standby too. Okay, gentlemen." He scanned the assembled HRT operators. "Let's talk tactics."

Three cars pulled out of the embassy gate. From the backseat of the middle vehicle, David stared out into the 6:00 a.m. darkness. At this hour, the thirty-mile drive to Bagram shouldn't take more than an hour. But snow had fallen during the night, and morning traffic would be horrendous. The usual snarl of cars, donkey carts, bicycles, buses, and taxis would reduce movement to a crawl, at best. He couldn't afford to be late for this meeting.

With Monica's location pinpointed, David knew the major hurdle to her rescue had been overcome. He would have preferred the FBI to rush in at once, but he understood the need for prudent, careful planning and was doing his best to curb his impatience. To trust the men charged with saving his daughter.

It wasn't easy.

But he took some comfort in the knowledge that a rescue operation was under way.

He wished he could say the same about the other three hostages.

Twenty minutes later, as his driver finally eased away from the burgeoning crush of traffic in the city, David's cell phone began to vibrate. Bob Stevens, according to caller ID. Fumbling to flip the cover, he pressed the phone to his ear. It could be an update on the secretary's arrival . . . or information about Monica's rescue.

It was neither.

"Good news, Mr. Callahan. Your trip to the bazaar paid off after all. A message came in this morning providing us with the location of the hostages."

David's grip on the phone tightened as he struggled to find his voice. "Is it authentic?"

"We think so. The informer referenced the previous delivery method, which hasn't been publicized. He also knew a couple of details about your daughter's abduction that haven't been released to the press. We think he included that information to validate his message."

"Where are the hostages?"

"In a small, obscure village near Kandahar. I've already spoken with General Adams. He's mobilizing the Delta Force teams that were deployed in anticipation of a rescue operation. Coordinating a clandestine rescue in a handful of hours in such an isolated area will be tough. But he's convinced they can pull it off."

A great weight lifted from David's shoulders. "I can't think of better news to take to the secretary."

"There's more. Our informer was also kind enough to tell us not only who the mastermind is but where he is."

"Why would he do that?"

"Who knows? Maybe he's disenchanted or angry or looking out for number one. Frankly, I couldn't care less about his motivation. Capturing the leader will be a tremendous coup. A Delta Force team has been deployed to that location as well. They want to pick him up first."

"Who is he?"

"A name you might recognize. Tariq al-Hashemi."

The memory of his single encounter with the cold-eyed, corrupt official remained vivid in David's mind. He would never forget the palpable hate that had emanated from the man. "One of the high-level officials we exposed in the government scandals a few years ago. For bribery, I recall."

"It appears he has a long memory too."

"You think Monica's kidnapping was a vendetta of some sort?"

"My guess is he used it because it dovetailed with his plans and appealed to him on several levels. I recall him as being a very cunning character. I'll be glad to see him put away."

"That makes two of us."

"I understand from your security escort that you've just left the city. Safe journey."

"Thank you. I guarantee it will be a far more pleasant one than I thought."

Outfitted in body armor, Coop checked the video screen. In the past two hours, while his team had chalked out the motel room on the floor of the warehouse and rehearsed their assault, there had been little activity in the spartan room.

The arsenal was still arrayed on the bed, and one of the abductors had done a meticulous check of each weapon. He was now sitting near the head of the bed, his head tipped back against the wall, his eyes closed. The second man remained half out of sight, seated against the wall between the rooms. Monica hadn't moved from the bed. To Coop's relief, there was no indication they were preparing for an imminent departure.

"Team ready?" Les joined him, scanning the screen.

Coop surveyed the men. Attired in black flight suits, Kevlar helmets, and body armor reinforced with ceramic trauma plates in the front and back, the operators were armed with MP5 submachine guns or assault rifles. They wore their primary pistols in low-slung tactical holders just below their hip, and each man had a second .45 in a cross-draw shoulder rig. The member designated as breacher was equipped with two strip charges. He and Mark carried flash-bang grenades.

"Yes."

"Okay. Let's do this."

With a nod of acknowledgment, Coop was starting to turn away when a movement on the screen caught his attention. He paused to watch as the man sitting on the bed rose, his angular posture radiating tension and leashed energy. A dangerous combination.

The kidnapper prowled the length of the room. Stopped at the foot of Monica's bed. Looked at her. Spoke.

"Translate," Coop barked.

The conversation in the room had been sparse, leaving the translator in Quantico with little to do. Now she went to work, interpreting via speaker phone to those watching the monitor in Harrisonburg.

"He said he needs something to relieve his stress."

Coop's fingers clenched into fists.

"What's up?" Mark joined them.

Shaking his head, Coop's gaze remained riveted on the screen. The man walked up to the side of the bed. For a few moments he stood over Monica. Then, in one swift movement, he yanked the bedspread down.

As Monica recoiled into a tighter tuck, Coop stiffened and sucked in a harsh breath. He felt Mark's hand on his arm. Shook it off. Listened as the translator interpreted.

"Your face is not so pretty, but the rest of you . . ." The man

250

lifted the hem of her sweatshirt and shoved a hand underneath. Monica's gasp had the effect of a scream in the sudden silence of the command center. "Very nice."

As she tried to twist away, he removed his hand long enough to grab her wrists, crushing one under his knee and pinning the other over her head. Then he resumed his aggressive groping as she writhed on the bed. "You still have a bit of fight, I see. Good. I like resistance."

Coop uttered a word he rarely used.

"Later." This from the other man, who remained out of sight.

"We have only a short time left."

"Four hours. There is plenty of time for your games. I promise you a go at her before we kill her."

The man didn't remove his hand at once. When at last he did, those assembled around the monitor had an unobstructed view of Monica. Her chest was heaving, and her face was a mask of terror and revulsion.

As Coop struggled to regain some sense of professional distance, Les spoke, his tone grim.

"My take on that last comment is that they never intended to release her alive."

Coop had been so focused on the other part of the man's blood-chilling remark that the more lethal phrase hadn't even registered. But Les was right. No matter David Callahan's decision, Monica's fate had already been determined.

"We need to move in. Now." His steel-edged words came out in a growl.

"Agreed. Once you're in position, I'll keep you apprised of the movements of the kidnappers. Let's get this done and send the lady home."

In silence, the operators climbed into the Suburban that would drop them behind a manufacturing facility a couple of hundred yards from the motel.

As Coop settled into his seat, Mark slid in beside him. "At least we're in the final stretch."

While he appreciated Mark's attempt at encouragement, Coop wasn't buying. "We're not home free yet. Too much has gone wrong with this assignment."

"I hear you. But we've handled far tougher assault situations. This should be a piece of cake."

True, Coop conceded.

But until he was holding a living, breathing Monica in his arms, he wasn't going to count on anything.

Their little motorcade had made good progress, David reflected, checking his watch. In ten minutes they'd drive through the gates at Bagram, fifty minutes before his meeting with the secretary of state. The snow hadn't slowed them as much as he'd expected.

The ride had also been far more peaceful than he'd anticipated. Instead of agonizing over the fate of Monica and the other three hostages, he'd been able to breathe for the first time in days. While the situation remained volatile, he knew the best teams in the world were committed to rescuing all four of the hostages. He had to trust—and pray—they would succeed.

Closing his eyes, David took a moment to do just that. And to give thanks for the positive turn of events.

The explosion came without warning.

One second, the car was quiet, the ride uneventful.

An instant later it felt like Armageddon.

A blast roared through the car, hurling David against the door.

Glass shattered. Searing light blinded him. Pain shot through his head. His arms. His chest.

He heard screams.

Realized they were his.

And then the world went black.

20

Staying low, Coop and Mark covered the last few yards to the end of the building where Monica was being held prisoner. Cued by Les, who was monitoring the kidnappers' movements on the live feed, three other assaulters were already in position behind the car parked outside the door. The remaining two were concealed next to the car belonging to the agents in the adjacent room. They would remain there unless needed.

The job could have been handled by three or four operators, but Coop assumed the commander had drafted the whole group as a precaution, given the high-level nature of the abduction. Likewise the decision to call in three snipers versus one or two. Coop didn't mind the overkill, considering all that had gone wrong with this mission. The more hands on deck, the better.

After verifying that his team was in final position, Coop fitted in his earplugs, adjusted his goggles, and lifted his wrist to his mouth to alert the Tactical Operations Center they were ready. "HR-35 to TOC. We're at yellow."

"TOC to all units. Stand by to copy." Les's voice sounded in his ear.

Flexing his fingers on his Heckler and Koch MP5, Coop waited for Les to count down the assault, his adrenaline pumping. Behind him, he felt Mark shifting his own submachine gun into position.

The seconds ticked by. Ten. Twenty. Thirty. Coop frowned at the delay.

"TOC to all units. Hold."

At the clipped instruction from Les, Coop tamped down his impatience. Ten more seconds passed. Twenty. Thirty. His patience gave out.

"HR-35 to TOC. Request an update."

"TOC to HR-35. One of the targets has moved too close to the hostage."

"HR-35 to TOC. How close?"

"TOC to HR-35. He's standing by her bed."

"What else is he doing?" Coop's fingers clenched around his gun and he gritted his teeth, aware that his question violated normal communications protocol. For one thing, he should have prefaced the query with his operator number, as he had in the previous exchanges. For another, it wasn't up to him to call—or suggest—the shots. He was out of line, and he knew it.

Les's terse tone when he responded made that clear. "TOC to HR-35. He's not hurting her."

That depends on how you define hurting, Coop countered in silence as a muscle clenched in his jaw. "HR-35 to TOC. Request permission to move to green."

"TOC to all units. We're not going to rush this unless the hostage's life is in imminent danger. Stand by."

Unable to see—and helpless to stop—what was happening on the other side of the wall, mere feet from where he stood, Coop tried to block out the nauseating scenarios playing in his mind. Did his best to focus on the play-by-play plan they would soon implement. Struggled to swallow past his thirst for vengeance.

Failed.

In the end, he turned to the only tool at his disposal during this agonizing waiting game.

God, please protect her.

The seven-thirty phone call didn't surprise Tariq. This was the big day. There were many plans to implement, most of them contingent on David Callahan's response to his demands. His people were awaiting instructions, and he'd expected some of his lieutenants to check in.

But the caller ID told him the man on the other end of the line was a key informant who'd played little role in this operation. Tariq used him more in his opium business. And he had little time today for those matters.

Yet the contact often provided valuable, opportune information, he reminded himself. Two weeks ago he'd tipped Tariq to a raid that would have cost him several hundred thousand dollars. It might be in his best interest to answer.

"This is Hissar. You have information?" The man knew Tariq only by that code name.

"I have learned that David Callahan's car was bombed this morning en route to Bagram. I thought that would be of interest to you, in light of your present activities."

Stunned by the news, Tariq groped with the implications as he fired off questions. "Who did it? When? Is he alive?"

"My source tells me it happened thirty minutes ago. No one has claimed responsibility yet. I have no report on his condition."

"I am anxious for more news. You will be compensated for any information you provide, as always."

"Thank you, Hissar. It is a pleasure to do business with you. I will let you know if I learn any more."

As the line went dead, Tariq began to pace. And process. There could be only one explanation for the bombing, he concluded. Mahmud.

His key Kabul lieutenant had questioned Tariq's plan almost from the beginning. Yesterday he'd raised concerns that David

Callahan might be leaving the country and pushed Tariq to kill the diplomat while he had the chance. And he'd admitted he wasn't convinced Tariq's decision to kidnap Monica Callahan had been sound.

Tariq had rebuked him, assuming he'd toe the line until this was over.

Instead, it seemed the man had taken matters into his own hands. And possibly ruined all of Tariq's plans.

Anger began to seethe inside Tariq. He should have listened to his instincts and pulled Mahmud out of this operation weeks ago, when the man's insolence first manifested itself. Instead, he'd decided to give him a chance to prove he could be trusted. And controlled.

That had been a mistake. Instead of learning his lesson, the man had grown more brazen. And now he'd become a liability.

Was he foolish enough to think such insubordination and treachery would go unpunished? Tariq wondered, astounded by the man's boldness. Or was it conceivable that Mahmud thought Tariq would have a change of heart, realize the error of his ways, and thank him for taking the initiative to disobey what Mahmud considered to be erroneous orders?

The questions didn't matter, and Tariq dismissed them. He didn't intend to waste time or energy trying to understand Mahmud's motives. He had already decided there would be consequences for the man once the operation was over. Now they would be more dire. And more immediate.

His lips settling into a thin, unyielding line, Tariq tapped a number into his cell phone. He needed to canvas all his sources to find out if David Callahan lived. But first, he planned to send a message to Mahmud and the rest of his lieutenants: defiance will not be tolerated.

Fifteen excruciating minutes after the HRT commander issued his hold order, Coop's earpiece crackled back to life.

"TOC to all units. The subject is moving away from the bed. Stand by to copy."

His fingers tightened on his weapon, and Coop angled a look over his shoulder at Mark. The other man gave an almost imperceptible dip of his head and edged around Coop.

"TOC to all units. One subject is at the back of the room, near the sink. The other is at the computer against the inside wall. We're at green. I have control. Five . . . four . . . three . . . two . . . one."

As the last number echoed in their ears, Coop and Mark were already moving. Mark rounded the front of the building and passed under the window in a crouch, stopping on the far side of the door. Coop took his place under the window, aware their position was fully exposed. But as he'd told Monica, his teammates had earned his trust. The long-range precision fire of the three concealed snipers would cover them if they were detected.

One of the operators hidden behind the kidnappers' car had already moved to the door. Working swiftly, with a quiet efficiency reflecting long hours of practice, he attached the rubber strip charge and primed the end of the detonation cord. As he fired the charge and moved aside, Coop shielded his eyes.

The blast exploded in the quiet night, buckling and bending the door as it pulled the locking mechanisms from their catches. Explosive breaching alone was often sufficient to shock and stun suspects. But for good measure, Mark lobbed a flash-bang grenade into the room as the door fell inward, shouting "FBI" at the same time.

Two-point-seven seconds later, the room erupted with brilliant repeating strobes and high-decibel noise designed to debilitate and disorient for up to five seconds.

Coop was the first one in, as rehearsed. Mark and two other operators followed, fanning out. The imploding door had knocked the kidnapper at the computer to the ground. He wasn't moving. Coop's gaze went to the second man.

A pistol shot rang out, startling him. He felt a sting on his arm.

More shots followed. From HRT automatic weapons.

The kidnapper at the back of the room reached for the gun at his belt. Coop aimed. Pulled the trigger. The man jerked back. Toppled.

It was all over in eight seconds.

As quickly as the room had erupted with noise, it went silent.

While the other operators verified that the kidnappers posed no additional threat, Coop strode toward Monica, wrist to mouth.

"HR-35 to TOC. Scene is contained."

"Copy, HR 35. What is the condition of the hostage?"

"Checking that now. Get the EMTs in here."

"They're on the way. Any operator casualties?"

Without breaking his pace, Coop did a quick scan of the room. "No."

Yanking out his earplugs, he pulled off his goggles and leaned over Monica. She was curled into a ball on her side, her eyes wide. Dazed. Unfocused. She was also shaking badly. No surprise there. Flash-bang grenades could destabilize people in good condition for up to a minute. After everything she'd been through, Monica didn't come close to falling into the good category.

Aside from the lingering effects of the flash-bang, however, she didn't appear to have been injured in the assault. To verify that, he reached for the bedspread, intending to pull it back. But her hands convulsed around the edge, gripping it, and she whimpered.

With a jolt, he realized his actions must have reminded her of the slimeball who'd harassed her.

Leaving the cover in place, he sat beside her and pulled off his helmet. "Monica, it's Coop. You're okay. It's over." The words came out hoarse and uneven as his gaze locked with hers. With a gentle finger, he stroked the back of her white knuckles. "Monica? Can you hear me? I just want to verify you're not hurt."

She blinked. Squinted as if trying to focus. Blinked again. And then, all at once, she emitted a soft sigh, went limp, and loosened her grip on the covers.

"Good girl." Coop wanted to gather her in his arms, reassure her the nightmare was over. But he settled for a gentle stroke of her cheek.

"HR-61 to TOC. We have two dead subjects."

Mark's voice reporting to Les pulled Coop back to the job at hand. He eased the bedspread down, did a cursory scan. The blood on Monica's pink sweat suit was dried. He saw no additional signs of trauma.

"HR-35 to TOC. Hostage was not injured in the assault."

"Copy, HR-35. EMTs are on the way."

Motioning to Mark, Coop pulled the cover back over Monica. "Handle the cleanup here, okay?"

"Sure." Mark glanced at Coop's shoulder. "Looks like you got winged."

Frowning, Coop noted the bloody crease on the outside of his upper arm. Remembered the pistol shot. And the sting. "It had to be the guy by the door. I can't believe he managed to get off a shot in all that chaos."

"He must have had his gun out for some reason when we breached and taken a wild shot. You better have that checked out."

"Later. Monica's first in line." He spotted two EMTs in the doorway and waved them in, stepping aside as they took over.

Someone had already briefed them on what was known about her condition, but Coop hovered nearby as they eased her onto her back, snapped on latex gloves, and went to work. One of them wrapped a blood pressure cuff around her arm, another prepared to start an IV.

"Seventy-seven over forty." The technician removed the blood pressure cuff and checked her heart. "Pulse is rapid, weak and thready."

At Monica's sudden flinch, Coop took a step closer. "What's wrong?"

"I'm having trouble getting the IV in. She's in shock and shows obvious signs of dehydration. Not a good combination if you're trying to start a line."

Coop recalled enough from his first-aid training to know the EMT was probably dealing with collapsed veins from restricted blood flow. But it didn't ease the knot in his gut when Monica flinched again as the man tried a second time.

"Look, can you take it easy?" The words came out in a low growl as Coop edged in and reached for her free hand, scrutinizing her face. "She's been hurt enough today."

"The IV will ease a lot of her discomfort once we get it in." The man kept working, tapping the inside of her elbow, trying to raise a vein. On his third attempt, the needle slid in. "Got it." As he taped the needle in place, he spared the HRT operator a quick look. "We were told she'd been drugged. My guess is she's thrown up and hasn't had any fluids replenished. The IV will help."

"She'll need some stitches in her chin." The other man spoke as he tested her pupils with a penlight. "It appears she might have a mild to moderate concussion. Plus assorted bruises and abrasions."

All at once, Monica drew in a sharp breath. Her features contorted, and she struggled to sit up, her eyes hazy with pain.

261

The EMTs reacted at once. One held her in place while the other attempted to discern the cause of her sudden distress. "Ma'am, we need you to lie still. Can you tell us what's wrong?"

Her breathing grew more labored, and she thrashed at the restraining hands. "Hurts." She gasped out the word.

"What hurts?"

"Leg."

"Which one?"

"Right. Calf."

The EMT pulled the bedspread all the way down and pushed up the leg of her sweatpants. "Muscle cramp. Common with dehydration." He looked at Coop. "Can you do some gentle stretching and massage while we deal with the other problems?"

"Yes." Standing around watching her suffer was agony. He was glad he could do something—anything—to alleviate her pain.

Bracing himself on one knee on the bed, he kneaded the rigid spasm that had convulsed her muscle. It was tight and hard, contracting beneath his fingers, and he worked it with steady, even pressure until at last he felt her tension ebb and her body went limp.

"Okay. We're ready to transport." One of the EMTs stood and motioned to another technician hovering in the doorway, who moved a gurney beside the bed. In one smooth motion they transferred her.

Coop knew a medevac chopper was standing by to take her to Richmond. He'd heard it land a few minutes ago. And he intended to hitch a ride.

"I'm going with you," he told the EMTs as they started to wheel her out. "Give me three minutes."

The technician facing him acknowledged the instruction with a nod.

As the gurney disappeared out the door, Coop surveyed the room. For the past few minutes he'd been oblivious to the activity taking place behind him. He cast a dispassionate eye on the two kidnappers, still lying where they'd fallen. He focused on the one who had harassed Monica. Perhaps he should feel remorse for taking a life. He didn't.

"Is she okay?" Mark joined him.

"She will be. I think." He turned away from the bodies. "I'm going to Richmond with her as soon as I clear it with Les."

"It's cleared."

"Thanks." Coop shot his partner a grateful look as he stripped off his body armor.

"Les wants us to remain on security detail for the next twenty-four hours, anyway. After we grab a few hours of shut-eye. I'll join you when we finish up here. The Richmond office will also have agents at the hospital to keep out the press."

"Good. The last thing she needs is a bunch of reporters in her face." Coop worked fast, shedding the bulky assault gear. There were few people to whom he'd entrust his equipment, but Mark was one of them. He slid his Glock into the holster on his belt. "I'll see you in Richmond."

"Count on it."

The chopper was waiting, and Coop ducked into the prop wash under the blades, climbed aboard, and found a place next to Monica—near enough to see her but out of the way of the EMTs. Despite the warm blanket they'd tucked around her, she was shaking again as reaction set in. She needed medical treatment, a quiet place to regroup and heal, and lots of TLC.

And Coop intended to see that she got all three.

21

Forty-five minutes later, as the chopper settled on the roof of the main hospital at VCU Medical Center, Coop's BlackBerry began to vibrate. Pulling it off his belt, he checked the ID. Les.

"Cooper."

The noise of the rotors overpowered the commander's response. No small feat, given the man's booming voice.

"Sorry. We just landed. I'll be inside in sixty seconds. Can you hold?"

A garbled "yes" came over the line.

The chopper door slid open and the gurney was moved into position for unloading. Coop knew a team from the Level I Trauma Center was standing by, and he was grateful the physicians' skills wouldn't be taxed tonight.

Once inside the hospital, Coop fell into step behind the gurney as he talked. "Okay. Now I can hear you."

"I have news. An effort is being made to contain the information as long as possible in light of the looming hostage deadline in Afghanistan, but it may leak, and Ms. Callahan needs to be prepared. Her father's car was bombed this morning while he was en route to Bagram for his meeting with the secretary of state."

Stunned, Coop's step faltered, and he fell back from the gurney. "Is he alive?"

"At last word. He's being treated at an army field hospital. They're trying to stabilize him for airlift to Landstuhl."

Only the most severe battle casualties were sent on to the U.S. military hospital in Germany. He had to be critical.

"What happened?"

"According to initial information, it was an IED."

Improvised explosive device. Better known in the American media as a roadside bomb.

"Was it related to the hostage situation?" Even as he asked the question, Coop was struggling to make sense of this latest turn of events. After all their efforts to coerce David Callahan into persuading the U.S. and Afghan governments to meet their demands, why would the terrorists attack him on his way to meet with the secretary of state?

"At this point, no one knows. I'll keep you apprised as details become available. But you need to inform Ms. Callahan. If this breaks, it will be all over the media."

Propping a shoulder against the wall, Coop wiped a weary hand down his face and watched as they wheeled Monica through a set of swinging doors farther down the hall. "I don't know how much more she can take today."

"You pick the timing. But it would be unfortunate if she overheard the news in a conversation or saw it on TV."

"Yeah. Listen . . . on another subject . . . what did you see on the live feed when you put us on hold during the assault? Did that scumbag—"

"No," Les interrupted. "He didn't. Not while we were watching. You'll have to ask the lady what happened before that."

A muscle jumped in Coop's jaw. "I plan to. As soon as I get the chance."

"Mark will be heading your way in about fifteen minutes. Is security in place at the hospital?"

"I haven't confirmed it yet." Coop pushed off from the wall and scanned the area around the double doors where Monica had disappeared. Two men in suits stood close by, one angled

265

away from him. "But I see a couple of guys who have all the earmarks of agents. I'll verify that after I hang up."

"I'll be in touch."

As Coop slipped the phone back into its holder and approached the two men, both turned his way, posture alert. One of them was Nick Bradley.

"You look a little the worse for wear." Nick glanced at Coop's arm.

"Not compared to Monica."

"Yeah." Nick frowned and shifted his attention to the double doors. "I got a quick glimpse as they went past. How bad is she?"

"I didn't hear the EMTs mention anything more serious than shock, concussion, and dehydration. But I'm about to confirm that. Mark's on his way too. You guys will be out here?"

"Our instructions were to stick close all night."

"Keep an eye out for media."

"Hospital security has been beefed up. But should a reporter get this far, I've perfected the 'no comment' routine and the intimidating stance." He folded his arms across his chest and glowered.

One corner of Coop's mouth quirked up. After the horror of the past twenty-four hours, Nick's touch of humor was welcome.

Turning toward the swinging doors, he prepared to push through—and almost got decked as someone shoved one his direction. His arm shot out and he took an instinctive step back as a fortyish, dark-haired nurse swept through. He estimated her height at five-foot-three, tops, and he doubted she tipped the scales at much above a hundred pounds.

Nevertheless, she planted herself in front of the doors and folded her arms across her chest, her stance an imitation of the one Nick had just used. Out of the corner of his eye, he caught the agent's amused expression.

"This area is restricted." The woman didn't appear the least bit bullied by his height advantage or the Glock on his belt, Coop noted. "Only patients are allowed in trauma rooms."

"I need to see Ms. Callahan."

"She's being evaluated. The waiting room is down the hall."

Widening his stance, Coop settled his fists on his hips and stared down at her. When she didn't budge, he withdrew his credentials and displayed them. "I need to ask her some questions."

The woman gave his ID a quick, dismissive perusal. "Is this a matter of life and death, Mr. Cooper? Or a national security issue?" She didn't surrender a single inch of ground.

Coop debated his strategy. He could lie. He could bluff. He could bluster. But he had the distinct feeling none of those tactics would sway this nurse one iota. Instead, he opted for honesty.

"No." He tucked his credentials away and relaxed his aggressive stance. "I just need to see her. She's been through hell, and she took me along with her. I failed her once in the past twenty-four hours. I'd like her to know I'm standing by now."

For five long, silent seconds, the woman assessed him. If he hadn't been watching closely, Coop would have missed the almost imperceptible softening in her features. Pursing her lips, she inspected his arm. "That needs attention."

"It will keep."

"We don't like people bleeding all over our waiting room, Mr. Cooper. Why don't you let us stitch that up?"

"I'd rather see Ms. Callahan."

She moved closer. Close enough that they'd have been nose-to-nose except for the height difference. "Mr. Cooper, we stitch people up *back there*." She hooked her thumb over her shoulder. "The place where we take *patients*."

Her strategy finally penetrated his fatigue. "Okay. I guess I do need a few stitches."

"That's what I thought. This way." She pushed back through the swinging doors.

Coop followed without another word.

Mahmud sipped the last of his coffee, nodded to the owner of the tiny café, and stood. He was a regular at the shop, and it was important to maintain his routine on this critical day. If David Callahan didn't use his considerable influence to convince his government to meet Tariq's demands, Mahmud could be called on to eliminate the man. Today. And he didn't want a change in pattern to raise suspicion or suggest he had any links to the diplomat's demise—or to the current hostage situation. He had ambitions once Tariq regained power, and caution was his ticket to achieving them.

As he left the café, he pulled his robe closer to his body. It would be interesting to see the outcome of the meeting with the American secretary of state, he reflected as he tramped through the snow that had blanketed the city overnight. Tariq believed the pressure he had exerted would work. Mahmud remained unconvinced.

Communicating his doubts about strategy to Tariq, however, had been a mistake. One he would have to amend after the current situation was resolved. He hated groveling, but it might be necessary. Whether or not Tariq's plan succeeded, the man wielded considerable influence and power, and he'd built up a remarkable covert organization. In time, Mahmud believed Tariq would reach his goal of regaining a position of influence in the government. He couldn't afford to alienate the man.

Yes, an apology was in order.

His head bent against the wind, his thoughts turned inward, Mahmud didn't realize he had company until a man drew up beside him, matching him pace for pace. His hand instinctively went to the gun concealed in his robe, closing around the handle.

"I have been sent by Tariq."

Startled, Mahmud looked over at his unexpected companion. Though a scarf covered the lower part of the man's face and his head remained in profile, Mahmud recognized him as one of Tariq's men. His hand relaxed on the gun. They'd met once, during a summit with the leader. Mahmud didn't know the man's name, only that he was playing some role in the hostage situation. Since Tariq always cautioned his people never to meet in public, Mahmud was taken aback by the man's presence.

"We should not be seen together."

"This will be a brief meeting. I have a message for you from Tariq."

"Why did he not call me himself?"

"He requested that this be delivered in person." The man tipped his head toward an alley ahead on their right. "Let us pause for a moment where we will not be observed."

With a worried glance, Mahmud scanned the narrow side street. Few people were about, but talking with this man was dangerous. Better to get the message and part company as soon as possible.

Striding ahead, Mahmud took a few steps into the shadowed alley and swung toward the messenger. "Let us not linger. Tell me what—"

Mahmud saw the gun and heard the muffled pop . . . once, twice, three times in rapid succession . . . before the man's intent even registered. He staggered back, stunned.

Fell.

Watched the white snow turn red as the world faded to black.

She could focus again. Sort of.

Blinking, Monica stared at the ceiling above her. She felt as if she was finally coming back from some no-man's-land. A nightmare place where people were intent on hurting her. Where fear clawed at her throat. Where hands touched her with malice and evil intent.

Her fingers curled into tight balls, and she fought back the sudden panic that swept over her. She wasn't in that place anymore. It was over. Coop had told her that. His comforting voice was her one clear memory from the past few hours.

Nevertheless, it took several slow, deep breaths to slow her pulse. Once it returned to a more normal pace, she inspected her surroundings. The curtained cube told her she was in a hospital. An IV hung by the side of the bed, and she followed the tube down to her arm. The black and blue skin suggested someone had used her arm as a pincushion while inserting the needle.

But that was the least of her complaints, she decided, as she took an inventory. The vision in her right eye remained a bit fuzzy, but a gentle probing explained why. The lid was swollen half shut. She brushed her fingertips over her forehead and discovered a sensitive, sizeable lump. That accounted for the dull, aching throb in her head. Her nose was tender to the touch too.

Working her way down her face, she stroked an exploratory finger over her cracked, puffy lips, encountering a scabbed-over cut. There was a strip of gauze taped to her chin and another smaller bandage on her neck. Her fingers lingered there for a second as she wrestled into submission the terrifying memory of the knife pressed against her throat.

Okay, so much for her head. Based on the glimpse she'd gotten of herself in the mirror at that motel room, there were no surprises there.

Shifting slightly, she tried to assess the condition of the rest of her body. Every inch ached, but there didn't appear to be any serious damage. When she tried to roll a bit to one side, however, she gasped in pain as her hip encountered the mattress.

"Big bruise."

With a gasp, she jerked her head toward the voice. A black-haired nurse entered the curtained cube and began checking her vitals. "Sorry. I didn't mean to scare you. How are you feeling?"

"Like a truck ran over me." Her words came out in a raspy croak.

"Close enough. You met up with some very nasty characters. Would you like a drink of water?"

"Yes. Thank you."

The woman retrieved a cup from the small table beside the bed, and Monica took the straw between her parched lips, drinking greedily. She emptied the contents.

"Better?"

"Much. What can you tell me about my condition?"

"Concussion, dehydration, assorted bumps and bruises, a few stitches." The nurse refilled the cup from a carafe and set it back on the table. "My guess is you've had better days. We're waiting for a couple more test results and the X-rays from your nose, but nothing we've found so far indicates any serious damage. If everything comes back okay, you should be fine after a few days of rest."

The woman draped the stethoscope around her neck and checked the IV drip. "By the way, there's a man prowling around our hall who is going to go ballistic if I keep him out of here five more minutes. Do you feel up to a visitor?"

"Is it Coop?"

"If you mean Evan Cooper from the FBI, yes, that would be the man. Patience is not his long suit."

"Maybe not. But I think he saved my life."

"Not a bad credential for entry. Shall I send him in?"

"Please."

"The doctor will be around to talk to you soon. In the meantime, I don't think you'll be bored." She winked and pushed through the curtain that offered the barest modicum of privacy to patients in the trauma center.

Two minutes later, Coop swept the drape aside, his gaze probing, assessing. When he spoke, his voice was several shades deeper than usual. "Hi."

"Hi." She tried to smile, but it hurt too much. Yet she wanted to reassure him she was okay. Wipe the worry from his eyes, ease the lines of strain around his mouth, erase the fatigue from his features. "I'm okay, Coop. I won't win any beauty contests for a while, but at least purple is one of my colors." She did her best to adopt a teasing tone.

His Adam's apple bobbed, and he shook his head. "You are one amazing woman."

The compliment surprised her. Touched her. Threw her off balance. Coop had struck her as a man uncomfortable with verbal expressions of emotion or compliments. Why the change? Unsure how to respond, she countered with levity. "Have you been reading my book?"

"I haven't had much time recently for leisure pursuits." He shoved his hands into the pockets of his slacks. "But I absorbed a lot that first night. And I learned quite a bit about communication from an excellent lecture I attended a few days ago too."

The man was full of surprises. After everything he'd been through, she'd expected him to be more taciturn than usual. Instead, the experience seemed to have had the reverse effect. It was a pleasing change, but she wasn't up to a personal exchange yet. First she had to figure out why her feelings for this man were so potent, given that he hadn't even been in her life until a week ago.

Once again, she retreated behind the armor of humor. "Did you come to spring me?"

"Nope. They're waiting for a few test results before they admit you."

"I don't want to be admitted. I want to go home."

"Not an option tonight." His tone brooked no argument. "May I come in?"

"Of course."

He stepped inside, turning to pull the curtain behind him. That's when his attire registered. He was wearing the top of a pair of green surgical scrubs, she realized. And there was a large piece of taped gauze near shoulder level, on the outside of his arm.

"What happened to you?"

He moved beside her. "It's just a crease. I needed a few stitches."

"How many?"

"I didn't count."

"Come on, Coop. How many?"

He shrugged. "A dozen, I think."

Coop had suffered a bullet wound because of her. And he may not have been the only one. She drew in a shaky breath and braced herself.

"Who else got hurt?"

"In the rescue operation? No one except the kidnappers."

"Before that."

"We can talk about the details later, Monica."

"No, now. I need to know."

He scrutinized her, debating how much to share. Considering the other bad news he needed to pass on, he'd prefer to postpone this recap. But her intense expression suggested she wouldn't go for that. And he couldn't lie to her. "The police officer patrolling the road behind the safe house. And one of the agents on perimeter patrol."

"How bad are they?"

"Last I heard, the officer was critical and in surgery."

"What about the agent?"

A beat of silence ticked by. "He didn't make it."

"Oh, God." The agonized words came out half prayer, half lament, and she squeezed her eyes shut. "All because of me." Her voice broke.

"None of this was your fault, Monica." He took her cold hand in his, infusing her fingers with his warmth. It wasn't professional behavior for an on-duty operator, but he didn't care. Her need for consolation outweighed protocol.

Tears leaked from beneath her eyelids. "Can you get me an update on the officer's condition?"

"I'll work on it."

He brushed a few strands of hair off her forehead, his gut clenching at her misery. She was struggling to keep her tears in check, and he wanted to tell her to let them flow. She deserved a cleansing cry. Needed one. Her fierce grip on his fingers was a clear indication of the coiled tension begging for release. Unfortunately, the news from Les was only going to exacerbate her stress.

All at once a memory of Joey Brummett, the vicious, cruel bully in his grade school, flashed through his mind. There were a few things Coop found difficult to tolerate. Preying on the innocent and defenseless was one of them. And kicking someone when they were down ranked near the top of his list. That had been Joey's modus operandi. Nor had his sadism been confined to people. Coop had found him once poking a sharpened stick at an injured puppy he'd confined in a wooden shipping case. Though Coop had rescued the furry little critter, its pitiful whines had echoed in his mind for weeks afterward.

Trying to balance the scales of justice so the grown-up bad

guys of the world didn't win was one of the reasons he'd joined the FBI.

Except at this moment, as he regarded Monica's battered face and prepared to pass on the information Les had shared, he felt more like Joey Brummett.

"Monica, before I check on the officer, we need to talk about a couple of things."

She searched his eyes, her own filled with apprehension. "Okay."

He propped one hip on the edge of her bed, taking care to jostle it as little as possible, and kept her hand in his firm clasp. "We used a fiber-optic camera in the air duct to monitor the activity in the motel room where you were held, and we saw one of the abductors touch you in . . . an inappropriate manner." Soft color suffused her cheeks, and a shudder rippled through her. He tightened his grip, his gaze flicking to the ring of bruises on her wrist before it locked on hers. "Did he do anything else to you?"

"No. He just . . . touched me." Her reply came out in a whisper, and she shuddered again.

"Were you unconscious at all?"

"Not after we got to the motel."

He let out a long, slow breath as the tension in his shoulders abated slightly. But not much. He still had a difficult task ahead.

"I have some news from Afghanistan." He stroked the back of her hand with his thumb, wishing there was some way to break this gently. But the harsh fact couldn't be softened.

"The hostages . . . did the terrorists . . ." Her complexion paled and her voice trailed off.

"No. As far as I know, they'll be okay for another couple of hours. This news is about your father."

"Did he have the meeting with the secretary of state? What did they decide?"

"He never made it to the meeting, Monica." He took a fortifying breath. "His motorcade was hit by a roadside bomb."

What little healthy color had survived in her cheeks disappeared, leaving the ugly bruises stark against her white skin.

"He's being treated at an army field hospital and will be airlifted to the military hospital in Germany as soon as he's stable."

"He's alive, then." Her words came out choked.

"Yes. But he is very, very critical."

Tears pooled in her eyes. One leaked out to trail down her cheek, and Coop brushed it away with a gentle finger.

"We were going to have dinner together. In Washington." Her voice choked.

His own throat tightened as he searched her stricken face. He wished he could promise her everything would turn out all right. But the best he could do was hold her hand. Through whatever lay ahead.

"I'm going to Germany, Coop."

Taken aback by her startling announcement, he shook his head. "You're in no condition to travel, Monica."

"I can make it." She squeezed his hand, her eyes reflecting a compelling urgency. "Don't you see? He went into that marketplace for me. I have to be there for him. Will you help me make the arrangements?"

He wanted to refuse. Every protective instinct in his body urged him to shelter this woman from further trauma. To tuck her away in a safe, quiet place where she could rest and decompress and heal.

Yet he understood her feelings. Saw the resolve in her eyes. And knew she'd find a way to make the trip.

Suddenly the curtain was pushed aside and a white-coated figure walked in. Coop retreated to the corner of the cubicle, grateful for the interruption. And hoping Monica might have a change of heart.

But when their gazes met, the determination in her eyes told him it was a lost cause. She was going to Germany—with or without his help.

22

Why wasn't Nouri answering?

Tariq pressed the end button on his cell phone, his brow furrowed. Since learning that David Callahan had been injured, he'd been too busy trying to get information on the diplomat's condition to check in with his nephew or Sayed until now. Nor had they bothered him. The two men shared that worthy trait. They let him initiate contact unless they had an urgent matter to discuss.

But they always answered their phones when he called.

Nouri's silence unnerved him more than Mahmud's treachery. He didn't doubt his nephew's loyalty or diligence. There had to be a good reason he wasn't responding. And Tariq suspected it didn't bode well for their operation.

He punched in Sayed's number next. With the noon deadline a mere two hours away, the hostage guardian would be awaiting instructions.

As he waited for Sayed to pick up, Tariq considered his options. The most he'd been able to find out about Callahan was that the diplomat had survived the blast and would be transported out of the country for treatment. No one had been able to confirm if he was conscious, but on the off chance he was, he would be in no condition to negotiate.

That left Tariq with two choices. Extend the deadline on killing the hostages, or let it stand. He was undecided which option would serve him better.

The phone continued to ring, and Tariq frowned. After five more hollow intonations, he hung up.

Why would two of his key people not answer his calls on this critical morning?

The phone began to vibrate in his hand, and he checked the caller ID. One of his sources in Kabul, who was trying to ferret out information about Callahan's condition.

"Yes? You have news?"

"Not of a medical nature. But the Taliban has just claimed responsibility for this morning's bombing. They say they planted the bomb weeks ago when the American vice president was supposed to travel that road. After he cancelled his trip, they waited for an opportunity to take out another high-level official. It seems they found out about David Callahan's visit with the secretary of state and chose him as their target."

Stunned, Tariq stared at the dingy wall in the sparsely furnished bedroom of the hovel that had served as his home and command center for the past few days. The Taliban was responsible for the bomb?

"Hissar? Are you still there?"

"Yes. You will be compensated for the information." He stabbed the end button.

How ironic, Tariq mused. Mahmud had died for a crime he didn't commit. Yet he felt no remorse. He hadn't trusted the man anyway. The disruption in his plans caused him more distress than his lieutenant's unjust demise. Yet even that was overridden by worry over his unanswered phone calls.

Something was wrong. He felt it in his bones.

Moving across the room, Tariq opened the door to the living area, intending to summon Anis. They needed to switch locations again, and Anis handled those details. At least the man had learned not to interrupt him, to wait until he was summoned. There might be hope for him yet.

But the room was deserted. A quick glance confirmed that Anis had not prepared tea nor paid his daily visit to a bakery to pick up the flat bread sprinkled with cumin seeds that Tariq favored for breakfast.

The silence in the apartment was unnatural, and the tingle of unease that had started at the base of his spine suddenly zipped to every nerve ending. Tariq could almost smell the danger. It was imperative he leave. At once.

But his instincts had kicked in too late. As he strode toward the door, it burst off its hinges, and he lifted his hands to shield his face from the splintering wood. Two seconds later, the room erupted with noise and light. The scene froze in his vision, like a snapshot, and he swayed, struggling to regain his equilibrium.

After the noise and light abated and the freeze frame came back to life, the scene had shifted. Half a dozen American soldiers surrounded him, their automatic weapons pointed at his heart.

In the blink of an eye, he understood three things.

He wasn't going to die. If the soldiers had meant to kill him, he'd be dead already.

He had been betrayed.

And his dream of regaining power was history.

From the corner of the tiny curtained cubicle where he'd wedged himself, Coop observed the doctor's conversation with Monica. He hoped the physician would discourage her when he heard her plans.

"Considering how this could have turned out, you are one lucky young woman." The man scanned a printout as he spoke. Like many trauma doctors, he looked permanently sleep deprived. There were deep creases around his eyes, and Coop suspected the prominent gray in his dark hair was premature. "Mild concussion. You may have a headache on and off for the next couple of weeks. An over-the-counter pain reliever should help."

He flipped to the next sheet of paper. "Nose is bruised but not broken. Six stitches on your chin. The IV is helping with the dehydration, but we need you to keep drinking fluids too."

"What did they drug me with?"

"Chloroform." Coop supplied the answer.

She shifted her attention to him. "Isn't that kind of old-fashioned?"

"It does the job."

"It also made me sick."

"The concussion contributed to the nausea too," the doctor interjected. "You threw up?"

"Several times."

"That's another reason you were dehydrated." He shuffled the reports together. "We're ready to move you to a regular room. I'll check with you in the morning, and if everything looks good, we'll release you."

As he prepared to exit, Coop realized that Monica didn't intend to tell him about her travel plans. He stepped forward. "Ms. Callahan is considering a trip to Germany, Doctor."

He sensed her surprise. Understood her displeasure at his interference. Ignored it.

"When?" The physician directed the question to his patient.

"As soon as possible."

"You need a few days to rest and recuperate before you consider major travel."

"It's an emergency, Doctor. I don't have a few days."

"We'll discuss it again in the morning." It was obvious the man wasn't used to having patients balk at his instructions. "In the meantime, get some sleep—if you can. Hospitals aren't the quietest places."

Monica didn't even wait for the drape to settle back into place after the doctor exited before nailing Coop. "You aren't going to help me make the arrangements, are you?"

"I didn't say that." He moved back beside her. "But you're in no shape to travel."

"I need to do this, Coop. If you won't help me, I'll find someone who will." Despite her prone position, he caught the slight stubborn tilt of her chin.

The black-haired nurse pushed the curtain aside to admit an orderly, once more interrupting their conversation. It was like Grand Central Station in here, Coop thought in frustration.

"Okay, we've got a nice, private room all ready with a very hot-looking man guarding the door. And another one here. You must rate." She directed her next comment to Coop. "You can come up after she's settled. Room 312. Give us fifteen minutes. And there's a guy in the hall looking for you."

Mark, Coop figured.

"I'll see you in a few minutes, and we'll finish our discussion," Coop told Monica.

"Midnight is no time for discussions." The nurse shooed Coop out. "This woman needs some sleep."

"I'll be waiting." Monica kept her gaze fixed on Coop.

He watched while they wheeled her toward an elevator, then headed for the waiting room.

"Everything okay?" Nick turned toward him as he exited the restricted area.

"Yeah. No permanent damage." Of a physical nature, anyway. "They're moving her to a room."

"I know. My partner for the night is already up there."

"Is Mark here?"

"In the waiting room."

282

"Thanks."

"Both of you need to get some sleep. Two of us are on security detail, and I can promise you no one will bother her tonight. I plan to stick very close."

A bone-deep weariness was settling in, and Coop knew Nick was right. There was nothing more he could do here, and Monica would be in good hands with the two agents standing guard.

"Mark and I will probably cut out once she's in her room."

"Okay. See you up there."

As Nick forked off toward the elevator, Coop continued toward the waiting room. Mark was slumped in one of the uncomfortable chairs, fatigue weighing down his shoulders, but as Coop entered he rose.

"How is she?"

"Minor injuries, but enough of them to produce a pretty significant cumulative effect. They're moving her to a room, and once she's settled, we can go get some sleep. Nick's on the security detail tonight."

"He's a good guy. She'll be well protected."

"Yeah. I got that feeling."

"Les told me about her father."

"Any updates on his condition?"

"No."

"Monica wants me to arrange for her to fly to Landstuhl."

Mark arched an eyebrow. "Is she up to that?"

"Not according to the doctor."

"Any chance of talking her out of it?"

"I wouldn't put any wagers on it. But I intend to try."

"From what I've seen of the lady, once she makes up her mind, she's not easy to persuade."

"Tell me about it." Coop sighed and raked his fingers through his hair.

"Les passed on some other interesting news." Mark glanced

around the deserted room, motioned Coop into the corner farthest from the door, and lowered his voice. "The informer who promised to provide the location of the hostages came through."

"Wow. I didn't expect that."

"Not only that, he provided the name and location of the mastermind, who's already been picked up. Delta Force is preparing to free the hostages as we speak."

"That's some of the best news I've heard all day."

"I agree. By the way, we got fingerprint IDs on our kidnappers. They both had clear terrorist connections."

"No surprise there." He checked his watch. "They should have Monica settled by now. You want to come up or wait here?"

"I'll wait. I doubt she wants a parade through her room at this hour."

"Give me ten minutes."

When Coop stepped off the elevator on the third floor and turned down the hall toward Monica's room, he found Nick planted outside the closed door. And his watchful posture suggested he had no intention of moving. The other agent was a bit farther down the hall, with a clear line of sight to her door.

"Is she alone?" Coop paused beside Nick.

"Yes. The nurse and orderly left a couple of minutes ago."

With a nod, Coop opened the door and stepped into the darkened room. He gave his eyes a few seconds to adjust to the dim light, then moved to the bed. Monica lay unmoving under a blanket, and at first he thought she was asleep. But her eyelids fluttered open at his approach.

"It's Coop." He identified himself immediately. The last thing she needed was a shadowy figure sneaking up on her in the dark.

"I think they spiked my IV." Her words were a bit slurred, and he could see her struggling to remain awake.

"Good. You need to sleep."

284

"I want to finish our discussion."

Even drugs couldn't dilute her single-minded determination, Coop reflected. "You've been through too much, Monica. I'm not in favor of this trip."

"I know you aren't. And I appreciate your concern. But I'm going. Can you arrange it?"

"Why don't we wait until tomorrow and see where everything stands?"

"I don't want to wait. That will delay the trip." Frustration nipped at her groggy words. When she continued, however, her tone was more conciliatory. "But I'll tell you what. If the doctor finds any reason to keep me hospitalized tomorrow, I'll reconsider. In the meantime, you set things in motion. Okay?"

Her voice was fading, and Coop had to admire her tenacity—and her ability to bargain—despite the effect of the drugs dripping into her bloodstream. Considering her threat to find someone else to help her if he didn't, his options were limited.

"Okay. I'll see what I can do."

She groped for his hand in the dark, and he wrapped her slender fingers in a warm clasp. "Thank you." Half a minute later her grip grew limp as she succumbed to the oblivion of sleep.

One minute ticked by. Two. Coop continued to hold her hand, reluctant to break contact. In the end, however, he forced himself to listen to reason. He, too, was in desperate need of sleep, and though his heart urged him to stay, logic told him to leave.

But before he slipped out of her room, he did what he'd been wanting to do from the moment they freed her.

He bent down and pressed his lips gently to her forehead.

From his last position of cover, Captain Jack Logan trained his binoculars on the two gun-toting guards outside the hut that

285

stood a bit apart from the handful of scattered hovels that constituted the tiny desert village. One was gesturing in an agitated manner with his free hand. The other's posture was stiff.

Their intelligence had been sound. This was the place.

He scanned the barren terrain, looking for any sign of the fifteen men from the three Delta Force teams summoned for this rescue mission. Even with his trained eye, in broad daylight, he saw nothing. Masters of the art of infiltration without detection, they'd low-crawled into position, melting into the desert in their camouflage gear and face paint. A couple had managed to work their way into an abandoned structure a short distance away from the hut containing the hostages.

Now, they waited for his command. Snipers had the two guards in their crosshairs. Every assaulter knew exactly what he had to do.

A third guard from inside the hut joined the two at the door, and Logan hefted his HK416 into position. According to the informer, there were four guards on duty, two outside and two inside. If that information was correct, only one guard remained in the hut.

The time had come for their diversion.

Logan initiated the rescue with a single command that echoed through the speaker in every team member's ear. Within three minutes, smoke began to billow from a storage shed behind the abandoned building where the two Delta Force operators were concealed.

One of the guards pointed to the shed, and the three began an animated conversation. They summoned the fourth guard, who exited the hut, gun at ready. The group conversed some more. Finally two of the guards edged toward the smoke.

The triggers on four rifles were squeezed to within the last ounce of resistance as each sniper verified a clear line of sight and confirmed his target.

Jack issued a second command.

Shots echoed.

Guards fell.

In the eerie silence that followed, the assault team moved in.

Four minutes later, Logan dropped down on one knee beside the huddle of three grimy, terrified hostages.

"I'm Captain Jack Logan with the U.S. Army. We've come to take you home."

23

Eight hours after he left Monica at the hospital, seven hours after he set the wheels for her trip to Germany in motion, and six hours after he passed out on the bed, Coop jolted awake, heart racing, adrenaline pumping. He grabbed his Glock. Bolted upright. Identified the noise that had awakened him as the shower.

Sagging against the headboard, he lowered the gun. He was in a hotel. The nightmare was over. Monica was safe.

He drew in a slow breath. Let it out. Repeated the process once, twice, three times. As his pounding pulse subsided, he consulted his watch. Eight o'clock. Six hours of sleep wasn't enough, but it had helped.

"Morning." Mark came out of the bathroom, a towel draped over his hips, his hair spiky with moisture. "Did I wake you?"

"I needed to get up."

"What time did you finally crash?"

"A little after two."

He grimaced. "The shower's yours if you want it."

"Yeah. I want it." As Coop swung his legs to the floor and stood, he couldn't imagine anything he'd rather have right now than a hot shower. Well, perhaps one thing, he conceded, as he padded across the room, the hint of a smile softening the tension around his mouth.

"Want to share that thought?" Mark propped one shoulder against the door frame, blocking Coop's access to the bathroom. "I could use a smile too."

"Sorry. It's private."

"Hmph." Mark pushed off, allowing Coop to pass. "Must be about Monica."

Coop shut the door in his face.

Mark called through it. "That's what I figured."

Sometimes his partner was just a little too cocky, Coop decided, twisting the faucet and shedding the clothes he'd slept in. And a little too insightful.

Although he'd have loved to spend half a day under the hot, tension-dissolving jets of water, he gave himself a mere three minutes. Les had informed them about the successful hostage rescue last night, but he needed to check in with the commander for an update on David Callahan. He also wanted to run by Monica's house and pick up some clothes for her to wear home from the hospital. As far as he was concerned, they could burn the pink sweat suit.

When he emerged from the fogged-up room in a cloud of steam, Mark was already dressed.

"Give me five minutes." He rubbed a towel over his hair.

"No rush. I talked to Nick. Everything was quiet last night. And he arranged to have someone clean up Monica's place. The housekeeping service was there at seven."

"I owe him one for that." He'd planned to do a cursory cleaning himself before they picked her up. The ERT was thorough, but the fingerprint people typically left powder everywhere. As for the bloody lingerie drawer . . . that had been his first priority. The fewer reminders she had of that trauma—and the ones that had followed—the better. "We'll only have to stop long enough to grab some clothes for her."

He dressed with speed and efficiency, scanning the contents of his suitcase as he sorted through clothes. One clean shirt left, he noted, adding laundry to his to-do list.

"If you drive, I can check in with Les en route." Coop secured the last button on his white shirt, tossing the keys to Mark before slipping his arms through the sleeves of a charcoal gray suit jacket.

"Piece of cake compared to some of the assignments I've had in the past few days. Let's go."

Once in the SUV, Coop tapped in the number of Les's cell phone. As usual, the commander answered on the first ring.

"We're on our way to the hospital." Coop buckled his seat belt as Mark exited the hotel parking lot and pulled into traffic. "I wanted to get an update on David Callahan."

"He's been airlifted and is scheduled to arrive at Landstuhl within the hour. A surgical team is waiting. I understand he has very serious head and chest wounds. I was told the odds of him pulling through are fifty-fifty at best."

Another piece of bad news to pass on to Monica, Coop reflected, wishing he had a better prognosis to offer her.

"Any idea who was behind it?" He tapped Mark's shoulder and gestured toward a fast-food chain up ahead. He was desperate for a cup of coffee, and a couple of egg and sausage biscuits didn't sound too shabby, either. He couldn't remember the last time he'd eaten. Maybe a stale donut at the safe house? It seemed like a lifetime ago.

"The Taliban is claiming responsibility. No connection to the hostage situation. According to the ballistics experts who are investigating the incident, the bomb appears to have been detonated by a cell phone."

Mark swung into the drive-through. After being paired with him on missions for close to three years, Coop didn't even have to tell his partner what to order. Mark had it down.

"I also have an update on Ms. Callahan's travel arrangements, assuming she's released from the hospital. We've got her on military transport out of Andrews at seventeen hundred hours. You and Mark can escort her to the plane, and State Department security will take over from there. Let me know as soon as you confirm it's a go."

"Okay. Thanks." As Coop ended the call, he snagged a biscuit. Mark had already inhaled half of a breakfast sandwich, he noted.

The two men wolfed down the food in silence. Not a crumb remained by the time Mark swung onto Monica's street and surveyed the neighborhood. "I don't see any media vans."

"You will once she's released."

"We'll be with her. That should put them off."

"Let's hope so."

They spent no more than fifteen minutes at the house. Once Coop verified that the cleanup crew had erased all evidence of the break-in, he snagged a pair of jeans and a sweater out of Monica's closet. The sanitized lingerie drawer was empty, but he found a few folded undergarments in the laundry room. He grabbed them all, adding them to the duffel bag he'd dug out of a closet in her spare bedroom.

"Okay, we're set." He emerged into the foyer and retrieved her coat from the closet.

"We have company already." Mark was peering through the blinds he'd cracked in the living room. "Someone must have tipped the press that there was activity at the house earlier this morning."

Setting the items he'd gathered on a side chair, Coop joined him. A van with the call letters of one of the national network news affiliates was parked near her driveway. "That was fast."

"This is big news. It's all over the headlines."

"There's no way out of here without being seen."

"That doesn't mean we have to talk to them."

"And I don't intend to. Let's go."

They were out the door and in the car before the news crew realized they'd exited. But as Mark put the car in reverse, a reporter and cameraman stepped into the driveway. Instead of slowing his speed, however, Mark accelerated. The news crew quickly moved aside, conceding the game of bluff to the FBI.

The two men made one more brief stop en route to the hospital. Mark waited in the car while Coop went into the store, grinning when his partner emerged five minutes later carrying a huge jar of M&Ms tied with a red bow.

"She'll love that."

"I figure she deserves all the comfort food she can get for the next six months. At least."

The media was out in full force at the hospital too, and Mark veered toward the rear of the building, parking near a service entrance. They flagged down a passing employee, who admitted them with her access card after they flashed their credentials.

Nick was still glued to Monica's door and greeted them with a status report. "No problems. Everything was quiet last night. The doctor just left, and word is she's been cleared for release."

Considering her impending travel plans, Coop didn't necessarily consider that good news.

"You guys can take off now if you want to," Mark told Nick. "Coop and I will escort her home. We appreciate your assistance with this." He shook his friend's hand.

"I second that." Coop, too, extended his hand. "And I also appreciate the extra mile you went to get her house put back in shape."

Nick gave his hand a firm shake. "I didn't want the lady walking into that mess. She's been through enough."

"Amen to that."

"Okay. We're out of here." Signaling to the other agent down the hall, Nick gestured toward the elevator. "See you two around."

As Nick headed out, Mark folded his arms across his chest and faced the hall. "Go on in. I'll watch the door."

After a soft knock, Coop stepped into the room, pausing just inside to set the duffel bag and Monica's coat on a chair. He hid the jar of candy behind his back. "It's Coop. May I come in?"

"As long as you don't flinch."

She tried for a joking tone, but Coop heard the slight unsteadiness in her voice. Letting the door close behind him, he moved into the room. Bruises and abrasions always looked worse the next day, and he tried to prep himself.

But he hadn't factored in the merciless effects of harsh daylight. The sun streaming in the canted blinds highlighted every contusion and every nuance of the red and purple hues on her nose, her brow, and around her eye. The large pieces of gauze on her forehead and chin had been replaced with Band-Aids, but he could see the ends of the jagged cut on her jaw peeking out on either side of the latex strip. She'd regained very little color overnight, and her eyelid remained puffy and half closed. The lines of strain around her mouth, and the skin stretched taut over her cheekbones, gave eloquent testimony to her uncomfortable night.

In other words, she was a mess. And in no condition to travel to Germany.

"I look that bad, huh?"

So much for trying to mask his shock, Coop berated himself. Forcing his lips into the semblance of a smile, he strolled over to the bed. "Well, I doubt *Vogue* will be coming by to take any cover shots today. But maybe this will help console you." He pulled out the jar of M&Ms.

A delighted smile eased some of the strain in her features. "The perfect thing. Thank you." She held out her hand, and he walked over to take it, sitting on the edge of her bed.

"You're welcome."

She touched the jar, stroking a finger along the smooth glass. "I have a feeling these will come in handy in the next few days.

How's my father?" Trepidation rippled through her voice as she met his gaze.

There was no way to sugarcoat the facts. He passed on what Les had told him, though he eliminated the odds the commander had quoted without minimizing the seriousness of the situation. "It's not good, Monica. They'll do their best, but there are no guarantees."

"I know. I'll just keep praying, like I did in the motel room."

"I did some of that myself."

Surprise parted her lips. "I didn't think you were a believer."

"I'm not saying I am. But I read a bit of the Bible that night you loaned it to me, and it piqued my interest. After you were snatched, I couldn't think of anywhere else to turn for help. I decided it couldn't hurt to ask for divine intervention."

"A lot of people first seek the Lord in adversity."

"We've had plenty of that in the past few days."

"But things are improving. I heard about the hostages. And did you know I'm free to leave as soon as they take out my IV?"

"I heard."

"Were you able to get my trip set up?"

"Yes. You're on a military flight at five o'clock. But I think you should delay this."

"I can't, Coop."

A nurse bustled in, interrupting their conversation with a bright smile. "I hear we're going home today. Let's get that IV out and send you on your way." She moved to the side of the bed and pulled on a pair of latex gloves, studying the huge black and blue blotch on the inside of Monica's arm as she began pulling off tape. "Looks like someone had trouble getting this in."

"I was dehydrated."

"That'll do it. Okay, I need to press this cotton ball against your arm when I pull out the IV. With all that bruising, it's going to hurt. Ready?" At Monica's nod, the nurse extracted the IV and put pressure on the puncture. Although Monica didn't flinch, Coop felt her stiffen, watched as she bunched the sheet in her fingers.

"You did good." The nurse disposed of the needle. "Keep the pressure on for a minute. I'll be right back."

As Monica slid her fingers over the cotton ball, Coop realized she was shaking. Moving to the other side of the bed, he took over. "Let me."

She released her grip without argument, and he cradled her elbow with one hand, maintaining even pressure with the other. "I brought you some clothes." He hoped conversation would distract her from her discomfort.

"Thanks. I'd hate to have to go home in this hospital gown." She tried to smile, but he caught the glint of moisture in her eyes. She was hurting, and the fact that there wasn't a thing he could do to ease her suffering didn't sit well with him.

The nurse came back in, peeked under the cotton ball, and slapped a bandage over it. "All set. Do you need some help getting dressed?"

"Yes." Coop answered for her.

"Okay. A wheelchair is on the way."

"I don't need a wheelchair," Monica protested.

"Hospital rules. Sorry."

"I'll be outside with Mark," Coop told her.

As he slipped through the door, his partner sent him a questioning look. "Well?"

"Not good."

"Does she still want to go to Germany?"

"Yes."

"Do you think she can manage it?"

"I'll let you form your own opinion."

Ten minutes later, after an aide wheeled Monica into the

hall and she greeted Mark, he fell back and glanced at Coop, shaking his head.

It took both of them to help ease her into the backseat of the Suburban. Mark took the wheel, and Coop slid in beside her, reaching over for her seat belt. She winced as he pulled it across to insert it, and he froze.

"Sorry. I have a big bruise on my hip."

And where else? he wondered, scrutinizing her battered face. She'd had the sheet pulled up to her chin in the hospital bed, and her arms and legs were encased in denim and wool now. "Any other spots I should be aware of?"

His question came out husky as her warm breath caressed his cheek. Their eyes were mere inches apart, and all at once soft color flooded her face. He could feel her quivering and debated the cause—her injuries or their nearness? He settled on the latter for one simple reason. He was having the exact same reaction.

She dipped her chin and focused on a button on her coat. "No. All of my other injuries are visible."

He took his time securing her belt, fighting an urge to gather her into a comforting, protective hug. But at last he eased away and buckled himself in.

"We'll need to leave your house by one for Andrews." Mark spoke from the front seat, flicking a look at Monica in the rearview mirror as he pulled into traffic.

"That's not a problem." A slight quiver ran through her voice. "I won't need more than an hour to throw a few things together. Can you fill me in on what to expect on the flight and at Landstuhl? I'm not very familiar with military operations."

For the remainder of the drive, they briefed her. She was in the middle of a question when they turned down her street, and as the news cameras came into view, her words trailed off.

296

"I didn't expect that." She frowned at the vans as Mark drove the short distance to her house.

"Don't worry about them. There are consequences for trespassing, and we aren't going to linger in the driveway," Coop assured her. "Stay where you are until we tell you we're ready."

After pulling as close as possible to her garage, Mark set the brake, slid out from behind the wheel and strode toward the front door. He disappeared inside. A couple of minutes later the garage door opened, and when he reappeared Coop got out of the car and came around to her side. Mark positioned himself to block the view of the reporters on the sidewalk as Coop opened it.

"Seat belt off?"

"Yes."

"Six steps, we're inside. You okay to walk?"

"Sure. I think so."

Noting the caveat, he moved closer. "Okay. Swing your legs out. Then grab on to my arm and slide out."

She did her best, but once on her feet, she had to clutch at his suit coat to steady herself. Coop slipped one arm around her waist, and with his support she moved toward the refuge of her garage, away from the shouted questions of the reporters. Mark brought up the rear. The instant they stepped inside, his partner pushed the button for the garage door, and it rumbled shut, blocking out the media circus on her sidewalk.

"Let's get you inside." Coop helped her up the single step that led into the laundry room, and Mark closed the door behind them. He could feel her trembling. "Why don't you lie down for an hour before you pack?"

"I might have to. They gave me a pain pill at the hospital, and I think it's making me sleepy."

Perhaps. But her quick capitulation and pinched features

297

told him the simple trip home from the hospital had also taxed her to her limits.

"Let me help you." He started to guide her toward the hall, but she shook her head.

"No. Thank you. I'll be fine. But if it wouldn't be too much trouble, I'd appreciate a cup of tea."

Understanding her need to prove to herself she could function without assistance, he released her. "No trouble at all. I'll bring it down in a couple of minutes."

With a brief smile of thanks, she moved down the hall, slow, stiff, cautious, the fingers of one hand brushing the wall to steady herself.

Once she disappeared into her room, Mark shook his head. "She's not up to this trip."

"I know. But I'm not having any luck convincing her of that. Why don't you try?"

"If she won't listen to you, I guarantee she won't listen to me."

Coop expelled a frustrated breath. "I'll make the tea. And try again."

Except five minutes later, as he approached her room carrying a steaming mug, he could see through her cracked door that she was already asleep. She hadn't even bothered to pull back the bedspread. Setting the mug on the dresser, he retrieved a throw from a chair by the window and gently draped it over her.

Mark was eating a piece of toast when Coop rejoined him in the kitchen, mug in hand.

"What's up?"

"She's already asleep."

"Must be a powerful painkiller. But she needs the rest."

"I agree. I'll try to talk to her again about the trip after she wakes up." Coop set the mug on the counter. "Any more bread?"

"A whole loaf in the freezer."

Half a dozen pieces of toast and three cups of coffee later, Coop pushed aside his plate as Mark reached for his BlackBerry.

"Les," Mark relayed, checking the caller ID.

The conversation was brief and one-sided. And Mark's sober expression didn't bode well as he ended the call.

"What's up?" Coop gripped his mug of coffee.

"Les tried to call you first. Your battery must be dead." Mark took a deep breath. "David Callahan didn't make it."

24

Monica's eyelids flickered open, but the room was fuzzy, and she felt groggy and disoriented. Jumbled images of an anonymous safe house, a bare-bones motel room, and an antiseptic-smelling hospital swirled through her mind, confusing her. As her focus sharpened, however, she realized she was in her own room. Lying in her bed.

Had all the horror, all the trauma, been no more than a bad dream?

She rolled to her side, and the sharp jab of pain in her hip, along with the dull throb in her head and face, answered her question. The nightmare had been real.

And it wasn't over yet, she recalled with a start. Her father was critically injured. She needed to pack for a flight to Germany.

Lifting her arm, she squinted at her watch. Blinked. Looked again. Panicked. That couldn't be right! She remembered Mark saying they needed to leave by one o'clock for the drive to Andrews. It was five after twelve! And she hadn't packed yet! Why hadn't Coop awakened her?

Propelled by a sense of urgency, she swung her legs to the floor and stood. Too fast. The room tilted, and she groped for the bedpost, clinging to it until the world steadied. Moving with more caution, she worked her way down the hall, her fingers again splayed on the wall for support. The house was quiet, and for a moment she wondered if Coop and Mark had stepped out for some reason. But as she rounded the doorway into the kitchen, she found Coop staring out the window into her backyard, his profile pensive, a mug in his hands.

"Coop? It's after twelve! Why didn't you wake me?"

He turned toward her, his eyes narrowing a fraction as he scrutinized her. The flicker of some emotion she couldn't define produced a subtle shift in his expression, and he set the cup on the table before walking toward her.

"Let's sit down in the living room for a minute." He took her arm.

"Coop, we're going to be late!" She resisted his gentle pressure and sent him an alarmed look. "I need to pack."

"We have time."

"No, we don't! I'm not moving that fast today." She tried to tug her arm free, but he held fast.

"Trust me on this, Monica." His gaze locked on hers, and he repeated his previous comment. "We have time."

His tone held a trace of . . . dread, she decided, and sudden panic squeezed the breath from her lungs. "What's wrong?"

"Let's sit."

A feeling of impending doom swept over her, and she didn't resist his third attempt to guide her toward the living room. After easing her down on the couch and finding a pillow for her back, he took the chair at right angles to her and leaned forward, clasping his hands between his knees. He'd shed his suit jacket and loosened his tie, and the haggard planes of his face reminded her she wasn't the only one who'd had a rough few days.

"Where's Mark?" Delaying the inevitable wasn't going to change Coop's message, but all at once she didn't want to hear what he had to say. Not yet.

"He had a few errands to run. He'll be back soon." Taking a deep breath, he wove his fingers through hers, his gaze never releasing hers. "I have some bad news, Monica. My boss called a little while ago. I'm sorry to tell you your dad didn't make it."

She heard the words. Understood them. Couldn't accept them.

"I thought you said he was in Landstuhl."

"He was. The operation was in progress and going well. But he went into cardiac arrest and suffered a massive heart attack. There was no way to save him. I'm sorry, Monica."

Silence fell in the room as she processed the news. She didn't want to believe it was true. Not when everything else had turned out so well. But Coop wouldn't lie to her.

Deep inside, she felt something shatter.

"Now we'll never have a chance to try and forge some kind of relationship." She choked on the last word, swallowed, swiped at the tears threatening to spill from her eyes. "Before the bombing . . . did he know I was okay?"

"He knew we'd located you. And that a rescue operation was in progress."

"I'm grateful for that, anyway." She looked down at their clasped hands, grateful, too, for the presence of this man at this moment. "What do I . . . what happens next?"

"Someone from the State Department will call you in the next few hours to discuss arrangements. They'll handle all the details."

"I don't even know what my father would want." The knowledge saddened her.

"Given the dangerous nature of his work and his reputation for thoroughness, I suspect he may have left some instructions. Don't worry about that unless you have to."

His BlackBerry began to vibrate, and he automatically reached for it. Checked himself.

"Go ahead and get it. It might be important."

Conceding the point, Coop pulled the phone out of the holder

302

and scanned the caller ID. "Cooper . . . yes . . . yes . . . that's fine." He slid it back onto his belt. "Mark will be here in a couple of minutes."

"I guess you guys need to get back to Quantico."

"It's Friday afternoon, and I have the weekend off—if you'd like some company."

The offer surprised Monica. And the warmth and caring in Coop's eyes touched a raw, aching place in her soul. Facing the weekend alone would be torture, she realized. There would be decisions to make, red tape to deal with, grief to process. Coop might be new in her life, but she already knew his strength and quiet competence would bolster her in the days ahead. "Are you sure?"

"Yes." There was no hesitation in his response.

Nor in hers. "Then I accept."

He lifted his free hand, as if to touch her face, but the doorbell interrupted them.

"My partner always did have impeccable timing." One side of his mouth hitched up in a wry half smile. He let his hand fall away, and with a gentle squeeze of her fingers he rose to admit Mark.

The murmur of quiet conversation sounded in the hall, and a few seconds later Mark appeared in the doorway. He walked over to Monica, dropped into the chair Coop had vacated, and took both her hands in his. "I'm sorry about your father, Monica."

"Thank you."

"I know Coop is staying this weekend, but if you need anything after that, don't hesitate to let us know. We'll do whatever we can to help."

"I appreciate that. And everything you guys did."

"All in a day's work." He flashed her a brief smile, squeezed her hands, and rose.

After Coop showed him out, he returned holding a pizza box. "Mark brought us some provisions. You need to eat."

"Later." Food held zero appeal for her.

"Did you have any food yesterday?"

"No."

"How about today?"

"I had breakfast at the hospital."

"Hospital food is an oxymoron. You need real food. And I don't like to eat alone. Come on, try a few bites."

It was hard to refuse, considering all he'd done for her. In the end, Monica capitulated to his entreaties.

And that's how the weekend went. Coop cajoled and bartered, somehow convincing her to eat a decent amount of food. He persuaded her to watch some of the old comedies she had in her DVD collection. When the State Department called about funeral arrangements, he sat by her side, holding her hand as she worked through the details.

She also managed to put quite a dent in the jar of M&Ms.

Mostly, though, she found herself falling hard for a dark-eyed HRT operator—and wondering what would happen to their relationship now that his mission was over.

On Sunday night, when Mark drove down from Quantico to pick him up, Coop wasn't ready to leave. Not even close. As Monica walked him to the door, he turned to her. Her movements weren't as stiff today, and a tiny bit of her natural color had returned to her cheeks. The puffiness in her eyelid had subsided, and her lips no longer appeared swollen and cracked. But her bruises hadn't faded one iota. He hated to leave her alone in such a battered condition.

"I could take a couple of days off." He'd offered earlier, and she'd refused. He wasn't certain why he'd brought it up again.

"No. I've monopolized your life too much already. I'm sure you had better things to do this weekend than babysit the walking wounded."

He thought about what he'd have done on a normal Saturday and Sunday in Quantico. Gone to a couple of bars. Had a little too much to drink. Shot some pool. Talked up some pretty women. Once upon a time, he would have considered that a perfect weekend.

Not anymore.

"No, Monica, I didn't. There's nowhere else I'd rather have been."

His candor surprised him as much as it seemed to surprise her. Open, honest communication with the opposite sex was new for him. He didn't typically reveal his deepest feelings to anyone—female or male. But he felt safe with this woman. It was a new—and unsettling—experience.

"Thank you."

Her earnest, whispered response tugged at his heartstrings, reaching deep inside him to reawaken once again the long-buried protective instinct she'd managed to tap into from the moment they met. And her proximity didn't help matters. She stood close enough for him to catch the faint, fresh fragrance emanating from her hair. To feel her warmth. To see the glints of gold in her green irises and the spark of fire in her russet hair.

Coop had had no intention of kissing her this weekend. Her emotions were in tatters, and taking advantage of a woman who was still reeling from a traumatic experience didn't strike him as an honorable thing to do.

But over the past two days, as they'd chuckled together over old movies, as he'd comforted and consoled when unexpected tears overwhelmed her, as he'd fended off the press while she'd braved their blitz in order to attend church, as they'd shared pizza and M&Ms and confidences, he'd found his resolve wavering.

Now, as she stared up at him in the dim light of the foyer, he could see she dreaded this parting as much as he did. Perhaps not for quite the same reasons, though, he reminded himself. With all she'd been through, it was only logical she would have welcomed a protector this weekend in her violated home. His presence had helped her feel safe.

Yet he read more in her expression than that. More, he speculated, than she was aware of. Tenderness. Caring. Longing. Invitation.

All of which he found impossible to resist.

Without breaking eye contact, he lowered his bag to the floor and touched her cheek, his fingers whisper soft against her skin. He heard her sharp, indrawn breath, felt her go still, but she didn't pull away. Nor say a word. She wasn't in any condition for much of a kiss, let alone an embrace, but he couldn't leave without erasing any doubts that might be lingering in her mind about whether he'd considered this weekend an imposition.

Resting his hands lightly on her shoulders, he leaned down and touched his lips to hers. The contact was gentle, caressing. Yet the impact of it reverberated through every nerve in his body, leaving him feeling as unsteady as a newborn colt. He'd shared plenty of kisses with lots of women through the years, but the unexpected potency of this one jolted him.

Shaken, he pulled back a few inches. Her lips were parted, her respiration shallow and rapid. He was pretty sure she didn't realize she was clutching the front of his jacket, bunching the leather fabric in both hands.

"I-Is that part of the job too?" She sounded as wobbly as he felt.

"I'm not on duty now, Monica." His voice came out husky,

intimate, as he kneaded her slender shoulders, his fingertips tingling from the warmth of her skin radiating through her blouse. Touching her felt good. And right. Walking away felt wrong. But he knew staying wouldn't be wise, even if she'd accepted his offer. In fact, it would be dangerous.

Calling on every ounce of his willpower, he released her and stepped back. "I'll call you tomorrow. And I'll see you Tuesday at the funeral."

"Okay."

Bending, he hefted his bag and stepped through the door. He heard it close behind him as he strode toward the car where Mark waited, and when he glanced back, Monica had disappeared.

But as he climbed into the car and Mark pointed it toward Quantico, Coop knew that no matter how many miles separated them, she wouldn't disappear from his heart.

Today, tomorrow, or ever.

25

The pure, plaintive notes of "Taps" floated through the still air, sending a chill up Monica's spine that had nothing to do with the thirty-one-degree temperature on this late February afternoon. Unlike most of the mourners gathered around her father's flag-draped casket for the graveside committal at Arlington National Cemetery, she didn't even feel the cold air. She was too numb.

So much had happened in the past ten days. Too much to process. The events had a surreal quality to them that was heightened by the ethereal rendering of "Taps."

But the words of the navy chaplain who'd conducted the service, the rifle volley that had preceded the playing of "Taps," the presence of the secretary of state a discreet few steps to her left, and the flag-draped casket waiting to be lowered into the cold ground confirmed that every nightmare moment had been all too real.

At least she'd been spared the ordeal of planning the details of this service, she reflected. As Coop had predicted, her father had outlined his wishes for this eventuality, freeing her from the burden of all but a few decisions. Besides, as she'd discovered, the military was thorough about such matters. They had procedures and protocols for everything, down to the minutia of which seat was reserved for the NOK—next of kin. Left front. Where she sat now.

In most circumstances, Monica would find such rigid strictures oppressive and stifling. But on a day like this, when her brain wasn't operating at full efficiency, she was glad the strict protocol rendered thought unnecessary. They'd even sent a limo for her, freeing her from transportation logistics, and supplied an escort from the State Department to guide her through the ceremony.

The only thing they hadn't provided was a shoulder to cry on.

As the bugler sounded the final notes of "Taps," she searched the small crowd for Coop. He and Mark had been waiting in the background when she arrived at the cemetery. They'd attended the nine o'clock service in Philadelphia for Terry Minard, the agent who'd been killed at the safe house, and driven straight from there to Arlington. She'd wanted desperately to go to the agent's funeral too, but the secretary of state had expressed a strong interest in attending her father's service, and one o'clock today had been the most convenient time for him. She'd caved under pressure from the State Department—and regretted it ever since.

She found Coop in the spot he'd claimed near the back of the crowd. He was watching her, as he had been whenever she'd looked his way during the ten-minute service that had seemed endless. She could read the concern in his eyes even from a distance, and that did more to warm her than her heavy wool coat.

The final note of "Taps" faded, and she refocused on the scene in front of her. The members of the navy honor guard, in their dark dress uniforms, folded the flag into a precise triangle. The flag bearer presented it to the chaplain, who saluted it and approached her.

He had a kindly face, Monica thought as he drew near. One that had surely witnessed this exercise thousands of times. Yet she sensed he hadn't become immune to the turbulent emotions pooled in the small groups of people who clustered each day in tight knots of grief on these quiet, solemn hillsides. The duty hadn't become routine for him. She appreciated that.

He stopped in front of her and offered the flag.

"On behalf of the president of the United States, a grateful nation, and a proud navy, this flag is presented as a token of our appreciation for the honorable and faithful service rendered by your father to his country and navy."

Monica hadn't expected the formulaic wording to move her, but as she took the flag she felt the pressure of tears in her throat, behind her eyes. "Thank you."

He nodded, saluted the flag, and moved to the side.

An older woman, accompanied by a navy escort in full dress uniform, took her turn in the well-choreographed service. Monica had been briefed to expect an expression of sympathy from one of the "Arlington Ladies"—wives and widows of military personnel who attended every service in the cemetery. The woman's quiet, sincere words of comfort touched her too.

Finally, a man in civilian attire stepped forward. "The service has ended. You may now return to your cars."

As Monica stood, the secretary of state approached her. She'd often seen the man on TV, but his real-life presence added to the surreal quality of the occasion. He held out his hand, and she found hers taken in a warm clasp.

"Ms. Callahan, I want you to know how much all of us at the State Department respected and admired your father. He was a man of the highest integrity, and your loss is shared by all of us."

"Thank you."

"The president and vice president asked me to convey their deepest condolences as well."

Monica acknowledged the expression of sympathy with a dip of her head.

The formalities attended to, the timbre of the man's voice

shifted. "On a more personal note, I considered David a good friend and confidante. I'm not a man whose trust is easily earned, but your father had mine. I'll miss him very much." He cleared his throat and reached inside his overcoat to withdraw a thin, legal-sized envelope. "When the embassy staff in Kabul was collecting his personal items for shipment back to the States, they found this on the desk in his quarters. I wanted to deliver it to you myself." He handed it to her. "I'm sorry for all you've been through, Ms. Callahan. If there's anything the State Department can do to assist you, please let us know."

"I appreciate that. And thank you for attending today."

"Considering all David Callahan meant to this country and to me, I couldn't be anywhere else."

Once the secretary departed, a steady line of sympathizers moved past Monica. A few of her colleagues from the university had come up for the service, but most of the people were strangers. Residents of her father's world, members of an elite circle she knew nothing about.

Coop and Mark brought up the rear, waiting until the crowd had dispersed before stepping forward.

"You're shivering," Coop greeted her, a worried frown furrowing his brow as he scrutinized her. "You need to get out of the cold."

As if to reinforce his comment, a sudden gust of wind whipped past, bringing with it a few icy pellets of sleet. "I just need a minute to say good-bye."

Without waiting for a response, she tucked the envelope the secretary had handed her into a side pocket of her purse and walked over to the casket. The bleak, gray sky was fitting on this somber day, she reflected, as another pellet of sleet stung her cheek. It mirrored her mood. For a few brief days, she'd allowed herself to hope that perhaps she and her father could find a way to reconnect. But that hope had died with him, on an operating table thousands of miles away. She would never have the chance to reconcile with the man who'd been her father in name only.

"I'm sorry we never had the chance to mend our relationship," she whispered, leaning close to touch the polished mahogany, fighting back tears. "And I'm sorry for all the years we missed. I guess I'll never know why you preferred your job to Mom and me. But I choose to believe it wasn't a personal rejection. And that maybe, in your heart, you never stopped caring about us. That despite our estrangement, you loved me. And I also want you to know I forgive you, as Mom did long ago."

Pausing, Monica fished a tissue out of her coat pocket and dabbed at her tender nose. Then she closed her eyes and spoke in the silence of her heart.

Lord, I ask that you bring my father home to you. Despite his faults, I know he was a good man who did important work. Please forgive him for his failings in this life, as I have. And grace him with your forgiveness and peace in the next.

When she turned back, only Coop and Mark remained at the gravesite. Her driver stood attentive and waiting by the back door of the limo that had picked her up. The Suburban Coop and Mark had driven was parked farther down. All of the other mourners had departed.

They came forward to meet her in silence, each taking an arm to guide her toward the waiting car. She stumbled once on the uneven turf, and their grip tightened, steadying her.

"Are you okay?" Worry roughened Coop's voice.

"Yes." She kept her head down, blinking back the tears that had blurred her vision and caused her to trip.

She didn't speak again until they stopped a few steps from her car. Mark released her arm, but Coop's grip remained firm. "Thank you both for coming. It can't have been easy to attend two funerals in one day."

312

"We needed to be at both," Coop said.

"I did too, considering Agent Minard died trying to protect me."

"His family understood. They mentioned the note you sent. And we saw the flowers."

"It seems like such an inadequate gesture in light of their loss."

Another gust of wind whipped past, hard enough to rock her, and Coop urged her toward the car. "You need to get out of the cold. What are your plans for the rest of the day?"

"I'm going to stop by my father's apartment."

"Are you sure you're up to that?"

"No. But I'd like to see the place he called home."

"Would you like some company?"

Her eyebrows arched. "Don't you have to go back to work?"

"I do," Mark chimed in. "But Coop took the day off."

"If you'd rather be alone, though, I understand."

She searched his face. "If you have the time, I'd appreciate it. And I have the driver for the whole day. He can drop you off at your place before we head back to Richmond."

"Sounds like my cue to exit." Mark took Monica's hands and leaned down to brush his lips over her cheek, his expression sober. "Take care of yourself."

"I will. Thank you for everything."

With a half salute, Mark strode off toward the Suburban.

Once in the car, Monica gave the driver her father's address and settled back in the seat. As she set her purse beside her, Coop startled her by reaching for her hands and stripping off her gloves. "What are you doing?"

"Warming up your hands." He cocooned her fingers between his and massaged them gently as he issued an additional instruction to the driver. "Stop at a Starbucks, if you don't mind. This woman is in desperate need of a cup of hot chocolate."

"Yes, sir."

"Coop, that's not necess—"

"Yes, it is. Your hands are like ice."

"They're getting warmer now." As were other things, she realized, watching his strong, lean fingers caress her skin.

Thirty minutes later, fortified with the hot chocolate, Monica inserted the key in her father's small apartment. When the door swung open, however, she hesitated.

"What's wrong?" Coop rested a hand on her arm from behind.

"Now that I'm here, I feel like an intruder invading his personal space."

"You're his only family. There's no one else to do this. But it doesn't have to be done today."

"There's no reason to put it off, either." Straightening her shoulders, she stepped across the threshold and into the small foyer.

Coop followed, shutting the door behind them. He took her purse and helped her off with her coat, and she crossed to the living room, surveying the austere, modern furnishings. A sleek buff-colored leather couch. Side chairs in burgundy. A glass-topped coffee table resting on a carved stone base. A couple of unusual steel lamps. No clutter. No personal touches. No sign that this was anything more than a display unit.

Her shoulders drooped a bit in disappointment. Monica had hoped the apartment would offer a few insights about the man who had fathered her. But nothing in this cold, impersonal space provided a clue about who he was as a person.

"It doesn't look like anyone even lived here." Disheartened, she checked out the galley kitchen and small dining area, speaking over her shoulder to Coop.

"It's the tidiest bachelor pad I've ever seen," he concurred, shoving one hand in the pocket of his slacks while perusing the living room furnishings.

The cooking and eating areas carried out the same contemporary, minimalist theme, and Monica dismissed them with a cursory sweep to head down the small hall. The first door she opened revealed a chair and a small desk with a tangle of wires underneath, suggesting her father had used this room as an office during his brief stopovers between assignments.

That left his bedroom.

Considering the lack of personality in the rest of the apartment, she had little hope it would offer any hints about what made him tick, either. And at first glance, it didn't. The queen-size bed was covered with an off-white comforter, and a dark-teal-colored bolster pillow was propped against a beige leather headboard. A glass-topped table edged in chrome stood beside the bed, topped with a sleek clock radio.

Her attention was caught, however, by an ornate wooden chest, Middle-Eastern in design, that stood at the foot of the bed. It was the only thing she'd seen in the apartment that hinted at his global travels. The piece must have had special meaning to him, she speculated, moving closer to run her fingers over the smooth relief carvings and inlay.

Curious about the contents, she bent to lift the lid as she gave the rest of the room a quick scan. And then she froze. On the otherwise-bare top of a chest of drawers stood a framed photo, the faces dated but instantly recognizable. Her mother and father stood close together behind an eight- or nine-year-old Monica, and everyone was smiling. They looked like a perfect family.

The chest forgotten, Monica walked across the room and picked up the unfamiliar photo. She had no recollection of posing for it, nor could she remember ever seeing it. The color had faded a bit, washing out the skin tones. There was a ghostly quality to the image, as if the camera had captured a scene that didn't really exist.

And, in truth, it hadn't, Monica acknowledged with a pang,

fingering the edge of the frame. They had never been the happy family depicted in this frozen moment.

Yet all these years her father had kept this. And the fact that it was the sole personal item on display lent it added significance. Did its presence mean he was sorry he'd lost the family represented in this photo? Did he look at it last thing at night and first thing in the morning and regret what he'd thrown away? Did he wish the picture represented reality rather than illusion?

As she pondered those questions, Monica set the frame back in its place and returned to the ornate carved chest at the foot of the bed. It, too, seemed out of place in this sterile environment. Did it contain a few more clues about David Callahan, the man?

Trying not to get her hopes up, Monica lifted the lid. And almost dropped it when she found a copy of her book staring back at her.

With a hand that was far from steady, she picked up the volume. It was well-thumbed, she noted, as if it had seen much use. Had her father not only read it, but reread it? Several times?

Her mind whirling with unanswered questions, she focused again on the chest. It contained one more object, she discovered. A leather-bound scrapbook. Placing her book on the bed, she lifted the album and sat with it in her lap on the single chair in the bedroom. It took her a full sixty seconds to work up the courage to look inside.

And there she found a chronicle of her life. School pictures, obviously forwarded by her mother. Copies of report cards. An invitation to her high school graduation. And numerous press clippings. About her fellowship, her appointment at the university, a talk she'd given, her book.

There was only one conclusion to draw. Her father had followed her life. Had participated in it. As a spectator, true, but he'd participated nonetheless.

316

She was stunned.

How long she sat there, grappling with the implications of what she'd discovered, she didn't know. But finally a soft knock on the half open door drew her attention. "Monica? Everything okay?"

At Coop's concerned question, she drew a shaky breath. "Yes. Come in. I found some . . . interesting . . . things."

He pushed open the door, and she gestured to the photo, her book, and the opened scrapbook in her lap. "My father did have a few personal things, after all."

Coop glanced at the items the diplomat had held most dear. Reminders of a life he'd given up . . . and a decision he'd perhaps come to regret. "It's not much to show for a life on a personal level, is it?"

"He had his work. Maybe that was all he needed. Maybe that's all a lot of men need." Her voice was tinged with sadness.

"I used to think that. I don't anymore."

At his quiet response, she looked up at him, her gaze searching, seeking the significance behind his words. But he shuttered his eyes and held up the envelope the secretary of state had handed her. "I found this on the floor in the foyer."

"It must have fallen out of my purse. The secretary gave it to me after the service. He said the embassy staff found it on my father's desk. Do you mind if I open it now?"

"Not at all."

She put the album and book back in the chest and closed the lid. The chest, its contents, and the photograph she'd keep. The rest of the furnishings meant nothing to her. Nor to her father, she suspected. "Let's go back in the living room. There's nowhere in here for you to sit."

He followed her, but instead of claiming one of the chairs he walked over to a window and stared out at the view while she sat on the couch, slit the envelope, and began to read.

My Dear Monica: It's one in the morning on Thursday. In seven hours I meet with the secretary of state. In eleven hours, if we choose not to deal with the terrorists, they will begin executing hostages.

Attempting to sleep this night is an exercise in futility.

As I struggle to discern the right course of action, I find myself recalling our brief phone conversation earlier this week . . . and thinking about the words I should have said. But expressing emotion has never been my strong suit. It has always been easier for me to consign my feelings to paper than to verbalize them. Tonight, as I pray that the current crisis will be resolved with no loss of life, I also ask the Lord to allow us to keep our dinner date in Washington—and to give me the courage to tell you face-to-face what I script here at this late hour.

Many years ago, when your mother gave me an ultimatum to choose between family and career, I believed the world would be a better place if I gave my life to the diplomatic service. In my arrogance, I was convinced my contribution would be worth the sacrifice to me and to my family. And much as it pains me to admit it, I was also selfish. The excitement of life in the fast lane, of hobnobbing with the world's power brokers, appealed to me. My choice had nothing to do with my feelings for you and your mother and everything to do with misplaced priorities. Neither of you did anything wrong; the fault lay with me.

As the years passed and the glamour of my job faded, I recognized the egotism behind my motives and realized my mistake. While I achieved all my professional goals, my personal life was empty. Elaine kept me informed of your activities, and after she died I continued to follow your career, relishing your accomplishments from afar. Often I was tempted to call you. But I understood your resentment and could think of no way to bridge the gap between us. As you so aptly put it in your excellent book, I didn't know how to talk the walk.

318

I still struggle with expressing emotion. And I expect I always will. But I've resolved to at least attempt it when we meet. I've wasted too many years watching your life from the sidelines instead of participating. If I can convince you to forgive me, to give me the second chance I know I don't deserve, I will do my best to tell you how sorry I am for the choices I made. And to tell you how much I love you.

I hope the Lord grants us the oppor—

The letter ended mid-sentence, with a line that squiggled across the page.

For several minutes after she finished reading, Monica stared at the handwritten page. She'd had no idea her distant, reserved father had harbored such deep feelings. Had he given voice to them sooner, they might have reconciled long ago.

But perhaps not, she admitted. In fairness, she couldn't lay all of the fault for their long estrangement on him. Her resentment had run deep, and despite her faith, it had taken the recent traumatic events to compel her to consider forgiveness.

Now she'd never know where her change of heart might have led.

Nevertheless, her father had given her a priceless gift, she realized. An expression of love in the personal effects he'd left behind, and an affirmation of love expressed in words.

In the end, he'd talked the walk.

Monica didn't notice the tear trailing down her cheek until a gentle touch wiped it away. As Coop sat beside her, she blinked to clear the moisture from her eyes.

"You okay?" He stroked a finger over the back of her hand.

"Yes."

She ran her thumb across the letter, tempted to share the personal document with him. She wanted Coop to know her father had regretted his reticence. And that he was sorry about some of his choices in life. Perhaps the message would resonate with the strong, tough, high-achiever sitting beside her, who kept his own emotions on a tight leash. Who had admitted that as a boy, his fondest wish had been for his undemonstrative, distant father to simply notice him. Who'd decided, after that wish had gone unfulfilled, that pinning his happiness on someone else's approval and acceptance was too risky.

If Coop was willing to learn from her father's mistakes, she had a feeling it could change his life.

And hers.

If he wasn't, it was better to know that now.

Summoning up her courage, she held out the letter. "Would you like to read it?"

For a long moment, Coop looked at the handwritten message. "Are you sure you want me to?"

"Yes."

He hesitated, grappling with the significance of her gesture. Knowing his response would have a huge impact on their future. And then, making his decision, he reached out and took the single sheet of paper.

As Coop scanned the note David Callahan had written to his daughter, he realized that the diplomat had been more similar to his own father than he'd suspected . . . and similar to him in many ways, as well. All his life, Coop had favored stoic strength over emotions. It was safer. Once you let someone get close, exposed your deepest feelings, you became vulnerable. Susceptible to control—and hurt. He'd taken that risk as a child with his father, only to get burned. It was not an experience he wanted to repeat.

But neither did he want to end up like David Callahan, isolated and alone because he couldn't find the words that would connect him to another human being—nor the courage to say them.

The term "crossroads" flashed through his mind as he read the words the diplomat had penned alone, late at night, in a sterile room thousands of miles away from home. He stood at such a juncture now. If he continued down the path he'd been traveling for thirty years, he'd lose any chance of connecting with Monica. Her book was clear on that point. Nothing less than full disclosure in a relationship would suffice for her.

Could he live up to that expectation? Could he overcome the fears about trust he'd articulated to her earlier in the week, during their discussion about faith? Fears about whether commitment diminished freedom and chipped away at individuality, and which pertained as much to human love as to divine? Yet she'd countered by saying such trust and commitment were liberating. That they freed a person to be exactly who they were, without fear or pretense.

That concept was foreign to Coop in everything but a professional setting. There, in the field, he'd seen it demonstrated. Because he trusted his fellow HRT members with his life, he was able to accomplish more on missions than he would ever be able to do alone. His team allowed him to be the best he could be.

Could the same be true in loving relationships?

Until Monica entered his life, he'd never met a woman who piqued his interest enough to raise such questions. And a week ago, testing that theory would have scared him more than any of the explosive situations he'd encountered since joining the HRT. But he was smart enough to recognize a good thing when he saw it. And he saw it now, sitting next to him. Monica Callahan was the complete package—innate intelligence, strength of character, and a tender heart all wrapped up in russet hair and deep green eyes and a trim, toned body that kicked his libido into overdrive. If he let her walk away because he was afraid, he knew he'd regret it to the day he died.

Setting the letter aside, Coop looked at Monica. "That's pretty powerful stuff."

"Yes, it is. I wish he'd had a chance to tell it to me in person, but I'm grateful I got the message, no matter the form."

"With all the negotiation he did, it's hard to believe he had such difficulty with words on a personal level."

"Talking about feelings is a whole different ball game." She tilted her head and regarded him. "And the strong, silent types seem to have the most problems with that. But you know something? I've learned a lesson too this week. As important as it is for people to talk the walk, it's just as important to learn to listen with the heart as well as the ears."

This was it, Coop realized. Time to fish or cut bait.

Drawing in a slow, deep breath, he took the proverbial leap of faith.

"What are you hearing now?" He searched her face as he asked the question.

"Why don't you tell me?"

He should have figured she wouldn't make this easy for him. He tried for a teasing tone. "Is this a test?"

"No. More like a challenge."

"HRT operators thrive on those."

"I kind of suspected they might."

"Okay, you're on. I'll give this a shot." He took her hand, lacing his fingers with hers, all levity vanishing. "I'm not all that great with words, Monica. And I know you'd prefer a guy who is. I read your book last weekend cover to cover while you caught up on sleep, and that message came through loud and clear. I can't promise I'll ever be in the world-class verbal communications league. But I'm willing to work on it—if you're willing to continue seeing me."

"You didn't do too badly at the safe house, when you told me about your childhood."

"I'd never shared that with anyone else."

"Do you regret telling me?"

"No. That's why I know you're special." He picked up David's letter. "I don't want to end up like your father. Alone, with regrets."

She lifted her hand and slowly traced his lips with her finger. "I don't think you're going to end up like my father, Coop."

"Does that mean you're willing to give this thing between us a chance? See where it leads?" His question came out hoarse—and hopeful.

The woman who believed in the power of words said nothing. She just smiled and leaned into his arms, giving him his answer in a language far more eloquent . . . and timeless . . . than the spoken word.

Epilogue

Five Months Later

Coop slipped into the back of the church and scanned the right center section for Monica. They always sat in the same area, and he quickly spotted her about halfway down. It was hard to miss the coppery highlights in her hair, which were burnished by the late-July sun streaming in the tall, clear windows.

As he walked down the side aisle toward her pew, he nodded discreetly to members of the congregation who looked his way as he passed, many of whom he'd met over the past few months. Although he'd debated skipping church to snatch an extra hour of sleep before tackling the hour-and-a-half drive to Richmond, he was glad now he hadn't. He'd missed few Sundays since they began dating, and he relished his respite in the Lord's house each week. He was making steady progress on this faith journey, and the hour on Sunday, supplemented with private Scripture readings, helped center him. Half a service was better than no service. Even if it came at the expense of sleep.

Besides, Monica's expression as he slid in beside her more than compensated for his hurried shower and too-short night. Surprise softened to delight, and she gave him that warm, intimate, welcoming smile he'd come to love. The one that made him feel more like a man than any of the physical demands of his job or the macho off-duty pursuits he used to enjoy. She reached for his hand, and he twined his fingers with hers, giving them a gentle squeeze.

The service was uplifting, the sermon inspiring, and Coop did his best to focus on worship. But he couldn't help stealing a few glances at the woman beside him, admiring the teal green silk dress, belted at her slender waist, that outlined her soft curves. As he traced her profile, he said a silent prayer of thanks that the only reminders of her trauma were a thin white scar on her chin and the nightmares that occasionally disrupted her sleep, leaving a dull headache as a morning souvenir.

Honing in on the faint shadows under her eyes and her pinched features, Coop suspected last night hadn't been one of her more restful slumbers. Nor, perhaps, had the several previous nights. A few weeks ago, after he'd pressed her, she'd admitted that she struggled more with nightmares when he was away on missions. Not that she ever complained or tried to lay a guilt trip on him. But considering all she'd been through, he hated to add to her stress.

After the service ended, he commandeered her arm and headed toward the exit, responding to greetings with a polite smile and a few pleasant words without slowing his pace. As he hustled her out the door, she grinned at him.

"Can't wait to get me alone, huh?" Her tone was playful, but the strain in her voice was telling.

"That thought did cross my mind. But in the spirit of open, honest communication, you look like you need to lie down. Bad night?"

Her smile faded. "Kind of."

"How many in a row?"

"Three." She summoned up her grin again and touched his cheek as he guided her toward her car. "Nice tan."

"Thanks."

She didn't ask more. He didn't offer. They both knew the rules of his covert job. Besides, she didn't need to hear the sordid details of the dangerous mission that had taken him back to the jungles of Puerto Rico to flush out a drug lord. She had too many nightmares as it was.

"I'll follow you home." Opening her door, he leaned down for a quick kiss. "That's just a sample," he promised, his lips hovering close to hers.

His comment elicited a throaty chuckle that spiked his blood pressure. "I'll hold you to that."

Twenty minutes later, after following her into her house, he made good on his promise with a lingering kiss that left them both a bit breathless.

"I missed you." He murmured the words against her hair, inhaling her fresh, distinctive scent.

"Not as much as I missed you."

"Mmm. That's good to hear." He held her close for a couple of minutes, her head nestled against his chest, then extricated himself to shrug out of his sport jacket and loosen his tie. "Okay. First things first. Did you take anything for the headache?"

"I didn't say I had one."

"You didn't have to. Did you take anything?"

"No. You know I don't like medicine."

"An admirable trait. Medicine should be used judiciously and only when needed. Go sit in the living room while I get you a couple of pills and a glass of water."

"Did anyone ever tell you you're bossy?"

"Never. Go sit down."

She propped her hands on her hips and stared him down, trying to scowl. "You don't intimidate me, Evan Cooper."

"I could try a different kind of persuasion." A slow grin teased his lips, and he took a step toward her.

"Okay, okay." She backed up. "You win. I'm going. But you caught me at a weak moment. As soon as I get my strength back, you may have to use some of that persuasion."

"I'm counting on it," he countered with a wink.

After he rejoined her, she swallowed the pills in one gulp and gave him an apologetic smile. "If I'd known you were coming, I would have taken these before church. I hate to forfeit one second of our time together to a headache."

"I didn't know I was coming, either. We didn't get in until four this morning." As he talked, he tugged off her pumps and lifted her legs to the couch.

"How much sleep did you get?"

"Three hours." And only four the night before. But he left that unsaid.

"You should have stayed home, Coop. You must be exhausted."

"And give up our Sunday? No way." He plumped a cushion and set it on one end of the couch. "Just rest for a little while, until the medication kicks in."

"This seems like such a waste, after you drove all the way down here to be with me." But she didn't resist when he pressed her back into a prone position. He took a seat at the opposite end of the couch and settled her feet on his lap.

"I don't consider it a waste to spend my Sunday playing with a beautiful woman's toes."

She gave a soft chuckle and closed her eyes. "Mmm. That feels good." She snuggled deeper into the cushion, and within a couple of minutes she'd drifted to sleep.

Two hours later, when she stirred, Coop's eyelids flickered open. It seemed they'd both needed sleep, he acknowledged, rotating his neck to get the kinks out.

"Hi." She blinked, her voice husky from slumber.

"Hi yourself."

"What time is it?"

He checked his watch. "One-thirty."

"Already?" She swung her legs to the floor and scooted closer to him. "Why did you let me sleep so long?"

328

"You needed it. I did too. Feel better?"

"Yes. Much."

She did look refreshed, he decided, assessing her. The lines of strain had eased and the shadows under her eyes had faded. "How about a late lunch?" Most Sundays, they went somewhere for brunch after church. But a quiet, elegant, leisurely lunch dovetailed better with his plans. Assuming all went as he hoped.

"Sure. Let me freshen up a little."

Heading for the bathroom, she gave her hair a quick brush and did no more than reapply her lipstick, loathe to give up one more minute of her precious time with Coop.

When she returned, she found him waiting for her in the living room. He'd retrieved his sport jacket from the kitchen, and she hesitated in the doorway, assuming he'd want to leave at once. But he surprised her.

"Sit with me for a minute. I have something I want to show you."

"Okay." She crossed the room and dropped beside him, attuned to his odd inflection. He sounded almost . . . nervous. Not the kind of vibe she often picked up from this confident, decisive man.

"Do you remember saying last February that once the crisis was over, you were going to go someplace that had white sand, palm trees, and sunshine for some R&R?"

"Yes." Some of her animation faded. "But I wasn't in the mood right after my father was . . . after he died. By the time I'd regrouped, I was committed to teaching summer school. I guess it wasn't meant to be."

"I think it was. Your timing was just a little off." He withdrew an envelope from the inside pocket of his jacket and handed it to her. "I found the perfect place for you to unwind."

Curious, she opened the envelope and withdrew several pages

of color printouts. The sheets were filled with interior and exterior shots of an elegant house, surrounded by palm trees and tropical flowers, positioned on a small rise above a pristine, empty white beach.

"Wow! Where is this place?"

"A private island in the Caribbean."

"A private island." She scanned the photos again, puzzled. "Even if I could afford it—and that's a big if—how would I get access to a place like this?"

"Through me. It belongs to a high-level government official who was grateful for my assistance during a dignitary protection detail. He offered to put it at my disposal any time for two weeks. I thought it would be a great place to spend Thanksgiving."

"You want me to come with you?" Up to this point in their relationship, he hadn't pushed her beyond her comfort level with intimacy, respecting the old-fashioned values her faith espoused—and which she thought he'd come to share as his own faith blossomed. But the invitation threw her off balance. If she'd misread him on this, had she misread him on other things too?

"Yes. But there is a caveat. You'll need a credential only I can supply." Once more he reached inside his jacket.

Monica stopped breathing as he withdrew his hand and she saw a small, square, satin-covered jeweler's box resting in his palm.

"To take advantage of my once-in-a-lifetime offer, this has to be on your finger. Along with a matching band." He flipped open the lid.

She stared at the perfect solitaire flanked by two square-cut diamonds. "You want me to marry you." Dazed, she tore her gaze away from the ring. She'd known they were heading this direction. She just hadn't expected things to move this fast.

"Yes." He leaned forward and took her hand. "I'll never be a silver-tongued wonder, Monica. I'm afraid it's not in my genes.

But I love you with every fiber of my being. I can't imagine a future without you, and I give thanks to the Lord every day for your presence in my life."

During the months they'd been dating, Monica had learned much about Coop, whose profession of love filled her with a joy as radiant as the spring sun after a long, dreary winter. She knew he could be trusted to keep his promises and honor his commitment. That he could open up and share what was in his heart—with her, at least. She cherished his strength and kindness and sensitivity, admired his intelligence and humor and capacity for tenderness, and loved him for stepping out of his comfort zone to woo and win her.

In the past, on the few occasions she'd allowed herself to daydream about the kind of man she might marry, someone like Coop hadn't even been on her radar screen. Yet now she couldn't imagine sharing her life with anyone else.

When the silence lengthened, Coop shifted. She saw an emotion resembling panic flit through his eyes, but before she could reassure him he spoke.

"I want you to know that if my job is a deal breaker, I'm prepared to hand in my resignation tomorrow. The HRT isn't a long-term gig, anyway. Most operators leave after five or six years. I'd be moving on in a year or so, with or without you in my life. If I have to accelerate that timetable, it's not a problem."

Over the past few months, Monica had visited Quantico often and had met many of the HRT operators. And she'd come to understand the tremendous commitment, perseverance, and hard work it took to get on the elite team. It was not a membership given up lightly. Or too soon. Coop's willingness to walk away from the job he loved sooner than he'd planned was yet more evidence of the depth of his love.

For a moment, Monica was tempted to take him up on his offer. She worried constantly while he was on missions. The margin for error was slim, and as she knew firsthand, a life could be snuffed out in an instant. Every time he left on a mission, there was always a chance he wouldn't return.

Yet people were killed every day crossing the street too, she reminded herself. Coop was well trained. He was careful. In exchange for a lifetime of love, how could she deny him the work that, for now, helped define him? She'd lectured him once about trust. Now it was her turn to put his welfare in God's hands and have faith the Lord would keep him safe.

"I wouldn't ask you to give up your work, Coop."

"I'm willing to do it, if that's what it takes."

"No. It's part of who you are."

He gave her an uncertain look. "So . . . is that a yes or a no?"

"To what?"

"My proposal. I asked you to marry me."

"Not in those exact words."

As he caught her subtle teasing tone, some of the tension in his face eased. "We're back to that word thing again, huh?"

"Most women only get to hear this question once in their life. I don't want to feel deprived."

"Okay. Then we'll do this right." He dropped to one knee and cocooned her hand in his. "Monica Callahan, will you do me the honor of becoming my wife?"

In response, she leaned toward him, aiming for his lips. But to her surprise, he backed off.

"Uh-uh. This works both ways. Yes or no. A man deserves to hear the answer in words."

Grinning, she put her free hand on his shoulder and leaned toward him until their noses were almost touching. "Yes, yes, yes, yes, yes. Good enough?"

"Good enough," he confirmed.

Then the room fell silent.

Because words, after all, do have their limitations.

ACKNOWLEDGMENTS

Back in the summer of 2006, when I decided to dip my toes into the world of suspense, I was a total rookie. I had no background in police procedure, criminal investigation, or FBI protocols—let alone any knowledge of the elite Hostage Rescue Team.

As a result, this series represents a ton of research. I spent hours at the library, online, and talking to experts in a variety of fields. For their help with book 1 in my Heroes of Quantico series, several people deserve special recognition. I offer my most heartfelt thanks to the following individuals.

To Pat Bradley, for reviewing the Afghanistan sections. In general, I visit all places I write about, but for Afghanistan I relied on research material. I asked Pat to double-check my descriptions to ensure I portrayed the terrain and the "feel" of the country accurately. And he would know. Through International Crisis Aid (ICA), which brings food, medicines, and supplies to desperate people in places other organizations cannot or will not go, Pat has made many "under the radar" trips to the world's trouble spots in the name of humanitarian aid. He does this as a volunteer, and at great personal risk. He has my deepest gratitude—and respect. (For more information on ICA, visit www.crisisaid.org.)

To Steven Buckner, PhD, chairman of the chemistry department at St. Louis University, for his impromptu chemistry lesson. He told me his colleagues deemed my break-in scenario "chemically and physically realistic and sound," and I consider that a great compliment. But it wouldn't have happened without his input.

To a former FBI agent out West who reviewed my entire manuscript and gave it a thumbs-up for accuracy. Since he didn't change a word, he felt he didn't contribute much and declined any recognition. But his blessing on my research contributed greatly to my peace of mind! He knows who he is, and I thank him for plowing through all four-hundred-plus manuscript pages when he had far better things to do.

To the wonderful people at Revell, who have welcomed me so warmly. To my editor, Jennifer Leep, for her insights and belief in my work; to Cat Hoort, who has now moved on, for her enthusiasm for this book during our brief association; to Cheryl Van Andel for her incredible responsiveness to my cover suggestions; to Kristin Kornoelje for her superb copyediting; and to all the other folks I met on my visit whom I haven't yet had the pleasure of working with as I write this . . . I look forward to a fabulous partnership.

To gifted author Dee Henderson for her graciousness and her fabulous endorsement for this novel.

Last, but by no means least, to my agent, Chip MacGregor of MacGregor Literary. Thanks for believing in this project, for your perseverance, and for finding the perfect home for my suspense debut.

Finally, on a personal note, I'd like to pay tribute to three people who have had a tremendous influence on my writing career.

To the special man in my life—my husband, Tom—whose love and support mean the world to me.

And to the greatest parents (and proofreaders!) ever, James and Dorothy Hannon, who have always encouraged me to reach for the stars.

Irene Hannon is an award-winning author who took the publishing world by storm at the tender age of ten with a sparkling piece of fiction that received national attention.

Okay . . . maybe that's a slight exaggeration. But she *was* one of the honorees in a complete-the-story contest conducted by a national children's magazine. And she likes to think of that as her "official" fiction-writing debut.

Since then, she has written more than twenty-five romance and romantic suspense novels. Her books have been honored with the coveted RITA award from Romance Writers of America (the "Oscar" of romantic fiction), the HOLT Medallion, and a Reviewer's Choice award from *Romantic Times BOOKreviews* magazine.

Irene, who holds a BA in psychology and an MA in journalism, juggled two careers for many years until she gave up her executive corporate communications position with a Fortune 500 company to write full time. She is happy to say she has no regrets! As she points out, leaving behind the rush-hour commute, corporate politics, and a relentless BlackBerry that never slept was no sacrifice.

In her spare time, Irene enjoys hamming it up in community musical theater productions. A trained vocalist, she has sung the leading role in numerous shows. She also regularly performs with a six-person musical review troupe and is a cantor at her church (where she does *not* ham it up!).

When not otherwise occupied, Irene loves to cook and garden. She and her husband also enjoy traveling, Saturday mornings at their favorite coffee shop, and spending time with family. They make their home in Missouri.

To learn more about Irene and her books, visit www.irenehannon.com.

Don't miss the next book in the Heroes of Quantico series

When a reunion turns deadly, the killer's target is a mystery. . .
but the hunt is still on—and time is running out.

COMING IN SEPTEMBER 2009

Revell

a division of Baker Publishing Group
www.RevellBooks.com

Available wherever books are sold